1

LINGERING MORALITY

A Nonfiction

By Rémy Roussetzki

There are too many moments these days when we cannot recognize our country... lawless behavior has become standard practice since Sept. 11, 2001.
Editorial, *The New York Times*, Monday, December 31, 2007

Nonfiction is a form of literature that lies halfway between fiction and fact.
Scott. F. Fitzgerald

Log 1

"I'll lay low for a little while but don't worry, I'll be *there*."

"For how long?" she asked. She is thirteen years old.

"For as long as it takes, Isabel."

"Those who are after you *this time*, Dad" she continued in her thin, frightened, but probing voice, "are they the bad guys or the good ones?"

The words "this time" entered in me like a dagger. She demurred and lowered her chin and was about to cry, her face all shriveled up like when she was a little girl. How much does Isabel know about the game of hide-and-seek I've been playing with the Lagrange family for a couple of years now? As much as the general public, I assume, no much beyond catch phrases found in Nathaniel's famous *corridors* and publicized by pundits and admirers.

"I cannot say who's good who's bad anymore, not after the bad news," I told her. After that, we exchanged a few banalities just to hear each other's voice and see our faces a while longer; I offered my excuses and, to not have her witness my crying, switched us off. Isabel remembering the long face of her father; her keeping this sorry image of me was already more than enough.

Gabriela, her mother, was too upset to talk to me; she lurked in the depth of the screen.

I am in it up to my neck *this time* and confused as to what to do. Should I change skin and like in the movies rethink my outfit and haircut? This is unfortunately not the tentative script of a movie. And it does not matter what I look like. For a few nights, I've used an alias and checked in this expensive Upper East Side hotel. I have painstakingly covered my tracks on the Webwork and spoken meaningful words to no one. Automatic doormen and service robots don't count, do they? They could provide details if someone is asking. Is someone asking? Nobody is asking about me or I'd be under arrest. No one is after me that I can detect. But perhaps they are around me in a different way, to learn from me.

I could return to Gabriela and Isabel—who would not, in my shoes?—and not open this file, not throw my life away pursuing you, Nathaniel, and besides you, the Lagrange family. Yes, I could resume with teaching short stories and great classical drama and call the last turbulent couple of years a sabbatical. And then, I could live as happily as before, as though nothing occurred; even when my consciousness, what's left of the moral fiber in me, is about to boil over.

But if I don't do anything, if I wait passively, they'll come for me sure enough one day and break my pleasant world. Say, if I finally get cornered, I could hire the best lawyer my money can buy. I could then go back home and be with Isabel and my wife, would make no difference as to my case—but not now, I cannot drag my family into this, not when the Lagrange affair is like a fresh wound full of sharp nails. I have to weather this horror by myself without them being constantly reminded that I am a part of it. If I were recording this in 1800, I would say, a gulf has opened under my feet; the risk of not reaching the other side not only body but soul intact should only implicate me.

You've heard about the crash. It caught your fringe vision one morning as you opened the screen. I need to preface my description of what happened over the Hudson River and on the side of New Jersey by making a political, geopolitical, even historical statement. The crash immediately reminded everyone of 9/11 all over again; one more version of 9/11. Think of it— it's been nineteen wildly spinning years, violent and ugly as far as the planet is concerned. Brutal dictatorships are back everywhere as the better solution to managing vast numbers of humans. The economy serves mostly to enrich a few ultra-rich families that intermarry like the aristocrats of yore and live as separated from us as if they were their own specie. All this means waning abundance for the rest of us, disorder, police state and popular despair. It's 2020 and we still are one disaster away, reeling from the aftershock of the disaster at World Trade Center 1 and 2. Kids were not born when the colossal towers collapsed, but you don't need to tell them what happened. Isabel was born six years later, and we didn't go visit ground zero for a good ten years after that—even though it's one subway ride away from our home uptown. I do not remember, however, having to explain 9/11 to her. 9/11 is the given, the horizon, what she has to take into account.

This time it was different, and it was the same. One plane was full of Venezuelans, Europeans and Americans going to Caracas. The other, borrowing the same corridor but coming in the opposite direction, came from Sydney. It was full of young, middle-aged and elderly Australians, several orthodox Jews and their families. In the first, three Arab families had attended a wedding; in the second, one Manhattan bound newly-wed couple was returning from a honeymoon in Sydney; in both you had businessmen from Brooklyn, Queens, Westchester county and Long Island. In both there were babies, kindergarten children, two first graders twice, three middle-school students, five college students…

There was not enough space in that breezy corridor going through the clouds for two jumbo planes occupying it at the same time while going out of trajectory would have meant risking worse accidents in other corridors. We know now that the pilots in both planes had seconds to figure it out; they tried and veered and almost succeeded; but jumbo planes are unwieldy. Their tales tangled and sent them spinning.

This is not public domain, the media have only been informed that there was a technical failure at JFK's command center, not hacking; classified information. Nobody is allowed to look into it too closely for fear of panic. There is an investigation, period.

However, the moment the news of the "accident" reached me, I sensed having something to do with it. Like a tremor starting from the feet; like a punch in the stomach. Bullshit! Erase *I sensed* and replace it by *I knew*. This file is for me to be honest somewhere. Me to myself. Catastrophes are not missing in our skies, but that does not attenuate *my* responsibility. This one "accident in the sky," it was not simply *their* fault—the crazy fanatics that day were not *them*; it was my friends who triggered it. And to a degree, it was I, ex-Professor Etienne Zeltzki.

It was I who did this ignoble thing. In this secret file, I'll admit it's easier to confess to nobody. Dozens of bodies to dispose of, the warm remains of a massacre. Incapacitated families, innocent flesh, energies—myriad beings, consciousness(es) eradicated without reason, natural cause—and I am involved. Me who is only a couple of generations removed from the worst of abomination, I am among those who bring a new kind of abomination. I cannot ever let this one atrocity in the sky pass me by. I will have to mourn these dead as my own, and find I don't know exactly what ending, what solution and closure to their lives.

If you are gaming the encryption protecting this enough to read continuously, glean what you are looking for and forget the rest. I am not worthy of attention, and anyway, it's probably not for me that you make the effort of cracking this: you hope to learn more about Nathaniel Lagrange. You're smart, and not merely technically equipped; you're morally right if you treat me as background character of an apparently grand but ultimately sordid affair you hope will soon be forgotten, like I am some negligible vermin whose head you will kick back in the cesspool where he writhes as soon as you muster the courage of shrinking this to a resource-file. In the meantime, though, be aware that I might wrap around you Dante and Shakespeare and all the philosophers, so you condone my errors and imagine you're entering an intellectual paradise.

It's not white collar crime, my category; it's theoretical malevolence, idealistic nuisance, nefarious virtual influence. If I met you in the flesh on the pavement grey of 2nd Avenue, I could find a way to introduce myself, insinuate my good graces, have a drink, a bite with you, perhaps; but certainly not convince you to look into the most extreme positions, I mean this existentially. I am a good talker; but in the flesh, you would not follow me. I am too ordinary, a nobody. How different it would be if I met you through a cypher in some trendy corner of the Webwork. Especially if you guessed how close I have been to Nathaniel Lagrange.

Nathaniel has changed the bottom-line for cohorts of people without moving from his chair. He has convinced them to desist from beliefs, from attachments, projects, sense of belonging, essential possessions they took for granted.

Me, I was merely involved at several steps removed; I was not in the room, it's not me who pushed the key and triggered *Josephine*; but, yes, I am part of the terrible mess because I was there at her birth, fed her with schemes when she was an infant, stood next and encouraged her monstrous heads to acquire digital proportions.

This realization weighs tons the moment I wake up in my too-large bed, then look at the advantageous mirrors around me. I correct instinctively and see the old man, his jaw flaccid, his waist thick, big neck for his modest height. This formless man is me; and I am not quite sure which undesirable category best classifies my soul.

Even if no one links me to the "accident," if no jury condemns me, if no police agency persecutes me and my name never *surfaces* at all in the Lagrange affair, I am part of it. And you know why? Because I know I am.

There must, there will be one agent who suspects how close I have been to the Lagranges over the years. A professional, young FBI agent, journalist or graduate student who will insist that I be counted among the causes since my ideas—the consequences of my ideas, to be exact, my ideas once amplified by Nathaniel's megaphone—brought us here.

Guilty as hell; yet guilty of what, precisely? If I could answer this question, I would go straight to the closest police station and confess. At least in a court of law the accused confronts the accusation and the verdict. He may clear his chest. My crime can be concealed so well that I am no longer sure there is crime—while I also vividly remember there was, and I'll show you there was.

Logically, if I am not punished, I have to become the punisher. Someone has to pay for the slaughter. Someone has to pull over to himself the bloody shroud; and if there is no one to act this generously, then, let's have one to blame, the most likely culprit. It's the ancestral, proven solution and I see no reason to change that.

I can only imagine the grimace of disgust when the news pierced their eyes and ears. I was not in the room with Gabriela and Isabel when they met on our crystal panel the familiar Lagrange faces and saw them handcuffed, faces averted, wincing, Nathaniel blinking in the glare of lights—Kathy and John right behind him, stooped, ashamed, escorted by police. Our friends, my employers, on national TV at news hour, exposed as villains, a new breed of demons. This was too close to home!

I will confront my girl and my wife when I come back; by then the outrage will have faded some. I won't evade my guilt but acknowledge it head on. Tell them when they ask. No I was out of the loop when it came to JFK. Yes I have been responsible of monstrosity on the Webwork. It will be a relief. My direct participation has remained professional, and in the realm of ideas. When I'm back they'll excuse my mistakes like his father absolved the prodigal son. I'll cry in their lap. They are what matters to me. There will be another day. It may sound corny, but there is no other hope, no other goal. We'll talk again, I'll hold them close and we'll be our little family. If I don't die before this story ends.

I am entering the growing crowd of the elderly, but I'm not finished because I have this interface to pull off, this dangerous game of invisible Go to play with you, Nathaniel. I am sure you don't yet realize that I am after you to get you; you don't imagine your old friend *that* devious; and this is already an advantage. You never thought I was a man of consequence; you always loved to minimize my contributions. Me who was content with acting the figurant all my life, including among your following, I may become in my old age the one bringing you and the whole thing down.

Log 2

I slept poorly, tossed about like the damned in his circle of hell—mouth full of a bitter substance, lead pouring into my brains—and suddenly, beep! Isabel's smooth, open face is on my screen and it has this readiness to pardon me as always.

She is somber, my thirteen-year-old, the dark shade in her skin is pronounced, her lips pursed, her eyes dilated and red. I suppose they have cried a lot together with her mother. Isabel is immensely hurt; but she has slept, unlike her mother, probably. Isabel is still the happy child, confident in the future. There's got to be an end to the tunnel her daddy is in; we'll wake up together at the end of his nightmare.

"So, daddy, are you getting on better with the good guys?" She is repressing a smile and a sob.

"Not sure yet, as I told you."

"Yes, but that was already a week ago."

"Isabel, no reason to cry, I'm not accused of anything."

"Not yet."

"Maybe never," I said, adding in my mind, if I can arrange it.

We sort of laughed and then cried. She knows I'm doing this, breaking us apart and leaving her alone with her mother, to protect our home. She has seen clips of the catastrophe on her phone. She's overheard the mob connections; the accusations of racketeering and dirty hacking practices the name Lagrange has suddenly been associated with. It used to be one of these refreshing brand names coming out of the Webwork. It had made her proud of her dad, surprised and flattered that he was treated like a friend by cool people, the Lagranges being considered responsible of a whole attitude, more than a fad, almost like a way of being, a practical philosophy on a level with yoga or Zen, popular and not only among nerds. She had long thought her father went over his head when demonstrating at dinnertime ideas bigger than himself; and look, indeed, he was part of something much bigger than himself.

She doesn't know to which extent her dad and the "accident" at JFK are linkable; and Gabriela could not clarify that for her. It's to not have to clarify the extent of my involvement that I am not back home. I don't want Isabel to ask questions and having to lie. I have never lied to her. White lies, but not outright construction. However, one day, when she is grown, she may look for it and find incriminating evidence. I have worked for the Lagranges and been friends with Nathaniel way before the whole nasty affair started, before one talked about Desistence, before one defended the nebulous idea at all costs and even took great risks for it. In fact, I could boast of being the thinker behind it all. It's me who first provided the highfaluting references Nathaniel has plastered the walls of his *corridors* with; me who gave birth to the seeds of résistance he's seduced his young following with. But what would be the point of shouting it? Who cares about the creator and originator? The only man the crowd remembers is the one who sold them the idea.

Now, of course, it would be better not to be considered the Doctor Frankenstein of this monster. Anyway, the long story short, after years of friendship, we lost sight of each other; and it's when he reappeared in my life out of the blue, that I realized (at first incredulous) the phenomenon he had become. Placed in the best of circumstances, that is, helped by his family and Suzan Friedman, Nathaniel had propelled himself into fame. I could not begrudge him extraordinary talents when it came to cajoling his myriad listeners, to organizing the shrewdest youth on the Webwork; but, again, and I'll prove it to you, intellectually, Nathaniel is my creation, he is my student. And if you still admire him after all that's happened, you might call me the Socrates of this Plato; I inspired to his last musing on the Webwork.

It is also true that this inspiration occurred a long time ago, in our first friendship. Most of my intellectual input occurred when I was a young man, a bachelor, a grad student. It was long before *Josephine* straddled her *worms* and unleashed them unscrupulously.

Gabriela suspects that I could be brought to account for the catastrophe in some business-like capacity. But she will not ask me for explanations, not now, not until I am ready. She trusts me. She understands that I am trying to spare her; that whether I did something wrong or not, it was ultimately for our small good—and I love her for that.

There remains a diffuse threat: we, excuse me, the movement is responsible for having inserted *logic bombs* in digital hubs that regulate water, gas and electrical supply to neighborhoods of New York, preferably the Upper East Side and the West Village, Tribeca, Battery Park because they are more affluent. We could, in effect, threaten to starve among the richest people of the planet. We were not the first and, as a matter of fact, the *worms* Suzan Friedman tightly interconnected and called *Josephine* were just empty shells ready to serve, available to anyone willing to investigate online ([1]). Not that the Lagranges and their associates harbored a visceral anger against the rich—we'd become quite rich ourselves at this game. But exceptionally rich people are more exemplary victims than others, more convincing as victims. Who cares if you threaten Everyman, the one who pays his taxes and hardly gets by? He is frightened and already a victim. We chose the rich who'd carry the threat all the way down the social ladder. Meek, poor, pale people like to see the happy few tremble. Menacing the filthy rich and putting them on the grill made Desistence more popular.

And one more thing, let's imagine that we were forced to abandon our daily tribute to Desistence, threatened by some authority to reveal and dismantle the phalanges that work in the dark, what they bring of treasures to be safely deposited in our exclusive message board, *Josephine* would come handy; she would tie the hands of the police. They'd have to learn from us how to undress her.

They called it class struggle when I was a teenager. French people would whisper "La lutte des classes!" around me as though they were in awe of some golem coming from the dawn of time. Nowadays there is struggle, obviously, but it's group against group; it's every race and color and nationality and religion and income tax bracket against the other. And so, *we* feel—and I share strongly this feeling— that there is no reason why the rich men, women

---

[1] Suzan Friedman liked the name *Josephine*, code name of a famous hacker (presumed to be an adolescent male) from the heroic age of hacking. In 1974, *Josephine* used the New York Subway System's electronic board to say hello to *her* friends: "Go on hackers anonymous, let's eat them. It's our day!" This on all the bulletin boards, in scintillating letters above the crowds walking to destination that day.

and their children included, should be let off the hook. They're to be brought into the fray, the nitty-gritty; they've taken advantage, robbed the banks and walked out for too long scot-free.

Though a peripheral actor, a guest of the core group and not the source, the technician, the inventor, not the one more brilliant than me who came up with the digital knots and bolts, I repeat, I have been in favor of *Josephine*. I have known the danger she brings; and I have justified her in front of my own scrupulous conscience because she was necessary to us and a question of survival. I have participated in her breeding and felt the thrill of her getting strong enough to present a threat on a large scale.

I need to explain this notion of threat, central to the teachings of Nathaniel and to our strategy. It will shed a light on the particular kind of hacking Desistence has been committed to.

There is mention in *The New Yorker* of "tampering with the core managing system of clinics and major hospitals with the intention of disrupting the most profitable services and of affecting selectively the privileged patients, those who are presumably better treated than the rest of us."

Correction: we had no "intention of disrupting... profitable service," and no intention of hurting anyone; only the intention of threatening vital services if the authorities didn't get off our backs, didn't let us be the anonymous and busy bees that we are—until you did the unthinkable, Nathaniel.

Of course, *Josephine* was bad news from the start. The simple fact that one could concoct poison as elaborate, indirect and concealed as her. It was part of our selling pitch, even as the details of our deterrent remained secret: we were, if not dangerous, playing with danger; but hardly more than all kinds of financiers who threaten to bring the system down if they don't get their way. Until that moment when you blew your top, Nathaniel, until then, I was not associated with fanatics; in fact, Desistence is a response to terrorism. Nathaniel's on-going *Fragments* posted on the Webwork are all about what fuels fanaticism and looking for a response other than repressive. "Is it possible to counteract terrorism in the heart and mind if those who are about to perpetrate horror?" asked Nathaniel not long ago.

"How to show them the futility of their act? Not by mocking their god; by making clear that Desistence goes beyond any threat and any act of terror; it does away with religion and walks ahead of the dirty bombs and of any threat since it is about giving it all up."

"Desistence is about the power to terminate the process, whichever it is, and using that end, anticipating, betting on it, using, gambling on it all along."

Elsewhere, "Do you remember, perhaps from high school, the story of Diogenes of Sinope? Do you recall that one day Alexander the Great paid a visit to the famous beggar, usually represented sprawled in his rags inside the obscurity of a smelly barrel, itself half-wrecked on the sunny beach of a Greek island? So you remember what Diogenes said to Alexander: 'Please, get out of my sun.' To my mind this is ultimate freedom and defiance, and it resonates to this day. One can imagine old Diogenes in his filthy barrel full of garbage, and young Alexander dazzling in his cuirass, patronizing, paying homage to the scandalous philosopher. The most powerful man on earth bowing to the intellect of the least. Who came out the winner after Diogenes asked the emperor the move out of his sun, do you think? Did Alexander get out of Diogenes' way *like that*? Or someone in his personal guard put a hand on his sword. Alexander stopped him since nowhere is it said that Diogenes died then and there. The philosopher offered his life; of course, the emperor didn't take it. He knew better than to make of Diogenes a martyr."

I must say, Nathaniel excels at using common, even tired knowledge and bringing it to mean something new. One found correct considerations on *HighGunsOnTheSierra.com*, refined scholarship, daring, cavalier, yet also rigorous intellectual forays; and on top, one got the exhilarating feeling that it was not just a site full of *corridors* where people exchanged ideas before going back to more important business. One's browsing scratched the surface; what one bought into was only the vitrine of a machinery employing myriad busy bees harvesting for the long winter. There was a fervor to the site.

There was something protean about *HighGuns,* which offered the Lagranges and Suzan Friedman a platform for a constellation of things. They sold benign products: subscriptions to enlightening forum and modish chat-rooms centered on Nathaniel's last *fragments*; next to that, you had closets of virtual memorabilia bearing the signature of famous white hat hackers, preferably adolescent male heroes of the early 1960's, pioneers who showed the way. Deeper in the site you could find the basic hacking tools you needed to start exploring. Our front was a boutique for would-be hackers and Webwork tourists thirsty for *exploits* they would never dare. But they understood when buying our stuff and listening to Nathaniel, that inside the building there were hackers busy at work. It was not mere academic talk.

Today a popular site confirms that the Lagranges inserted malware able to scramble the distribution of dividends pertaining to select families, important investors on Wall Street, retirement-fund managers and union organizers living lavishly in Greenwich, CT. "They have designed *Josephine*," I quote. "It's a refined version of what was called *Trojan horses* by previous groups. It is aimed at crippling police, firefighters and ambulance phone lines at certain intervals. The Lagrange group has also implanted the latest version of an *Octopus virus* conceived to overdub official news, make anchormen say the contrary of what they say. This is something akin to summer 2008 when, one may recall, many heard liberal TV programming while on conservative cable; and the reverse happened as well: articulate, considerate liberal anchormen were insinuating oppressively macho, preposterously dated, racist, chauvinistic, homophobic and provincial conceptions. And this did not occur in one or two neighborhoods as it would have in an earlier stage in the already long history of hacking—this happened all over the tristate area. And it lasted as long as the *octopus* was not taken apart, flushed out of Webworks that absorb and digest maladies to grow more immune."

"Also, beware," I continue to quote, "selected computer screens and televisions are posting obscene subliminal *graffiti* invisible to the naked eye. Moving fast inside the quiet image, the icons on the toolbars, hard-core scenes of subjugation, abject oral and anal intercourse, multiple penetrations. Again, this affects one's device at unpredictable intervals and may be glimpsed at by whoever happens to be in front of the screen. Stay out of the screen's *face* and you may be safe. In another realm, apparently not connected, selected solar panels on top of selected buildings have emitted a kind of black light swallowing all the energy they were supposed to dispense. Again, until the last strand of malware is digested, one may protect one's console (for a fee) and one's roof; for the time being, until the process of destruction activated by the malware is better understood by the engineers, entire districts of the city, particularly those of the Upper East Side and the West Village, advise parents to unplug all means of communication, switch off IPhones and spare children."

All this would be funnier if it were not happening to you.

I sent a message to Gabriela to not worry about it, I do not think that Isabel's device is affected. We are talking about people who belong to a much higher bracket. However, what I've said so far doesn't sum up what parents, rich or poor, should worry about. Who has not heard about the Lagranges *teachings*, especially among the young, and including the young at heart?

Isabel has. It has to do with archaic ritual, with sacrifice, human and animal. Even if teens overhear tidbits and lack the frame of reference to comprehend, there is this vogue, this trend. And here I must again tip my hat to Nathaniel, his ability to question the long history of ritual sacrifice; he has pointed to a link between modern-day terror—rampant, everyday terrorism around the world nowadays— and the ancient traditions of sacrifice, fundamental to all religion. "Whereas in olden days one sacrificed the virgin, the goat, the bird to heal the collective wound and pacify the future," Nathaniel posted not long ago, "now one explodes oneself to access the end and annihilate in the process as many humans as possible. Whereas archaic sacrifice staunched the flame; it now inflames it—but it is still sacrifice."

Memorable lines. I will not shy away from what we owe to Nathaniel Lagrange. He is a criminal *and* he is one of the most influential thinker to come out of the Webwork. However jarring to my ears these twin facts, I must keep them together as I go on with this account. Without the computer, Nathaniel Lagrange would have stayed forever the loser I met late in the last century. Nathaniel and whatever he stands for, his *Fragments on Desistence* and his *Treaty of Self-Slaughter* are creatures of the Webwork. Desistence is contemporaneous with the coming of age of the digit.

Nathaniel has developed—more or less coherently, I will leave that to you my keen reader—what I had found in the French philosophers of the late XXth century. I told him about the Lacanian notion of *manque à être*, the idea of a fundamental non-being. I translated the sentences from the incomprehensible French psychoanalyst for him: "It's on the lack-of-being that the human subject hangs," I told him. "Or you could say, there is a bottomless being, call it a lack-of-being, which each one of us furnishes with imaginary objects and real torments." I transmitted to Nathaniel this Freudian sense among French forward thinkers that personal history is born in loss and grows around repeated failure—that as you gain in imaginary identity, you lose, give up on parts of your body and soul; you forget whatever does not fit in the adorable picture you must uphold. The price to pay is a pile a debris and refuse which trails you and that cannot be so easily forgotten.

Nathaniel absorbed all that and much more, and years later, in a world plagued by explosive terrorism, searched for the kind of self-sacrifice that could counter the bloody ones, the sacrifice to end all sacrifice. After all, the atomic bomb had rendered impossible full-out world wars by presenting the maximum threat. It may sound crazy, but many human beings could present the maximum subjective threat without moving from their console. He remembered what the two of us had talked about walking the streets of Manhattan; and to make a long story short, he came up with the idea of self-retreat, disengagement of self in all kinds of so called important collective pursuits. And, on the contrary, he called active, even aggressive Desistence—which, for instance, consists in learning the ins and outs of the digital substructure surrounding us—the solution to all our problems.

One phrase comes to mind: "If people reversed the fright instinct and, instead of fleeing, looked for the terrorists, found them in their lair and told them 'explode me, go ahead, I'm ready!' What would they do, your terrorists? What terror could they spread?"

Nathaniel, it seems to me, came up with this idea that the désistant is someone who accesses his lack-of-being, turns it into a resource. By not fleeing and freaking out in front of it, one makes of one's death a power. One can dwell for a long time on not-being, on refusing to be. One can hang there without having to reach for easy remedy.

Well, of late, it's been so appealing that this train of thoughts has filtered down to kids. Desistence has become some cheap wishy-washy ideology that gives credit to any kind of laziness and distraction.

Log 3

"Your friend is cool," said Isabel to me a month ago. She was probing me, she's been probing me since she was four.

"You mean *was* cool. I'm no longer with him, he's gone too crazy for me, you know that."

Chin down, she was pursing her lips, doubting my denegation. In my heart, I still was with the Lagranges. Frankly, I still admire Nathaniel and envy him to this day. And I regretted bitterly having split from the group and living like a lone wolf again. And my thirteen-year old could read me. Nathaniel and whereabouts is where it's at. The Lagranges are still out there *doing* it, even if they have to hide because the noose is closing around their necks. Nathaniel is not hiding alone, scheming alone like a creep.

"I guess he is cool because he is himself, doesn't pay obedience to any institution," I answered Isabel, hesitating and not about to tell her more than she could chew.

"He's the only thing that makes sense," said Isabel, taking stock of a long experience. She knows no more than what she's overheard Gabriela and me talk about; like everyone else she has surfed into phrases, expressions attributed to Nathaniel, whose flamboyant style has permeated the Webwork. Gabriela and I talked at dinnertime about the provocative blurbs coming out of *HighGuns,* my modest participation in the flow, my comments in the throng of his followers. I had a singular acquaintance to his thoughts, which helped me play the fiddle to them. Nathaniel could be enigmatic or his wording brutal. Gabriela worried, early on, about the despairing tone he affected, the threats he conjured; she was concerned by the fierce defiance she detected in his speeches. I would try to show her how interesting that day Nathaniel's pronouncements, quips, jests, jokes, retorts. Why Nathaniel's rebellious side has been so appealing to the young. He is the romantic hero of old literature, the loner and loser turned sage and, many believe, prophet. The family Lagrange had so much allure on the Webwork before they closed us; when our site hummed like a well-tuned engine. We were *HighGuns!*

"You're a third-generation Holocaust survivor, Dad! No wonder you're, excuse me, a little fucked up!" Her mother not being around I didn't have to reprimand her.

"I never think of myself that way... I mean, not the part about 'fucked up,' the one about third generation."

"But you are third generation, Dad, your granddaddy went to Auschwitz and never came back and your father was what you called yourself a drifter and a womanizer, not ... and you, well, it's not clear yet, is it?"

She blushed but she looked at me straight. She enjoys her version of what she has learned from me over the years. What you get in return when you give your child an honest education. I've evaded her questions about my family sometimes, but for the most part I have answered up to the point I thought she could take. I've told her what happened to Joseph, my Jewish grandfather who sneaked into France with his family as a child before WWI in order to escape the Warsaw pogroms—same grandfather who by the middle of WWII was given by French authorities to the Germans, along with his brothers and sisters.

I have told Isabel how my father, hidden during the war, spent his childhood in the countryside, came back semi-educated and grew streetwise in the streets of Paris. He divorced my mother when I was twelve and left us, left France and ended up in the tropics, hopping from island to island, selling small sail-boats so fast he didn't have to stay at anchor.

I have also told Isabel how on my mother side, they were all a little crazy, traumatized, but by the exact opposite experience, that of having gone through the war and survived when everyone else around them had died.

I kept to myself how I became some kind of educated drifter, a peddler of ideas that were no doubt great but did not pay the rent—an opportunist and a small-time gigolo. *Drifter*, I could not use that word to self-describe in front of Isabel. My grandfather should have left France to save his skin. I had to leave France and migrate to find more solid grounds. By immigrating at twenty-eight, I finally got somewhere. I planted my tent in a corner of the

English language and settled. My English still does not have the background, the thick roots that come from childhood familiarity; but I am okay with being a foreigner in this language. It was clear to me from the start that immigrating to America was going home, my second home, homemade.

My wife also is an immigrant who for other reasons couldn't make her home where she comes from. All this we have explained to our little girl in various ways. There were aspects not easy to impart: I didn't want her to carry the dark saga of Joseph and his eleven brothers and sisters, yet I still had to tell her some. She had to be aware of that terrible past; otherwise she would not be prepared for a shaky present, and I did not dare look into the future.

My faults she will have to deal with; but I cannot tolerate that my personal errors poison her future, constrict her prospects. This is why I am thinking about a grand solution.

I sit alone in this room orange painted. Fluffy, hairy brown carpet under my naked feet. I thought at first it would make things even worse, but I switch off all the lights and let darkness come in the middle of the day. My suite being on a low floor and the hotel ensconced between mammoth structures, there is little natural light. And yet at dusk, for a minute or two, a ray of sunset from the red-hot sky comes down to me. It is so strong that it pierces higher windows nobody cleans. Then, I open the curtains.

And me, who liked binges! Once married I'd given up on affairs, but I'd indulge otherwise. I had moments of excess, drank single malt and Pouilly-Montrachet. Now, for the last two weeks, I mean, I starve on healthy stuff and comport myself like an angel, I drink juices. Exquisite Zen dishes are brought to my lacquered table on a silver tray. I need to be in shape for this last one. I have to lose weight and muscle up. If possible regain some of the handsomeness.

Even without moving from my bed, a doctor told me he can send nanobots up my bloodstream that will eat up greasy molecules and putrid tissue, and make me pure as a baby. For a price, I was promised that the laser touch would rejuvenate to the cells of my marrow. I will be the same, but only in appearance. The exterior will remain that of an old man because that's who I am, unless I choose to re-skin head to toe, which I don't want.

"I am who I am," I told this doctor, "just make me strong *inside*."

Beautiful young people they have in hotels like this, and quite willing, for an extra fee, to add natural charm to the laser, procuring highly-needed relief. It used to be only in Third World countries that populations resorted to the selling of sex. I let the cute nurse do her job without looking at her legs for fear that I could not resist because I can pay the extra fee.

I pass on each opportunity politely, "No, thank you, another time, maybe" and don't pursue the smile girls hardly a couple of years older than Isabel send me down the avenue. Whether in the lobby of my hotel or just outside on the pavement, even on an affluent block between Madison and Park Avenue, they come in pairs, light like birds of prey; they flutter around you, migratory birds. They lower their slender body and whisper gaily in my ear, "Hey, young man, wants some threesome piece of youth this evening?" Offerings of life burst inside panties and modish brassieres; young love is for sale. I refuse to yield to the flattered impulse in me, not out of purity or devotion to my wife, but because I inevitably perceive the humiliation in their eyes—I am talking about the twenty-year-old college students who are throwing themselves at me; and I think about Isabel not having to throw herself at anyone any time soon, not ever if I can prevent it. And I feel blessed and not in the mood to fuck this young person.

I may regret it during the night, but that's how I feel on the spot.

The diverse police outfits roaming the Webwork have so far succeeded in keeping secret from the general public the long-term threat posed by *Josephine.* They have also caved in to the demands of the "cyberpunk terrorists" and let them go. I am no longer physically among them, but thanks to the contacts I keep, I know that in exchange for their escape, Nathaniel and John, the younger brother, and sister Kathy Lagrange have collaborated and helped overwrite *Josephine.* Not all of her, not the squirmy saliva she leaves behind once squeezed empty. Who can tell if some avatar is not sleeping in an image on my screen or on yours, reader? Say, you are with your child and you are expecting to watch the pumpkin metamorphose into a beautiful six horse carriage deserving of a princess, and instead, the pumpkin stands up, splinters, turns into a porcupine, who invades the screen and pop! there is no more image, no more screen and no more machine. This is benign; but it may not be. Some viral string may use your laptop and make of you a blind accomplice, fooling you, abusing your intention, borrowing fingers who write innocent lines. Many now go on working knowing they unknowingly toy with dangerous messages out there ([2]).

I should not use this machine at all. But how could I *not* use a computer and try to make sense of my predicament? I look into the crisp white electronic page and I fear revealing not enough and too much. I spare Isabel by not telling her the fix I'm in while all I am going to say here is for her, for me one day to be able to talk to her. Meanwhile, will I not build a case against myself?

---

[2] *Logic bombs* implode at the mere evocation on screen of a sound, a date, a time, a name, the wrong spelling of a word, the foreign turn of a sentence. Once triggered and roaming at large, *worms* and *rabbits* are prone to enjoy a kind of independent life. With or without your consent, metastasis of the virus may attack sensitive tissue—emergency codes, alarm systems, personal records, insurance accounts, property records. They behave on the Webwork like out-of-control cells do in a human body.

Log 4

Being alone, no longer among family and friends, is nothing new. I was mostly alone during my ten years in Paris; alone when I emigrated and lived uptown Manhattan in a rundown apartment. I didn't have yet what you call a home. Not that I was homeless; I was by myself. And then, late in my life, at forty, something occurred, actually related to my encountering Nathaniel Lagrange, and I transformed into a professor, a husband and a father. I passed my degree and published.

And now again, at sixty-two, I am back doing it alone and in the shadows. This time, I want my existence to become cloaked in the thickest secrecy. I would like to not weigh more than a cypher. Having cut the branch that supported me, I progress in a deep fog; but I progress and learn. I keep telling myself that I have not lost but merely loosened the ties that bind me to everyone who's dear to me; but who knows.

"For how long?" she said. Will I ever be able to show this file to Isabel? I keep contradicting myself; but no, in fact, I should not show her. This will remain the unseen Nathaniel Lagrange, classified testimony on the dark side of his reputation and, as far as I am concerned, a defense against no accusation where I run the risk of exposing myself.

You didn't do it any more than I did it. That's what you tell yourself. It was not you, Nathaniel; you were part of a group that went too far reluctantly, *à leur corps défendant*. The Lagranges acted against the grain. You must pretend to yourself (as you pretend to your following) that you were manipulated by the police, as though your computer had been forced into a *blotnet*. And maybe it's true, they forced you to consider measures of reprisal, your following was asking for them, you had to show spine and muscle, you fell into the trap of the puppet-leader; but I have been too close to you to not see how you enjoyed the power *Josephine* placed in your hands. She aggrandized your influence over many lives—how much you liked to influence and right down control people, Nathaniel. Strange for someone who had made of Desistence and manqué-à-être the cornerstone of his teaching.

I am no longer as impressed by your rhetoric as when I met you, about twenty-five years ago. You no longer fool me, Nat. When the shit hit the fan and you blew your top, you were under no other influence than your own inflated self. You didn't have to satisfy your following; you could have taught them otherwise, you could have quoted your own *Fragments* and showed restraint. You could have desisted.

My understanding is that you were at the command of *HighGuns*, Suzan Friedman worked under you, and everyone else doted on your last word. And it's to enjoy this empire and gamble it all that you woke up *Josephine* and pushed the key.

Luckily for me, I had jumped the boat by then; and so, my hands are clean, if not my mind. I would lie if I said that I quit because of *Josephine*. It's not like I had the choice. I didn't quit, Suzan didn't give me the boot either, the group simply didn't have the same need of me.

Would I have pushed the fatal keystroke if I had been in Nathaniel's shoes? Probably. Probably not, to start with because I couldn't be in his shoes. I couldn't be the leader. I could whisper in the leader's ear, but my kind of malice works better in the shadows. I can assist, work toward dire circumstances. I can respond with rage to perceived affront; I am relentless in revenge and sadistic when I get a chance to screw my enemy; however, making the move to directly risk a killing is another level of engagement. Sorry for the cynicism but giving death requires a hot temperament professional intellectuals like me can rarely boast of. Nathaniel is a rare kind of intellectual and not a professional, never finished his degree.

Again, it's not that when angry your professional may not envision the most vicious angles of a killing spree; I contemplate the destruction of fellow human beings once in a while with a smile on my face. Let's be honest, there is a fair amount of people I would indifferently keep or wipe out because I don't see the reason for their being. My bias is not racial, religious or nationalistic, idiots come from all walks of life. Only, I could not do it; I would not be the one putting theory into practice.

We talked about the intolerable possibilities *Josephine* placed in the hands of morally troubled and emotionally fragile, to not say neurotic and a bit perverse and psychotic—individuals like, well, like you, Nathaniel, and drunken brother John, and our friend Jacques the Cynic, and overweight but cute sister Kathy, and ambitious Suzan Friedman. And I should count myself here. The Lagranges were a pretty self-conscious bunch. To spy on, temper with and sway private lives in undisclosed directions, isn't that the traditional role of corporations, administrations and governments? How could *we* crush dreams, frustrate desires, mess with people's activities and intentions? No way. And if the *worms* were excited, programmed to discharge, how could we handle the idea that it might cost a few New Yorkers not merely their bank account, their virtual identity or the store of their medical records, but their limbs and perhaps their lives? This was unthinkable. Harming anyone was disgusting, unbearable the idea of ever being the cause of pain in another. The cause of anything wrong.

It's not that we were Robin Hoods taking from the overfed to feed the deprived, but we robbed—if the kind of hacking we did had anything to do with robbing—only from the well provided for, the surfeited. And we never robbed for money. I am talking about the phalanges that still deposit their loot in the BBS of the Lagranges as we speak; I am not talking now about what Suzan was doing with her own team of crackers; nor am I looking into *Josephine* at the moment. Under the banner of Desistence, the phalanges inspected, copied the algorithms that were taking over the management of information in every aspect of life on earth. And if, to give a proof of our potential, we happened to complicate the lives of the few who had too much, it didn't amount to more than a bad joke. Until—

Here is the contradiction on which I break my head. Nathaniel has taught his Webwork viewers never to commit violence on other than on themselves, and this self-inflicted ferocity to remain metaphorical—unless it comes to last resort, if they are at a loss, pushed into a dead-end, humiliated or otherwise subjugated. Accept to lose, be the loser, give up, but don't give in. Retreat is our slogan, give up a limb, retreat physically and in yourself, *worldwide* Desistence we call it.

My reader may have skimmed his ideas, applauded, even commented if he is young and curious. Nathaniel has professed of modern-day abandon-of-the will to succeed, the desire to achieve—the desire *period*. It's Schopenhauer for the Webwork. At one point agreed upon we refuse, we give up, we prefer not to... Not to what? We lift our hands from the keyboard, switch off the console, put it on lull; and yet, at the same time, keep a wary eye on what's going on, keep track and record, but without intervening. Buddha and ancient Stoicism mixed together for the enlightenment of the geeks. Sweet negative power, we don't say no and act upon it, we merely threaten to do so. We inspect the recondite workings of the Webwork and amass knowledge of its redundancies and weak points to become potentially very effective.

Everything hinges on this potentiality.

Please, anyone, don't act on theories. Not even the old-world theories, not even the thousand-year-old thoughts that now sleep in their dusty digitized copies—let them sleep. There is a metaphysical gulf between thought and action, theory and practice—the Greeks asked their Gods for assistance before acting—and nobody has bridged it unscathed.

Between the sharp examples of Desistence you gave daily and the horror of the "accident" you precipitated, between Buddha and Schopenhauer, *and* the bodies that video clips show burning on the grounds amidst carcasses of planes and exploded buildings, the juxtaposition is grotesque, incomprehensible. And yet *there is* a connection since it is the same man who participated in both.

I have already confessed there was something exhilarating in living on the safe side of a threat, of having the power to rock the boat and hold on to it—of trading danger for the advantage. Such a secret gave you a high, even to someone like me who did not comprehend the technical side of hacking and easily resorted to attractive metaphors. More corporations, groups and institutions were protecting themselves aggressively. Big companies were unassailable—why not us?

I remember Suzan Friedman chiding Nathaniel: "It's a deterrent, Nathaniel, which, as its name indicates, has the power to freak them out as long as it's proven, shown as effective, but not used. How do we prove to them *in the virtual* that we have a digital bomb of magnitude, leave that proof to me. No need of a dissertation. You're so much the hippy or the Trotskyist or I don't know what they called people like you last century. We cannot trigger *Josephine*, and the call is not moral; it's business, not in our interest, bottomline, *point à la ligne*." She could pronounce French syllables clearly enough for her American intonation to shine through. "We can't afford *Josephine* messing everything up. She has the power to unleash hell if we let her. So, we won't use her *worms*. We'll trade their formula when the time comes."

She was still the boss, then; and she was good at bluffing—herself, to start with, assuaging her own fear. If only to prove to our enemies that her threat was not in jest, not merely virtual or at an embryonic stage, at some point her *worms* had to show their ugly head and discharge a sample of their secretion in the environment. That's what Suzan called *the proof*, maybe not the Big Bang, but some nasty little mess all the same. Don't weapons call for war like scientific theories demand experimentation? Tell me of one weapon that rusted in the warehouse forever. Suzan could marshal our tacit agreement and our silence (we had no other choice), but all involved felt that statistical crime was brooding as soon as the membranes inside *Josephine* breathed in their unnatural cocoons. She was the reason why Suzan couldn't sleep. And that was before she realized how much the danger came from *within*. That it was you, Nathaniel, she'd have to fight off.

I could no longer sleep and I was nowhere near you, in the eye of the storm.

Oh! I'm sure, Nathaniel, the carnage went way beyond your intention, even as you raved over the keyboard and spat too many words a minute. You never dreamt of the devastation in your worst nightmare. I never did —though, since I'm telling the truth here, I did dream one night that planes lost control and brushed past each other over the Hudson River. And one night I dreamt that there blew an icy cold wind of utter panic as a jumbo airbus and its 550 passengers vanished in a black hole far in the galaxy. However, the plane was saved in my dream when a female-looking angel descended from on high (she looked exactly like a younger Suzan) to bring the air-traffic controllers back in communication with the pilots, directing him through a maze of conflicting false-truths and fake information. But I never dreamt something like an international airport whose phone lines and radar screens go blank for several long minutes.

Suzan didn't find the way to get into the system at JFK for quite some time, and not for lack of skill or not enough computing power. It is always possible, at least in theory, to open top security apparatus by cracking access codes. It is, however, quasi impossible in reality to operate damage inside self-contained networks like those that control airports: too many layers of protection, it would take years and vast teams harnessing the power of gigantic *botnets*.

Luckily—erase this… Lately, the air-traffic controllers (like those who persisted in my dreams) were deemed too expensive, unreliable and their political affiliation unsavory. They were replaced by advanced electronic devices effective at sorting zillion data per second, decisive when drawing consequences and taking apolitical and unemotional decisions. Problem is, being machines, their intelligence is penetrable, and they have no say, no qualms.

For Suzan, the solution did not consist in cracking their codes, however; but in speaking to one of the executives in charge of the airport. What she told him no one knows—I guess, what she told us, that she needed a bargaining chip. Anyway, it was not easy, I can assure you, airport executives are guarded, well-paid, scrupulous, honest individuals. She discovered looking at bank accounts that someone had been squandering money like there was no tomorrow. Money is the purveyor of destinies. He gave her enough information for her to break in. You will understand that I don't give the man's name; it's not my intention to accuse anyone in particular—save you, Nathaniel.

Nor will I get into the technical details of how *Josephine* operates, the ones I have come to understand. Do not ask me to contribute to her multiplication. In any case, by now, she can be had on the dark side of the Webwork for a price; you may scotch her entire brain to your drive without much of a sweat.

Once she had put *Josephine* together, Suzan could let the authorities detect what kind of catastrophe they'd have *on their hands* if they senselessly insisted in bothering us. And we'd dismantle *Josephine* limb by limb, buying time, immunity, freedom to operate outside the country. But you're not like Suzan, Nathaniel. You're not good at bluffing. Once you took charge, you had to act like the redneck that you've remained, you had to brag and bluff and show your cards. The police didn't play with you. Aggressors tend to feel aggressed, so you're convinced and have convinced your troupes that they forced you into retaliation. And again, I keep revisiting this and looking into the data, maybe they did. But whatever you did (just a few clicks in your case), you did it as a free agent so that the hecatomb, the fumes of massacre—it's all yours.

I, for one, want to make sure it is.

Last week your names were in *The New York Times*, your family portrait on the second page of the *Daily News*: "Hardly two weeks after the catastrophe, Nathaniel Lagrange, the head of the group, his brother John and sister Kathy Lagrange, all three well-known for organizing the movement called Desistence, plus their attendants and service people, all have vanished. Nothing has been reported of their whereabouts since." Half of the front page of the *New York Post*: "Read how the cyberpunk rascals skip town!" And in bolder print: "With top cop approval!" Blurb on the portal of *The New Yorker.com*: "This time they are not your usual young disheveled air-heads. They may be disheveled, but they are mature white old males and females—a bunch of old beards. Picture them like some kind of comfortable old hippies loafing on the strip of quaint Woodstock, NY. Long gray hair flowing like in the case of the leader, Nathaniel. With one big difference, this group has the looks but it does not act relaxed and does not give you ideological buzzwords; the Lagrange family may be tanned, forearms tattooed, but they don't spend weekends on their motorbikes. They practice their dark power in nitty-gritty New York City, perched at the top of luxurious towers, where their aliases take risk for them so that they can make tons of money while also discussing great ideas in their chat-rooms like old school philosophers. They come complete with masters in computer sciences, engineering and Ph. D. degrees in Philosophy from elite institutions. "

They explain your schemes on TV, they research your antecedents. Nathaniel, John, Kathy Lagrange have become household names. Interestingly enough, though, nobody mentions Suzan Friedman; she has succeeded in remaining undetected. They comb your respective childhoods, and among tech and terror specialists assembled for *The Lehrer News Hour*, debate the kind of alarming precedent you set for future generations.

And I am associated with you, Nathaniel, which flatters me and gives me importance; and makes me feel anxious to the point that I cannot stay for long in my room. I spend nights walking down 2nd Avenue, visiting coffee shops, hotel lounges, *Barnes and Nobles* and *Starbucks*. I sit alone, surrounded by the brouhaha of the café and enjoying my anonymity. Or else, I settle outside on the terrace, in front of this creamy white, super slim Mac, and plunge deep into the strident noise of sirens and honks, the constant crowd moving like a controlled sea on the pavement. I fool myself into imagining that all these innocent people are protecting me by their ignorance, taking care of me unknowingly, my complicated secret.

And then I look into my IPhone and neither Gabriela nor Isabel has called for days. Whenever I dose off, I can see myself walking back home and kissing Gabriela who prefers to direct the conversation toward some interesting task Isabel has to do for school. Nevertheless, I am kissing Gabriela on the nape of the neck, at the root of her dark hair where she has a beauty mark, which always gives her the frisson. There is the cherry color of the solid wooden floor we have added, and the cherished pictures and things we've accumulated over the years. It's Isabel's turn, she kisses me on the cheek once and fast. "Hé dad, how you're doing?" She gives me a complicated handshake that cracks me up. She is comfortable in the skin of the Upper West Side kid and can afford to copy the ghetto black and the Hispanics from El Barrio. Not mock them, just play with the lingo. A second later she is the preppy girl who speaks French to her dolls since she was an infant.

But then I wake up. I will not call them... I should not call, better to remain absent and benevolent. Gabriela has to protect Isabel. Until my plan works, I have to protect them through tokens of my affection.

Where are you, Nathaniel? I need to find you and dissociate myself from you before it is too late. If you were dead, your fame would be assured, you'd be flying high, excused from the roll call that pins us down here, white as snow, sanctified as the archangel who bears your name. Desistence is still massively behind you. Your hacker friends keep considering you their hero. It's a matter of pride—how could they be so wrong when following you? Many argue on the Webwork that it's the police who meddled and fumbled, and again, yes, no doubt, if you look at the clips and listen to the tapes, they did—yes, it's the police who put you between a rock and a hard plate. As it is, however, no one associated with you is immune to the foul breath, the ripple of muck that you exude.

There is a reason why nobody is barging in on me. It's not that I didn't do actual damage and could pass for a mere "thinker," blogger endowed with a wee bit more insider information—in the end, no more than an antecedent and an accessory to the crime. I can't help but think that they have let me hide behind this version. For now, they don't bother me and prefer to monitor my moves in the hope that I will lead them to the Lagranges. They spare me to use me later. Being the old friend that I am, I will help them track and bring the family down without violence and too much publicity, they think. And they are right; that is what I intend to do, bring Nathaniel down, and if I am lucky enough, hand him in person to the police. I want to find Nathaniel and see the end of him.

Log 5

It is about time I describe my first meetings with Nathaniel. At first there was only Nathaniel. This was in 1995, long before he was anything. I am going back to the beginning, to even before there was the possibility of Nathaniel ever meeting someone like Suzan.

He was the salesperson at the Annex of the Griffith Bookstore. Since then, the store on Broadway and 82nd St. has gone bankrupt and the Annex transformed into luxury condominium. Bookstores, let alone second-hand bookstores, have become a thing of the past. They were already on their way out in the early 1990's.

A block away from Riverside Drive, the Annex occupied the top floor of an old and stately Upper West Side high-rise. Ivy covering the stucco and the rose bricks, drive-in rotunda, marble reception like for an ancient palace, doorman elevator wearing copper buttons on his dark blue uniform. Entering this building was like revisiting New York City half a century earlier. The Annex occupied a seven or eight-bedroom apartment tucked right under the monumental eaves of the roof. Shelves were stacked with books up to the ceiling, even in the two bathrooms, the storeroom and the kitchen. I wondered how the bookstore's owner paid rent selling second-hand masterpieces for a buck.

There were few clients, and they came mostly for the salesperson who knew, or gave the impression he knew, about every single one of the hundreds of thousands of books. In two jumps he was at the one you were looking for, got hold of it and perched on the highest rung of the ladder. There, he would curve his back and lean head and shoulder against the ceiling. He'd flip the pages of the book between yellow fingers and look you right in the eye. Then, in a tone of confidence and personal attention, he'd talk at length about it, making boundless digressions and unlimited parenthesis.

Not that he had read cover to cover every book, but he could relate its title, its lasting influence or its debt to other books. He'd elaborate on its obscure and difficult origins, tell you the tormented life of its author and the dire conflicts pregnant in its context. Unless it was a book that had no reason to be, a pale duplicate of a theory better elaborated somewhere else, a showy and empty gathering of words only meant to obtain at your expense instant fame. "Piece of trash, the binding has more value than the content, inexistent as work, as thought, as anything, and yet printed material paid for and robbed from more worthy writers who were not allowed to see their work in print."

Aiming at the trashcan across the room, he'd mimic the gesture of throwing the book in it like a basketball, and tell the client to consider better choices. And if this client got offended by so heavy-handed an attack against his selection, then Nathaniel would not retreat: "You asked my opinion and I gave it to you… if you know better, you do what you want, naturally." On his way down the ladder, he'd give the book back to the client and go sit on the stool near the cash register.

Now, if it was what he considered an essential essay in theology, philosophy, literature, psychoanalysis, archeology, anthropology, ethnology, geology, physics, thermodynamics, chemistry or astrology (!), he would delve into a protracted discussion, especially if you contradicted him in any way, and in particular if you were a young blond person studying hard at the nearest college up Broadway, Columbia University.

You didn't have to be curious about him like I was, to notice that he loved to impress young blond and very white women, fresh from Indiana, Idaho or Nebraska. He could be very helpful, become indispensable even. He could rewrite the term paper for you.

Standing behind a high shelf, I heard him read out loud from a page someone had dared submit to him. He trashed every aspect, including the commas and the exclamation points. And the more he savaged it, the more the young woman loved it and asked for more. I wondered whether the process of rewriting these elaborate compositions involved a touch of natural tenderness after his shift or only a modicum of money.

More than a few owe Nathaniel a great deal in this respect, who have not and will not come forth—and not only young blond things.

Later, when we had become friends, I showed him a draft of the introduction to my thesis. It was courageous of me, given that I expected him to scoff at the haphazard look of my paragraphs and the shaky syntax. Of course, I'd come late, in the last hour of his shift, making sure no other client lingered in the Annex. He'd slide the ladder next to the high window, from where, even at my low level, you could see a sliver of the river beyond the mountainous trees of Riverside Park. Up the ladder I imagined that the dark river must have glistened with lights.

Come spring, by the time I'd enter the Annex and look through the windows, trees were tender green and the river orange from remnants of the sun sinking beyond the hills of New Jersey. I've always been touched by dusk, and it was splendid at the Annex. I'd drag a stool from under the cash register and sit at the foot of the ladder, looking at shredded skies outside and hearing the voice from above.

He read out loud sentences of mine that I didn't recognize. They were felicitous until they made me wince. He'd shout invectives at my writing, accuse me of sloppiness and of juxtaposing ideas without method or destination. It was a hard school, learning with Nathaniel. But then, to write a thesis in English when you have been educated in another language is hard anyway. As a second-language learner you had to grow a thick skin, the first layer of which I'd developed the moment I set foot in this country. Bit by bit, night after night, Nathaniel ended by giving me important advice regarding both form and content, and, in effect, rewrote (orally) key segments of my dissertation. He didn't let me off the hook until it was impeccable. There were weeks I'd come talk to him every day and, strangely, he seemed always as interested by the topic, as involved and invested in the process of clarifying my thoughts as I was. He was looking forward to bringing my work to fruition.

He had an amazing generosity of mind. As long as you offered the framework, institutional format and deadline, and provided you came with a circumscribed argument he could not blow out of proportions, Nathaniel was an incomparable resource. He never corrected my words on the page or scribbled in the margins like professors did, but he was a remarkable editor, and a much more effective teacher than those who "occupied" (to speak like him) the teaching positions at the graduate school where I'd matriculated. Not only did he give you his deepest consideration, his heartfelt encouragement if he liked your pursuit, but he thanked you for sharing the discoveries, thanked you for the flights of thoughts you afforded him. He loved to learn and to wrestle with age-old topics, the more arcane and arduous the better.

New to canonical English literature, I needed to sink my teeth into John Milton and some of his following, the British romantics. One page written by Milton would be more than enough material for an essay of three hundred pages. I had to find that page; and then, not merely understand it, but get an angle, cut through the centuries of commentaries and become a specialist full of original thoughts concerning the great Milton. I went to him in search of the best available edition of *Paradise Lost*.

He acted as though I was looking for his favorite writer ever, the one he had permanently on his mind. Then he ran along the shelves and, without hesitation, grabbed the edition that in the eyes of the connoisseur stuck out among the row of its lesser siblings. Book in hand he climbed the ladder.

From his funny position, with his angular chin and nose, his piercing blue eyes and bony frame, the fact that we were at dusk... it struck me that he resembled the bird of prey about to fly into the night—some animal not as domesticated as the rest of us, still free to wander in the forest of ideas. Nathaniel was a tall man, past the prime of his youth, thirty-five (about my age), though he remained thin, muscular, nervous and as full of electric energy as a young man. He had a way to make you instantly understand that he stood *beyond* what you saw of him, outside this low, unrewarding position he occupied (as a salesperson); and if you found him crouched against some dark corner of the ceiling in an obscure second-hand bookstore on the Upper West Side it was because he had chosen to do so for reasons of convenience. He'd given up long ago on climbing the social, professional echelons one climbs when one indulges in phony self-aggrandizing and compromising.

He had given up, resisted, opposed climbing that ladder for the sake of purity of purpose, I presumed, purity of soul. The more I visited him in the Annex, the more he looked like a racing horse who'd chosen to confine his jumps to these modest stalls for fear of breaking his exquisite legs running too fast in the open. He reminded me of Baudelaire's Albatross that flies faster than hawks and eagles, but whose majestic wings prove awkward and make him look ridiculous once on the ground. To finish with grand comparison, he made me think about an unknown and forever obscure Rimbaud, who'd been brilliant beyond measure earlier in his life.

This first time, flipping through the thick book back and forth, and then looking in the distance at the river and the dark sky, he took his time to come to the matter. We were facing an Everest of literature, and so, before the climb, we had to take a stroll in the valley, gather provision and flex our muscles on the approaching slopes. In guise of introduction, and to test my personality (he had, no doubt, detected my accent and wondered if I was as snotty as French people were rumored to be), Nathaniel took an unexpected direction. He confessed to daily strumming on his guitar tunes by Bob Dylan, Elvis Presley, Muddy Waters, the Beatles and such.

"Great stuff, right?"

Indeed, abundant blond hair still wavered on his head like he were a mature Rock n' Roll star, some Brian Jones that hadn't died prematurely. On the spot, I didn't know what to think of Bob Dylan, Presley and the Beatles. I loved their music, but over the years my taste had moved toward Jazz and Classical music. Yet I also sensed the trap. So, I told him that, as a good boy in France, I'd received piano lessons.

"You could probably teach us the notes, then?" he said in a relaxed manner. I felt the sting. "Me and my friends, we play by ear."

"I could probably, yes, read notes by Bob Dylan but never play by ear," I answered, repressing the remark that perhaps soon-to-be-middle-aged men and strumming early pop songs all day didn't mix well together, unless you'd long made a name for yourself, of course. Or you had children in whom you cared to instill the worldview of your own childhood in the 60's.

Though he practiced a lot alone and among his few friends, Nathaniel admitted never performing in public: "I don't care for the show. It's the spirit that counts; and very few capture it, don't you think? They're too busy playing the crowd."

I let this flourish pass. You were allowed to smoke indoors, Nathaniel chain-smoked, his corner up there was thickened and made blurry by volutes of smoke. He combed his hair between smoky fingers, smiled and let me see the irregular tip of his gray front teeth. You could tell that his vertiginous side was not that of a star, who may die of overdose tomorrow, but whose teeth are sparkling clean today, and the nails impeccably done. Nathaniel had this frown of absorption and self-pity I have seen on the faces of angels who've fallen on hard times.

I must have satisfied to his test by saying nothing and waiting patiently for his verb to flow (the snob not being who you expect), for there was something of a wild call, an illumination in his eye. Nathaniel was excited by the version of *Paradise Lost* he was selling me and for so very cheap.

"Boy oh! Boy!" he said, "if there is a book worth reading it's this one, in this edition. You can throw just about everything else in the garbage …" He sent a denigrating glance around. "We need to talk after you've read it, make sure we do."

"Yes, let's make sure," I answered, "and which aspect in particular should I consider?"

I could see that half of his face smiled while his penetrating gaze tried to evaluate my level of preparation to John Milton. "Are you familiar with his views on the Enemy, the Arch-Enemy, Satan?"

"My teacher in Grad School is only at the beginning of the book," I answered.

"Where exactly?" he asked, apparently without noticing the supercilious tone in my voice.

"In the third book, where Satan is this enormous, black, winged monster who lands in Paradise, this *Alien* (he beamed at my reference to the film) who diminishes in size and transforms into a lizard, a serpent and finally a toad—small enough to crouch at the tender ear of Eve… "

I was trying to undercut the didactic tone, somewhat difficult to sustain. He smiled at my attempt but was not laughing.

"I know," he interjected; and then, raising one index finger and serious as a professor emeritus in a crowded amphitheater, he said: "While she sleeps, you get that, while she is out, unconscious, dreaming, Satan infiltrates her hearing… he sneaks his dirty little tongue into her aural cavity… He squirms, he croaks, he whispers flattering words in there, using his 'wiles,' Milton writes, 'to reach/The organ of her fancy, and with them forge/ Illusions as he list, phantasm and dreams'… Hum, what a great passage!"

"Man, you know this stuff!" I acknowledged in admiration.

"Yes, I do, and do you remember that Satan has fought against Him, His virtual Son and their grand plan regarding the Creation, Fall and Redemption for more than 10 000 years, by now?"

I had not factored in this number and thanked him for reminding me how deep-seated was resentment in the armies of fallen angels, the rebellious souls led by their leader, the Archangel, previously the most beautiful among those who sat in conclave around God.

He resumed after a deep drag on his cigarette: "Satan is nobody and he's everybody. Satan is able to occupy anyone's shoes. He knows what *you* want… He'll introduce into Eve dreams of grandeur like we all share"—he looked at me—"The toad crouching at her ear makes her believe she'll lead the revolution against Him and His vapid Son, who forbid her to learn. She'll teach Adam and show him in turn what she has learned eating of the fruit, and, of course, being female, she likes that."

Ah ah! Nathaniel rolled his eyes and observed me like a chess player his competitor. Though nothing tangible was at stake, my intellectual honor was, my intelligence. This was more demanding than graduate seminars where you scribble doodles in your notebook, look outside the window when there is one, and daydream.

His lips were sealed. No more from him, it was my turn. Trying to get even, I said: "At this point also, don't forget, Eve in her waking state has already noticed *the fruit* and heard the injunction not to sink her sweet tooth in it. Adam has told her of a casual chat he's had with angel Gabriel—not to touch, not to suck on it... Soon the Serpent will stand high in front of her and demonstrate the virtues *of the fruit*..."

I succeeded in saying all that, but Nathaniel had to have the last word, which was okay with me. This store was his domain. "*The fruit*, as you so justly say, you're right, it's the word used by Milton... well, what is it about that fruit? It is like an empty shell, the empty signifier of our post-moderns. In other words, it can mean anything you want. Notice, it's Satan who gives meaning, justification to the interdiction, saying it comes from a jealous God, who does not want men and women to know more than they do. In the Bible and in Milton, no reason is given by God (or his angels) why not to eat of the fruit. Why the apple? Why not kiwi or banana? No reason. It's just the way it is. There is a limit to knowledge, beyond which starts respect, religious respect. Milton lived in the seventeenth century, man, when the sacred still had a place. Don't touch. Don't argue anymore *there*. If it were kiwi and banana that were forbidden, you could ask the same question and there would be no answer. Except from the mouth of Satan, *who loves to fill the void that God leaves behind.*"

Where had he read that? For more dramatic effect, Nathaniel had suspended his speech. Although the word "God" sounded out of place, what he said resonated in the day to day. "Look, says the Serpent to Eve, this apple is full of fantastical properties. It's morphine, a rapid way to reach Nirvana and fulfill the wishes you didn't even know you had. Satan entices Eve in the forbidden zone where we know and she knows she's trespassed for the best reasons, to learn and teach to her progeny, yes, but also for the sheer pleasure of trespassing. Later, look into Book IX, when the epic poem has become tragic, that's where she will sin, there is no denying it... But what I want to say is that, ultimately, *in the eyes of God*, Satan brings mankind down and merely accomplishes his part in the grinding cycle of Fall and Redemption. The irony is that meanwhile Satan is also played. The dominance of evil in the affairs of mankind will not last forever. At the end of time, for Milton, but also right now, in every second that we live and in every grain of sand that we touch, if you read Blake, there is Eternity. Infinite freedom."

He waited for me to catch up. Then loudly, proudly, sanctimoniously: "When you get to it, remember what is said in Book XII, toward the end of *Paradise Lost*—that the divine plan must be accomplished, we must owe it to Him, His self-sacrifice, to be reborn. It has to go full loop, and at whatever cost. Milton doesn't spare us the details: for instance, have you noticed that in this *Book III* you study now, God puts his angels to sleep and lets Satan creep into Paradise in broad daylight?"

"Satan then," I jumped in, "is a mere operator, an instrument to reach deep into Adam and Eve, break them, humiliate them, have them live in guilt, their progeny, generations after generations waiting patiently for His second coming—dependent, hostages of His choice time and place at the end of time..."

Smiling, Nathaniel waited patiently for me to finish before he added: "At the second coming, there is no longer a need for Satan. At the end of time, God doesn't even destroy Satan, He dispenses of him, sends him to the junkyard of History... You're only in *Book III* and there are *XII* of them..."

"You're right."

We detached our eyes from each other. I felt excited by our foray. It was more interesting than photocopying footnotes and accumulating bibliographies. Nathaniel was excessively proud. Down to his worn-out sneakers, his suspended body shook like the magic rod in the wiry hands of a prophet. That was enough for me. I was ready to pay and take the book home. But Nathaniel was not done.

Invoking the authority of the shelves around us, he continued while he unwound and came down: "To implant in you while you sleep dreams of accomplishment, isn't that seduction at its best, possession in the traditional, magical sense? Supernatural possession since Satan does not die. Let us say, then, that the Serpent of Milton *possesses* Eve. He doesn't have her sexually, worse, and here, one should add, it'd be plain stupid to bring to bear psychoanalysis like they spend their time doing in school... That the Serpent coming up to Eve who is, by the way, naked, looks like a penis in erection...etc. Of course, he does. And so what? It's of no interest. What matters is that he owns her spiritually. Satan has her soul, he *is* her, you see, at the moment of the Fall?" Could it be only for my progress in Miltonic Studies that he spoke so loud, so forcefully and relentlessly? Perhaps he deemed me slow of understanding...

This was getting to be more than enough, yet he felt compelled to add: "So the conclusion, for now, is that Satan works like a virus of the mind, okay, that's what I said earlier. He gets into her synapses. He makes her reason like him. How dangerous is dialogue with the wrong people!"

He considered this witty and nodded his appreciation.

"Eve is very smart in Milton, but she is outsmarted by his Satan, who is outsmarted by God. *Paradise Lost* is a cautionary tale for smart people. By the way, you know, don't you—perhaps you don't—that young Milton was at the forefront of Cromwell's Revolution and paid the price for it the rest of his life? Politically, the British people went as far as one could before everyone else, didn't wait for the French, did they? They beheaded their king, come to think of it, two hundred years before Robespierre. Quite a gifted people!"

The long nail of his thumb scraped his throat. "*Readiness is all*, I guess. Which, between you and me, goes a long way into explaining why they were ahead in dominating the world. Once you've cut the head of your king, I guess, the world is yours to take!"

Although I'd read about early English expansion, having taken credits on the topic, I thought it better to keep quiet at this point.

As a conclusive gesture, I put my dollar and fifty cents on the massive desk, next to an old cash register that looked like it had survived the Civil War. Instead of cashing the money right away, though, he accompanied me pensively to the door. I was wondering how to get going politely when he stopped on the threshold, still holding the book: "John Milton and William Blake, this strain of radical Protestantism you don't find in France, nowhere, never—or do you? Tell me. Not in Racine, not in Montesquieu or Voltaire, not in Marquis de Sade. Not in Corneille... whoa! Racine! Can't read him in the text, but!"

He licked his lips. Having no idea of what William Blake would take from John Milton, no exposure whatsoever to radical Protestantism, I was completely at a loss. It was embarrassing. Nothing in French literature remotely prepares one for Blake and Milton. Humbly ready to concede this shortcoming, I took a peek at the inviting stairwell, silent and cool. Mistake: you did not *not* pay attention to Nathaniel. He made a brash move and grabbed me by the elbow.

"Corneille!" he repeated. His pronunciation was terrible. "Something, eh! No Protestantism in France, pushed out, given the boot. If they don't like you, they kick you out, the French. It's simple and practical. That way, they keep the generous social regime all to themselves... Is that why you're here, because they kicked you out?"

He let go of my elbow.

"No, they didn't kick me out!"

"Not literally, of course."

I blushed. Fortunately, I didn't have to explain myself further, unless we became friends. Had France spat me out? He had found the right spot to apply pressure. I kept telling myself that I'd chosen to live the migrant life. But what if I was embellishing? What if I sounded French and thought like a French person after almost thirty years *there*, but remained a foreign body *until I finally realized it and left*?

Very pleased with himself, he finally passed me the book and turned around. I looked back into the store and realized that standing behind a shelf, there was a client, a young blond woman Nathaniel must have noticed earlier from his perched position. The man was not as self-absorbed as I thought, not as self-indulgent. It was for her sake that he had spoken so abundantly and forcefully—to reach her auditory faculty. Evidently also, she knew he'd tried to impress her. I didn't exist anymore, and neither did Milton and Blake. Nathaniel was wholly absorbed by what he said to her, fascinated by her conversation, taken by the topic she'd frame for him. I didn't take it personally and fled down the stairs.

Log 6

Nothing else to do now, but wait and hope for a mistake on the part of the Lagranges—or that one of the diverse police lower their guard and lead me to them inadvertently. They make as much noise on the Webwork as their counterparts in *noir* movies when rushing after criminals wearing two-color shoes and fedora hats. It is taking more time than I thought. Nathaniel has been sucked away by some foreign land, I suspect his family and their dependence have been absorbed by the wrinkles of some ancient soil. It could be France. The Lagranges are somewhere in France. It's the more unexpected that, in spite of their name, no Lagrange is conversant in French. True, French hackers have little need of French. And besides, their local connections are likely to be cosmopolitan Arabs and exiled American Jews.

Why did I go for his friendship? I began to see Nathaniel very often. Having not much to do other than read demanding books, write academic papers and look for someone with whom to share the results, which hardly occurred in the doctoral program where I was matriculated, they just graded you and scribbled laconic comments in the margins. I simply found myself walking down Broadway at the first occasion, eager to take the elegant elevator all the way up to the Annex. I was happy to hear from below the flow of demonstrations thrown down at me like a torrent let loose. I took mental notes of his rhetorical moves, his expressions, his references and his suggestions. I learned from Nathaniel what I could have learned in an American school during the first life I never lived in America.

In between two frenzied flights of thought, he'd sometimes show curiosity for me, my past, the first life I must have had *over there*, in France. He'd ask the usual questions about my immigration. Coming from him, though, these questions didn't bore me. How come I had left, and not at the youngest age, and not because of a career move nor the kind invitation of a parent, such a rich, culturally endowed and socially generous country as France? Was I not born

French? Yes, I was. Had I lost any of the protections and public support that surround the full-fledged citizen? No, I had not. Truth is, as I told him, I hardly worked in Paris. I showed up at the unemployment agency around the corner to receive a basic check on the first of the month and registered in speculative studies in some little-known department of the Sorbonne officially supposed to prepare me for a depressed job market. Was it about anti-Semitism, then? No, I answered, ignorance and neglect of all things Jewish were too subtle to present an obstacle. Then what?

"Hard to say, it didn't work for me *there*... Nothing clicked, no direction. I didn't have what it took, born under the wrong star, with the wrong pedigree."

"No direction home... Funny, same feeling here, whether in Florida, Tennessee, California, New Hampshire where I was raised, Brown University, Rhode Island, where I matriculated... Don't need to come from far away. New York is the city of exiles."

"The end of the line..."

"Yeah, the last exit..."

He could not simply let me have the immigrant experience all to myself.

I told him about arriving in New York with one suitcase and $1500 rolled in my underwear. And how I was shaking in front of the custom officers. In that summer of 1984, the Socialist government had forbidden exiting France with more than $1200 in cash.

"They said they were fighting 'capital departure'—as though people like me could ruin France! Just goes to show the kind of petty nationalism and thrifty economy I come from."

"If you can't corner the big fish, catch the small fray. It has a name," Nathaniel said, "Random Retaliation Syndrome..."

"Not as random as that," I added after reflection. "It tends to fall on the same kind of small fray or..." I groped for the right word, one that would not feel overused.

"Or scapegoat?" he concluded.

Yes, though overused, 'scapegoat' could do.

I told him about fighting landlords at the dirty corner of 109th St. and Amsterdam Avenue, the underworld of crummy tenement buildings where I had landed a few years earlier. How I occupied a three-bedroom apartment without paying rent, putting $6000 away while my case dragged in lower court downtown. I'd learned at a tenant association that the street was *warehoused* by a couple of shady owners. To warehouse is to keep buildings empty, or at least not tied to leases, and get higher price at the moment of selling. Empty buildings are worth gold In Manhattan. Before selling, however, landlords are not against making a buck, if only to pay the bills; and so, they give the street to unscrupulous characters, who, without signing any lease or sublease, find occupants they can evict at will. The dedicated volunteer lawyer told me to change the lock on my main door if I was ready for the fight of my life. 'They're animals, you know, up there,' she told me in a whisper. 'And they won't appreciate your exposing their scheme, even if judges don't go after warehousing. It's perfectly illegal but hard to prove and expensive.'"

"Now," I told Nathaniel, "it's not that I'm a courageous person, but I changed the lock. I had no choice, for one thing, couldn't afford anywhere else. And, there is something else, I don't like to be played."

"Who does?"

"I figure there's got to be a way to outsmart the smart."

He smiled intensely.

"A couple of big Hispanic guys came in the middle of the night to bang on my metal door, safe as in a safe—'Get out! Police!' They wanted to throw me out and all my stuff in the cold of February! They would have... Piece of cake, they thought, I mean, the son of a bitch who'd sent them, a naïve French intellectual, what's easier to fool?"

Nathaniel laughed wholeheartedly, so I continued: "I saw their bulk in the peephole, heard them fuming and swearing and groaning through the lock they couldn't open, and I jubilated inside." Saying this and vividly remembering the picture of desperation the two big idiots made, I actually jubilated and rubbed my hands again, me, the same man cozy inside. "What's more fun than fuck the fuckers at their own game?"

"Nothing, I suppose." He giggled.

"I called 911. The police came. Someone yelled from the street and they scrambled. It would have taken destroying the wall to get me out. The next day I went to court and obtained restraining orders against the false Jew who had rented me the place in the first place."

"How do you know he was Jewish?"

"His name: Abraham Rabinowitz."

He nodded, sucked on his cigarette, grimaced, sucked on his teeth, combed his hair and giggled some more.

"It was a noisy and dilapidated apartment, but after that not paying rent made my immigration a lot easier."

"Understandably." He lowered his chin and looked at his feet. It was my turn to teach him something.

"No, I mean, I was not spending the money. It was legal, deposited in an escrow under my lawyer's supervision. And yet, to see the money pile up was a boon. Since the escrow communicated with my regular checking account, here I was, hardly stepping into America and already building a small capital. Money circulates, it's the great virtue of money, isn't it? One moment it's here in one form, the other it's there in another."

"And what's the outcome of all this, if I may ask? The morality, if there is one?"

"I was illegal, no papers. Tourist visa had expired. But judges didn't consider your immigrant status back then. 1987, just a few years back. Strange to associate this date with freedom, but America was still a free country in 1987." He didn't object. "Thirty-days occupancy and you had rights to the apartment, at least the rights to defend yourself." He didn't know this basic rule. He'd never had to fight his way in. I wondered where he lived in Manhattan, with whom, which money, who paid for him, given what could only amount to minimum wage. "I remained the *de facto* occupant," I said, "until, after numerous motions, postponements and adjournments, my lawyer told me that having no lease, he could not defend me. 'Not a good idea to enter plea when you don't exist on paper.' His exact words."

"But you had been living in there for three years!" Nathaniel slapped his knee.

"Yep. I had the right to breathe in there and they couldn't evict me, and the escrow could reach the ceiling, but I didn't have the right to claim one square foot of the 5D, 203 W 109th St. under my name."

"Ah! America! America! You're more complicated than Dun Scott the scholastic. Which brings to mind..." He made as though to look around the ladder for the Middle Ages section which, fortunately, was not on hand. I wanted to finish my story.

"I had better accept the deal the new landlord would be willing to offer. And that's how, eventually, I became the legal tenant of an apartment next door, the 3F 205 W 109th St. Two small bedrooms which... (I hesitated here: should I dare? What would be his reaction?) not even a year after taking possession, I decided to vacate for personal reasons. Next thing you know, I was subletting the 3F to two ingenuous immigrants, taking their deposit and adding my 15% fee to the rent. Just like that, for good measure."

"Son of a bitch yourself! False Jew!"

"Eh! You do me; I do you. This is New York."

He regained his composure. "I envy you," he said after reflection. "No longer the chip on your shoulder one presumes you carried overseas."

"No longer the same chip, you're right," I whispered. And what is *your* problem? I was about to lash back: why this dead-end job? Where does the chip that weighs *you* down and pins you like an insect in this dusty museum come from? But I didn't say anything, preferring to spare him. It was clear that his inflated ego came with a thin skin—and a lot of frightening emptiness inside. I surmised that he'd surrounded himself with this pyramid of books and like buried his talent and enormous energy alive to protect them from hard exposure. If he was a racing horse confined to these dead-silent walls, it's not because, as he let it float, *they* had prepared special difficulties for exceptional people like him, but because the competitive field had been too dangerous for his fragile legs. The man was weak.

It took me some time to realize that Nathaniel lived in the future and his own studious past at Brown, where he'd been great before they broke him and generated in him jealous spite, envy of his peers, resentment at the institution, hatred of the system. But one day, after years of moving the axis of thought in the company of fresh blond recruits and alien foot soldiers like me, Etienne Zeltzki, he'd regain the heights and live at the top of that selfsame system. He'd straddle the institutions of high learning and squeeze their flanks like it were that of horses running to win between his slender legs. Somehow, in one jump, after a decade of hesitation, one day he'd command the panorama. They'd have to admit their mistake and make room for him, Nathaniel Lagrange.

Soon in our conversation, I'd lose track of what he said, however profound it may have been, and looked at him. He was so wrapped up, such a sucker for attention and, in a way, a fool. The problem with avid speakers is not so much in what they say. They don't take time to sit back and look at themselves for who they are. He was like a Kabuki performer who'd not aim at slashing the air but at building fortifications on the quick sand of thought. The conversation flitted by and the logical chain of his argument ended. And yet he still had to rebuild the castle up from the foundation. The more he talked, the less his construction stood. Slaving job, if you ask me, Sisyphus task, sterile, useless, unrewarding. Useless to him, I mean, for I personally learned a lot at his contact.

What had gone so wrong at Brown? I tried to steer the conversation toward personal matters. It was not easy. Nathaniel was cautious and secretive regarding himself. It took a couple of years for me to learn that he lived with Anna Otlaf, a Scandinavian woman of almost forty like him, and that his many books and sheets of music, the guitars and the suitcases of notebooks, all his belongings crammed her miniature studio on Waverly Place. He wouldn't invite me in when we happened to walk through the West Village. In spite of his brash disposition and careless appearance, he was ashamed of his living conditions, his borrowed roof.

A couple more years to discover that he led a double life, steeped as he was in a steamy affair with a young British person who worked at the main store on Broadway. Nathaniel had a life uptown and another downtown, and they were not the same. In fact, they excluded each other. They excluded his friends from one another.

Log 7

Since it was crucial for him to have ample time on his hand, and since I was as well a man of leisure, having then only to teach few hours as an adjunct and attend a couple of graduate seminars, we'd regularly walk from the Annex all the way downtown, to the West Village, and further down, to Battery Park in front of the Statue of Liberty. He'd have the butt of a joint in his pack of cigarettes: given by a thankful client after one encyclopedic insight, or a colleague in the main store who had decided to go clean. We'd make sure to smoke it before the long walk in some leafy and discreet corner of Riverside Park, although the city was nowhere as policed as it is now. Misdemeanor was no crime, back then. We had our spiritual moment under spectacular beams of light piercing rococo clouds over the Hudson River. It was uncanny how our usually far-fetched conversation communicated with the element around us: the fluid and relaxed gatherings in Central Park; the lurid, compact and anxious crowd on 42nd Street; the West Village parade of gay men whose savage looks we spurned while hunting the concept; and finally, the agitation, the vehemence or calm repose swelling the bay of New York.

It's not merely that Nathaniel believed a little too much in his eventual contribution to the triumphant drumbeat of important, though difficult and contorted ideas. I could detect in him the ominous core, the dour madness of personal resentment that had anchored him to failure. He had few kind words for the professional of ideas, the paid and promoted thinker who occupied the scene, the specialized professor whom he called "bloodsucker, one who profits from the great dead, quote *them*, excerpt *them*, then paraphrase *them* and all the while denies he pays luxurious rent plagiarizing *them*. Accredited and affiliated thinker who doesn't bring anything to dinner, ventriloquist who doesn't have the courage of his ideas, evil breed that lives on the back of the dead like vermin on the living!"

Though the metaphors were exaggerated, I could only applaud. I did not harbor any particular admiration for the academic profession either. Getting a Ph.D. was a necessity, in my case. And a comfort; for instance, it provided a safety net against the type of aimless life my friend led.

"They have no substance, your professors (the irony, not lost on either of us, was that I was becoming a professor under his mentoring), their bloodstream hardly shows any distinctive quality in the strict philosophical sense, the one which the high middle age has taught us, scholastic definition. Think about it, Etienne, they are just like Satan in Blake, transparent and empty. Have you seen the way he draws *him*: the one shape that can take any shape, the figure of all figures, mere contours, the form that takes any form, transparent and empty? Satan is the one who sucks you right out of your life and takes your place, fucks your mistress, and perhaps your wife, takes care of your children in the bargain, without you noticing any of it..."

I had, by now, seen Blake's illuminations to *Paradise Lost*. And yet, unaccustomed to Blake's visual style, I had failed to notice the transparent form ready to occupy any form, the figure of night and death about to frighten any living figure out of day and life. Coming from him, this marvelous insight surprised me. Usually Nathaniel only had a second-hand appreciation of Art works, what theoreticians had squeezed out of them. There were entire periods of Church paintings and Classical music where I would find comfortable refuge for he had no clue. Abstraction, Modern Art was undignified in his eyes, manifest proof of miscommunication between the rich and "us, the poor..." (he included me here, though as an adjunct teacher I already made much more than his minimum wage). Much of Art today, he often contended, only served masturbatory habits in their creator and money laundering purpose in their buyer. He was rigid and had had limited exposure to classical music. Adventurous Jazz he loathed, whose complexity made a joke out of his gumbo of Rock and Blues. As far as the luxuries, refinements and beauties of this world were concerned, he was working class, and proud of it. I then realized that a good part of his ranting against successful people was a way to turn to his advantage his low social extraction. It escaped from his lips that his father had been a corporal and, before retiring, a sergeant in the US army. Interesting piece of information: Nathaniel had been the poor boy at Brown, the son of servants, as it were. Not the son of an officer.

No wonder he had a terrible time in the Department of Philosophy where he matriculated: junior Lagrange was too serious, too keen, had too much to prove. Without mentioning his lack of manners and of proper style, even if his spoken English was first-rate, and his knowledge of philosophy, admittedly, deep, he must have been too eager, rushing things, speaking too much.

But when it came to British literature, he was solid as a rock. And he loved to read the old masters. And so, at Brown he'd read all Milton and all Blake, attending courses in the English Department he couldn't get credits for.

"It was all fucked up."

"You couldn't transfer?"

Sorry I asked; this was technical question beneath Nathaniel.

"Your teacher make his outstanding career on the back of the living," he repeated. I am aware that central characters should change and progress in the course of a well-written story; but this is neither a novel nor a short story. This is a file where I am collecting the memories of Nathaniel that live in me. People act (or don't act) the same way over and over; they do repeat the same things in life as they do in files.

"Teachers suck the marrow of whom they need for reason of advancement. And the more tiny, puny and irrelevant the subject matter the better. One of the bones, one tendon in Milton's left hand fuels the publications of dozens of promising scholars, who can't find anything interesting to say, so they have decided that that tendon, that muscle in the left hand of Milton would be *it*, the new *it* in *Milton's Studies*! And since they control the publications, the idea spreads. Anybody who's somebody in English Literary Criticism believes that there is nothing more urgent to uncover than the after-effect of acute pain in the left hand of nine-year old John Milton!"

This was funny, somehow, and I was about to laugh, when he made as though to masturbate. The idea was clear enough, I thought. There was this vulgarity to him I was not quite ready to settle with.

There was something in what he said, however. He loathed the sedate, comfortable graduate students who'd slashed papers of his they were vastly unprepared to read. He had no downgrading enough vocabulary for his peers and roommates, who'd grown long teeth abiding by trendy talk at Brown. The problem with Nathaniel is that he was a snob. Among the contemporary luminaries, he only admired French thinkers like Foucault, Deleuze, Derrida, Lacan... exotic names, people who didn't pay taxes to Uncle Sam, thoughts that washed up on American shores after a long voyage, clean and free, he assumed, from the compartmentalization, the regimentation and auto-glorification practiced from the top down by AA, American Academia. There was this blind fury, this see-through resentment in Nathaniel that made me laugh inside, even when I was shocked by the directness of his expression. For many reasons, to start with my not finding a way into the *Grandes Ecoles* of France anymore than him at Brown, we had what it took to like each other. I only had the advantage, I felt, of being the one aware of it when looking into the mirror he tended me. We simply were two losers trying to regroup.

Part of his power over me came from my not being able to put a word in edgewise—the violence of his speech. I noticed that Nathaniel exhibited what psychiatrists call *logorrhea*: words couldn't leave his mouth fast enough, his face reddened, sweat pearled on his brow and he literally spat in your face. There was this rage in him to make his thought stick to thin air. It happens when one's mind is homeless, one's words without a roof. When one gives up on the proper forum, the adequate format where thought will accumulate like any other product. Why doesn't he write all this? He said he was and he'd show me one day. I didn't know yet what dizzying ocean of difficulties surged in front of him when he looked at the white printing-paper page.

When I insisted, he turned nasty: "Why do you feel it necessary, because you write appendages to secondary literature and brochures for school, to think that actual dialogue, living word of mouth, speech among individuals in flesh and bones is shit and conversation useless when it comes to deal with interesting questions? Don't be such a snob about *le texte*, Etienne Zeltzki!"

He gave me the example of Socrates, who used to hang out on the *agora* and never wrote a word. I didn't retort that, were it not for Plato's talented and extensive writings, we wouldn't have a name like Socrates. Did Nathaniel really believe that he could, *hic et nunc*, reach the core -- the noteworthy, the important insightful core of truth? But the truth has to be heard, and by more than one.

He was right, I did not trust the word of mouth. I didn't trust the living to speak the truth. I had not spoken French in years, and didn't miss it for a second. If one could simply say the truth nobody would bother to sweat it out on the page, transcribe it into a score or shoot it onto the screen. Between flesh and blood individuals, words of mouth are good to carry business information, personal secrets, justification, seduction, dominance, entrenchment, slap in the face and mutual destruction. They may, at times, convey tenderness, okay, until they translate into emotional clichés. Actually, Nathaniel didn't deny that that could happen and, indeed, that that was the dominant mode of exchange. But he claimed to be looking for something else, another kind of dialogue. Something that was fresh and new because it sliced through the mountain of crap like a knife cuts into butter.

He was not, he would never be paid so many words an hour like me, adjunct professor Etienne Zeltzki. He'd skip the politeness to colleagues and the obsequious pleasing of Vice Presidents and Acting Deans. He'd jump altogether over the tedious stuffing of rows of yawning and empty heads, the painstaking grading and correcting of clumsy papers according to hand-me-down standards. And, unavoidably, the curtailing the imagination and raw inspiration of your rare gifted student. He had refused that "easy" solution when he could have had it much more comfortable than me. I was starting a career in an obscure campus belonging to City University, while Nathaniel could have been invited to prestigious private establishments from East Coast to West Coast. Did he not regret his precipitous retreat from Brown? I, for one, would bitterly cry over not having finished a Ph. D. in the Ivy-League. And not finishing it for one unfinished paper, as he confessed -- only one unfinished paper, and a thesis of 200 pages, bibliographies and endnotes included. He had enhanced, expanded and clarified dozens of papers for others. He claimed to have his fine and florid handwriting cover thousands of pages in his notebooks. Reduce the juice, man, say more by saying less -- why can't you condescend to do that for a terminal degree at Brown?

But me, of course, who was I to tell him what to do? I was an ordinary little bourgeois, pragmatic and tenacious -- a relatively well-informed middle-of-the-road kind of guy. "No extreme for you, Etienne. Nothing too cold or too hot -- no tragedy, no risky heroism." I have to say, I resented that. "Which is okay, in your case," he hastened to add. "You're an immigrant, you have to make sure your feet stay planted on the ground. Me, I may fall hard and brake my nose, but I should fly high above the ground! I have to… It's my parents that walked all the way from Canada who took the pedestrian road for me."

His squinting told me how smart he thought this remark was. We were actually walking down 6th Avenue, the double colossus of the WTC straight up in our sky and surrounded by a dazzling morning of late spring. He rested his arm on my shoulder to smooth the frown on my face. Being almost a head taller than I, for a minute he was like the brother I never had, the big brother showing me through town.

He was right again. American-born makes all the difference. Me, I had to go back to school at thirty-five, and I had to get a tenure-track job, and I would soon get married, live in a co-op uptown and become the father of two lovely kids. That's what you had to do as first generation, impregnate the new world, make sure you belonged. Of course, if possible, I wanted to kneel at the border of the chasm, peep down the cliff of staggering thought, feel the age-old wind ruffle my hair—not, however, if it meant jeopardizing all that my future identity as an American promised to offer.

So much the better if there was no memorable future to his verbal flights, if he disappeared before existing, his grand gestures in vain, his formidable thoughts unclaimed, his story untold. Nathaniel would become a tragic hero in a world long stripped of true tragedies and of true heroes -- or he would cease to exist, without ceasing to have been a hero anyway, all unto himself. Prometheus unbound, forever falling happily into the abyss after taking 500 years to cut with his teeth the ropes that attached his demigod body to the beast eating his liver.

No country for old men on his horizon: the more staggering the cost and sweeping his sacrifice of career, health and security of mind, the more real his intellectual commitment. Perhaps I am lingering for too long on this hollow period in the life of Nathaniel Lagrange. If this were destined to a reader from Mars, he'd have already gotten the picture and grown tired of dwelling on a grandiloquent nobody. But, precisely, Nathaniel is not destined to remain nobody on this Earth. Not quite a speck or a statistics. It's fascinating for me to see how his entire trajectory into glory (some would prefer infamous notoriety) was present from the beginning: his romantic and megalomaniac views of himself, the obsession with victims, victimization as a process, which could be reversed, turned against itself—an idea which has now produced his highly-publicized meditations on self-sacrifice, his well-attended calls on the Webwork for *self-slaughter* on a cosmic scale. What he calls the mother of all threats.

And yet, at the same time, the man was so far, so near and so far from what he'd become one day. He did nothing back then, and the little he did, whatever he did amounted to nothing. Though he said little about his family, he told me enough to guess that among his siblings, even compared to his sister Kathy, the lawyer who-never-practiced-the-law and who lived at mammy's at thirty-three, even next to his brother John, the construction worker who had eloped at twelve, drank himself almost to death... even among fuck-ups, Nathaniel held his own.

Father had dragged the family from training camp to military base all over the country. No consistent education for the Lagrange kids: backwater, messy, rowdy and mediocre schools full of southern rednecks or northern roughnecks. And yet, here was Nathaniel at nineteen, declared a genius, accepted at Brown University.

I tried to imagine the narrow-minded, overbearing and severe man who had left a distorted version of himself in the superego of his son. But Nathaniel's number one problem was probably not his father. Of his mother, he said nothing, except to lash back, when I played the psychoanalyst and insisted with my personal questions: "Just a housewife, nice, good, loving, serviceable, obedient and extra demanding like they make them in New England. How about yours, Etienne? Mothers. Don't they make them similar, in France?"

How she must have loved her first born, her big blond and blue-eyed boy, that mother. How intelligent he must have sounded to her unschooled ears. How much ambition and yet also how much need of constant reassurance she'd injected in that boy.

Boy oh! boy, yes, Nathaniel was demanding to himself. Between his sublime idea and the expression of it one biographer might read some day in one of the frayed and boyish notebooks he always carried with him—between the intimation of immortality, the vistas into infinity he experienced at the reading of someone else's acclaimed creation, and the trivial bits of realization he produced on his own, there was a difference of scale he could not begin to bridge. He would not let me look at his notebook.

"You know, just a few notes in preparation for the *magnum opus*," he'd say, blushing in false modesty while rapidly leafing through it. I glimpsed incredibly dense, compact, seemingly endless lines without punctuation or paragraphs, and so diminutive a handwriting as to require for anybody else, without exaggeration, a magnifying glass. Perhaps writing the next end-of-the-century masterpiece of literature was not his thing, but he didn't know it yet and you'd better not tell him. Maybe he was a man, not of thought, but of action...

He liked to say, in a pastiche of Shelley: "The insight that the gods did not have in store for you, Etienne, you have to snatch it from their greedy hands, and by force. It's what polite people like you don't understand, by force! Not by attending boring seminars and writing acceptable papers. Poetry occurs, if it does, in the second before the burning coal of imagination cools off—as you, I mean, the writer, hold that flame of inspiration in your puny, shaky and bashful hands."

"Paltry also?" I ventured. He realized that I was making fun of him.

One time that we were particularly stoned, he raised his hands in mock-expectation of a diffuse thing coming from above, some ecstatic light sent from the portion of sky corresponding to the clamoring intersection at 7th Avenue and 8th Street. A mystic gift descended on him, pushed away the clouds and bore a shaft of unreal silence in the chemical sunset. I remained just outside, witness to his elevation, loafers glued to the pavement. Ok, it was no more than the pose of a pothead, but it threw an unsparing light on the egomania raging in him, it made plain his being locked up inside like a larva unable to come out of the chrysalis. I felt sorry for him. And nevertheless, I must confess that this pathetic show, this gaping flaw didn't detach me from Nathaniel. I felt it shouldn't be hard to accrue power over a puppet. He could always speak his head off and not let me put a word in edgewise, I'd have him eat in my hand.

"Imagination," he resumed, "gets one crack at it. After that, it's too late. Petrifaction has started in the bones of the poet, who may well finish in the hospital, or at the bottom of a lake…" He meant Coleridge in rehab at 30 and Shelley going down at 33…

Was he a poet? In what way and what kind of poet? Older than the oldest kind. Nathaniel confided to me in the tone of imparting a revelation that he was working in the direction of a gigantic epic, Miltonic in scale, complex and ambitious in its composition. He showed me a page full of amazingly vague and ornate lines—unheard of verses of thirteen stressed syllables. The work was, he observed, in its incipient phase, which explained why he was reluctant to divulge it. This work in progress (on which, as it leaked in the conversation, he had worked in secret for several years already) should engulf description, dialogue and peroration, demonstration and narration, satire and caricature, sublime and grotesque, all in one compelling breath. After that, no field of knowledge, no style, no issue would remain the same.

What to think of his *monstrous opus*? I didn't tell him but personally, I was glad to write pompous papers with long bibliographies, so as to get honorable grades and have done with graduate school. How easier you make it on yourself, I realized, when you limit your campaigns to a career in some humble institution uptown. No wonder the man couldn't breathe, and between syllables he had to smoke cigarette after cigarette.

Log 8

We continued talking about Milton as though there was nothing more urgent in the world. For me and my dissertation, there was actually nothing more urgent.

I found an extraordinary passage in *Book IX* of *Paradise Lost*. Along the promenade of Battery Park, in view of the Statue of Liberty battered by the waves on a windy afternoon, I shared with Nathaniel my reading of one central passage. I said that half a millennium later one page of that book was still overlooked, underestimated, misunderstood by readers and critics, even by the most fervent admirers of Milton, women. They are the last to read these lines. Radical Feminists are not ready to follow Eve in the darkest corner of ontology, and that is when she refuses to live, when she calls on suicide in common and says no to procreation. Our educated women today love Eve's intelligence, her defiance and her suspicions, but they lack the courage, they're chicken in comparison with the tragic grand dame Milton has created.

Only someone like Nathaniel could have taken me seriously. And so what? We didn't do no harm. It was only he and I, the calm waves of the bay and the mute statue solid and proud in the distance. We could speak crazy, we could let the bravado out, be men, have balls for once, we could make grimaces and assume poses standing against the salty wind of the bay. The dark passage we delved into is at the beginning of *Book IX*, after Milton writes modestly: "These notes turn to tragic." I had to refresh Nathaniel's memory. Even *he* couldn't remember off hand the details in that passage just off center, just past the center of *Paradise Lost*. And since my unlikely reader may not have the whole episode fresh in mind either, let me make a parenthesis. According to Milton, once Adam and Eve eat of the fruit, they indulge in an orgy of the pleasures their pure new bodies can procure. Result: they wake up the next morning bloated, bluesy, in a funk and like suffering of a hangover. Now, for the first time in Paradise, they look at the genitalia they've overused, and they don't find them so appetizing.

It's then that Eve proposes to Adam a challenge to God. She doesn't want of His plan of action, her necessary Fall, Adam's going to Hell as well as all the children ever to come out of her. She doesn't care for a Redemption that'll take centuries and shall depend on the sacrifice of, as Nathaniel liked to say, His vapid Son... Eve doesn't sit comfortable in this saga, this overextended story of pain and dependence. She tells Adam that since God lets Satan stalk his victims in so-called Paradise, then why not go ahead and grab the monster by the jaws?

I recited from memory the fantastic lines and it was clear that in spite of my accent, Nathaniel listened: "Tired of lamenting the loss of their purity, Eve tells Adam, enough contrition, *Childless thou art, childless remain... both our selves and Seed to free --*

> *Let us seek Death, or he not found, supply*
> *With our own hands his office on ourselves;*
> *Why stand we longer shivering under fears;*
> *That show no end but Death, and have the power,*
> *Of many ways to die the shortest choosing,*
> *Destruction with destruction to destroy.*

"Since they are to die now, and die to go to Hell as they are told, live a kind of living death, since God expedites them to guilt and sin, atrocious agony for generations to come, since they're fried anyway, why not forestall the move? Why not attempt death 'on ourselves' and see what comes?"

"It's the old philosophical suicide of the Romans, the Greeks, the Japanese," interrupted Nathaniel. "When humiliated, about to be made a slave, one should resort to suicide. Dead perhaps, but free!'

Not agreeing this time around to let him finish for me, I said: "One may imagine that she carries a knife, a screwdriver (ha-ah), some such sharp instrument she's snatched in a previous scene from the cook or the gardener, so as to defend herself if Satan crept back into her conjugal bed and tempted her into more delirium. This beautiful lady is so alone, she feels so defenseless in Paradise. She's already suffered such abuse."

"She's a tormented romantic. It's great," exulted Nathaniel. "Thanks for letting me in on this! You're right, this passage gets shortchanged, it's like a dark fold in the poem you easily overlook since you're sure of the outcome, you know her killing herself is impossible. We wouldn't be here to read the book if she had, would we? Adam will easily convince her it's better to wait and please Him until kingdom come…"

"Better than what?" I asked. "What is the alternative?"

"Than go straight to Hell!…'die the shortest choosing'…"

"But they are going to Hell anyway since they have sinned. The reader knows that and so do Adam and Eve. She's ready to sacrifice her young life, her beauty and fertility, her dreams, her love for hubby Adam, his for her… all of God's gifts…"

"Yes," answered Nathaniel, "but Adam is not hundred percent wrong either in believing the Theodicy, God's overextended story as you call it. They will receive in *Book XII* the promise of a better world to come – it's true, after many generations have gone to waste. Nevertheless, in theory Eve's seed shall re-enter one remote day a better remake of Paradise -- if both wait and pray on their knees, as they show due respect, of course. The first parents have first to go and multiply, supporting the hard life, working, killing and dying of natural causes, as they say. They have to let their nasty kids propagate the mess until there comes the Flood!"

"Nevertheless," I said, "Eve's speech in favor of dignified self-extinction, her calling for primal immolation, self-slaughter in common, that's subversive. A married couple saying no – don't forget Adam and Eve are married (I could see he nodded). It's dramatic, and not in any way melodramatic. It's high tragedy. Eve's attitude is one of total defiance: she's ready to annihilate humanity *ab ovo* -- don't forget in her womb there is all of human life…"

"I don't forget."

"She proposes, she defends, she argues for, then, not genocide, bigger scale, the scale of all scales, beyond which there is no more dimension: humanocide…

Nathaniel seemed quite taken by this neologism.

"Undo the original sin by annihilating its consequences: 'destruction with destruction to destroy.' Before there were generations, all gone! *Coup de Theatre* before the show began. Quite a drama… We know that Milton would have loved to go to the theater in London if the Puritans had not closed it. He admired what he could read of drama from Plautus and Seneca, to Corneille." No small pride in showing Nathaniel my recently acquired erudition. "You see," I said, "one should have written libraries about this decisive moment, Eve's self-immolation, *their* self-annihilation. Instead of which, silence -- Adam's coward response will force her to relent and come down from her heights. And yet this page remains the high point indispensable to the thousand pages Epic."

"Right," Nathaniel piped in, giving me a tap on the back. He was excited and impressed. "This stuff is excellent, she's articulating a Gnostic stance Milton must have read about… He knew every heresy there was…"

Of course, my point could not be our last word. So I let him have it.

"The Gnostics thought," he started and paused. We stood at the elegant new fence they had built in front of the Hudson River to guard people from falling in agitated waters. I had nothing against being again, after my day at school, the student and taking mental note as he camped the foot of a specialist in the matter. "Most Gnostics, you had all kinds, but most seem to have shared this that the created world is Satan's creation, the very devil's product. Evil permeates and without possible remission – no Christ buying our sins with his bloody flesh for the Gnostics – foul is the fabric of Nature around and inside of us, including our breath. What we do and what we say is harmful, *nefas* (a Latin word Nathaniel knew). So, what other choice do we have but to call it quits *en masse* (and a French one)? Remedy to all our woes, attrition of being, 'darkest corner of ontology,' as you so justly pointed out, Etienne. Man, it's so well put…"

"Thank you!" I said, blushing.

"Nothing personal," he laughed. "It's smart on your part, that's all... *Resistance to being*, let's undermine the created world by all available means, let's explode the sucker. Let's mine the heap of shit! Such was the Gnostic credo. No children, less generation -- sex, yes, *en veux tu en voilà*, but no *procréation*. We are too many, they thought, and that was 2000 years ago!"

Again, nice and rare use of French on his part. The re-playing of this conversation sounds so strange. In our pompous and goofy way, we were so close to what is the universal theme now, the obsession.

He mused: "Come to think of it, it's like in the porn movie where sperm must flow outside vagina, not inside. And it was a flow, let me tell ya! They have dug out recipients in the form of rivulets carved in altar stones. At night, Gnostics appropriated to their orgies the very churches destined to glorify during the day Christ and the progress of generation. For the Gnostic, remember – and in this they agreed with the Jews -- Christ is not the Messiah, who has not arrived yet, not finished, not started perhaps on his return voyage." He verified my interest and my understanding.

I nodded in agreement to have him finish.

"The false prophet who's been among us in order to be crucified, this one was the anti-Christ, cunning and self-serving devil parading as Messiah. It's the same son of a bitch who's plotted his self-immolation on the cross to impress his future public with a show of pain and the model for abnegation. This Son of Joseph is the one who expects our subservience, our kneeling in humiliation for the centuries to come, until He'll decide on his own timing to come down a second time!"

I never knew how to take his bluntness. Okay, Christ was not the Messiah, but that didn't mean you didn't have to respect his name, what he stood for. It made me feel awkward.

"There are two gods, not one, that's the bad news," he proclaimed in an amused tone. "And of course, to make matters worse, we take the bad one for the good one. He's quite convincing, he knows how to fool us at every turn. It's the bad Eon that's responsible from before day one... since the dawn of time the pure Eon has retreated in His purity, retracted out of time, refused to be pinned down to space and time, out of reach in eternity..."

"So as not to wet His hands?" I asked.

"Not wanting to leave behind a vacuum that Satan shall exploit, remember!" I remembered his demonstration. We had a past, Nathaniel and I. We laughed, however, not quite wholeheartedly. His detachment, usual irony and didacticism didn't fool me. There was a vibrant note in his voice, a tremolo that made me wonder whether he shared the Gnostic extremism. "Fuck this world, mess with sacred life!" he said, "have finished with life, don't do anything good with it, waste it, stop it! No prolongations! Consummation of all things is now!"

"*Machiach* now!" I ventured, to relax the atmosphere, and to assist him: "Close to the Cabbala in spite of all the distance..." I'd only read second hand sources on the Cabbala, which presented daunting obscurities, my Hebrew being limited, but I wanted to teach him something. "There are four worlds and we progress in the lowest one in terms of substance and degree of transparency. We are in the most opaque sphere there is, refractory to His light..."

"Naturally..." Nathaniel smiled from ear to ear. He loved this stuff.

"That's the reason why practicing Jews thank God upon waking up, even before opening an eye, thank Him for giving them back their soul..."

Nathaniel asked me to elaborate.

"While sleeping you travel in higher," I said, "more creative worlds where it's easier for your soul to circulate among images and ideas. An angel has to convince the sparkle in you, the *neshama* to return and wake up in this clumsy body, these difficult, if not morally troubling and inadequate circumstances. And do not forget the *yetzer ara*, Nathaniel, the bad impulse, the ineradicable tendency to do bad and be bad just for the sake of it..."

"I don't forget!" he whispered.

Nathaniel spoke eloquently about *Fear and Trembling*, Kierkegaard's meditation on the sacrifice of Isaac. "Abraham is asked to commit a crime on the person of his son in the name of God. Abraham is ready to sacrifice the dearest, cutest of his possessions." For the sake of his argument, Nathaniel mimicked what you'd have expected him to have no clue about: the warm embrace of a loving father. "Abraham is ready to cut the throat of Isaac," Nathaniel said. "Isaac does not resist his father, doesn't think he's gone off the cliff. Not at all, the teen-ager submits, kneels down and offers his neck to the knife of his father. He believes also. There is suspension of the ethical, says the philosopher. It's mad but it's not madness. It's a religious call and it goes higher, deeper than the good and the bad. It's the proof that Abraham believes in God no matter what, beyond any reason, any morality. It's about faith and It's totally irrational, incomprehensible and indefensible in front of any court of law—and yet here you have Abraham's grace in the eyes of God. After that, God hands him the tablets."

"Not so fast, Abraham is chosen among the chosen," I agreed. "But a token sacrifice is still required of him, there is ritual business to attend to, a goat to bleed on the altar…"

"Yes there is, you're right," he said. "But what God claims is not the corpse of a son but the ardent belief inside a father, belief so strong that it can push him to gamble it all, jeopardize his sanity, risk the future of his family… Throwing family and fortune away, Abraham is also sacrificing himself as a father and a man, sacrificing his humanity as a human. He could not live one second after he had cut that throat."

Voice full of overtone, Nathaniel was looking at me. We sat in lotus on his bed, I mean, Anna's bed, drank *Jim Beam* and smoked marijuana, and then, speaking a storm, we left her pad and walked breathlessly, elbow to elbow, as fast as permitted the crowd and the traffic of Lower Manhattan. Walked all the way to Battery Park, there to stand in the strong wind coming from the ocean beyond Staten Island. On this side of the protective fence we admired the glittering flame in the right hand of the Statue.

Him so voluble ordinarily, he turned his face away and blushed when he spoke about his family. His parents whispered Canadian French words between themselves in secret, he told me. What they didn't want their three turbulent children to understand was whispered between the parents in their French. Mother presenting the mother tongue as not allowed to her children, that's cruel. The Lagrange parents were of that old generation of immigrants who believed children should not lose their time with the original tongue and speak English exclusively. The result was that strange situation of a mature Nathaniel devouring French thinkers in more or less effective translation and for no clear purpose, any goal he could account for or explain to himself. There is no way you are going to say anything interesting on a thinker whose language of thought you don't have access to. It's more imperative than for a novelist, perhaps. Nathaniel knew the French words floating in educated English, add to this, some German, peppered words, barely able to label correctly the concepts he referred to whenever he talked to people like me.

As we slowly approached Midtown's high towers, at some point or other in our walk Nathaniel could not resist visiting with me, a layman, some basic scientific law. He had a predilection for thermodynamics. Entropy, the loss of energy, the evening off and cooling off of the atmosphere stationing in a given cube, the growing disorder, disorganization, deliquescence of matter. How matter goes less diverse and contrasted, more homogenous, tight as a fist, and cold.

"Take that volume of air," he said slashing the air ahead of us as we walked rapidly down the avenue, "and study its composition on a microscopic and statistical level. Now, imagine one minuscule creature able to enter the cube to pick and choose among the particles that are cooling off. Some he *chooses* and puts aside, in a different room. Isolated, these chosen particles will cool off faster than the bulk of the others..."

Nathaniel sends a big smile in my direction to verify that I follow.

"Our little demon ushers the flock of the chosen in another room through a small device, which he controls, from where they can be released in the larger atmosphere whenever he so chooses, the little devil—control of energy, harnessing of the force—here you have in a nutshell Maxwell's Demon, and no less than the industrial machinery born during the Industrial Revolution, from the steam engine to electricity!

"If we had the book I'd show you," he said, "how Maxwell speaks of his black monster, his intelligent demon, who is a robber, a sneak, usurper of Nature, black as Hell, up to no good. The demon is our bad shadow, our specter, our proxy because he does the job for us. " Large negative grimace on his face. "And, nevertheless and by the same token, the Demon is our good angel," beaming smile, "because he turns to our advantage the pessimistic laws of thermodynamics, the ineluctability of energy loss, Nature steady decline. The fact that it is already fucked up and can only get worse. The Demon allows for rapid, immense expenditure of energy that benefits us. Between you and me there is no thermodynamics without demonology, without theology. No science without a religion imbedded in it." He rolled his eyes in my direction.

I had to say, this was interesting stuff, although I couldn't help wondering whom he was quoting.

Log 9

I have met Suzan here, in Paris. She made it look like I bumped into her at the Closerie des Lilas, a famous café for the old-time writers and intellectuals that used to come here fifty years ago. And then, I've discovered a way to trace her activities on the Webwork to a three-stars hotel on rue de Rennes, few streets from mine. We sat at a terrace under the ballooning sun and ordered two cool *kirs*, and then again two and two. She told me that Nathaniel was even more demented now than when I had left the group. It's Nathaniel who had brought destruction when she was about to explain *Josephine* to the police in exchange for our immunity.

Nathaniel is the monster. If someone should fall, it's him, along with his brother and sister. "The reason why I came here," I told maliciously Suzan, "to see him take the blame that he deserves and exempt us all from it by the same token." I'm charmed by Suzan and so, I should be cautious in her presence and keep my cool. My finding and denouncing the place where the Lagranges hide before she does would seem to anyone a long shot, remote possibility. She does not see me able to move faster than her, and she has made her deals with the police, who have left her off the hook, never arrested her. She has not even been mentioned to the large public in connection with the Lagrange affair.

For the first time in my life—me, nobody, a teacher in a Community College!—I may get the decisive advantage. But I cannot explain this to you and introduce Suzan the way she deserves to be, showing you the unique woman she is at this point of my account. I need to proceed with that obscure past before Nathaniel met her and show you how unlikely it was for him (and me after him) to ever encounter someone like elite hacker Suzan Friedman.

I remember nasty piques at my comfortable life after he helped me complete the dissertation. He made me feel that I owed him the favorable events that followed like getting a full-time job, the positive changes like feeling committed to one particular woman, my getting married, which had nothing to do with him. He took credit for everything. And I don't need to mention the smirk on his face when he spoke about *people like me*, the professors.

"You understand now to whom they owe the promotion, right? Usually some sharp personality is left behind…"

He had the nerve to envy me what he had turned his back on! The more I streamlined my second life the more he alienated his first. I no longer wanted to be his friend. If it was him calling I didn't pick up the phone. He was digging himself a hole. He would self-destroy—which did not stop the fascination he exerted on me. I learned by remembering conversations and speaking to our few friends that he had one girlfriend for everyday use and one for the perfect occasion.

The next day it's me who called him to learn more. The story with Kathleen Miller, the British woman, seems to have started when I met him and lasted until Nathaniel left New York. I observed that Kathleen and her roller coaster of a life took a lot of his energy and most of his time. Because of her he stopped trying to write free-floating stuff in his notebooks. He even stopped reading for long stretches of time. The end was abrupt, shocking, especially for me, who didn't have access to the developments. After several years of a steamy affair with him, she married a British subject and a highly professional young man. I kind of remember he was rumored to be a promising diplomat. Even though Nathaniel had done nothing for this not to happen and even though he knew it was going to happen, it was a terrible blow. It's what brought him back to mother. In other words, this Kathleen Miller also entertained a double life and Nathaniel fell in her crocodile jaw. Nathaniel and Kathleen were similar in their duplicity, but she had the edge. Similitude is the seducer. She seduced him, and when she had him flat on his back, she confirmed that her life was free and safe from people like him. Goodbye Nathaniel.

There was a teenager in Nathaniel, or he was in his mid-life crisis early, I don't know which, maybe both. Kathleen was the kind of crazed and doomed passion anyone in his right mind realizes right away he is lucky if he survives without losing too many feathers. Nathaniel making pocket money at the Annex, he depended on Anna for a typewriter—he refused the computer—for basic food, trips and vacation. I don't want you to go imagining Nathaniel a hippy starving. He simply used Anna's money. He acknowledged living like a pasha at Anna's, like an aristocrat centuries ago on the old continent. At her place—Anna not around generally—we ate take-out food from the West Village; we drank single-malt Whiskey. In between two warm embraces, early on Kathleen must have realized the state of dependency Nathaniel was in and it gave her a cold sweat. A body speaks. Between the sheets something to her of his anxiety and his limitations must have transpired.

There are patches in Nathaniel's life I reconstruct from what I've gleaned. He told me little of Anna Otlaf and for quite some time didn't introduce her to me. She was half British and half Scandinavian; her family had been rich, and still owned a small island off the coast of Norway, but her father had lost millions in pounds sterling during the oil crash of 1973. Nathaniel explained that Anna worked a lot, made good money. She loathed corporations and, like Nathaniel, capitalism—although, when I finally met her, Anna had nothing to say against her easy-going employer. The difference with Nathaniel is that Anna accepted the yoke. She was a good girl, she endured to wade knee-deep in the mud so as to offer the appearance of a home to Nathaniel, the artist and thinker. Anna Otlaf had to sustain herself while providing for her inspired and more driven friend. Let me tell you how Nathaniel thanked her for her generosity: not only could he diminish the woman in front of his few friends for accepting to work *merely* for money, the money that bought his lifestyle—but her long-hour schedule made it easy to cheat on her. There was a creepy element, sides of Nathaniel that grew on you as you became aware of them. The crudeness of his speech, his graphic behavior…

Though he was clean and well-groomed, shaven, in a good mood when sober, Nathaniel changed blue jeans and sneakers once in a blue moon. No more than coins in his pocket, just enough for cigarettes, a tic-tac box, a new notebook from the mini-Market on 7th Ave. You could not go to a concert, to a restaurant or a game unless you paid his ticket. And yet, I envied his availability. Though he was not Jewish, I respected his *rutzpa*, his evading Academia—his living in the West Village with an interesting woman while fucking uptown the most beautiful thing, for what he said. I did not meet the girl, but his boundless passion for her made me imagine her beautiful and more than shrewd.

Nathaniel had no intention of presenting Kathleen to us, his regular friends. We corresponded to a lower level of energy, to Anna's flat-footed world. "No reason to mix apples and oranges," he said one time that I stupidly insisted on meeting Kathleen. I belonged to the square, the official plane with Jacques (it's five years after we met that Nathaniel introduced his closest friend, Jacques Manassah, to me). At some point in our promenade, Nathaniel would declare that he was in love with Kathleen Miller, dreamt of giving her a child. He suddenly thought about finishing his degree at Brown because of her. He went as far as saying that he would return to his *Alma matter*, where there slept his aborted career; and get accredited. He would accept to be affiliated. For a couple of weeks it seemed that the impossible dream of a comeback, the mending the fences and rebuilding the bridges was still possible for Nathaniel.

After all, he was not so far gone, I thought. If they could go far away from New York, and while baby was coming out of Kathleen he could finish his Ph.D. in the Midwest somewhere. And they would not need much money. Back in England, Kathleen's parents wouldn't have to approve. The couple and their baby would not need their money. It was too good to be true.

Nathaniel would provide the basics, and Kathleen might go back to school at twenty-two. "Life is not so bad on a campus, you know," said Nathaniel to me, at thirty-five, after having resisted for fifteen years life on campus. It was surprisingly predictable of him. Was he exactly the same Nathaniel? He would become a regular guy for her sake. He'd buy the system wholesale. So strong and healthy was their affection, their love-making. Nathaniel didn't make it a secret that they had tremendous sex. "That's been amazing," he said. "We're the two of us the moment she steps in the store."

For a time, Kathleen worked a couple of shifts a week at the store on Broadway; for the fun of it, not for the money, which must have been ridiculous in her budget. Adding to his regular shifts at the Annex, Nathaniel worked the shifts when he could be with her. "We avoid touching for eight hours but we speak in silence and we don't detach our eyes... the clients are aware of it, everybody. Nobody thinks about breaking the spell. We run to her pad... Hard to explain, it's like new each time, no staleness, no habit, no yawning while you're at it." Here Nathaniel affected a wide and animal-like yawn, which he covered by the palm of his hand in a manner that seemed cruel to me. Nobody could have competed with what he gave Kathleen. Nor what she gave him. Nobody did, until—she got married to a successful man her age.

And there was no longer mention of a baby. There had never been a baby, not even in the making. Stupidly, madly, Nathaniel went all the way to a small town in Wales, England where the marriage was happening, using his recent credit card. He stalked around the wedding party like a character out of *Whuthering Heights,* tried to speak to her before and again after the ceremony. What did he tell her? Maybe he didn't even speak. She freaked out and called the police, and he became furiously mad at this ultimate betrayal. One can understand her. Nathaniel must have been half-delirious. But then he came back incognito to New York and to sleep and eat at Anna's. And after a couple of months during which he disappeared inside Anna's place without answering phone calls or opening the door, he returned to us, his few friends, as though nothing had happened. Nathaniel didn't seem to feel in the least guilty regarding Anna. And Anna still didn't know about Kathleen. Didn't want to know? He had sex with the two for years.

Anna was different from what you'd have expected. She was fun and interesting, having lived in Europe and in the United States. She had paid herself a year of English Literature at Yale on some money she'd inherited, and it had been a wonderful and nurturing experience. Nathaniel, of course, sneered on the side and winked to me when she said that. They could not have met at Brown. Nathaniel would not have engaged proper and studious Anna Otlaf at Brown, where he frequented the self-appointed underground, the small fish that lives off of the generous whale and resented it. Nathaniel and Anna had a common friend in New York, Jacques Manassah—another would-be writer. Someone who could write, though; and Anna also could write. And what is bizarre is that for some time this little world believed hard in the talent of a man who couldn't.

Jacques had been Anna's lover, and then he desisted for Nathaniel. How did Jacques find her is a matter of conjecture. Jacques had a way to find the people he needed. Anna went for Nathaniel head over heels, to the point of having him smoke cigarettes like there was no tomorrow in her few square feet, enjoy all day long and each day of the week her fridge, eat up from the fresh vegetable, the wine, and the compartment of Norwegian meat sauce she was acclaimed for, jams of all sorts, candies, cookies and nuts. Nathaniel liked to nibble while drinking his single-malt. The atmosphere was more intimate and relaxed between us at Anna's than in the Annex. I appreciated him letting me have my binge now at Anna's as well. We could dig in his personal library *ad libitum*. Everywhere on the walls, his makeshift shelves gave under heavy loads.

Anna was another voracious reader, but of a different kind of books. Theories let her cold, she said. She didn't understand why women were into such stuff at the university. "They want to prove they can think *also*—" Anna had this great British pronunciation whereby she rounded the lips and filled her mouth with the syllables of the word. She continued with a resonant laugh and a jerk of her round, somewhat formless shoulders: "As though theorizing was the only way to prove it." She was interesting, but she was not beautiful. Not the cute young thing Nathaniel pined for. She was not that young; she was like us, in her thirties. She was short, somewhat plump, alive and attractive as far as her green eyes were concerned. She had the goody, hearty face of an English girl, who turns pink, red and purple when she drinks and when she laughs. The blond hair of a Londoner for father, the extreme whiteness of her Norwegian mother. No matter which stylish product she put on them, Anna said, her hair was not responding. She had this self-diminishing modesty that is so common to people born, if not in wealth, at least in comfort and ease of mind. Money should not be a problem. Anna had no financial boundaries for her friends, and less as you got closer to Nathaniel. She'd invite us to a concert, a show, French restaurants in the West Village. It felt awkward since I, for one, was making decent money; but she insisted and moralized the situation like a teenager: "I have it easier than most. Money doesn't count for me, why should I count it *for* you, Etienne?"

For someone like Jacques—men, say, more of her size than Nathaniel, for someone whose taste in women was less specialized than Nathaniel's, Anna was a very fine woman. Though it is true that her hair fell flat on her front, as long as she kept in shape at her gym and didn't eat too much, didn't depress, she was spirited, curious, full of words. We never got close, I mean physically, though there was a time when I would have liked to take her from Nathaniel, giving her her due for one night. She was too taken by Nathaniel, who had her for granted. Naturally, the more he was absent, the more she was throwing herself at him. Unrequited love is a powerful chain.

The studio was cramped but it had the old New York style: stucco around the walls and the tin-pressed ceiling, the heavy bathtub serving as table, dancing small squares of black and white ceramic tiles in the bathroom. The outside of the red brick house was covered in summer by rich ivy, and booming roses on Anna's fire exit landing welcomed you from down the street. For a recalcitrant, resented, resistant entity like Nathaniel, it was smart to adopt elegant simplicity and carefree privilege where it didn't cost. For hours on end he'd sit reading, smoking, listening to the universal noise coming from the fire exit—right in the heart of the most coveted neighborhood.

I confess being an interested friend. I overlooked Nathaniel's eccentricities and pretended to take him seriously, making him believe that I took him 100% seriously. And somewhere I took him seriously. I needed his encyclopedic mind, his attention. Whether I picked him up at the Annex or at Anna's, he was always enchanted to have me join him. Anna at work from 9 am to 8 pm, including part of the weekends, Nathaniel noted his thoughts and read extensively (until he was tormented by Kathleen), then listened to MTV, watched the news—and then, he'd take a long walk outside, in the Village and on the peers with me or someone just like me.

He was open to discussion, to argument, any issue you might want to feed him or question him about. Thankful to you for giving him food for thought, he embraced it wholeheartedly, made it *his* and served it back to you all cooked and spiced as though it were his. This was his rare quality. Nobody else could do that for you, dress up your mind so well. He had so much time on his hands, he didn't know what to do with it but wait for *the* original idea to pop up from within. Which never happens, not without solicitation from outside. So, he regularly lived off of someone else's inspiration. And otherwise, there was no reason why he should ever accomplish anything. Months went by while he reread Hegel's *Logic* for the third time. He was never sure he had read enough, taken enough notes before tackling his *magnum opus*.

We were in the late 90's and there was this effervescence about computers. Anna bought a flat screen whose liquid picture was vivid and sharp, answering in-your-face, asking you to proceed and choose. Nathaniel kept it off. He couldn't stand the impeccable screen watching him, sending a reproach to his mess. He loathed the requirements and filing of electronic forms you had to comply with to first establish access. He didn't pass that stage. According to him, it was clear that the machine favored the rich, the white, the articulate and the young. It was the last manifestation of a society gone alluringly open, free, even berserk. "A society," he said, "that coaxes you, cajoles you rather than orders you, a society that convinces you to participate voluntarily, eager and happy to be in good standing..."

"To be in what?" I asked to punctuate his sentence.

"In the masquerade of late 20th century's triumphant capitalism."

This was below him. He saw from the corner of his eye that I despised the cliché and he tried to elaborate: "You know, the Web, what has it got in store for us if not more buying and selling. The universal babble is only the wrapping. You have no choice but to buy, and to buy what it wants you to buy in the way it makes you want to think that you are free to buy. You take an educated pick among their options, you have a choice between *their* choices. You turn computer-wise or not. And if not, you are out, among the have-been."

He was renting against the machine—but, strangely, when in the heat of conversation I succeeded to switch it on and got too close to the screen, touching the crisp liquid surface, he became very nervous, overbearing, bossy: "I've warned you about the screen, last time I say it, don't do it again!"

"But look, it erases the touch and reforms its cells around the blow like a wound..."

"Don't fuck with me!"

He was green, jaws clamped, tight-fisted. What kind of threat was that? Last time of what? Nobody can simply refuse technology and he, Nathaniel, should have been aware of this more than anyone. He was not, and it was a surprise for me to witness this blindness in my friend. Nathaniel was in awe of the computer and despised it only because for some neurotic reason he couldn't master it fast enough. There was no patience in him. Same problem he had with learning foreign languages, which took the ability to survive weeks of weakness and childishness, the patience to go through basic skills while stumbling and feeling inadequate to the task. Nathaniel couldn't afford to stutter and fumble like a baby, even temporarily. His self-esteem was too fragile.

Nathaniel's romantic stance against the ravage of technology gave way in front of the computer to good old peasant attitude. He was afraid of the magic. He couldn't be bothered by a new way of arranging things when it had taken so much for him to master the old intimate note-taking, the scribbling-of-thoughts in the spur of the moment. In there Nathaniel was like a snail, lived in his carapace. Just when most people claimed that it was helping them to write better, the computer was of no use to Nathaniel. It represented an attack on his experience. Why notebook and computer could not cohabitate, one coming after the next in the writing process? I didn't understand. He blanked in front of the dead-living whiteness of the screen. Maybe he didn't use the right keystroke, forgot to save, un-saved after saving. He got in a loop, his words looked at themselves. I have learned typing as a teenager, in France. Due to an administrative mistake, they threw me in a technical high school, and so I practiced the low-key skill as if I had been a future secretary, one of those people who didn't get jobs in France. I am thankful for the mistake: typewriter typing is as essential as moving the jaws and the tip of your tongue the right way when you have to speak a foreign language. Nathaniel Lagrange couldn't type. A guy accepted at one point in the elite didn't type fast enough, he refused, didn't care to learn so as to be comfortable in front of the screen. The entry test at Brown was not computerized yet.

Nathaniel despised the overrated performance of the computer almost everybody was mad about. He was not entirely wrong. You had this dotcom generation full of itself, people our age, commandeering the known world from California, and in the media and in New York everybody was looking at the phenomenon with indulgence. Start-ups pretended to represent *the* up and coming way of life, what the future had in store. Of course, we were in New York and the dotcom inflation was bringing money to Wall Street, nothing wrong with that. But not for Nathaniel, who didn't profit, didn't want to profit and was perhaps the worst case of die-hard leftist breathing. From my angle, as I said earlier, envy was writ large in his rejection. Spurn what you can't get, it feels better.

Nathaniel loathed the dotcom generation. "Opportunists, profiteers, generally from exclusive origins, Wellesley, Stanford." He also acknowledged and in the same breath that it was the last expression of freedom of the century. The last dream of communality, however distorted. People really thought that through the Webwork a window to easier communication, direct dialogue between random individuals was possible thanks to a loose network thrown over them like a myriad cells of electronic brain extending their own. Open sources, the archives and libraries of the planet, stratospheres of brochures and books, films, pictures and music, the universal encyclopedia turned over, miniaturized, compressed, encrypted and made accessible free or for a nominal fee, downloadable in high speed communication at the touch of a finger. Utopia ushered in, made available by what we, people like Nathaniel, had thought wrongly was not human: technology. In its rudimentary stage, maybe, technology had been the anti-thesis. Now it went hand in hand with us. Better: it extended our hand. The frontier was up for grabs again, invite your friends. No corporation could control the Webwork. They were right, nobody could. No monopoly and hardly any police on the Webwork, back then.

I faced further proof that my friend was a serial failure, a pretense, some weird snob. Nathaniel had an old friend from Brown, not another timid radical like him, Tony Wumster was a man from Queens who had started a career in Hollywood by working for Disney. Nothing wrong with that. Tony had kept in touch from L.A. and was inviting Nathaniel to contribute to his sparklingly brand new Web site, shiny like a gift out of its wrapping, and called euphorically *Rockets to the Uncharted: the Unannounced Fleet*.

Under this heady heading, Nathaniel could contribute among a growing number of blog writers, screenwriters and Webwork thinkers, designers and journalists, friends of Tony Wumster. "The way the Webwork operates, can be any kind of writing," said Tony to Nathaniel. "Any quantity. From your essay on Hegel to the last entry journal. We hardly edit what you send us, you say what you want to say the way you want to say it."

Nathaniel was paralyzed by this pleasant turn of phrase for weeks. First, he remained for a couple of weeks dry over his new notebook, untouched as of yet by his furious remarks and notes. After hours of torturing the words "uncharted" and "unannounced," he ended having them resonate in his head like empty cans of tin. Against all logic, Nathaniel maintained that Tony's words amounted, not to a carte blanche, as they appeared to at first sight, but to an injunction, a cruel order. Nathaniel was ordered to find the way he wanted to say things. What had been Nathaniel's pretense: to say "it" the way he wanted to say "it," that was what he couldn't do to the page. The page was not his habitat. He didn't fit the format and style of organization required by the page. Nathaniel didn't know any better and so he came back banging his head against that wall.

Apparently, Tony had just told Nathaniel what Nathaniel wanted to hear. He'd offered him the solution on a silver-platter. This was the worst thing you could do to Nathaniel. In his blindness, he didn't see that Wumster was not asking him for pages. A blurb on the Webwork is not made out of pages.

And then, I learned in the next walk we took that all doors had opened wide, it was like diarrhea. *Une coulée de lave*, the slide of a burning lava carrying away fences, doing away with sentences and periods, breaking paragraphs and pages. Nathaniel was writing non-stop, day and night. He was elated and exhausted, skinnier than ever. "Good fatigue," he said proudly, "like after good hard work, creative and rewarding in the country, like cutting wood or milking cows."

The funny thing was that he *was* wearing a checkered shirt and he had suspenders clasped to his waist like a boy from the farmland of New England. His name Lagrange did have white trash resonance. He did wear his blue jeans high on his lean abdomen, like a redneck and a jerk. The difference was that, of course, in Nathaniel's case the look was intentional. Nathaniel loved to look like your regular guy.

He tried to smile, but looked haggard, smoked out. His pants were coming apart at the seams. He had puffed at the marijuana stubs Jacques was feeding him every morning. Jacques lived on Leroy Street, about three blocks away. Nathaniel squinted behind his glasses. He looked like a gnat that's gone too close to pulsing light. Someone who's not only traveled through the passage where life transmutes into death, but also through the more daunting return, the reverse voyage, the making life out of death.

However, in contrast with Mary Shelley and other writers of monsters, who created life out of death, Nathaniel succeeded in creating nothing out of plentiful life. Nothing that he could show anyhow. It was terrible. Not that he lacked material, he had too much of that, he was agonizing over the compression he'd have to inflict to his inspired draft in order to transfer it to the flat screen and on the printed page. This flight of thought that, according to him, linked from Hegel to Laplace, from Lavoisier to Maxwell and Planck, from Hegel to Schelling and Fichte, while looking at the symphonic forms coming to maturity and exploding in Haydn, Mozart and Beethoven (!)—this net of flaming thoughts linking thinkers, scientists and artists who had not been linked previously, this risqué research into concepts taken from fields thought to be worlds apart—this complex and but one living thought would have to be streamlined, framed and made to serve a tame argument. Whether or not he'd ever heard Haydn's symphonies, Nathaniel didn't doubt for a second that he had an argument. It was immoral; it would be criminal for him to betray his inspiration. His mental dive into deep currents should remain primitively ebullient.

He was right, of course, computers put their stamp on what you confide to them. They channel thought process, they come with their format for allowing thought to circulate in a looser state than it did on the traditional paper page. But the medium imposes itself anyway, and Nathaniel's mind, for one, needed badly the nimble alliance of formatting and flexibility one finds on the screen.

Result? Nathaniel didn't send anything to Tony and that was that. He didn't even produce something we could read, Jacques Manassah and I. Jacques was not surprised. He told me they had shared an apartment in Brooklyn. They'd agreed on a challenge: to convene at the end of the week and read to each other ten pages typed. Jacques came up regularly with the desired pages, even if imperfect and hasty. Nathaniel didn't come up with anything and ended demolishing Jacques' intrepid essay. Jacques knew Nathaniel before I did and more intimately. Now, when the three of us happened to meet downtown, Jacques would send funny signals to me, telling me in Nathaniel's back, don't believe him, he's not what he seems, cannot do half of what he brags about.

I'll present Jacques later, give you his take on Nathaniel.

Finally, the fifteen pages destined to Tony that Nathaniel let us borrow a copy of one evening, I tried to read them and I didn't understand, didn't see the point. There was no point. No introduction: readers like to be taken by the hand, ushered into the moment you offer them. But for all his talk about the moment of grace, Nathaniel was not offering anything, no reason to make it easy for you. On the contrary, you should be happy to get a glimpse. As though you had to know the reference and Hegel was part of the air you breathed, in the first sentence he addressed you with a contorted mention of *Wirklichkeit* (as opposed to *Realität)* in the *Phenomenology of Mind.* In the next long sentence, this distinction, which he hadn't established, was connected to the triad of notions found in the system of the French psychoanalyst Lacan, difficult to read even for his French followers. There were *the real, the imaginary,* and the *symbolic*, and Nathaniel bandied about these three words without bothering to have them mean something and until they were not merely devoid of meaning but each weighing a ton. All that would still have been okay if the complication had been called for, motivated by an argument. I couldn't, Jacques didn't—I think nobody could have sorted out his argument. Nathaniel had none. I want to add, none that one could make out. It was there perhaps, entangled in the parenthesis, confused by the circumlocutions. Perhaps there was a dazzling idea, but it was dimmed, covered by complications like a jewel wrapped in a rag, like a scenery in thick fog, like the blurry features of a statue still in the rock, *un chef d'oeuvre inconnu* like the one Balzac wrote about. What Nathaniel had done was play on words, sound play between words, undercutting his attempt at expression and meaning. I could not quote anything my friend wrote back then, before he reached the Webwork. That would be an insult to his memory. Sad. What kind of friend was he that I couldn't help where it mattered?

Nathaniel was aware of all this, he was not stupid. He knew his so-called essay was impenetrable, he had wanted it that way. William Blake had complicated his epic poems to the point where no one progressed in them unscathed; similarly, walking through Nathaniel's lines was like straddling dunes of sand whipped in your face by a fierce desert wind. Without consideration for a minimum of orientation, not caring in the least for the comfort of his eventual reader. And you know what was the result of all this uncaring? His reader felt under no obligation to proceed. No one can force another to read. Who wants to sweat, and perhaps risk getting bored or hurt grasping nothing that was addressed to you?

Aware of all this, Nathaniel nevertheless expected against hope some kind of encouragement from us, he forced us to speak about his thirty-five pages, which he claimed he had paired down from a much bigger source. I tried my best. This strained our relationship. Jacques avoided the topic in Nathaniel's presence, which infuriated him. Nathaniel and Jacques had terrible fights when I was not around.

Nothing new, told me Jacques. The two had spent hours in Brooklyn (where they lived before Jacques got married), shouting to each other down Flatbush Avenue. They'd walk on opposite sidewalks but in the same direction, and for hours they'd slander, scold, undermine and thrash each other, depending on the gradation of the fury.

Jacques and I shared information about Nathaniel's passion for Kathleen, what he told him of impending disaster—while he still never said a word to Anna. It was becoming clear that he would leave New York because of Kathleen. We, in turn, being good friends, kept Nathaniel's secret from Anna to the end, and even after the end, after he left and seemed gone, we didn't speak to her of his consuming passion for Kathleen. Anna entertained to the end a purer idea of

Nathaniel. "Why break the spell?" said Jacques smartly. "Maybe not you or me, but some people need to see purity in their lives and around them, often where it's least called for."

Because of what he interpreted on my part as cold shoulder, Nathaniel never confided in me the more salacious episodes of his affair with Kathleen Miller. I would have liked to spy on their more piquant episodes. The disaster gathering speed around his head, Nathaniel about to take the last entry curve. Witness, be there at the end of his day, the wrecking of his life—yes, even back then, when nothing had happened. It's *Schadenfreude*, relief that it's happening to him and not to me. I could have assisted his demise. Oh! Not provoked the crash of his personal life, but accompanied the move.

For a long time there was no way to learn more about him. Nathaniel maintained no electronic log back then and I was no hacker. I developed such a curiosity in Nathaniel that I became jealous of his relations, his friends Jacques and Eric. No longer could I simply retreat and not take it personally when it came to Kathleen, who remained shrouded in secrecy from me. I didn't have anything against the young blond Kathleen Miller, but against the fact that he shut me out.

How I still miss walking with Nathaniel downtown. Our running after mercurial truth all the way to the egg-shape of the metal statue symbolizing the globe at the foot of the World Trade Center. There, just between the two colossal sky-scrapers scintillating into the sky, we would sit, regroup, smoke some more and talk about Deleuze or Derrida.

I have been two-face with Nathaniel—critical, dismissive *and* needy, without forgetting curious and envious. I have been afraid for him and I have pitied him. At present, I am horrified...

But still I miss him. I would like to be where he is, at the center of things.

Log 10

Hardly sleeping since the catastrophe, whether in New York or in Paris I've moved around in a state of exhaustion. In order to win against confusion, I mean mental confusion, I've spent my time surfing, learning, mapping and sequencing data around that same catastrophe; I have also delved into what people who've known Nathaniel, close friends of his, filed in the privacy of their laptop. How to understand what has happened, Nathaniel's final crack up, otherwise?

Jacques' hard drives since the day he bought his first computer lay open to my search. Kathleen's log and Anna's Web pages, both digital writers in their own right and much earlier than Nathaniel, which is not to his credit. It took a long, rugged and circuitous route for Nathaniel to reach the Webwork.

"Hey Dad? Where are you?"

"I'm in Paris." I turn the device around for her to get a good look at venerable Paris.

"I know, but what are you doing in Paris?"

"Do I have to tell you that?"

"Oh! It's true, sorry Dad, I forgot we are in a detective story of cosmic proportions!"

And then her face pales as she remembers that if there is a detective story and of some proportion, it's not one that the daughter of one of the heroes can afford to read comfortably settled. In the next moment, the darkness in her skin comes back. She has a genuine question for me; and it's not a question about me and my concerns and troubles, but about herself.

"Yes Isabel… what is it?" I say.

"I'm not sure what I want to become?"

"Man," I tell her, "you have all the time in the world to think about that!" And then I realize that it's not true to her perspective, I'm just babbling to cover my nervousness. Whether one is fifty-nine or twelve, one contemplates the same amorphous, unclear and unavailable horizon.

"No," she insists, "the thought I have is that, though I still love you and admire you, Dad, I don't want to be in the same line of business as you!"

"You won't have to…" I say.

She looks perplexed for a few seconds. Then her contrite little face relaxes and she smiles at me. She is sorry to have called me and happy at the same time."

"You know, maybe it's better if for a while you wait for me to call you…"

"Yes, I know, Dad… better if I don't call you… you're not ready yet."

"I'm calling you in my mind all the time."

"I know, Dad…"

She has this frown and her mouth is contorted because she is about to cry. When I'm about to cry, I disconnect.

In Paris now, it's the same feeling of loneliness I had in my first life here. Except that I am after several known, loved and admired individuals and that makes me more alone. I look at the old façades of stones and open my laptop to find you, Nathaniel. It's the same old bridges and castles and churches, the same proud 1900 buildings, same Art Nouveau street lamps—except the new lamps have no light inside, but some device that dazzles and projects a white light, more effective for the million discreet cameras of surveillance that populate the old city. The same slated roofs, glistening under a fine haze. Only, everything has been renovated and gentrified on the outside—and inside, France is so Americanized, and what I mean by this is, so full of gadgets, you'd think you're in some oddly preserved and quaint corner of a mid-size town in New Jersey. When I was a child the center of Paris was all black and blue from centuries of wars and pollution, riots and missed revolutions. It looked real old. Now it doesn't look old; it looks reconstituted. Now the renovated stones have a warm tobacco glow, and the apartments inside, or the lovely rooms like this one where I write are small, cozy and chic. And it's only if you get closer to the surface that you see the myriad holes, deep scratches and indentations, the dark recesses, all the indignity suffered by the old stone. No renovation can alter a savage past.

And renovation can do nothing against the new kind of summer heat that bathes *le bassin parisien*, as it is called. Remember that Paris is on low grounds, surrounded by hills. Pollution and heat mix well in this hollow. I do not remember Paris ever being so hot in summer, so humid. It's what I was always told growing up, how temperate the climate of my native country. Now It feels like the East Coast ten years ago: still much cooler than Georgia or Florida today, say Washington D.C. when I landed in 1985. Thirty odd years later, the French cover their old walls with fine panel screens that pump American series right into their bedrooms, but they are still advocating the "natural" and rightly pointing out to you when you complain that visible or invisible air conditioners only add to global warming. It's a point of honor with them, they still don't believe in air conditioners, too American, even the mobile miniature ones imported from China. They prefer to bake and distinguish themselves. Air conditioners do make things worse in the cosmic picture, and yet a discreet cooling system pulverizing fresh odors and basic oxygen would not be luxury in my steamy little room; hard to appreciate the chic. I assume this old hotel has a few of its façade stones and a beam or two from its original roofing made circa 1600—yet it is computerized, service is mostly done by robots; and it is sealed from the outside world as if we had already reached doomsday and were the only survivors.

On my flat panel, I have digital access from water quality to sending a last-second message to the cook who scrambles my eggs in the kitchen. But it cannot indulge in a minute air-conditioner that could adapt to the more recondite and like microscopic aspects of my atmosphere. While I was not around and after bitter fights, they have even passed a law against air-conditioners! As a result, Parisians spend their free time in department stores that stay opened, like in New York, 24 hours, Sunday included. It's not like in the old days, when they worked only 35 hours a week

Inside the metro is so hot I prefer to walk, or else spend hours in a fresh taxi. There are still sections of Paris where you can walk and look at the ancient buildings. Le Pont Neuf is still the oldest bridge; le Louvre is still looking at you from the time of the kings Henry. But I do not remember seeing in my youth here so many people. Taking advantage of generous vacations as a professor, I've returned to France over the years. Gabriela loves France, the villages, the old cities, the atrocious history, the complicated French language; and Isabel catches the tone and the intention of about everything you tell her in French. Until recently, she didn't bother much with her French lessons at school; but then, when she understood that Europe might be our refuge, and that daddy would like eventually, for the sake of his old age, to return where he came from, she changed.

It has always seemed natural to me to be surrounded by hordes of tourists while in Paris; but it has reached another level. You can hardly move on the Boulevard Saint-Germain; stand elbow to elbow Place de la Bastille, clomping the ancient pebble-stones of the vast circular plaza where once stood a dark and infamous prison; you would like to think for a second about the famous prisoners of that citadel, destroyed during the Revolution. Marquis de Sade staying in a filthy cell for 12 years comes to mind; but you get tired of the brouhaha, the incessant conversations. And it is quickly uncomfortable to be squeezed, so you force your way out of the crowd. Yesterday, I took the train at Gare Saint-Lazare and visited the Château de Chantilly where my grandmother took me and my sister to throw crumbs at the carps in the thick water of the moat circling the castle. There were few ducks huddled behind meager bushes and in the corners of leafy shade—and no carps, the water being too warm and shallow. So many people and so many cars, in the suburbs and in the countryside, at any hour—it's like in New York where there are at least ten individuals waiting at the door and ahead of you and cherishing the same conceit, whatever you try to do.

White people are getting older on both sides of the Atlantic and in accelerated numbers. I may sound racist but it is striking to me that their young are not as numerous as the colored kids. White, Catholic France is fading as we talk. While many are dying in their attended homes like flies, you bump into more old people on the sidewalks of venerable Paris than ever before; and do not forget those in wheelchairs who, pushed by their nanny, are blocking the sidewalks.

Otherwise, there is this colorful mosaic of second and third generation migrants that loafs around and makes a lot of noise. Paris always harbored migrants; but these don't behave like their predecessors. For one thing, they don't assimilate. Better said, they make a point in not assimilating, in eating only their own food and dressing their own religious way. They come from East Europe, North and Central Africa, the last catastrophe in Asia, and they are wedged between the stones and the ancient wood like a pack of fresh worms. They are like a population of carpenter ants waiting for the moment when they have multiplied enough to swallow the edifice.

The *Daily News* was right, the Lagranges have fled New York to Canada and hence to Europe under the benediction of the authorities. And what is shocking is that, once in Paris, these officials have let the Lagranges settle right in the heart of Rive Droite, métro Strasbourg-Saint-Denis, there to operate and grow digital roots. As of today, the same incompetence has managed to let the Lagranges evaporate, most likely for a few days.

The international police, the CIA, the FBI and you name them, all the intelligence of France, and I'm probably forgetting the Arabs, the Russians and the Lithuanians, the armies of the virtual, and real eyes as well were monitoring the Lagranges—and they vanished in the Parisian underground. You would think I am writing a cheap novel. It won't be long until they are found, and that's why you find me in France. I'm an old friend; I'm like the Lagranges. It should be easier for me. I don't know their local connections, but I've learned their tricks on the Internet, especially when they take precautions. Their cell-phones have mapping systems, even if they disconnect them. Surely, they change cell-phones like I change socks; and when they intend business, instead of relying on a laptop, they call from old-time booths found in hotels and such, away from their lodgings. They have learned to rely on low-tech from Suzan, who liked to tell us, "low tech is what breaks down first, and it's also what you rely on at the end of the day. A good old line is what you cannot afford to lose. Wi-fi or no wi-fi makes no difference, your computer hangs on the wire like your rich fur coat on a flimsy and rusty hanger."

Log 11

Nathaniel felt excluded when the three of us walked downtown, which did not happen regularly. Jacques and I, how to put it, each much preferred having Nathaniel alone and devoted to his cause.

The Jewish aspect matters. The three of us together, the atmosphere could get almost unbearable, full of danger. Part of his respect for the new friendship between Jacques and I came from Nathaniel's *goy* perception that Jews have an aura, they are part of a convoluted but distinctive *thing* that's innate and radiates from them down the centuries. Jews are ponderous and resourceful individuals; okay, many are. They represent a high level of cultural mixture, a concentration of diversity, that's right. Coming from North Africa (fleeing Alexandria, in Egypte), Jacques' parents transited by France and that's where they married before coming to Florida. Jacques' parents never made of the French language a secret. As a teenager, Jacques spent summers in Paris, invited by his Sephardic family. As a result, he didn't have Nathaniel's problem with foreign languages. Jacques spoke a funny streetwise French.

"Alors comment ça va, ben mon vieux? Qu'est-ce tu fais par ici ?"

He neither spoke his father's Hebrew nor his mother's Yiddish, and he said that he had barmitzva-ed for the gifts and to please his parents. Jacques didn't express interest in Talmud and Kabbalah like we did, Nathaniel and I, but he liked bagels and matzo ball soup and the Jewish contribution to music, music-hall, cinema, theater... Jacques was on his way to meeting and marrying an Israeli woman and have two boys with her. I don't know if he's finally written the script he talked to us about back then—he imagined a long dialogue between two very interesting Jewish figures, Walter Benjamin and his friend and intellectual enemy Gershom Scholem. Friendship of this complexity doesn't easily make for a movie; but Jacques had a way to have you believe in his practical ideas.

Nathaniel was right to be jealous, Jacques was close to me even before I met him. The moment Nathaniel presented Jacques, he felt already familiar. He was small and stocky like a cousin of mine would have been. Was it the genes, the demure smile, the fine gesture? His grey-blue eyes, the placidity of his regular features, his hardly pronounced nose? Or something more painful that shined through all this—the lucid remembrance of a terrible past handed down to him and me, including through the efforts of our combined parenthood to forget? Was it the precipice we could only imagine, Jacques and I, but which we owned nonetheless, which we shared, it seemed, before we even breathed and talked? That Jewish past the Jew carries on his back like a cross, that saga Nathaniel felt he could study until he was blue in the face and never share.

There was in Nathaniel a genuine desire to learn more about Jewish thought, to be *in* on the garden of secrets. The American soil is more permeable to Jewish tradition than the European. For white middle-class college-educated Americans, it's as though Jews had been cleaned of impurity once and for all, and no matter how this one or the other behaves, whatever they think about the wars Israel wages, Jews are purified by their collective passage through the worst possible fire. They are the ultimate victims, you cannot outdo the Holocaust any more than you can overreach the speed of light. Add the strand of Jewish mysticism that involves adoration of each letter painted in the scroll and access to exclusive knowledge—and you'll understand why Jewish-ness entices the wanderer.

Another more trivial aspect was Nathaniel's jealousy regarding Jacques and me, his devouring curiosity as to what was said about him, Nathaniel, the *goy*, when he was not around.

Disregarding the rules that preside over impartial discussion, Jacques was offensive to Nathaniel in front of me. Jacques didn't think that Nathaniel had anything to say concerning aesthetic production. He mocked Nathaniel's taste in cinema, which had something limited and cliché indeed. Nathaniel felt obliged, Jacques said, to appreciate renowned works of Art because they were renowned; and to put down Jazz because it had lost its popularity. So, implied Jacques, Nathaniel was as false and untrue as the philistines he spent his time vituperating against. It amazed me that Jacques could be so negative toward Nathaniel while remaining a close friend. Though I shared Jacques' reservations regarding Nathaniel, I respected the man.

Nathaniel looked ridiculous. He acted as though Jacques' character demolition had not sapped him of his juice and cut the nerve. If their fencing had been for real Jacques would have cut the Achilles' heel of his opponent.

As we walked together down 6th Avenue, Nathaniel continued to pretend childishly that Jacques' accusations didn't count, didn't mean anything, didn't undo him. That was too painful to watch. Nathaniel would look for my approval sideways; I gave none and only pitied him. His best friend had pulled the rug from under his feet and made a perfect clown out of him. Yet Nathaniel sauntered gaily down Bleecker St. and even hummed a tune.

Beware of your best friends, they are your worst enemies.

I have discovered only recently that for a price powerful retrieval engines let you in on anybody's personal chatroom, present or past. If the digital trace you target was never intended for the Webwork but to remain inside a laptop, occupying bits on the hard drive, sending this disk to the junkyard will not entirely erase its content, which will have left an image in other computers.

In 2000 Jacques had probably no idea that his laptop could be copied from afar in all its details; he didn't suspect that a friend could one day, years later, read his log over his shoulder as it were. I myself didn't grasp in 2000 that they might do that to my machine one day. There is no future and no past in the universe opened by the Webwork, only an eternal present in which everything co-exists in a digitalized, and arguably, diminished form of existence. We didn't know back then what we were buying into, a universe where nothing counts or matters very much, good and bad are equal; but where also nothing gets lost. Nothing lays dead and as though it has never been—*it* cannot disappear altogether once it has been compacted in neat rows of zeros and ones.

We wanted to believe that our computers were these lonely machines, connected worldwide but hermetically isolated, fire-walled and virus-controlled. In fact, opening a file has always been like sending your soul to whomever shall care to search for it. And encrypting it and pinning it to your skin in a blue-tooth like I do does not protect you anymore than the most sophisticated alarm will spare your house if a professional thief is determined to break in.

Until November 2000 Anna's hard drive contains things like: "Nathaniel is at work every day. As soon as I leave him alone, I'm sure, he works. We have so little space, but we make do. He may really come up finally with some exciting ideas about Thermodynamics. I do not understand the technicalities but the philosophical and especially the moral undertones are wonderful. If only he could tame the demon and not project it onto my poor computer! My crystal screen is for nothing in the rigidity that comes over him as soon as he places his delicate hands on the keyboard. Why couldn't they teach him?"

"Never been so optimistic for him and for us, however. Something that greatly obsessed Nathaniel all these years has lifted. It's as though the clouds that competed to dominate his sky have dispelled, disbanded like a pack of wolves, gone in shreds to the winds. It's so beautiful to be happy with him like yesterday evening! Etienne is more able than Jacques to bring about the intellectual side in Nathaniel, that place where he shines. I had forgotten how great it was when we met, almost ten years ago! Because of him I could, as though I were thirteen again, read entire afternoons without feeling guilty for not *doing* anything. There is this exquisite ability in Nathaniel, this old-world quality I should say— when he is such a Yankee— the talent of turning *le temps perdu* around. What stuck up people call wasted time, he calls untaxed time. Nathaniel makes being with him, especially when we don't say anything, insightful and a wonderful experience. That is what denotes the aristocrat, the exception in him."

Anna must have written this once Nathaniel realized it was over with Kathleen. Not that he would not continue to gravitate around Kathleen Miller beyond that point—to this day, I'm ready to bet his passion for her goes unabated. Kathleen breaks with him early 2000. By the end of 2000, he has not overcome her but he's swallowed his loss. He's realized he never had Kathleen. Only *he* had imagined their union, and a fruit to that union, a child; she had not imagined him—she had seen him for what he was. And in spite of his despair, when the worst of the stinging humiliation had passed, Nathaniel was convalescent. He enjoyed nights with Anna. He was getting used to not having Kathleen, to no having her but still having her, absent. Making love to Anna was comfortable and not unpleasant, a bit like putting on old slippers. Nathaniel overlooked his never finding her as attractive as he would have liked. She was under his spell, attending to his whims (when Kathleen had resisted him, slipped under him, body and soul) and he must have felt good. But he knew there wouldn't be another woman.

Nathaniel came out of his affair with Kathleen washed out like Ulysses after ten years of high seas. Except that, I am ready to bet this minor hero felt relieved not having to face the music by going back to school, not having to grow older by becoming a father and a professional. He wouldn't have a child and wouldn't be a father. He would remain a son. He would go back to mother's.

This humiliating return was described to me in romantic terms. He justified the move for two reasons: nowhere else than at mother's could he find the strength to stop smoking, and nowhere else could he write the work of his life. There it would come out of him—or it wouldn't. And if it didn't, then he would either change direction, become a carpenter, like his brother or find a way to die the shortest way, dramatically. He used the words "overdose of something."

I heard in his going back to mother the last manic songs Don Giovanni sings in Mozart when, recognizing he is doomed and destined to visit hell very soon, he still asks for more food, women and wine.

By November 2000, Nathaniel has decided on his retreat to mother's, and Anna has no hunch of that. Nor does she have an inkling that I can detect of the existence of Kathleen. Anna is still blind when it comes to Nathaniel, the man who sleeps next to her almost every night. Jacques and I, we know: the oldest of the Lagranges is going home, and not for Easter or Christmas, but to stay, until he figures himself out. How ridiculous to come back to square one without a penny, clueless and soulless at forty, a man as independent as Nathaniel. Ten years is enough, Nathaniel can't stay at Anna's and he won't tell her why, won't even tell her goodbye. He'll leave like a robber in the night. What would he tell her to explain his retreat, anyway?

On second thought, it doesn't really surprise Jacques and me that Nathaniel goes back to mother's, there to live in the room of his childhood. No, it doesn't come as a total surprise. Nathaniel has refused to integrate the forward social fabric. He has no degree, no steady job, no insurance malady, no apartment and no perspective of ever getting any of these things.

Later in her log, as he is leaving her, Anna is still not aware of Kathleen, but her tone has changed. She is lacerated by Nathaniel's decision. And yet, she has to recognize that she thought something like that was coming, she had to, even when their sex life had resuscitated, even in the midst of enjoying the attention from him she had never received. Anna expresses an effusion of guilt at feeling in sum relieved because their inexistent relationship is on the rocks. As though she woke up from a long sleep, suddenly she has her survival in mind and that of her potential progeny. She could still bear child, with some help from modern medicine. Ten years into this fruitless agreement, she realizes that she has mortgaged her future. She doesn't quite express the thought that way but it is clear to her now that Nathaniel has confiscated her future.. She would never say, like Kathleen or Jacques, that the man is a parasite, a bloodthirsty animal who leaves you dry. But the idea is there. She is like me in that she feels sorry for Nathaniel. "Going back empty-handed, at his age." However, her pain is rapidly alleviated by the fact that, as she notes in surprise, this denouement is best: "There is no other woman involved!" She has nothing to accuse herself of, she is not humiliated—no woman could compete with mother, brother and sister Lagrange. This was the best of break-ups.

Anna writes: "The day he asked me that abortion in 95, even though I was ready for the abortion and it cannot be said he forced me in any way, I suffered greatly realizing we were not to marry, never to go the beaten path of children and family together. What path, then? Was there a direction for us, a place where to go, a future even? It doesn't seem now that there ever a future for us, and at the same time we have been together in my miniature studio ten lovely years."

"Nathaniel has never elected me, never placed me at the center of his life. Who is at the center? His center cannot be a woman, unless she is, yes, she is... Maybe, who knows, it sounds awful—maybe Nathaniel will find himself nearer his center when he lives between mother and father, and when brother John and sister Kathy are on visit? He loves his brother so. Taken one by one they're screwed, but the Lagranges are okay in a pack. It's the mother who worries me, she lets him do what he wants, she doesn't ask questions, and at the same time, she likes to criticize. Not Nathaniel, she wouldn't dare confront Nathaniel, but anything around him she can set her eyes on. He will feel depressed and drink and smoke to death, and then one day he will sit at the desk and write to me. I hope he doesn't squeal nasty stuff about us. It's true we were an odd couple, who for long stretches of time didn't have sex or any contact, didn't kiss and didn't touch, though we spoke abundantly before we slept and held hands. Few inches from each other, naked under the sheet, we've slept pretty much every night together for ten years. Nathaniel cannot stand a thread on his soft, hairless and childlike skin when he sleeps, and in New York the heaters are so damn hot!"

September 2000, Jacques writes: "And now Nathaniel would like everyone to be stunned by his musical production. Nathaniel and his brother John and Eric have just spent a month down in Atlanta where John and his rich girlfriend live among acres of virginal land, and all the amenities, including a professional recording studio. I thought brother John was another Nathaniel, a man disoriented materially as much as spiritually, but I was obviously wrong... The fresh and pride product of their most recent divagation is a well-packaged CD signed by the

Bush-Whack Group. It's something, it's more than Nathaniel has ever finished and done on his own, although, in my humble judgment, the tunes are left unfinished and need more work. Not that the said leader of the group, Eric Dumois, does not hit hard every time he is allowed irresistible grooves, but this depends on Nathaniel supporting and self-effacing in front of Eric's inspiration, and it does not always happen. Eric should just play his music while Nathaniel prepares his encyclopedia and we would all be better off!"

Very angry, Jacques. "We thought Nathaniel would do something, break into something, say something in the flow of interesting ideas, instead of what he competes with Eric for the lead in a CD destined to no more than five friends!"

"I have wasted so much time on Nathaniel—and Eric and Anna…"

Funny he doesn't name me, Etienne.

Log 12

I have long hesitated inserting the following log into this file. First, because I have no hard evidence to support my suspicions. Nathaniel Lagrange may or may not have committed a murder before he left New York, a real one, not through complex electronic means. Yes, a good old murder. This is too grave an accusation to not at least preface it with my acknowledgment that the crux of the matter in the events that follow is mere fiction on my part. Only suspicions and questions, but coming after meticulous research. Second, I still hesitate because if I were to develop my questioning too well, it may alter in my reader the sympathy, the interest he started to feel for Nathaniel. Who would want to continue reading about an utterly hateful person?

It's on January 21rst 2001 that Craig Thompson passed away.

"His head was at an angle," Nathaniel told me two days later. He showed me how by bending the neck down and against his chest. "His neck was twisted and his glasses floated in the vomit. He was like covered with crust, dried-up secretion… I didn't touch him, didn't move anything, I am not stupid. Nothing you could do for him. No condensation on his glasses, clear against his nose… We think death is violence, but how peaceful, you should have seen how quiet Craig was. I'm the one who called the police."

Nathaniel was not jittery and didn't seem anxious. He stood contemplative, both hands deep in the pockets of his jeans, one strand of his curly hair falling between his eyes, very serious and poised. I tried to imagine Nathaniel speaking to the police. He'd become unexpectedly responsible in the wake of the young man's death. Before organizing the funerals, he received the parents, who were shocked beyond repair, and he told them little of what he knew about Craig. That is, he told them about Craig sober on a regular Monday morning; not that by Tuesday their son was at The National, a dive on Avenue A, and for the rest of the week.

Craig was also working sometimes at the Griffith Bookstore. He was gifted and prolific: two articles on Belize and one on Myanmar's intractable problems had already appeared in glossy magazines; and he had not even moved from his flat in the East Village. He researched the incipient Webwork and consulted in public libraries. Why was Craig in a rut, suddenly? Something had severed Craig's abilities to write—the wire had gotten disconnected. He felt uninspired, betrayed in his platonic love for Kathleen, source of his inspiration. And not at all because of Nathaniel, whose passionate relationship with Kathleen didn't bother Craig. Craig had thought to find in Kathleen what Shakespeare calls in a sonnet, "the marriage of true minds" which survives all "impediments" of time and does not suffer ups and downs. Before publishing them, Craig had read his pieces over and over again to Kathleen and she had given him important feedback. As far as he was concerned, she was a thoughtful, genuine, indispensable friend. But then, he'd learned before Nathaniel did of her getting married to the diplomat in England and of her decision to move back there.

Sex not necessarily bringing people together, Craig and Kathleen were closer friends than Nathaniel and her. How she kept the diplomat at bay when she spent the evening with Craig and good part of the night with Nathaniel? I do not know. Nor can I explain how a young, educated, even well-read and well-spoken woman could play this perverse game for several years and get away with it.

Craig was found dead in his vomit, and the one who found him is Nathaniel. He told me the horror: Craig's head squeezed at an angle against the wall, "Must have fallen, slipped... I don't know." Craig, who was the ultimate bohemian, had drunk a-plenty, and sniffed coke. Perhaps even done crack. They had occupied two small tables in the pleasant garden on Twelfth Street and Ave A. The name did not indicate what you could do in that secluded place. Outside, The National looked like one more insufferable East-Village burnt-up dive, and indeed when you stepped in, you had to move through a wall of bass vibration to make you jump and high pitched hard-rock grunts to make you grit your teeth. I could not talk nor hear anything once we sat at the stools in front of the massive bar, whose dark wood seemed to exude and like perspire human sweat. Right away I was tired of having to shout to be heard, and not even. The apparent bricks of the walls were caked with wax and organic matter; the place looked intently dirty, graffiti layered, unbearably vulgar—but luckily, beyond the bar, which opened in fact to the garden outside, there was a small paradise. You were practically allowed to drink and smoke and do whatever you pleased in that garden. The National had few clients attracted to silence, and so, the place had an air of exclusivity.

You had to be introduced like I was once by Nathaniel and Jacques, to this charming secret of the neighborhood. The gravel creaked under your feet, flowers and ivy grew on trellises, atrocious music from the bar still vibrated under your feet but it came muffled to your small white table. Kathleen had been the queen of this gathering. Nathaniel told me later that she had once spoken of *Wuthering Heights*, and in particular she had asked him across the table and out of the blue: "Do you remember the bastard child, the servant's child, the orphan, the ugly kid, you know, the one who is rejected, feels slighted and, years later, comes back to haunt the family and claim the domain where he first entered out of sheer generosity on the part of his masters?"

In the brouhaha of the conversations and the general state of ecstasy, that had gotten little attention; but it continued to trouble Nathaniel.

What did she mean, Nathaniel asked himself, did she think of me as the bastard, the one who didn't belong, the parasite who in the end turns out to be the winner, kicks everybody out if one lets him in?

That Craig had no sexual interest in Kathleen Miller explains why Nathaniel was not offended by the intimacy manifest between them. Craig's care for Kathleen was innocent and pure; the tranquil comfort between them escaped Nathaniel. He was so full of demands concerning her; full of despair. In any case, it would have been stupid to compete with Craig, who was no more than twenty-two when Nathaniel was going on forty.

Craig had celebrated his birthday in the company of Nathaniel, Kathleen, Jacques and others just a week before.

Usually, Nathaniel and Craig had a great time together. They might finish the night in Kathleen's apartment, a small studio in a pre-war building on 110th and Broadway. When lucky, Nathaniel would see everyone go in the wee-wee hours of the night, and he'd stay to enjoy her. But sometimes Kathleen didn't express the desire to have Nathaniel enjoy her all night. The next morning she was busy (I assume, with the diplomat), and so, he drifted out of her place with the remnants of the group and finished the night with Craig. And when he finally went back home to sleep, he'd bump into Anna all perfumed, dressed, combed, ready to go to work. It was not difficult to find excuses and brush aside the timid offer of her body. She was relieved to see him, she wouldn't dare ask hard questions. On the contrary, she'd make every effort to justify him. Artists of the mind have to have pleasures. Nathaniel had to be wild and unfathomable to the rest of us; otherwise, Anna thought, what kind of an original was he?

I imagine Nathaniel that morning at 6 a.m. He is alone with the dead man. He does not touch anything, does not clean. Everything around Craig is frozen in time. It's only the parents who at the end of that week paid for a cleaning lady. Genuine and naïve old middle class folks from Massachusetts, they must have been horrified by the squalor. Craig's loft was a terrible mess, and not your nice young-bachelor-writer mess, a den for a mole, the floor incrusted with pieces of undergarment glued by foods—half-empty jars, moldy plates, shoes, casseroles, notebooks, books in a heap, stacked up to the ceiling and leaving hardly a stifling space where to sleep on his spread-out futon mattress. I had seen on TV a documentary about hoarders. Besides being disturbed, most didn't seem too bright. How could a budding genius like Craig be a hoarder? His apartment, which I saw only that one time when introduced to the group at The National, while we were passing by on our way back to Anna's, and merely from the door, left ajar—his way of living gave me the impression of a deep depression in its occupant.

Alone before the dead, Nathaniel probably remembered how Kathleen had said a few minutes after her strange remark on *Wuthering Heights*, "If these are your intentions, Nathaniel, to grab us by the neck one by one, to suck the juice and the years out of us and not give us anything in return, and then replace us by your big ego... if that's what you intend to do, then we won't let you."

Why had Kathleen gone into this shocking, hurtful address and in front of all their friends? No doubt Nathaniel remembered also that, vendors on the same shift at the bookstore, upon finding together a volume on *Paradise Lost and the Art of Blake*, to impress her he had attracted her attention—as he had mine—to the sublime way Blake represents Satan: not as anything or anyone in particular, but as a black hole of a being—empty, hollow, transparent—and therefore eminently adaptable, able to espouse the shape of any shape, assume the contours of any living thing, suck it dry of life and beauty *and take its place*.

Her turning his explanations against him in front of Craig mortified Nathaniel. It is true, Kathleen was drunk and stoned. Kathleen, rare feat in a woman, could be stoned on ecstasy, smoke, amphetamine pills, and yet retain complete lucidity of purpose and level of engagement. On the spot, he hadn't been able to make out what she meant fast enough to counteract. Now he understood her. By making inspired love to her, had he not hoped to insinuate himself into the inbred soirée, the world of cosmopolitan class and chic Kathleen belonged to? Belatedly, Nathaniel realized that she had then decided to return to her people, which didn't include Nathaniel. It was her way of telling him that once on a student stipend in some Midwestern campus with him, and a baby in the equation, forget chic and cosmopolitanism and class. Their dream could not work. It would suck all the substance out of her.

One may ask what he did that early in the morning in front of Craig dead. It was a Sunday. People sleep at six am on a Sunday, especially after they have used substances.

Three hours earlier Nathaniel must have left the same apartment without thinking about closing the door. And the building being one of the last to not have been renovated in that part of town, the main door didn't even have a lock.

At 3:30 am Nathaniel was back at Anna's. When she spoke to me during that week, Anna made explicit mention to me of this time frame. "Thank God Nathaniel called the police right away. He's been so helpful, and so patient with the parents. He had to repeat ten times the same information. Poor parents, just to witness the way Craig lived! And poor Nathaniel, to lose like that a very important friend."

Anna does not want to speak about a very strange circumstance: Nathaniel has told the police that he'd left Craig's apartment at 1, 1:15 am…

At 6 am that Sunday he buzzed his friend from downstairs, and not getting an answer, walked into the building and into the apartment without having to force his way inside. Nathaniel must have had a suspicion that something was very wrong with Craig.

Or he came back to make sure he had not left anything compromising at Craig's—I don't know, cigarette butts, fingerprints, his urine in the bath and the fine mud of his shoe. Was Craig dead or just too drunk, unusually incoherent, suicidal when Nathaniel had left at 3 am? Was it suicide? And what if Craig was pushed and shoved beyond consciousness? They had a mock-fight like it happens between brothers, a joyful struggle, and then, it went a teeny weenie bit too far and Nathaniel didn't realize the consequences and left, and came back in a panic to cover his tracks… In this case, he'd left Craig's apartment three hours earlier as a murderer already. He'd seen him dead and left, too stone himself to register.

Didn't realize, I wrote? How could he not realize that his friend was drowning in his vomit?

But there still is the possibility that Craig died alone later. He may have abused of more substance once Nathaniel had left, vomited and died between 3 am and 6… This is what the police has reported: Nathaniel Lagrange left his friend Craig Thomson at 1:30 and came back at 6 am because they had agreed to play music together on that Sunday morning. If the police had been suspicious they could have wondered why so early on a Sunday morning. But Nathaniel told them about their rehearsing for a CD and the police was not suspicious. The case was not even been classified as suicide, but as overdose, an "accident occurring while the victim was under substance abuse." The notion of murder his my own entirely and perhaps this Log reveals more about my intention to throw dirt at Nathaniel than it sheds light on what Nathaniel really did. Yet, I cannot help suspect the worst in whatever Nathaniel did before he became the Nathaniel that we know. Could he have killed with his own hands back then? Was he a killer? Is he?

Why kill Craig? Were they not both losers, about to lose equally Kathleen? Should they not commune in their loss? They did, and then they attempted to kill each other. Or maybe… and this is the worst of my suspicions, stone as they were they imagined together something like the ultimate act of Desistence. They didn't use the word, but they played with the idea because Nathaniel was by then all about Gnostic thought and William Blake, and Craig all ears when it came to far-fetched thoughts. They would reach nothingness together. They would glimpse at the beyond, get rid of their limitations and meet both at the same time bigger than their own. It would mean annihilation for their limited ego, "self-slaughter" as Blake wrote; but in the process, each would lose his shell, his carapace and grotesque covering; each would fuse into the consciousness of the One greater than the sum of its parts.

In their megalomania and drug-induced excitement, they wanted to join forces in death—and one chickened out at the last millisecond. Nathaniel stayed on this shore of life. Craig was the more reckless of the two. Nathaniel had not smoked crack as much as Nathaniel nor drunk as much of the fine cognac that circulated among the small white tables. Or else, being older, Nathaniel's metabolism was more tolerant to excess.

These are conjectures; but there is a troubling difference between what the police reported of Nathaniel leaving the apt at 1:30 am, and what Anna told me to my face of his returning to her at 3:30 am and acting as if everything was absolutely cool. Has Anna lied to the police as well? It does not seem that the police even questioned her. She was not there when the overdose occurred.

But why did Nathaniel lie to the police? Why shorten his stay at Craig's during that crazy night? Was Nathaniel afraid that they might question his participation in their excess?

Anyway, since neither the police nor anybody has asked any question and the overdose was blatant, and Nathaniel came off as the best of considerate friends, and Anna was overwhelmed by how much humanity there was in her friend—why should I continue to entertain irrelevant doubts about all this?

I can testify that Nathaniel would not give up if he fought you physically. Whenever we acted like brothers and played at pushing each other down the avenue, he was taller than me and he made me feel the steel of his muscle until I had to abandon and ask for merci. Once I invited him at the gym of City College to play squash and it was exhilarating to play with such a competitor; but soon it was also overwhelming: Nathaniel cannot lose. During the competition, in close encounter Nathaniel forgets to be a friend or even a gentleman; he only thinks about punishing revenge if you outscore him. He's the eternal boy, unbeatable physically.

Log 13

Back in 2001, at the time when Nathaniel went back to Rhode Island and his mother, Kathleen writes in her log: "I am in a terrible mood. I cannot forget Craig. Someone has to pay for the excesses of others. True, Craig was himself excessive. We all were. It had to stop. Perhaps someone had to pay for it for it to stop. Craig did. Him and Nathaniel, like boys at the cookie jar until it exploded in their face. More specifically, Craig was the boy, not Nathaniel. The older man abused the younger by competing in matters of dangerous enjoyment (I speak like Nathaniel now, his way of thinking clings on to me, pooh!). Craig overdosed. Nathaniel was almost as overdosed as Craig; but it's Craig who paid for the two of them. I sound sanctimonious… In the last I heard Nathaniel is going back to the Lagrange's estate. I mock him and I feel so bad for him at the same time. As much as I cannot explain why, I do not feel guilty. He had it coming. We had what was agreed upon, plenty of that. Too much of that. The last stolen moments of my youth. It's trite, I know, but the expression is correct in our case, we stole operatic afternoons of passionate contact. We enjoyed purple dawns over the flat, garbled rooves of the Upper West Side. Our last adolescent ardors satisfied, we didn't realize how we'd stolen shamelessly from those who really cared for us. Youth is abusive. Growing means to give back. Another day comes around when you have, if not to give back what happiness you stole, at least settle the debt, clean the plate by your abnegation and, God willing, pray on your knees that you get a new lease on life. That *they* accept your love again. That, through errors, betrayal and confusion, they have remained faithful; their love for you has not abated. I sound like an old hag; but perhaps there are moments in a young life when one has to grow old. Nathaniel is the inveterate boy. He cannot negotiate transformation. Not in his genius, not humble enough to learn from defeat. Anna was a much better woman for you than me, Nathaniel. Your origins have constricted your prospect. Your father economized on electricity and heat. Shoes and pants had to serve several brothers. You yourself called that "a Spartan diet in the family of a sergeant." I hope for you that economizing on the life you could have had is a thing of the past."

What a bitch, this Kathleen! She is so right about Nathaniel and she is so wrong about what he will experience at mother's. In fact, things had changed at his parents' and drastically. The Lagranges were doing better than when Nathaniel was a child; so much better that it was one more factor in his perplexity upon settling back.

Here follows my reconstitution after collecting input from the Lagranges who were present upon Nathaniel's return.

Modest expanse of well-groomed lawn, the automatic sprinklers every so often wet slats of wood painted in a fresh white color. There is a fine stucco comparable to lacework over the front porch and around the bay windows, which have been renovated in a slightly pretentious Victorian style. The pedaling car of a kid, colorful balloons... Like many well-kept houses of New England, in the middle of July the Lagrange house looks together nondescript, hospitable and charming. There is a barbecue near the garage and on the front porch lingers a big plastic Santa with his huge red hood. There are swings and a round inflatable swimming pool sits under the shade of a tree.

Inside, the house feels cool and roomy and of a large size given the recent addition of a slick veranda for mother's plants and flowers, two garages, a shed for father's tools, playrooms for young guests, a mini-gym for retirees, and extra-showers and bathrooms.

One hears child laughter from the pool. George and his wife Rebecca are inside. George, the second brother, is two years younger than Nathaniel and two years older than John, who is in Atlanta at the present. George Lagrange is a well-paid accountant in a public administration in Cleveland. He has never tried to understand what Nathaniel is about.

But Nathaniel has decided to play it cool. Forget the old grief. He sits in a folding chair in the shade of a tree and pretends to read *The Chicago Tribune* together with the *New York Times*. At his feet, there is a pile of magazines and books. A week back home and he seems to have recreated his adolescent world. Except that he doesn't read books now and hardly glimpses at the newspapers. He skims the magazines. He experiences a disaffection, a stunning disinterest for the written word. He seems to smoke less already; but he probably struggles hard not to smoke.

In the attic, he has piled away the boxes of debris, tools and memorabilia, opening a space for his mattress. His mother Justine has not asked one question as to his indefinite presence back home. Retired from army-camp, Jean-Claude, his father, goes to the lazy business of the day as though his eldest son was not around and what was lounging around all day long was an empty shell of his son. Jean-Claude—so French sounding a name.

Nathaniel is surprised, almost shocked, by the change that has taken place at the Lagrange's home. Father's pension has long been pegged on the stock market and it's been doing extraordinarily well. The TV is your last model, and so are the mowing machine, the portable stereophonic ambiance system one of George's kid blasts in your ear, the massive console freezer-fridge, the washer/dryer and the elegant and shiny set-up of a marble-topped, computerized kitchen. It liberates mother and she becomes more present in the house. Having more time on her hands, Justine is available. It used to be father who was in your face and asking questions while you had to seek Justine somewhere to get one minute of her time; she was so busy, you could only count on half the seconds for her undivided attention. Now, on the contrary, mother is also in the open garden, next to Nathaniel, and while they don't speak she hears his breath, she looks at him. Mother reads from another pile of magazines. Neither wants to have to speak, neither knows how to speak about his coming back. Is he coming back? What is he doing? Nathaniel has always dragged the shameful side, the old precarious past right back in.

Justine is a flabby woman of sixty-three, and it shows in her soft flesh and her false blond hair, but her ruddy cheeks tell you that she is young again. She catches up on all the years devoted to motherhood and does what daughter Kathy and sons John and Nathaniel have asked her to do for years, *do something for herself*. There is a sparkle in her eye he had forgotten she had. And again, but for other reasons than when he was a child, he senses that mother has no time for him and it would be ill-advised on his part to press for more attention. It's obvious she'd prefer not to have to hear the last episode of what must be, for a Catholic woman, the perfect image of degradation. Over- ambitious and brazenly selfish, in New York Nathaniel has practiced sloth and aimlessness and despair, even as she could forgive him casual gluttony and carnal lust—and the outrageous search of forbidden knowledge in all its forms. My son is a heretic ostracized all by himself, mother thinks. That a woman like Justine no longer goes to church and is recently liberated enough from the tradition to think about herself does not change an iota to the exacting nature of her judgment. It's different now in that she keeps her mouth shut. She has learned to be silent in front of what baffles her expectations. Justine intuits what is playing havoc with her older son, betrayed love, and what she doesn't fathom, she guesses. Nathaniel seems exhausted beyond reason; he is like a parched man looking for an oasis. She cannot deny Nathaniel a respite, a heaven, few square inches of saving ground.

Self-effacing and easygoing Jean-Claude Lagrange, fact is that father never was a bad man. This is spite of Nathaniel, John and Kathy demonizing him over the years. Jean-Claude knows his son Nathaniel's in trouble, nothing new here. It doesn't bother him as much as it used to. Last thing father wants to see is the reopening of the old wound, what they went through when Nathaniel was the adolescent master bull-shitter of the Lagrange clan. And Nathaniel and little John fought like vultures over the remnants of *his* carcass, so that after his day in camp he had to distribute harsh punishments and be the drill sergeant at home. This fueled resentment in his children, especially in Nathaniel, always in fierce and mindless resistance against anything that stands in his way. Has to fight you to the death, Nathaniel, and for no other reason than justify his failure to accomplish whatever he's at. These days are over, thank God. Jean-Claude hardly survived them emotionally. Now, he prefers to hide behind mother and let her do the talking to strangers, which is what his older son has become.

How does Nathaniel feel back in the room of his childhood?

In the middle of July, actually, that room is occupied. One of his teenage cousins needed a room for himself and his occasional girlfriend. Nathaniel sleeps under the roof, in the attic.

Here, I must rely on sister Kathy and brother John's logs; they both have a lot to say about brother returning home. John took trips to watch develop the new Lagrange phenomenon. Recently their old laptops and zip drives have been confiscated. But I have worked with them and was either privy to their Webwork forays or a team member. Their familiar laptops send me whatever I need, even switched off. The secret services acted fast against the sophisticated equipment of Lagrange incorporated; it's the local police who still don't understand the deep connection between computers and stack them plugged and cabled, all ready to serve.

Protected by the cozy home, Nathaniel, as always, behaved like a hermit, a recluse. But there was a difference: he didn't drink, smoked less, had no sex, didn't try to get laid, worked at the chores that a large family house entails, further liberating mom and pop, and even the maid and the gardener. He cleaned loads of clothing, mopped the floors, vacuumed and by the end of summer, had cut wood for the house and the entire neighborhood. This was good exhaustion for Nathaniel. He heard of handyman's jobs in the countryside, and oddly enough, him so urban and bookish, was eager to have it rough. He went to the boats and offered his services to the first captain who overlooked his frameless glasses, whiteness and soft hands. Nathaniel was no novice at sea; once the family had settled in Rhodes island, he dreamed of going fishing flounder, tautog, bluefish, striped bass, menhaden, Atlantic herring out of Narragansett Bay. As a student at Brown, he had relished when depressed by his underachievement any chance to embark. Besides quoting *Moby Dick,* Nathaniel could speak about the sea.

He'd return three days later exposed, emaciated and skinnier than ever, but with the orange light of a dawn-at-sea in his eye, salt on his lobster-like neck and bulging biceps. He was happy like a boy and a couple hundred dollars richer. The pad of hard-earned dollars swelled the front pocket of his tight jeans. He was young again, but that was not enough. He wanted to rewind his life entirely, re-enter the beginning, regress before his birth and hide in the woods inland or in the harbor, move like an amphibian animal, half wet, half dry, in the crevices between the big rocks of the jetty. He was no longer after singularity, he was after being a regular guy, self-effacing, disappearing, and not even a man... some form of life that when it dies leaves nothing behind, no word, not even its footprints on the memory of his family and friends. The labyrinth of his notebooks remained at Anna's. He had no intention of taking his books back, it would be worth the effort. Anna still complains of their overwhelming presence a year later.

Log 14

Hardly had Nathaniel settled at his parents, there was this collapse of the dotcom enterprise and September 9/11. Under the pretext of finally disposing of his books, which in the end he didn't even disturb, Nathaniel came back to New York for a weeklong visit in November 2001. I am still not sure where he slept during that week. We discovered he had nothing to say, for he had not been in New York, and on top of that, he didn't read anything.

He had not seen planes slice into the towers like into butter and bodies fall—in his space, not on a screen—from 100 stories high. You had to have been within 10 miles of the devastation and smelled the smell a week later; you had to have witnessed under your windows like I did the constant flow of professional refugees walking from downtown, most in search of the bridges uptown, which turned out to be closed.

"It's the revenge of the low-skilled over the high-tech Leviathan," said Jacques, who had seen the second plane crash into the second tower and the whole thing tumble down his sky on Hudson Street, where he had just dropped in school his 5 years old. Jacques had not run for his life with the crowd. He had gone back home on Leroy Street, taken his camera and shot photo after photo, hundreds of them, running in the direction of the collapse, unaware apparently of the danger in the clouds of dust and the tornado of computer paper that whirled from Manhattan to Brooklyn and Staten Island.

"It's David against Goliath all over again," Jacques said, "we are the giant and ugly Goliath, naturally, and they are the charming David. The terrorists are the victims, no matter how many died in the WTC. Dead don't all count the same. They have stolen our mojo, our magic, the fucking Arabs!"

Jacques was right, 9/11 meant a setback for the digital age and a revenge for low-tech, and for more than half the world the terrorists were heroes, it had been a very successful operation for them, whatever detestation they received from the media and the pundits, they represented the little man brandishing his pocket knife against tanks and planes.

Like Jacques, I was convinced that the collapse of the WTC was a resounding victory for the enemies of the United-States and Israel. The glove of the meek hurled in the face of the colossus, whose ankles are made of clay. In a medieval novel the obscure and unknown knight ends sending through the armor of his formidable opponent the fatal blow. And it is not so much a blow as a way for his sword to exploit a weakness; his sword finds a spot where it's easy to enter. The prowess of a few obscure individuals undid America's impressive armada. So from now on the famed knight bleeds inside the metal. What is too big and too effective is bound to fail. He dies but doesn't die so fast, he bleeds to death and for the remaining 200 pages. America will bleed from 9/11 for a long time to come.

We realized that we lived in an unsafe environment, surrounded by gifted terrorists and improvised agents. Without talking about the unpreparedness of the army during the multiple attacks, unprecedented in the USA was the depth of incompetence achieved at first by federal, state and local agencies, those called upon to intervene in the demise of the WTC. First, second generation Americans, third, fourth, one felt that there was no one at the center, no one had the answer, no one responded fast enough. Our baffled president looked lost for an hour after receiving the news. Would another president respond better? Maybe not. Nobody had the explanation and there were too many explanations, no one can respond appropriately to this kind of destruction.

Nathaniel didn't try to theorize about the three thousand dead in the disintegration of the WTC. The merit of theory was wavering. He wouldn't speak about 9/11 like so many people did, trying to explain it away, and we appreciated that. He was a redneck with a conscience. On a global scale, many people acquired a sort of consciousness around 9/11. They saw global violence for what it was, scary, unvarnished, unjustifiable, and nonetheless, irresistible. The old victimization on a larger scale. Violent is the defining moment. Global age took a direct hit. You had to have felt the tremor in your pants. Nathaniel missed the most relevant, to have been here when they took the rug under our feet, and this distance made him prone to believe— more than Jacques, Anna, Eric or I did—in the endless bombast roaring out of TV's, radios and newspapers. People were already looking for reprisal, for a quick fix while the sequence of the double collapse was replayed *ad nauseam*.

Nathaniel sounded so *mainstream*. Of course, in his case, there was always the possibility that he mimicked the mainstream.

He didn't express it this way but it was clear that, if there was to be a response, he preferred it to be strong and unequivocal. War was unavoidable. Him so against the war industry which the Republican establishment favors, he could not but sympathize with a president putting his arm around the shoulder of a firefighter, a president taking the megaphone like a foreman and shouting, "bring 'em on!"

Nathaniel admitted that populism and aggressive swagger were dangerous coming from a *de facto* strong man like our president, who had not been elected by the majority. And, nonetheless, he said that the image of the president elbowing Mr. Worker while speaking loud to the crews clearing the debris and the dead...that was something we all needed to hear. That was crass and brilliant at the same time.

"That was a great moment in American politics!"

Good old Nathaniel was back, mocking, joking about the most frightening. He was jumping around to hide the nervousness he always felt when among Jacques and I.

"Besides, the French and the Germans can look down at us and think we still are cowboys, they are mostly hurt in their secret contracts with Saddam Hussein, that's the only reason why they renege on the war," said Nathaniel looking at me sideways.

"A bunch of hypocrites," added Jacques without looking at me.

"They are losing their old colonial grip on the Middle East, that's why they are furious, the French..."

I didn't take the bait. "Don't look at me," I told both, "I agree."

For good measure, Nathaniel and Jacques mocked the owners of restaurants who had thrown French wine, champagne, cassoulet in the gutter.

We sat down at *Round the Clock*, a mixed venue where one could eat hamburger, pizza, and also expensive lobster, caviar, fish, and they had a long wine list, though Jacques and I preferred tacitly to abstain from wine and not make it awkward with expensive foods for Nathaniel.

In this cool place for rich kids near the elegant Cooper Union building there was a huge screen pumping the first victorious news, showing in real time the irrepressible advance of intelligent bombs; and everybody inside and outside on the sidewalk was watching, fascinated. Even as you strongly suspected we were going into it for the wrong reasons and this war could very well prove a disaster of epic proportion, it was exhilarating.

Even if you're against war and you don't have a TV or radio, there is a war, the vibe in the air. In the first winning phase, as *our* columns were moving in and trampling under foot some far-away, unknown land full of humans no bigger on our screens than rats or vermin, which we were told were the source of all our present and future trouble—I have to admit feeling personally buoyant and like walking a few inches above ground. Nathaniel would later call what occurred all over America "a collective relief of satisfied random aggression." In plain language, we had found scapegoats and we were punching the bastards, *bringing them down*.

When I asked Nathaniel about books, he told me without apparent unease that he didn't read, not like he used to. In the world he now inhabited books didn't make sense. "Books explain, they clarify things for the sake of future readers, the next generation, at least. I don't have a future, nothing to explain, no longer. No idea left in my head. And if I had any idea left in my head I wouldn't make the effort. Why care to clarify things when *they*, of themselves, prefer confusion?"

He was as smart as ever.

Nathaniel looked fit physically. Older, less somber. He smoked less. The living at mother's was good, after all. And yet, in a short while you realized he was the same wounded animal, the same crippled of the mind and worse. His small turf had shrunk further. He hardly went out, hardly met any women, drank, didn't smoke weed. In his attic, he said, he had started another pile of notes, this time, he mused, "from thin air." The air around him must have been thin indeed since he didn't read, didn't play music, didn't talk about anything.

Jacques and I, we were happy for him, we said, until he made the blunder of calling himself a writer. I found that tacky. Even when I became a published academic, I wouldn't dare call myself a writer. We were about to break apart after dinner, walking fast towards 14th St. on 6th Avenue and say goodbye, when I couldn't help but murmur, "To call yourself a writer you need to be published, Nathaniel, it's, you might call it, a requisite."

"Published in your mind is good enough," he answered between his teeth.

"Published out of your mind," said Jacques, who was giving me winks to tell me that now was the time to teach Nathaniel a lesson. "Otherwise that's too easy." We stopped around one lamp-post at the corner of 12th St. and 6th Ave.

"Easy to do what?" asked Nathaniel. "The rules of what you authorize your mind to publish may be stricter than any editor's out there..."

He had a point there.

Jacques took a couple of seconds to drag on his cigarette and answered from the corner of his mouth: "Yeah, Nathaniel, them inner rules can be mad-crazy demanding, you're right about that, but they're still *your* rules, and only yours—nobody else's. Nobody to estimate, value what *you* say. So, enough with you, they all say one morning."

"And so what?"

"Nobody reads or listens, nobody gives a shit about what you scribble in your idiosyncratic notebooks. We're not in the romantic age when some lord or lady might fish you out of anonymity because you're so inspired. Now, you've got to prove you're inspired over hundreds of pages, and not in the eyes of a random crowd of potential readers, but in the eyes of specific cliques of professionals who have particular tastes that make them decide for the rest of us if you're worth shit!"

If not for the hurtful tone, I could only second Jacques.

"No reason to become vulgar," he said. A call for moderation sounded funny coming from Nathaniel. After that, he didn't compete with Jacques, didn't show him off, didn't even try to redress in my eyes his hurt ego. He was hurt, admitted defeat, stopped finally to make a fool of himself. He retreated a few steps, walked backwards and looked at us with a contrite face. We didn't express sad adieux. It was poignantly awkward, until two blocks away we saw him tumble down the subway.

Then Nathaniel disappeared from our lives for several years. From time to time he'd call me, but without having much to say, asking me about the books I read. I was not interested in a conversation about books with someone who no longer read them. I would have liked to know more about his life at mother's, but that was not why he called. Why did he call? Nostalgia? Envy? He asked me to send him my stuff on Milton, now that I was, in no small part thanks to him—this he didn't actually say, merely implied—a PH.D. and a tenured professor who published articles in specialized magazines.

"At least," he said, "you owe me the right to see the final product of all this work."

I could not show much enthusiasm. The dissertation had been accepted *cum laude* and I was cutting it up for publication. After we hung up, I realized that he had not even left an e-mail address or a phone number. Typical in Nathaniel to make me believe he wanted to communicate while not providing the means to do so. I tried to spot him on the Webwork but there was no trace of an e-mail account he'd used. He still didn't use a computer.

In her log, Kathy laments the fact that Nathaniel is so intelligent, yet he doesn't seem to write something consistent enough to be read out loud, if only one paragraph, one thought.

"He achieves nothing," she writes, "gets nowhere. He's not more advanced than when he was a boy. Except when he sings. He's got like an endless repertory of songs."

But besides that, even for Kathy who simply loves Nathaniel, there was not much to say about Nathaniel. "My brother is a broken man," she writes, "who's coming for a cure, in search of a magic mountain."

The newness of his comeback faded, until he was part of the furniture, like a bug working the woodwork and crashing at night in the attic. A working man, a hand, he was both proud and ashamed to say so on Friday night when there was a soirée dominated by George's two big boys, and Kathy and John were staying for the weekend at the house. That's what he was, a helper. Father and mother employed a caterer, and there were a couple of Mexican servers busying around their table, which unsettled Nathaniel. But after Herculean efforts he kept his mouth shut and didn't criticize. He was a helper served by immigrant workers.

Rehearse in the silence of yourself before speaking so as to efface, scrub and like expunge the sardonic tone from your face, wipe the smirk, he told himself. Desistence will have to do with this inner discipline. To his surprise, he succeeded and was no longer bothered and irritated by every word. He went along the tacky and the overdone of opulent gatherings, he heard the clichés and smiled at the contradictions his dear family members and their neighbors and friends wallowed in. Even the silence of his mother and father, their reprobation, he accepted. To accept things as they are without illusion, without acting on the belief that they could be better is perhaps the most difficult.

His attitude was now the exact opposite of what it had been before, he went along. Nathaniel was like a porous, sponge-like material that adapted, submitted, wrapped itself around the shape of the event, the rare events that punctuated his premature retirement.

Nathaniel got used to being served at home, and not by mother. It did not seem to contradict his Zen detachment. Even after the third California champagne flute served by a very cute nineteen-year old Mexican girl, he simply enjoyed good old class difference and privilege. He didn't even indulge and try to flirt with the girl, even though she was bored to not have someone to talk to. She was studying anthropology at the local public university, they could have talked great anthropological theory after her shift. In a past life Nathaniel would have laughed and invited her to a drink, at least. No longer. I would not go as far as that Nathaniel is an emasculated man. He has not lost his aptitudes. He is rather like the stud at rest after a difficult competition, foaming at the mouth, breathing hard and hardly recuperating from exertion. At some point, Nathaniel did talk with the servant-student girl, who was very smart and surprisingly ambitious intellectually. He advised her on how to read Etienne Mauss, Levi-Strauss and Boas. All that for her own sake, without claiming carnal payback. No longer did he look in people, and women in particular, for a way to take advantage of them, suck knowledge or his own pleasure out of them. He was glad his working-class father and mother had acquired comfort in their old age. Who would take that from them, in the name of what?

Though John drank a lot and encouraged Nathaniel, there was no fight at the table. Nathaniel was too weak to fight. A certain shame regarding Nathaniel invades John and Kathy's logs after that. They speak less of their big brother, and soon, don't speak of him at all.

Log 15

Unexpectedly, three years later it's John who brings Nathaniel into the fold. John has given up on music and no more is there mention of Eric, the talk is about computers. John the ex-carpenter now preferably drunk and his rich wife, Suzan Friedman, are passionate Web surfers, hacktivists. Not your Sunday hackers, every day they spend hours trading information and techniques in select chat rooms and exclusive billboards. They volunteer their time, their equipment and their skills to help Chinese peasants suffering under Communist rule get their complaints across; or else they assist dissenting Uzbeks who want to send bombs in the corridors of the virtual—and all this from the suburbs of Atlanta, Georgia. It's a treat. Suzan has made money on the Webwork before, but with John, who is a gifted learner, they are on the cusp of doing so on a tangible scale. In his simple epistolary style, John sends a good old letter to invite Nathaniel for an open-ended stay in a wealthy suburb of Atlanta. Meanwhile he e-mails Justine, pleading for her to tell Nathaniel it's time to leave the parents. John doesn't give Nathaniel any bullshit reason; he simply says, it's springtime in Georgia and your younger brother needs you.

Nathaniel goes to Georgia; sister Kathy comes along. She is a big girl with an awkward gait, a boyish laughter and a struggling career as a family court lawyer in Boston. She is starting to think that, like her older brother, she could reside rent free on Rhode Island. She is considering her options at this point in her life, and being on the dull side of the law doesn't work for her.

Sister Kathy has been an addict of the screen and the keyboard since her tumultuous affair with an elite hacker from Boston. Her much older boyfriend was a peripheral member of the "Legion of Doom," group that created as early as the 80's its own databank, own access codes and exclusive BBS, its own hierarchy or phalange of hackers based on merit and cyber exploits. The Legion of Doom had created its own hermetic network far away from indiscreet control either from business or government.

As I discover when I meet her a few years later, Kathy is a blond baby almost as tall as Nathaniel, larger, voluptuously plump, full of whims and made of insatiable flesh; but the boyfriend has taught her a lot. She has learned the thrill of breaking into where she was not supposed to: personal accounts in banks, assurances, subscriptions, police records, court records... in other words, essential information about individuals, businesses and institutions. You hack rich vaults preferably, not only for the return (if you sell what you learn, which was not the case of 'authentic' hackers like Kathy's boyfriend), but because that makes you feel less guilty to enter where you're not supposed to. It's so cool to learn what the gilded corridor you exploit is keeping secret from the rest of us, in particular, the formula that made it so rich. Icing on the cake, there is the assurance of not leaving fingerprints behind, not even one hair, one cell where a hound bent on your trace might collect DNA. This is not a fairy tale where candies left on the way help Little Tom find his way back. No "cookies" left behind if you do it well. Perfect stealth: only the members of the Legion of Doom could access the bulletin board where they deposited the loot. Sharing among anonymous siblings potentially destabilizing, even subversive secrets, what satisfaction it must be!

Nathaniel has no clue what collective computer experience John, Suzan and Kathy are talking about with delight, envy and admiration. It's new in John, but what about his younger sister showing a daring side? Nathaniel has not paid attention to sister Kathy for years. He thought he had understood her, what she was after; now he realizes he hasn't.

Of course, nobody mentions before mother and father the mythical phreaks who, in the 1980's, had produced a 2600 Hz tone giving them access to a toll network where they could call free of charge, connect to powerful computers, download millions of dollars worth of software.

At first, Nathaniel shrugs the whole thing off as another fad, another shallow temptation for young people, another misadventure in the realm of predictable disillusionment. He thinks they are just talking like he has done all these years himself, just talking.

Nathaniel stands on the large acajou deck John has built with Brazilian wood for Suzan; and as though there were no tomorrow, he drinks beer after beer with his brother and talks with him among the high fern, the exotic flowers, the panoramic glass panels that move silently on aluminum wheels, the discreet screens that faded in and out of moveable walls. He listens at dinnertime to Suzan and would make love to her southern drawl if one could make love to a voice. He drinks again with John, this this time single malt or Armagnac. Next morning, he oversleeps and, in fact, goes through a sleeping cure of two lazy months spent in a vast bed where, without even changing clothes, he receives home cooked food made according to recipes from all over the world. He is attended by unobtrusive service people whose manners are pleasant and relaxed, but who keep to themselves and only materialize when you need them.

Nathaniel doesn't ask questions; he does not ask where the money to maintain such an operation comes from. He goes along. At the end of this first sleeping cure Nathaniel's attitude has barely changed regarding the computer. He's not in awe anymore, there is no magic to it. But it still is for him just a machine more complex than a typewriter. What is good about the computer is that you can switch it on and off at any time. You can eat in front of it and you can drink your heart content, the machine doesn't care. It doesn't crash when you go wrong and does not break down; it goes in a lull or in a loop, freezes; you unplug or reboot. What else? Of course, Nathaniel assumes there is much more to the computer since it gives access to the famous ocean or continent, or should we say, alternate universe, of the Webwork. Only, Nathaniel has not surfed on it.

At dinnertime Suzan speaks about a famously secretive 60's French group, the Situationists, individuals who gathered suddenly and met for a coup in the streets of Paris, then disbanded. Situationists would not rob or vandalize, no violence; they would change the disposition of signs and disconnect traffic-lights, alter the functioning of automatic doors in department stores, reverse escalators, cover commercial pictures with radical slogans, lude graffiti or apocalyptic announcements. "The Situationists wanted the urban crowd to break with oppressive routine," said Suzan. "They wanted to re-route, redirect the human flow, expose the multitude to change and possibilities, even chaos. Their big word was *détourner*: instead of looking straight ahead like sheep, they wanted people to meander, get lost. They were just like the Surrealists that preceded them, but less upper class, less about the bourgeoisie, more about the working man, which the Situationists hoped to shock out of his stupidity."

Nathaniel was surprised by the direction Suzan was taking and with such energy; the quality of her information, her exquisite delivery. He certainly did not expect a rich Southern woman to be that radical.

Suzan quoted Guy Debord. "I don't know if you know him?"

Nathaniel couldn't place Guy Debord, the artist-intellectual-activist Frenchman who called during the riots of 1968 for "transforming around us the urban signs of our daily servitude. *Changer la vie!*"

Another day, John showed Nathaniel what, without reading French, inspired hackers had done in the last twenty years, forcing electronic boards in the subways of New York and Boston to publicize *The Quaterly Hackers*; creating porn fantasies that pop up on the website of the US Armed Forces whenever a colonel or higher up accesses it; turning the FBI public portal into a salacious puppet-show attended by kids doing hard drugs and enjoying them; demonstrating global warming worst predictions on the webpage of right-wing meteorological stations; giving vivid illustration of Anarchist Anonymous predictions on the home screen of all the employees of the attorney general...

Nathaniel had vaguely heard mentioned the existence of super gifted teen hackers. John read to him the old *Hacker Manifesto* written by an adolescent calling himself "The Mentor" after he was arrested for entering the vaults in cyberspace of a major bank:

This is our world now... the world of the electron and the switch, the beauty of the baud. We make use of a service already existing without paying for what could be dirt-cheap if it wasn't run by profiteering gluttons, and you call us criminals. We explore... and you call us criminals. We seek after knowledge... and you call us criminals. We exist without skin color, without nationality, without religious bias... and you call us criminals.

You build atomic bombs, you wage wars, you murder, cheat, and lie to us and try to make us believe it's for our own good, yet we're the criminals.

Yes, I am a criminal. My crime is that of curiosity. My crime is that of judging people by what they say and think, not what they look like. My crime is that of outsmarting you, something that you will never forgive me for. I am a hacker, and this is my manifesto. You may stop this individual, but you can't stop us all... after all, we're all alike.

Childish enthusiasm, perhaps, but you could not read to Nathaniel something more akin to him. The Mentor had not stolen or destroyed anything, he had hovered in mid-air of the vaults, copied parts and passed them on to the cohort having access to his BBS. This had set the tone for generations of overachievers.

The name of Kevin Mitnick would reoccur in Suzan, Kathy and John's conversation. Kathy had to return to Boston and didn't stay more than a week; Nathaniel waited to be alone with brother and Suzan to ask candidly: "What has this Kevin Mitnick done to deserve so much attention?" He might as well have admitted that he knew shit, which he couldn't do in front of Kathy. He still needed to be the bigger brother to her.

He learned that Mitnick had had the chance to rob millions of dollars from credit card numbers, and he hadn't. Mitnick entered US Department of Defense systems—poked around, mused, copied and didn't destroy anything, didn't trigger any chain reaction, merely passed the information around generously.

"They had nothing on him," John added, "it took them years to build a case against Mitnick, and it's only when he was careless..."

Here Suzan preferred to keep quiet and the three to smile at each other. John was on his wheelchair; Suzan whispered niceties in his ear. Nathaniel lounged in a Scandinavian chair, the supple leather adapting to his nervous spider-like body and softening his jerky moves. There clearly was something between Suzan and him. If not for her age, and her not being cute and blond and naive, she was his type. Though older, Nathaniel could pretend to be a healthier version of John.

Nothing would happen between them, of course. Nothing was possible except an intimacy built on loving John together, on bringing John back to life together. Suzan was openly seductive with Nathaniel, she made it clear she wanted more of him, and it didn't bother little brother nor did he find it scabrous in his brother to have eyes on his woman. He understood why Suzan dressed more attractively, almost provocatively, each evening.

Suzan was not like the young women Nathaniel had favored before; she was an intense and powerful woman of around fifty. Her red hair was cut very short, which accentuated her bony and boyish frame. Narrow hips, flat chested; but she had the neck of a swan and an intelligent face. She was thin, tall and elegant in her manners; she was beautiful in that she was all there in front of you, occupying every inch of her skin while her green eyes paid 100% attention. Add to this a man's shirt in silk, perhaps a tie, two colors shoes like gangsters in *noir* movies... She was intriguing.

Nathaniel started to wonder if hackers were not renewing with what was lost during the last few hundred years of modernity. Hackers do what traditional people used to do: when the native hunter and his companions came back from the hunt, he shared the prey with his people, gave a dinner and invited every member of the extended family and clan. Upon returning from a victorious war overseas, the Greek general would split the loot among his army: jewelry, women, slaves, weapons acquired were shared among his soldiers according to their rank...

But there was another aspect to hacking, which was not so appealing to Nathaniel.

"Hacking is the perfect steal, man," said John one time, probably to test him. "You're in and you're out. And you don't even have to steal anything, you warn them about the problem they have, and they even pay you to teach them how to fix it. Nowhere else can you get more satisfaction for so little risk."

While lightly massaging his back from behind, Suzan added, "it's not *risk* you should call it, John... it's not been done before, you're the first taking this path, and actually there is no path, you invent the f... ! sorry, the forking path! If you steal you don't steal something some dude owns! Who owns what, tell me, out there? No private property out there; it's still the Far West and we intend to keep it that way... After all, the Webwork was created to facilitate communication among humans. Anyway, I'll tell you a little more—what you sell, if you are smart, are cracks, holes, ruptures, tear, negligence and insufficiencies in the control system of reputed networks, and you sell them to the managers of the selfsame systems, gents who have great interest in keeping the matter hushed."

She was quite convincing and skillful at lifting the curtain only so much.

Initially, Mitnick had gotten probation for his cyber penetrations, the downloading of priceless software; probation for disrupting phone lines and melting away the computers of his high-school enemies. "He imagined everybody hated him," said John admiringly, "hackers easily go parano—" "iac" Suzan finished for him, lowering her graceful neck to kiss him. John was his usual slob, dressed in his frayed checker shirt, baggy pants; and sitting sprawled in his motorized rolling chair. Plump, drunk and apparently numb John Lagrange, and yet, as delighted and astute a version of a Lagrange when facing the screen as you shall ever get. Nathaniel observed how the callous fingers of the worker ran like mad on the delicate keyboard. She'd venture on her own, then come back to John and massage his back. John and Suzan—and, in the main room, in *la salle des machines* as Suzan called it, a handful of youngsters who spent day and night poring over rows of numbers passing fast on their screens—all had the latest version of slim touch-screen Mac laptops. The compound boasted of screens, printers, scanners, optic and zip drives Nathaniel didn't even know existed.

Throughout, Suzan acted as the soothing messenger, adding to John's recent discoveries for the sake of the newcomer, the older brother, Nathaniel.

"Mitnick evolved into a professional, he didn't remain an amateur. That is what I am teaching John, to be careful, to clean behind, to erase his fingerprints."

"His fingerprints?" asked Nathaniel, uncomprehending.

"The fingerprints that his keystroke habits leave behind."

Nathaniel still didn't understand; she went on, "He cannot repeat himself on the Webwork. No redundancy. You don't know coding so I won't be technical. He has to become an artist if he wants to avoid detection. Any fall in style, superfluous flourish, they pick up out there!"

"And so," proceeded John after combing his long, oily blond hair out of his face and looking at Nathaniel, "to diminish the risk, Mitnick had associates send to other computers the denial-of-service or the *Trojan*. When the heat started to turn up on him, Mitnick indicated the way by acting through proxy. You're alone and then you're never alone out there, people do the job for you."

Hacking was perhaps risky, but the point, the thrill was to pull a stunt like the heroes of old, and have your screen-name come out scot-free, unscathed, "you"—your handle elevated to glory. The ultimate goal was the success of the group, the community of unidentified and independent searchers outsmarting the Webwork. If Nathaniel had been born a few years later, he'd have already developed a much more favorable attitude toward the computer. He'd have been a hacker, who knows, of genius. The sneakiness, the incognito of the steal would have appealed to Nathaniel, for you perceived there was a steal, no matter how you put it. He wouldn't be Nathaniel, he'd be "The Leftist," or "Angel Head," "Maxwell's Demon"… yes, why not, "New England Demon"?

Nathaniel had felt close to John at times, but not like this. It's John who now opens a world to Nathaniel—John the dropout who teaches erudite Nathaniel. John has been raised as a working-class boy, attending more or less technical high schools, messing up big time and too early with alcohol and drugs, rehab, correctional; and then in the work force. This quite unlike Nathaniel, who's never joined any work force. Early on, before his older brother and, in fact, more radically than Nathaniel, John wanted out of school and every standing institution. He could see firsthand that books and going to Ivy-league schools hadn't help Nathaniel.

The two brothers had drifted apart over the years, one drowning in a sea of books, the other rejecting the books and his wobbly feet apparently on terra firma but drowning in alcohol. Luckily for him, building decks for rich people down in the South has transformed John and given him luxurious tastes; and finding Suzan has afforded him nothing less than a new lease on life, a second chance.

Suzan fell so hard in love with him that the wood of her deck was still rough when they made love on it. She does not understand it herself; John is not the man of her age, wealth and education, the one she's been looking for. John is a redneck, even a roughneck; has not finished high-school; she went to Stanford and has learned the hard and long practice of hacking under excellent guidance. It's hard to explain why it fascinated her so that John was a crippled man, that there was something strange to the lower part of his body, his legs not proportioned, not sturdy enough for the bulk of it, inflated as it was by the constant absorption of alcohol. John drank as continuously as Nathaniel had smoked; and John smoked also. They were in this delightful compound and he had this beautiful and successful woman giving him everything she had and was; he learned immensely from her, but he couldn't help drinking before noon his six-pack beer nor would he start lunch without champagne, then wine and whiskey. His day went like that on a crescendo until midnight, when he'd doze on and off, every two hours ordering a beer or two. He walked supported by a cane, but preferred to stay in his automatic wheelchair.

Kathy and Nathaniel understood on their first trip to Atlanta that they had to save their brother, and do it together. They would have to stay at Suzan's to accomplish that, and Suzan would love for them to come back and stay, and that's how the Lagrange enterprise got created.

Nathaniel comes back from his trip to Georgia with a slick Sony laptop, which, at first, he doesn't use and pushes into the pile of debris to make his bed; but which soon enough gets connected by his young cousin, who sneaks up to the attic to send messages and watch porno.

Nathaniel forgets that he doesn't know how to type and finds himself clumsily sending messages to Kathleen in England (unanswered) and to Anna in New York (answered immediately). Then he communicates with John in Atlanta and sister Kathy in Boston about making a sort of "familial commune" in Suzan's compound: nothing to do with the communes of the 60's, he warns, "no orgies, no excess, no children allowed... what we need now is collective reflection, a close-knit group, an intimate gathering of spirits opened to the future."

Suzan likes this kind of lyricism and communicates to him that she would be happy to receive "all the Lagranges together"; and a week later we have Nathaniel's unsparing account of his experience in the compound.

It's strange he doesn't tear to pieces the few electronic notes which follow, doesn't sacrifice them to his temper nor finds them disgustingly trivial and imperfect. Strange he didn't inadvertently push the erase button.

"She loves my brother so well, he who has brought only his misery. What in him deserves such royal treatment? The fact that he decked the castle, built the actual floors, and otherwise brought to it his insatiable needs, wounds, inadequacies only augment her love for him, her devotion to my little brother. Suzan is of the self-sacrificing kind, another Anna—on a grander scale and without for one second losing sight of her interest and passion. Quite a handful of a woman, Suzan Friedman. I am lucky we can't get too close. Obsessive as he is, and shrewd, I have no doubt John is not a drag; he moves next to her on the Webwork, in her wake. I don't understand what he does, but what he does pleases Suzan. They go "out there" and they come back together. Suzan is without hesitation the smartest woman I have ever met. Yesterday at dinner, when John was fetching his third six-pack from the freezer downstairs, which takes him fifteen minutes, she confessed to me that his problems are so real her own 'routine anxieties' (her words) pale in comparison. She admits: 'It sounds terrible but I sleep like a baby after I put John to sleep. Deep sleep, though I have to set the alarm to make sure I wake up every two hours. In the morning, I feel like a flower taking the sun, I exercise, walk the dog and shower. Then I have Maria-Teresa prepare breakfast for when he wakes up. He's usually in a terrible mood, having slept badly half the night. But a couple of beers later everything is in order, we have fun surfing the Webwork. We have even more fun since you are here, Nathaniel.'''

"Suzan's basic wealth comes from her husband, Nathan Freidman, who made before he died a couple million, mind you, not by hacking, but by speculating in real estate. She has not squandered it. Nathan was also a known white hat hacker, and eventually, after they cornered him, a nasty cracker of consequence. He was never arrested, but he was one of Pat Riddle's friends, the heroic group who, wherever they squat, would fix it so that low-income people around them enjoyed months of free electrical and phone service. That was in the early 80's, before they came up with laws for computer crimes. When Mitnick got caught again in the 90's, he received seven years in jail, and as though he had committed a violent crime, confinement. Hacking is not as benign a game as they pretend; and of course, this is the reason why they like it. Without "breaking" the system and calling the full force of enforcement upon oneself, hacking would be reserved to squares. The flat-footed policemen of yesteryears are no longer flat-footed for the reason that elite hackers are regularly co-opted; the laws are getting tougher by the day; Secret Service is catching up. I am sure John and Kathy don't do anything as hairy as penetrating top NASA computers like the members of the Chaos Computer Club who either were indicted for espionage, betrayed each other, sold themselves to the FBI, worse: corporations—and, even when rehabilitated, died years later like characters out of Hitchcock. Freidman's prowess went too far, I suppose, and he got caught at forty-two. To the humiliation of an arrest, the prospect of years in prison, Friedman preferred hara-kiri, Roman suicide by the sword, overdose in his case. Suzan prefers not to talk about her late husband's journey through the fledgling Webwork back then, and why he died so young, rich and almost famous. That she does not speak of him only makes his early death more felt, I feel when around her, since it is obvious that she still grieves him. She thinks of him whenever she has to make a difficult choice, there is a fork in the cybernetic road ahead of her; or she wonders where to invest her money: what would have Nathan done?"

"John does not press Suzan, he lets her have all to herself her ex, so why should I bother her with questions?"

Log 16

For the last time, Nathaniel makes plans for a book he projects to write in the attic at night, when the work of the house and the job in the harbor are done. There is the last mention of a thesis on *Thermodynamics and Demonology*. He details Logs, table of content. He sketches a preface. At this point, his drive indicates repeated forays in the Library of Congress and he taps into the New York Public Library. But he soon runs out of steam, loses momentum, complains that he feels awkward doing research with the kind of life he has at mother's; and besides, his notes on the subject are no longer at hand. His suitcases crammed full of amazing thoughts for a masterwork that is essentially finished and done are out of reach. In all fairness, he cannot ask Anna to send his suitcases; he'd have to go back to New York, which is out of the question. For one thing, he cannot face Jacques and me empty-handed. He could also avoid us, that's true. But what if Anna has thrown the notebooks to the garbage? He does not dare ask her about them over the Webwork. He obsesses about the content of his notes, his ideas spanning fractal fields of knowledge designed to shed insight on a fractal world.

Again, he imagines an intricate plan to stay in New York for just one day, plan which he does not share with Anna and never concretizes, for fear of discovering the suitcases have disappeared. He's not wrong because his thousands of tiny pages of notes have disappeared. The suitcases are gone. And in Anna's studio, it's not like he's left Waverly Place after ten years of procrastination, it's like he never even set foot in the studio. Anna has another boyfriend by now, an Irish painter, who has gladly helped her clean to the last useless reminder of Nathaniel. Nobody is irreplaceable.

The book on *Thermodynamics and Demonology* was not for him to make. Nathaniel Lagrange is not about making books. It's by accident, inadvertently, that he will discover another format, other means of expression, and excel in them.

About six years after his leaving New York, out of the blue I receive a phone call from him. He is not asking about my readings. He does not want to learn about the last of my successes in minor league academia. There is a joyous alarm in his voice, the ring of unexpected success shines through the old blasé tone. He is in California. That's strange, I think, it's where he's refused to follow his old *Brown* friend Tony Wumster who, besides offering to post any of his work, had generously invited him to stay at his place as long as he cared to.

Questions rush to my mind: Is Nathaniel finally able to express his thought in the land of computers? Or does he still obsess about paper page, printed page and the Logs of his book? Has he been able to finally leave mother behind and move on? Even first-rate procrastinators do sometime get a second chance.

Nathaniel is in Los Angeles, in the vicinity of Tony Wumster and in the company of Suzan, Kathy and John. On the phone, he speaks to me only about John. Answering my questions, Nathaniel tells me it's not for the concentration of computer wizzes—he couldn't care less about the geeks—it's for John that he has accepted Suzan's invitation to live in California, because John needs a dense family-life around him, especially at this moment of fantastic break-through.

I let this last flourish go and asked about his family. I learn that younger sister Kathy Lagrange has also given up on her previous life in Boston and joined the core-group. They are a team, it's quite serious.

And like that, as a matter of course, Nathaniel Lagrange—the friend I thought lost and gone forever—is inviting me to Los Angeles, to stay a few days with him and his family "in a *dwelling* on the hill," which over there goes by the name of sierra.

I don't take this invitation seriously at first. It feels to me like his usual swagger, a way to impress me since a dwelling on the hills of Los Angeles could only be a very exclusive villa or, as he said, compound.

"You know, just like one of those prolonged weekends you guys have in your profession," he insists. "Say it's for a conference, a Webwork conference, that you are being trained in computer research and data processing by elite..."

We laugh. What does he want with me? Why does he care for me to go to his rich compound? He doesn't make me feel like I owe him the air I breathe as an academic. There is a mixture of nervousness and assurance in his voice, even a shrill note of triumph, like he has stolen the fruit and it's okay because he has found the Graal, and this time, without bragging, without having to put big words on it. What leaves me in a state of shock is that, if I say yes, *this time* he will be the provider; I'll be received at *his* family-without-mother home, the Lagrange scene redux and transplanted.

I hesitate providing him the pleasure of further impressing me. The invitation, however, is hard to refuse. When I go to conferences, which is rare, I do, like my colleagues, miss days of classes. Data processing could appear on paper as "computer training in educational interface..." Nathaniel assures me that they'll have Suzan Friedman and him sign any official paperwork I want. They are the two top administrators of *HighGunsOnTheSierra.com*, a reputed site on the Webwork.

Nathaniel is an administrator? The name of their site sounds folkloric to me, but not more than others.

Could I go for a week, smack in the middle of the semester, with an excuse like that? I probably could. There was a weakness among deans for whatever was computer-related just then. It would actually do very well in my administrative file that I went all the way to California to train in "educational interface" in a high-tech start-up on the sierra. By the mid 2000, computers and ever more computer classes and skills and distance learning protocols were all that mattered in campuses across this country. It's not what you taught to your students, but that you taught it with the help of computers, which, as everyone agreed, could only do a dazzling job at enhancing human interaction.

I say to Nathaniel: "My little girl is five years old and my wife needs me…"; but I say it half-heartedly since a week in California will not much interrupt my obligations as a father and a husband. Gabriela could manage for a week.

"A week in a select compound overlooking Los Angeles ?" he answers teasingly, and he adds in the fake voice of a commercial, "Are you ready to miss this opportunity?"

I cannot firmly say, "Sorry, I'm busy," for he seems busy himself, speaking with several people and postponing conversations on other lines to speak to me. I have not heard my friend laugh like this in ages. And nevertheless, I remain noncommittal to the end of this first communication.

In the next few days, there follow several rapid, almost business-like phone calls that sincerely evince in Nathaniel the desire to see me and renew long-standing intellectual ties.

"We've gone separate ways," he says, "remember, you had to make sure… but I don't think we've ever diverged. You'd be surprised to see what we think here, what we say on our website. It's a direct consequence of what we, you and me, talked about long ago."

This last phrase touched me. Confined to my academic duties, I had not even heard of a site which, after just a few clicks, sounded actually rather engaging and its forums—here called "corridors"—full of intricate posts at the cutting edge of several fields of the humanities and the sciences.

I decide to goof off and take the California sun in the middle of March under the pretext of a week of training at *HighGunsOnTheSierra.com.* The name sounds like the title of a Western movie to Isabel and Gabriela is surprised that they let me go at work just like that; but she is also intrigued by the reappearance in my life of an old friend she had seen in my company. I tell her that Nathaniel has changed and that's what interests me in this trip. "I want to see how much *really*, and how come. What has happened to him?"

"And what do you gain from that?" asks Isabel.

"I don't know yet."

During the last phone conversation before my boarding the plane, Nathaniel assured me that, by the end of the week, they'd write a letter on watermarked paper to my Dean extolling the progress made by Professor Etienne Zeltzki in high speed interface communication and Webwork data gathering...etc.

We laughed. How professional Nathaniel had become.

Log 17

Set beyond Mulholland Drive, a glamorous address, the houses Suzan and the Lagranges occupied were perched high and had no vis-à-vis, no neighbor blocked the view. It overlooked in dégradé other compounds that faced at night the lattice of lights and, during the blazing day, the glistening slopes of Los Angeles. From my bungalow, whenever the smog dissipated, I could admire giant cacti, baby palm trees and red dust, and beyond, the flat rooves of the city all the way to the vaporous ocean.

But once inside the compound you utterly forgot the outside world. What you saw through the window-bays of desert-like earth, tropical flowers and shrubbery was reminder enough.

The Lagrange family had the type of equipment I had only seen advertised on the Webwork. In my bungalow, I disposed of a laptop thrice faster and with ten times the memory of mine at home. Elsewhere drives disappeared in the cloudy-white foot of stylish flat screens; and their battery of compatibles and mainframe CPU seemed to me on a level with large business and administration. It is true that, back then especially, I knew very little about computers; I merely observed that already when stepping into the compound, before crossing the porch, the living matter of a crystal screen convoked you, called on you to poke your finger in there and make an imprint, create your password, nickname or cipher for the duration of your stay. You can be *in there*, and move and make choices with the cursor, and live via a proxy, an avatar of yourself, screen-name or 'handle.'

Screens ultra-dense with pixels always looked to me filled with immobile matter fast moving beyond common perception to take from you and suck you in piecemeal. These were everywhere in the network of bungalows surrounding the main house and its impressive *Salle des Machines*. Incorporated in the walls, on the face of consoles, on tablets, they came in all dimensions, whether you walked into a bedroom, a kitchen facility, or "the office," as it was called. That transparent bubble-like structure buzzing with young people stood next to my pad. It was not made out of wood like the other bungalows, but of high-grade Plexiglas and steel. In the following days, coming in to sleep or going out to drive along the ocean, before and after dinner with Suzan and the Lagranges, I saw geeks busy themselves in there like bees; the reasons being, I was told, they were accountants-in-training and the office boasted of high-definition printers, scanners and external drives attached to the best computers in the compound. What they were learning to account for, I didn't ask.

When I entered the *salle des machines* for the first time, the teams were not busy, it would not be the right word—they were absorbed, bent on resolving a problem, a puzzle and elemental enigma. In a far corner, several youngsters were facing wide screens and poring over rows of digits passing fast. It was like in spy movies where an agent has to crack the secret code and all the signs dance the rigmarole around him—until he discovers their order and they fall flat in neat rows. Here, in bafflingly random (seemed to me) series of digits falling down fast like sheets of water, they had to detect unsuspected harmonies—or the opposite, I guessed, notice anomalies, undue repetition, chaotic patterns.

They were so engaged mutually and with the network of machines, even those who, like Nathaniel, John or Suzan, didn't pore over rows of digits, that the floor could have slid under them and the house tumble over the cliff before they'd detach their eyes from the screens.

After some time though, Suzan probed Nathaniel into introducing me to her. John and Kathy kind of did the same. And later, in a meeting, Suzan introduced me flatteringly to the programmers and service people. You did not enter *HighGuns* incognito.

I was "an old friend of Nathaniel's; someone who was there at the start." She added with a question to Nathaniel and a gracious smile to me, "even way before the start, if I am not mistaken?"

He concurred. I wondered if it was to my credit to have been there so long ago.

She shook my hand and welcomed me, then pirouetted gracefully and turned her back on me while Nathaniel sent me winks that it was like that and it was okay. They were busy right now.

"Make yourself at home!" he said. He'd join me later. I went to my bungalow and unpacked.

"Welcome, Etienne, to our communal abode and research center," said Suzan later in the exaggeratedly low voice of an English lord. She gave me her thin and aristocratic hand. No jewels, no rings, no frills. Impeccable nails, but no make-up—beauty of a mature woman. In her prime years, she must have been gorgeous, I thought, and on top, fierce as a *replicant* in the movie *Blade Runner*. She had short and spiky blond-hennaed hair, a fitted black tee-shirt, tight blue-jeans, old tennis-sneakers. She looked like a doctoral student at Berkeley. When she said, "We have heard a lot about you," she smiled, then excused herself for the platitude. It was not tongue-in-cheek; it was sincere: she had nothing better to say to me just then.

How intriguing the "we" she used. It was not the arrogant, mock-royal "we," but the group, the community of searchers that spoke through her. Back to my bungalow, I surfed further into the site and stopped. It bothered me that the word Desistence, around which we had tip-toed Nathaniel and I for years, was now bandied about by all kinds of anonymous people as though it was their word, their invention. It was not clear how they understood it, but it was obvious that they had firm, effusive, passionate convictions about it. And what bothered me probably more was that the Lagranges, and particularly Nathaniel, were more than esteemed and admired along the "corridors" of *HighGuns*; they were revered; one did not refer to Nathaniel's last dictum without tremolo in the voice; and you could see in the video-clips that this young crowd was not retarded or uncouth; they were handsome young men and beautiful, interesting young women.

I was jealous; I felt robbed, our old friendship used for purposes other than radical defiance. Our "marriage of true minds" exploited, the product of our collaboration rerouted; taken advantage of by the site's following and by Nathaniel himself, who'd been building his fame, and now making a gorgeous living at reciting, recycling, simplifying, no doubts, reprocessing tidbits of our conversations. I didn't know which, didn't want to know. I stopped looking at clips, got bored reading fervent posts, switched off the console; then, came back to the main building to lounge not in front of a screen but apart. As a matter of fact, there was on one side a purple leather-couch the size of a Buick. Facing wrap-around windows running floor to ceiling, it was set for visitors so as to afford them the best views of the city. I heard the clap-clap of fingers and nails running on keyboards while I watched the rugged sea of desert-like earth go by the slick hull of our cruise-ship.

Without understanding in the least what the several groups scattered in the vast room were doing, what kind of statistical skimming of e-commerce, and without showing how much I would have liked to be in the know, I noticed that Suzan led the pack and orchestrated the activities in the room without having to say a word. They didn't speak much while they surfed. It was to be expected that she would lead John and Nathaniel, but she had spent long hours and practiced hacker techniques way before sister Kathy, and the young decoders and programmers learned their alphabet.

These looked like undergrads from Stanford, Irvin and UCLA. American kids and immigrants, in good proportion Asian-Americans. I went to sleep and came back after breakfast, and the same groups were at it. Time in the *Salle des Machines* was frozen; Suzan was drinking her coffee in front of her screen, and so were Kathy and John; the group facing fast-rolling waves of digits had not budged an inch—except, getting closer, I noticed that the individual geeks comprising their cluster had been replaced during the night. Suzan did not have to look for them, I learned later; she had to refuse them, close and lock the door of the compound, put guards in front of it. These kids were interchangeable and disposable.

Now, whether you wear a white or a black hat, whether you merely observe and copy, or you reroute and shamble, one thing about hacking, the grunt of it is time consuming, tedious and repetitive work. You don't find weaknesses in protected information systems without obsessing, failing, going back on your tracks, learning from past errors, being lucky. However, I did not at that time and in fact would never observe anybody complaining of exhaustion around the Lagranges, even less exploitation—none of the laziness that makes office work a tedium. At long last, and only when Suzan insisted because replacement was growing impatient, one gave one's cherished position in front of the screen, reluctantly and with a tinge of shame, as though one was an athlete forced by accident to abandon the field of competition.

Indeed, the undergrads competed fiercely for the few hot seats Suzan abandoned to their care. And once a job was done and the room exploded in relief, the nameless cluster of youth commented passionately on their own moves, derided, bragged, vain-glorified one another. The outfits, the boots, the leather and hair-cut of the punk on many of them, but none of the blasé disgust, nothing destructive in their attitude. Smart kids, who skipped school and dinnertime, and would have slept on the concrete steps leading to the *Salle des Machines* had Suzan let them.

I would learn that they worked for no pay and didn't even have the incentive of being the ones to publish the exploit in the BBS run by the Lagranges. I grasped that the team around Suzan made sure to replace them as fast as they came for them to not get too personal with the work, too attached. They worked for the Lagranges, and beyond, the movement of ideas called Desistence; the credit for their exploit, the recorded details and the loot of data produced by their memorable exploration of the Webwork went entirely to the Lagranges and to the followers of Desistence. If it was an important job, actually, Suzan would take over and exploit the weakness they had found, the crack in a device or a network.

I asked Nathaniel what made this youth work so hard then, to the point of forgetting the balmy sun outside and looking all pale, even the Latinos, Asians and the rare black youth.

"If their name doesn't show anywhere and no remuneration, why this energy, this determination, this sacrifice?"

His smile let me understand that my question was perhaps astute but it also showed where I came from, exactly where Nathaniel had left me years earlier, as self-centered and interested merely in my own progress as ever.

What motivated them to work like slaves was the secret, the intimate glory of being one day allowed to publish their anonymous prowess on the Lagrange's BBS, which was prestigious, reserved to the elite of Desistence. Or simply the joy of working alongside Suzan Friedman and pointing the way to her.

"May not make sense to you, Etienne, I myself have a hard time sometime getting used to it, but for them, this is glory. They feel they participate to bigger, the One bigger than the sum of its parts, you remember? And there are many *many* of them like them!"

I had not seen him smile before like this. He looked me down from the corner of his eyes with a sweet and gentle irony, like he was overlooking my shortcomings and somewhat arrested development.

Nathaniel was not the same Nathaniel; he belonged now. He was part of the Lagranges, among the chosen. He was endowed with grace and purpose. I was baffled by the transformation of my friend.

Log 18

Kathy was almost as tall as Nathaniel and double his size. Kathy was the kind of woman a man can take for granted. She was so miserable that she was yours for the taking. For this reason, few took her, even though she was a Lagrange and she had a cute face. She was voluptuous, and I imagined, though I didn't try to bring her there, most likely passionate in bed. For Kathy, exchanging business suit and high heels for gym suit and sneakers; and then flying the coop to land in the midst of family had been like crossing the Red Sea.

For Suzan *HighGunsOnTheSierra.com* was the same life, it meant money; only more interesting because surrounded by people who said interesting things. She had learned a lot from Nathan Friedman. She had also learned from not having Friedman around and that's called balls and talent in her line of business. I gathered from her conversation that she had matriculated at thirty-three in the same school where she had been an Art History student at twenty-two. Before finding who she was on the Webwork and what she wanted from it, she'd taken advanced computer science at Stanford, alongside literature and philosophy. She was Friedman's student and she was herself. There was this determination in her to do what she was doing, this inflexible, mature will to follow in the steps of her ex-husband.

She never talked of Friedman's suicide and nobody did. But in the Webwork nobody disappears; and some like Friedman acquire a name that's immune to slander or blemish. Rumor had it that Friedman, a mathematics professor at USC, San Diego, preferred an overdose of injected cocaine to embarrassment and legal pursuit involving his partners and possibly his wife. Dead, his crime disappeared with him; he remained the inflexible hacker, independent and proud. Arrested, imprisoned, he would have been nobody.

Even though she had this slight drawl, Suzan Friedman sounded to me more British than Southern or Jewish-American. In her manners, there was this upper-class ingredient that she had either learned to fake early on or had inherited right off the bat.

But I was not knocked down by her, and I have already hinted at the fact that I was not in awe of Nathaniel's last dictum circulating on the Webwork; nor that interested by what kind of hacking—white or black hat—went on in the compound; not that inclined to resolving the question of how much money Suzan made. I was just disturbed by the collection under the same roof of people breaking into exquisite private virtual property (in spite of what Suzan pretended, there were fenced estates and private stakes "out there") and milking, no doubt, hectoliters of profit out of that; while others living under the same roof were waxing lyrical about an idea, Desistence, that meant detachment, refusal, retreat... How did the two sides work together? One was legitimizing the other, I assumed, covering plunder with literature and theory. But the question did not really interest me. All this hotchpotch seemed nothing really new to me.

I felt useless in truth. Not unwanted or uncared for, but superfluous.

At least, I'd take a break from New York and enjoy the scenery, the climate. The compound disposed of a fleet of cars; I drove to Venice beach in a white convertible BMW, parked and ate in view of a ballooning orange sun sinking like a giant ship. Back in my bungalow, I changed into my best shorts and white linen shirt for after-dinner cognac and cigars.

Nathaniel asked me about New York. Sitting next to him on his side of the table, I could not help telling him what I knew about Anna and her boyfriend, an Irish painter devoted to his art and to her. He was glad for her, "sincerely," he said, "She still has a life or two to live." Otherwise, I added, New York had stayed pretty much the same without him, nothing much happening, same old. He didn't respond like he would have in the past to the supercilious tone in my voice.

He turned nostalgic, asked service to fetch us a bottle of "single-malt at least 15 years of age." He offered me a cigar. Nathaniel had had the time to adjust to opulence. When I tried to make him talk about the fast-lane, risky enterprise he and his family appeared to be in, he looked at me alongside his eyes and said, "Who's looking into *their* backyard? I have spent my life crawling under petty rules..."

I noticed nevertheless that he kept an eye on me when nothing was said. He wondered how I judged all this. Was that the reason for his invitation, for me to look him up close, so that he could see how he fared in my eyes?

He said he was putting together the elements of his system, but he was not bragging about it, didn't have to hold me endlessly at attention. He simply invited me to surf further into the site. We hardly spoke about big books; very little about ideas. Nathaniel didn't read, not like before, and not because he had no future but because he didn't have time anymore, he *was* the future. He was part of something bigger than himself for the first time.

"John also has a second breath, look at him!" Nathaniel said to avoid to plunge into more complex subject, and without remembering that I had never seen John before. Not that he could dance now, but John walked supported by a bamboo cane and drank only two six-packs a day. John was not merely in love with Suzan, he was in thrall, he needed her like a baby his mother. Nathaniel marveled at how little brother kept following her every move, lusting for her. Little brother drank less so as to be in better shape when he made love to his wife. It's only now that he could make decent love to his wife. She must have paid of her person before. And now, what did she do, what did she volunteer to do for him? On top of being a respected hacker (rare in a woman, cyber stealth is mostly a young male's turf), and besides being a consummate business executive, Suzan Friedman didn't forget to be a woman.

It's on her that the both of us arrested our eyes at some point. Nathaniel could see that I was looking at her as well.

"She's something, eh?"

I nodded.

We briefly talked about my burgeoning career and my small but growing family, not a jaw-dropping topic. He was happy for me, nonetheless, "it's sweet, and it's so clearly what you needed." Was he being ironic, condescending or merely friendly? Another day it was my turn to be genuinely happy for him when Nathaniel started modestly explaining that he still didn't understand anything to computers and merely contributed to the ideological side of *HighGuns*.

"Who can run a business nowadays without megatons of blah, blah? So I blah, blah, I speak… Now it happens to be on screen. You know me, I couldn't write if my life depended on it, but I can speak (he looked at me sideways). I always could, right? Except now, *they* listen. Some do, who are becoming quite a few. I live by my speech, you could say, like in olden days the minstrel, the troubadour played his lute and sang his poetry. One needs to give meaning to the ambient mess, and if it's not people like us, Etienne, who will?"

His arms swept toward the layers of purplish clouds and the inflated red balloon of a sun finishing his descent into the dark blue horizon. We sat on the deck overlooking the lattice of lights, the grid of scintillating streets invaded by blackness.

False modesty and real modesty were nothing new in Nathaniel. What was new is that he had a good reason to be proud. He ran the company's open bulletin board, a chat room and a blog where "messy and disorganized discussions," he said, "occur on any kind of subject, might call it, issue of the day. Give them their doses of metaphysics, they are famished out there because they no longer trust accredited channels or radios to teach them anything. And the strict diet of ideas imposed by overpublished academics don't sustain them either."

When I asked about the content of his blog, he said: "Last week was about *The Digitization of History*, the question of transferring libraries and archives into the Webwork. There are ethical, philosophical problems involved, as you know."

I didn't know.

"Who owns the manuscripts left by famous writers after the digital age settles in? The people who own the rights to digitalize them and have paid for them, bought the manuscripts? The widows and remote members of family? And what if you contest such right? What if you're skeptical of the concept of ownership when it comes to what an artist did a long time ago in the process of achieving his work? All the drafts and correspondence of famous men you find in the University of Texas at Austin, why are they not available on the Webwork? Because the curator, I don't remember his name, doesn't like digitization, he wants to smell the old paper, and scholars around the world to travel to Texas and kiss his hand."

He paused, observed the spirals of smoke coming out of our cigars.

"Who owns the rights? The executive who financed the writer while he was alive and now wants to be the exclusive executor? Or does it belongs to Google? There is a battle out there and Suzan wants to make a statement. She has the bloggers claim free access to every book and work of art and piece of information ever gathered on the Webwork: *let us gain access or we jam your filters.*"

"Even though Google is not charging to access its resources, she is bothering the company for buying the exclusive rights to whatever is great on this planet; she is threatening to produce enough *Googlegangers* to choke their social utility. Just to show her force, I guess. Anyway, you'll see... Next week it's about *The End of Time at Your Finger Tips*—if you have ideas about that theme, welcome!"

The topic left me blank. I was flabbergasted that Suzan could even think about confronting Google. I could not have named any entity that dared throw hardballs at Google.

"And tomorrow it's *Downloading restrictions and the Moral imperative in Kant...*" Again, he observed me underhandedly. Then he sneered at these glaring headings and told me to stay away from the chatroom, "All bull shit, kids who have no clue, who have not read one line from Kant, merely heard their professor give anecdotes about Kant, how he took a promenade through town every single day of his life, you know the easy way they teach these things in school."

Passing jab at my profession, hard to resist, even after these intervening years of success. He felt vindicated to have taken the difficult route, much less traveled by. It made him tremble imperceptibly, the same way he shook all over up on the ladder at the Annex.

Next time I looked into one of his corridors, it reminded me at first of the thick paper on Hegel Nathaniel had concocted for Tony Wumster. Only, it was worse, paragraphs had been cut up and phrases excerpted, printed in different fonts. A shower of fragmented ideas was falling down my screen like sheets of codes in front of geeks. As a result, the esoteric idea Nathaniel was conveying about the tired question of *the end of philosophy* became even more esoteric, purposefully incomprehensible, and that's precisely what attracted his population of piranhas.

negaTVté, that's great Mister northwestern demon I want u 2 find examples appropriate sweet kiddies, put your ass in the position of negaTVté and listen

There is an irony in History; political events of magnitude occur twice, as disaster, catastrophe, tragedy—and then a second time down the century as farce, brutally aborted comedy.

No originality there, it's a view of History one finds in Karl Marx.

What occurred after the Holocaust according to Karl Marx? Is everything a farce now? How more brutal can it get?

On the contrary, does it mean that when History is at an end, when class-struggle as would have Marx is taken apart, pulverized among billions of individuals, then there is no more irony, no more farce and no more comedy?

Sure there is, that's all there is, farce and grimace.

Just a long and endlessly boring sentence where there is no longer bourgeoisie and working class but violence, frictions between high numbers that cannot be reconciled and don't want to be...

Mr Hegel does not answer my question.

Hé, dude, and who says sister dialectic is alive at the End of History?

Dialectic grinds to a halt at the end of time.

Right. You're all perfectly right, including the hallowed halls of the Sorbonne today, March 10/2008, which are crumbling as we talk. No one dares wake up the blind owl of philosophy lest she flaps her spooky wings around the amphitheater.

No time, no class struggle, no style, nothing exciting at the end of History

A white page

Blank screen

u make me laugh when i go down the hall philosophy students at it all they prove without the shadow of a doubt is philosophy is dead and will not resurrect, Mr. Northwestern Demon, you're right to say science has taken over.

And on and on, adding to itself.

Whatever the content of his chatroom, Nathaniel allows people's thoughts to flow, that's news. He's paid to enjoy the panorama (the question of his being paid and how much hadn't come up) and writes myriad words that don't amount to an article or a book but that are read and answered on the spot by others. How to call it? Instant thinking, the same way we thought on our feet going down 6th Ave; except now he and his following leave a trace.

One good point, he seems to have given up on his megalomaniac dream of epic intellectual grandeur or at least able to joke about it. I gather from his conversation, which is measured and not at all excessive as before, that he is satisfied to be of help to his brother and to be, as he puts it, "a peg in Suzan's organization."

He is not a peg; he could be the captain of their cruise ship, but he has made a tacit deal with Suzan. He does not have to agree with her defending victims around the planet to give a good impression and cover for more dubious endeavor; she, in return, does not post in his corridors. Their enterprise is multifaceted, part of it submerged, part getting a lot of attention. There is room for the two of them. There is a lot of room on the Webwork. It's one of these organisms that multiply by branching off and self-duplicating exponentially. Where there is one forum there can be another, alongside. She does not discuss Desistence, not publicly. She lets him sharpen his teeth on this concept, itself mercurial and multifaceted. He lets her sell shocking images, devastating clips parading on the sleazy side of the site, called the boutique. I didn't mention yet that Suzan made pocket money by auctioning the most vivid images and audio-clips of disasters around the planet—images taken by reporters but not sold to magazines because too ugly and awful. Witness accounts, testimonies, proofs of ecological, political and social catastrophes, graphic consequences of wars, riots, massive accidents, and there were many, and bigger by the day. And many buyers.

I was jealous, okay, but by the end of that week in California, still not impressed by Nathaniel's corridors. No one says anything, I thought, since no one signs and claims what he says. Nothing is said that matters enough for someone to take responsibility for it. You cut wherever, it does not introduce, develop and conclude.

And yet, I had to admit, I itched to throw my own bits in the flow; it was not as though nothing had been said.

Log 19

It's only on the plane back to New York that I had the time, or took the time, to look into his more personal log and found it more interesting. On the side of the main lobby, Nathaniel had established a virtual vestibule where he decided who to take on board for a "private" discussion. Nathaniel's output, I started to realize, was like the Talmud, where the core discussion is surrounded by commentaries, themselves consisting in discussions, which receive a century later another circle of commentaries. You had to peel the exterior layers and get to the core. It was clear at first glance that he no longer beat the truth on you with a stick, he avoided forcefulness and managed his punches. He had acquired rhetorical tools but kept the cavalier style he'd used in our old conversations.

"We may want to consider the terrorist problem we have through the light shed by the archeology of religions. In archaic societies, you had sacrifice. Now, you may think that the sacrifice of a goat, a pig, a fawn—even a young virgin—for the festivity that marked a victory, say, or if the army was about to embark in a dangerous expedition, all that has a remote, obscure connection to the guy blowing himself in a popular Baghdad market today. Whereas in antiquity sacrifice of one helped many, this guy blows as many of his brethren as he can. Well, the link is unclear, and yet, keep looking at it, you'll recognize there is a link. The terrorist comes forward, but doesn't offer only his neck to the butcher like Isaac; he slits as many throats as he can. You feel without understanding that there is a twisted link; it's like a sacrifice gone awry. It's like the victim of the ancient sacrifice taking the knife from the hands of the priest, killing everyone around him and burning the whole temple down."

More didactically than I expected, he went through a short history of sacrifice.

"Take any group of men (and women)—actually, any group of primates; chimpanzees, orangutans organize themselves around a leader, who can readily become the next victim as the young want to take over. The first myths are about gods killing other gods and taking over. In Hesiod Titans are replaced brutally, hurled down precipices. The sacrifice of a creature is required in Euripides to propitiate Neptune, allow the god to save face in front of Agamemnon, who must pay a dear price because he has mocked the gods. The Greek fleet is paralyzed, no wind, no way to wage war to Troy. The sweetest flesh is offered to Neptune cooked and seasoned to perfection. The dearest of kin is sacrificed. Euripides dramatizes a situation that no longer exists in the Athens of 5th century BC. In practice the Greeks replaced human victims by animals and token sacrifices in the temple. Monotheism tends to abstract the sacrifice, to merely ask for its metaphor. An angel stops in mid-air the knife of Abraham. The goat's blood amply satisfies to the ritual; soon the priest will place the host on the tip of your tongue and you'll be one with the victim who walked ahead of his own sacrifice to take all your errors on Himself. Jesus is the victim who spends his time saying to his following, 'You're gonna kill me!' And they do; and after that they adore Him and fall on their knees at the wounds they inflicted on Him. Crazy story, isn't it? And their descendants go on killing like there is no tomorrow; it's easier once the Church has consolidated because to clean their soul of the blood all they have to do is put the host on the tip of their tongue. But it's less easy around the Mediterranean Sea to sacrifice humans, that's my point, even animals. There is a problem with sacrifice, a suspicion over it. It no longer works miracles; no god is satisfied. The sacrifice does the contrary of what it's supposed to do, it rips the community apart, pits brother against brother. By the time Jesus walks on the scene, the message is give the other cheek, shake hands with your neighbor before sacrificing in the temple. Don't sacrifice, don't make the move, feel the pain of sacrifice inside. Judeo-Christianity is about a purified sacrifice, giving up on ritualistic violence. In Jansenist France, you attain *sanctity* by sacrificing common forms of pleasure, by living like a saint in a Neo-Classical castle. The Church has often been shaken by demands of purification, in other words, demands for more personal sacrifice. Saint Augustine or Saint-Dominique are represented walking bare feet in the rugged desert of primeval temptations."

"By the middle of the Middle-Age, Augustinian and Dominican orders illustrate the necessity for the Church to resource itself, you are perfectly right... "

"...Christ had touched the poor. He had been among the victims..."

"What you say makes me think that the Reform only asked for stricter ethics and sacrifice, one more turn of the screw..."

"Exactly, the Reform meant a tightening of the subjective screw... no longer could the orgies of monks be accepted!"

"No oily satisfaction should hang on the walls of the temple."

"But what happens when the virtues of sacrifice no longer benefit the group at large? When sacrifice—metaphorical or literal, inner or physical—does not work? One sacrifices and nothing happens but the need to sacrifice more. It no longer helps the fleet to leave the harbor if you dispatch daughters and sons to their early death. You're still stuck in Iraq..."

"Rough! Then, we're in trouble."

During my years in graduate school I was obsessed with tragedies and had introduced him to the character of Iphigenia who, as a sacrificial victim of choice, appears in Euripides', Racine's and Goethe's plays. I had mentioned Robert Grobard and cutting-edge literature on sacrifice; Nathaniel had ripped through the bibliography and overreached me, of course. Now it gave him a cushion; he could fall back on what we had spoken about if informed questions came his way.

In one vestibule Nathaniel developed in detail Grobard's victimization process.

"The anthropological fact is that groups, small groups at first, found it expedient to project their problems, their errors and in particular the crass stupidity of their rivalry, on one member. The exception to the set helps the set define itself. Sacrifice is a social and sometimes political safety valve, it lets the steam of rampant violence out. Sacrifice offers ritualistic, ancestral and limited violence to control the random hatred inside the group, the cycles of vendetta which ravaged traditional societies and now destroy post-colonial countries. I am sorry if I move slowly here, Grobard takes hundreds of pages to explain the basic psychological mechanism of projection on the victim, who is first perceived as nasty, dirty, incarnation of evil, sole responsible for the mess the group is in. As soon as the adequate scapegoat is found because of some particularity on his body or his belonging to a sub-group considered pariah, the group at large consolidates, it knows what it wants and feels vindicated to be together in this needed purge. However, again, everything changes in the self-perception of the members of that group as soon as the victim bleeds. The marks of pain, the humanity of the creature make everyone regret their bloody act and attribute to the sacrificial lamb all kinds of virtues. After all, the scapegoat is good since it reconciles *us*. Soon wise men and priests arrange the process which took place and explain to the crowd that the victim was an exceptional man, his death has purified *us* and we should adore his memory, follow his precepts."

Nathaniel's face is on my screen, his cunning smile; he combs long hair out of his face with yellow-tipped fingers like he has always done; he lights a cigar, drinks water; then, wets his lips on a glass half full of single malt, and continues. "Consider Oedipus, thrown out of Thebes because he married mother and killed father; in the next play, we see the same Oedipus egged on by his son Polyneices to come back to Thebes so as to die in the city where he was once king. Ostracized Oedipus is asked now to leave his bones near the walls that protect the city against its enemies. The victim has gone full circle, from hero and king, to inhuman monster and pariah, and again hero, *post mortem*…"

Pause. Looks at his viewers. "Sacrifice works like homeopathy and modern medicine whose preventive methods consist in inoculating the disease into the body so as to prepare it and fortify it against a real outburst of the virus. Greek soldiers had the severed head of Medusa painted on their shield so as to turn the object of their fright against their enemies, same logic. Small evil against bigger one." Pause. Nathaniel looks at his notes, where he has not put down the whole content of his discourse, but useful pointers, specific examples to bolster his argument; Nathaniel comes prepared and delivers, and this is new.

He continues. "Those who follow my corridor on John Milton will remember how we discussed this line in *Paradise Lost*: 'Destruction with destruction to destroy.' In Milton, the first woman wants to end the world and stop humanity *ab ovo* after she realizes she will go to hell and forever, and all that for the mere eating of an apple. Eve says no. I can only refer you to our discussion here. And add today what William Blake will say in *The Marriage of Heaven and Hell*, that one has to use acid against acid, corrosive method against corrupt practices. Corrosive practices are beneficial when you are in Hell. You cannot eradicate evil, so you deal with it, you turn it against itself, you utilize Satan, you borrow from him, hoping to decide what you take from the encounter and what he keeps. Hoping to not be tainted by him in the fight."

The style was as desultory as usual, his argumentation loose and unprofessional, and nonetheless, it was fascinating. Naturally, I resented the fact that he had attributed to himself the discovery of that extraordinary "moment" in Milton, without once mentioning me, his old friend. Though why should he have mentioned me? This happened before my visiting the compound; he had all the reasons to believe I was definitely out of the picture. And besides, it was not a theft for him to borrow from a dissertation he had helped develop.

The goofy impromptu that worked against him before, now went to his credit. He was the thinker who thought on his feet, not in an impeccable paper full of footnotes. Nathaniel could be serious, referential, grandiloquent and funny. You didn't know with him where it would go. He was very well informed without being one of the pedantic faculty who told you what it was correct to think. You absorbed what fit your worldview, the clip was not framed or sponsored by any institution. And yet you learned, you came out of a Webwork "discussion" with Nathaniel Lagrange full of ideas about books to read and connections to make. Of course, you had to be a member of *HighGuns* to view this; but the basic fee was a nominal $14.99 a month.

The Nathaniel of the corridors was not the same Nathaniel I had known, and yet he was. Smoking just two or three cigars a day, he looked healthier. No longer did he put himself *before* his ideas; you didn't have to deal with a thin-skinned ego when you listened to him, and this also explains his success on the Webwork.

My sense is that he was inhabiting the gulf that, after losing Kathleen (and Craig), had opened in him. It was rumored that he never invited anyone in his bungalow. Despite his ascending the Webwork and starting to shine like a star, he remained a wounded animal, a loner—no woman, no child, no drunken nights, hardly any playing of the guitar. He was like living *near* his old inflated self.

Log 20

There was the answer to why my friend had invited me to come: he owed me. Maybe he had helped me with the dissertation, but he now spent his time borrowing from the wellspring of our collaboration. He needed me as a witness, he had to see in my eyes that it was okay to be where he was and do what he was doing *with our ideas*.

Back in New York, the question I returned to was where did all the money come from. The hard cash, the money that was not just a trick in the virtual, how did it materialize? Was it enough to sell dead hackers memorabilia to make a fortune? How did she do with the IRS? Did she declare the revenue from hacking/blackmailing? Exactly in what kind of business, lawful or unlawful, was *HighGuns*? When pressed, Suzan had said she was in the business of selling weaknesses in networks to their administrators. "You have a problem. I fix it for a price; otherwise I sell it to who is interested." Is it extortion, racketeering?

Suzan had maintained there was no law forbidding her industry; no jurisdiction, no infringement, therefore no enforcement, no punishment. No fault. They were simply "out there," as she repeated, "doing stuff nobody has done before." I remembered our last dinner. We were to say goodbye an hour later and she was a little tipsy. "*They* always call crime what *they* don't understand. And when they finally catch up with you, they want it from you. Eventually, they do punish you under some pretext, like Al Capone for tax evasion, and you know why?" I was surprised that, out of all the people sitting around the vast oblong table, she was looking at me. "So they can take it from you. They couldn't find anything by themselves, so they spy on us, hackers, robbing the very people they call robbers. Pass me the salt... By the way, Etienne, have you seen by Altman, *McCabe and Mrs. Miller*?"

I had not.

"The big developer from back East asks the local pioneer in Wyoming, brothel-owner Warren Beatty, great in that movie, to vacate for a comfortable price because they want the train to pass through, and he refuses. Beatty does not understand, he is too drunk to understand. In response, the big developer sends killers to eliminate him. That was in the 1880's but nothing has changed, Etienne, you have to understand this. Once the wet work is done, they take over, they steal from you and make the big bucks; and, of course, they're never the robbers!"

"Never, of course!" added a chorus of voices. *They*? Was she talking about the police now or the corporations? They sure used generously the pronoun "they" at *HighGuns*. But why did she have to justify herself in front of me?

I waiver in my narration and at times speak about the Lagrange family or group as all together, while at others, I single out Suzan Friedman as the leader, the power in the pack. This ambiguity is not of my invention: I am astounded by the fact that to this day no mention has been made of her in the media and that the Lagrange family has received all the attention. She has mastered the art of self-effacement, which entails having others do for you what you don't want to be pinned down for having done. While adopting a friendly, hospitable demeanor, she hadn't opened to me at first. She had had little time for me, was not much interested by my ancient contribution to Desistence. Perhaps she was not sure where I stood concerning hacking. Was she suspicious? She had no reason to be; had it been demonstrated to me that wrongdoing was committed in the compound, proven embezzlement, any by-proxy, anonymous crime involving computers, first I may not have understood it; second, I could not have reported it. To whom? My meek, humble public university colleagues? The police? What kind of police would even understand what I would be telling them?

To my wife and in the circle of my friends I only had praise for *HighGuns,* the intellectual and political work they did. I told them how unforeseen Nathaniel's ascension had been; and I also told them the opposite: that it was predictable. Computer geeks had lost all hope of learning something from professional intellectuals. The Post-Marxist and Post-Colonial professors were out of the loop. To speak like Nathaniel, what had "the patented thinkers" digested and explained about 9/11? Which light had they shed on the mounting waive of terrorism, the rampant violence engulfing not only African jungles and Asian swamps but good old American soil? I have only briefly mentioned the connection Nathaniel established between modern terrorism and a perverted kind of sacrifice; he said much more in his corridors, as we shall see, and I still consider his contribution to victimology masterful. Nathaniel's radical rejection of the professors and all they represented paid off.

I loved the scene at *HighGuns* and envied my friend's life. Supposing Suzan were to ask me to come back—but why would she need me, what for? Perhaps to keep company to Nathaniel like Nathaniel kept John together—supposing she did, I'd gladly take another break from my academic life; and I didn't dare imagine what I would do if she paid me.

Yet there was a problem in that I wouldn't feel comfortable bringing along my wife and child; I wouldn't settle the family too close to the compound. It was okay if they reaped the fruit of my association without having to sully their soul in the business.

Suzan must have read this desire in me; six months later Nathaniel called, they had spoken with John and Kathy about a job for me.

"A job at *HighGuns*?"

"Yes, you can do it for the most part from where you are, anywhere... won't take much of your time either; but you might want to show up... *show your face at the meeting* as they say in your milieu."

"What do I do?"

"For a start, you study the entry test on your campus, the ACT, Academic Competency Test, you know about it?"

I certainly did, that's all I knew at work.

"And you figure out if and how the remedial work they receive in your institution—how d'you say, the achievements of your students in the classroom are reflected or distorted by their result at the exit test..."

The relevance of such inquiry, the precision of his wording impressed me, so I kept my mouth shut. "Is it something you could live with?"

"Seems rather interesting," I said.

"Only you'll have to be discreet, don't talk to your colleagues and administrators about it."

"Why should I?"

"Suzan has agreed to help a competitor of the *Pheonix Testing Services*, the company that administers and computes all the results of tests at City University—you can well imagine, making millions of dollars. The competitor says that unfair monopoly is granted *Phoenix Testing Services*, and that the central cabinet at City College is in cahoots with the company. They are ready to bring corruption charges and prove the existence of kickbacks in court... anyway, you don't need to know all that, it stinks."

His breath was almost clear, I noticed, his voice nimble, unburden by smoke. If he happened to smoke, it was one cigar at a time.

"You make your research in your own remedial and non-remedial classes, those who pass and those who don't pass, take samples, document a cluster of students, how you see them personally, and send us the results, whatever they are. It's not your job to judge the information. Your sample will be small but only a professor like you could give us the *live* testimony we won't find on the Webwork."

How businesslike Nathaniel had become. It sounded like he was reading the memo a project manager had handed him that morning.

"Is that something you can live with?" he repeated.

I certainly could. The money was handsome for very few hours of work. "Then consider yourself a consultant of ours. *HighGuns'* junior consultant Etienne Zeltzki. You can put that in your resume..."

I didn't detect condescension in his tone. He was happy for me, it could only do me good to work for the Lagranges. It turned out to be a juicy job, indeed. Like my colleagues, I was already aware that results at tests had little to do with the actual "competency" of a student, whatever was meant with that word. Some very articulate students failed the test because they had too much to say in 60 minutes, the topics were small for them and trite. And conversely some very bad students, those incapable of a simple statement written in a complete sentence, and we are not even asking for consistency of tenses, paragraph organization and nuance of thoughts—well, these happened to do very well by *Phoenix Testing*.

I sent my report in no time, and I can tell you, they were pleased at *HighGuns*. The enemy of *Pheonix Testing* only had praise for the researcher, whose name was not mentioned. My report (among others, of course) could help their case in court, if it came to a trial. More likely there would be a settlement and *Phenix Testing* would have to loosen its grip on the profitable market of testing in public universities around the country, allowing competition to exist.

This was better than publishing an unpaid scholastic article nobody read. For the first time in my life I was involved in business, doing commendable work and not just talking to students. I started to make consistent money on the side of my employment at the university and, though nobody advised me in this regard, I decided not to mention my emoluments to the IRS, the reason being that the Lagranges did the same with most of the money they made and for obvious reasons. Since I didn't mention it on campus either to my colleagues or the administration, it was as though for a couple of years my association with *HighGuns* were developing in a parallel universe.

Example of another assignment: I was to "study the level of dissatisfaction and truancy among professors and staff" of a public university comprising 150 000 students and 79 000 teachers, full timers for one third and two-third adjuncts. I was not asked to provide statistical data but a personal and subjective account about the level of fatigue and disillusionment found in the gray matter, heart and limbs of my colleagues. I could include my own feelings; I was myself the topic, as an instructor of Literature teaching disfavored adults on a campus in the South Bronx. I could even be the only subject of study, didn't matter since I would remain anonymous.

Now, the City University of New York was obviously not what it used to be when it educated great writers and Nobel laureates. Faculty were not replaced, class size out of control; and across the board, from full professors to adjunct lecturers, pay had stagnated for years; that is, roughly, since September 11, 2001, at least according to my impression and that of many.

Who, what organism in the City University of New York paid *HighGuns* to study the level of dissatisfaction in the ranks? Maybe the teacher's union in order to bolster future claims to higher salaries and better conditions. Or maybe their nemesis, the board of directors, the central cabinet, wanting to learn more about avowed and secret resistance to the last directives among junior and senior professors, so has to have reasons to slow their promotions. I did not need to know that and that made it easier for me. I merely expressed in my report what does not get expressed in meetings and certainly not in front of Chairs, Deans and Madam the President. *HighGuns* bought my report and passed it on to his client. I cannot say if they edited out part of my complaints about the limitations of my job.

There was nothing suspicious in what I was doing for the Lagranges. It impressed me that from California they had landed such a perfect job for me. Suzan was resourceful; in order to lure me she had to offer me a project not too cyber oriented. It was one of many well paid and interesting such projects. What gets well paid can only be good.

Log 21

Come summer of 2009, I am invited by *HighGuns* to spend a month above Taos, in New Mexico. I am on vacation and my wife lets me go since it is work-related. We have had discussions about the nature of my association with the Lagranges and I have succeeded so far in presenting it as professional and fascinating. That there is more money on hand is not a concern; I am transparent and sincere and avoid making much of the fact that Suzan is an elite hacker.

She'll take a week from her job and join me at the end with four-year old Isabel. I thought it should be easy to separate private and professional life once they visited me in the compound. And if it didn't particularly mesh between Suzan and Gabriela, I'd take one of the cars and drive us around.

I try to sort out my memories of the ranch. The situation was splendid. On the horizon, the mountains of Colorado, and coming down in red waves of earth, steppes-like prairie offering sparse vegetation. My bungalow with its beams of rustic wood coming out of uneven white walls; Mexican style of service. This time I am received in a vast estate.

I was told by a Mexican-looking student upon presenting myself that the team was about to come back from a ride. A few minutes later I saw, trotting on their horses, Suzan and John trembling in the distance—a lighter, nimbler John Lagrange, straddling a small hors—and behind him, Kathy and Nathaniel, and a silhouette I didn't recognize at first, a small man approaching slow on the red-dusty land, trotting leisurely, meandering. Nathaniel at times looks back and his horse makes a semi-circle, confronts, then walks back along John's and Kathy's. They let the reins loose and the three horses snort, shiver and shake their necks; and now Suzan's horse also makes a circle and so, it takes a while for them to end their ride. From a distance, they seem so happy and together, the Lagranges and Suzan, plus the silhouette. Finally, they come down from the horses that two Mexicans overtake and walk in the red powder of the corral. Nathaniel turns around, lights up a cigarette and, like he always does, gestures to emphasize his idea. They are in the corral outside, beyond the enclosure of the ranch proper; up to this point, Nathaniel behaves as though he has not yet seen me. He is talking animatedly to Suzan and John. I am standing too far to hear. He walks against their walk like his horse did before, and this creates a funny commotion among the group. Red dust everywhere on their boots, pants and horse apparel. Having recognized me, Suzan smiles, she is radiant; they walk hand in hand, John is happy. Nathaniel has thickened; he is not so sinewy and falsely juvenile. He is more of a man.

And there comes Jacques, who looks from below and smiles at me the smile of the rascal he is. His attitude tells me, "Eh, Etienne, is it all happiness to see me?"

I can't believe Jacques Manassah got here before me. I have to repress the sting of jalousie. I have been jealous of Jacques and Nathaniel from the first, jealous about their playing folk music together and reading their writings to each other. This time there is also Suzan in the picture. Savvy as he is, Jacques is already Suzan's dearest friend, no doubt.

Elbowing me familiarly as they enter in a pack the living room, Jacques whisper in my ear: "You see, Etienne, you were wrong to be so negative about Nathaniel." And later his manners would tell me, get used to it, Paradise has not been designed only for you, Etienne. You're not the only child in the family.

It became clear as soon as we sat around the fluorescent table in the main living room that it was not only Nathaniel who wanted me and Jacques to come to the ranch, it was Suzan. Why? One reason is that I belonged to Nathaniel's past, when he was not yet Nathaniel Lagrange. I was at the birth of Desistence; and even if we didn't use the word, Nathaniel and I were the first to talk of Milton and Blake as prophets of a radical solution. The first to wonder what it would mean to seek in each day that goes by "the moment that Satan cannot find." To seek apocalyptic resistance by using to our advantage the menace of auto-destruction as Nathaniel was at time developing in his *Treaty of Self-Slaughter* and his *Fragments on Desistence*.

As for Jacques, he had been choosing, editing photos at his employer on 17th Street and 5th Ave, and Suzan cared to tap into that source. Jacques could write blurbs to accompany the photos, and edit narratives in English. Based in New York, far enough from the ranch, efficient, smart and not exaggeratedly principled—add to this, in constant need of cash for his two boys growing in a tiny apartment in the West Village, and to help his nonworking wife pay for a dance studio where to practice experimental choreography— Jacques was the perfect employee for Suzan.

She was aware of our previous threesome in New York. She was also aware that Nathaniel and Jacques had been enemies to the blood. In a very business-like way Suzan wanted to thank good employees like Jacques and me while entertaining Nathaniel, who had a following on the Webwork and yet, in actual life, seemed so lonely.

He was at the apex of the world and at home with Suzan, Kathy and John. Yet, he seemed to be as mad as ever, if not more. His madness had gone softer, more acceptable, even pleasurable: he was now extolling the exploits of the team for them. It was funny for us, his old friends, to witness this, because before it had been the contrary, Nathaniel could not praise anyone other than old French thinkers, British pop singers or great dead writers—or himself. Now, he praised his friends and family, *the team*! He mentioned the revolutionary way they had found to navigate millions of passwords and ferret out just the ones needed for their project; he said, "Your trick is like Maxwell's Demon who picks and chooses the particles he cools off in a separate chamber… no, really, you think I'm crazy!?" Everyone around the table denied they could ever think such a thing. He proceeded, "you pick and choose among the myriad of passwords the ones that serve your scheme. It's devilish; and at the same time, it's not because for one thing, you guys reveal the weakness, the crack, the place of impossibility and lack in any man-made system. This can only reinforce the networks by teaching them how to fend for themselves. Come Cyber Wars of planetary proportions, as they will soon, the American immune system will have survived more than its share of melted-down core defenses; it will be ready. And in any case, if it has weaknesses, then the network you attack deserves to be broken in and taken apart—and serve bigger purpose, be rejuvenated as Blake said, into a greater One..." He laughed and quoted Blake by memory:

To Bathe in the waters of Life; to wash off the Not Human
I come in Self-annihilation and the grandeur of Inspiration

He had the illuminated look on; and yet, his tirade was not wrong nor uninspired. Suzan being the queen, Nathaniel had no problem filling the shoes of the madcap, the jester at court. In fact, he joked about taking back the guitar and singing like a troubadour to the constant party around Suzan and John. Suzan encouraged his foolery but directed it to a more appropriate show, that of praising the team; Nathaniel obliged. Why did he so easily overlook what Suzan was really about? Was he under her spell like everyone else, subjugated by everything Suzan?

No longer was I useless around her. When I'd worked as an insurance-life salesman in Paris, the job had lasted three weeks, one in training me and two in getting rid of me. This business was different and it was made for me. I am not fast at the computer, but for one thing, Suzan dealt more often in euro and she needed my French. She presented the job as though she were asking me a favor. I started translating, interpreting messages in French and in Spanish she feared were misunderstood, simplified by her regular consultants. I welcomed a salary of $376 an hour and refrained from asking when did my work start and end exactly, did it include sleeping hours when I dreamt in several languages? These details she left to my discretion. All the hours spent in the compound, for all she cared. This meant, as long as my budget can absorb it.

"To start with, we'll see later what happens," she added with a malicious smile. She knew, of course, that part of my motivation in spending time at the ranch was not Nathaniel or his *Fragments*, but money.

Could I absorb the unexpected sums I was getting? This sounds like a rhetorical question but there remains a potential problem with the IRA; unless I considered there was no problem since hacking money does not exist anyway. Later, as Suzan made money, $376 became $410... versed to my account in euro. She wanted to make sure I was happy. Why? Because I was becoming more useful to her, and not only with my interpretations. She knew how privy I was to the doctrines Nathaniel defended. Bringing me into the business she would have me on her side. She was starting to take Nathaniel seriously and aspects of Nathaniel's speculative considerations spooked her. The self-slaughter idea was not merely an idea like you find in many thick books nobody reads. She could use an ally from Nathaniel's past, in case.

It so happened that there was a lot of talk on the Webwork about mushrooming social utilities. People built growing networks by connecting to the "friends" they didn't remember they had, and the "friends" of their "friends." The operating system was no longer in your computer but "out there," computing for you, searching, sending, poking others and extending connections, answering questions for free, bombarding you with publicities tailored to your moods. Your computer didn't have to work for all this, and so it ran faster.

These social utilities were making fortunes. I wondered (and later discovered I was not the only one) what would happen if one infiltrated networks with inexistent "friends" exchanging digitally-created photos, stories, ideas... Nothing at first probably; but what if these false "friends" multiplied, sending each other vivid messages, cross-referencing and comforting the tenor of their original and succulent stories toward existing "friends" out there. Inexistent "friends" would go prying into the group-rooms and walled activities of living and breathing Webwork "friends" and all kinds of profitable encounters (for the social utility) could ensue. I chose *Facelift*. The site had almost crashed six months earlier because of virtual prostitution and real extortion, and then, suddenly it had cleaned, purged itself, the "clean" participants denouncing "vicious" friends to the administrators. These smart administrators only had to throw away bad apples to please a growing need in this world for true friendship ([3]).

Facelift had rebounded and picked up subscriptions in Asia and Europe. I then wondered why it was popular there and not yet in the US. The possibility of building privacy by writing on a "wall" accessible only to a select number of your "friends" should appeal to the guarded Western Individual. The hierarchy or levels of "intimacy" permitted by the site also. The friendly list was selected for each participant out of his history on the Webwork and limited to 50. However, once the list of the 50 "friends" of these 50 "friends" is compiled, they reach to the millions, and the points of intersection between "friends" are so many that the site becomes the most attractive publicity board.

Suzan transformed my vague idea of the puppet "friends" into a brilliant way to be counted on the expense-sheet of social utility networks. She produced a regiment of dummies, and with the help of almost everyone in the ranch, she made them so varied, loquacious, interesting and attractive that she steered the entire population of users of several sites into sharing what the team deemed right. Computer-fed and therefore able to tap into unlimited information, such "friends" helped you in your social life and your professional life. "Friends" like that shared movies, news (a particular slice of news), music, lyrics, looks and outfits, recipes, personal photos, tastes, habits… Quickly Suzan found herself gently commandeering the buying power of a growing population of geeks.

Being generous, Suzan lavished gifts on me, the inventor of *Spacelift Redux*, as we called it. The executives at *Spacelift* bought us out eventually, we kept our mouths shut and helped them clean their system. They did not want their subscribers to ever discover they had been talking all along to fake "friends," conned and manipulated. Suzan agreed to keep silent if they doubled their amount.

---

[3] Although a direct source of inspiration, the inexistent "friends" I had in mind should not be confused with the *Googlegangers* Suzan threatened earlier to create. The latter were mere empty shells, doubles of existing members able to jam and saturate the utility; I thought about inexistent "friends" who would take on a true digital existence, acquire flesh and blood and feel more real and complex than characters in books and movies.

In the ranch above Taos no more students at the screen, no buzz from excited youth, a lean team, only the family Lagrange and Suzan. The core and their intimate friends worked on the premises. Delegating most tedious tasks and traceable moves to far away consultants, Suzan was more powerful than she had been in L.A. and at the same time more discreet, relying on few trusted servants and auxiliaries. She has always done so well hiding in their midst, covering her tracks, putting forth her troupes spearheaded by Nathaniel Lagrange. Suzan Friedman is still not considered the leader of the gang; she is hiding in plain sight and no one, except me, is interested in setting straight the record.

Between Nathaniel *and* Suzan, that seemed to be a match made in the cloud; but the only one sticking his neck out was you, Nathaniel. Couldn't you remember the lessons you gave on a Greek tragedy where the king and hero becomes in the span of one day victim and pariah?

The sprawling facilities cover several acres of cactus and golden, blood-dappled land. The soft red earth sticks to the soles and paints your shoes in a nuance of orange and cramoisy. The ranch is a comfortable and convivial place. I could stay alone for a couple of hours, walk toward the corral and remember the time when my father would bring me to Rambouillet outside Paris. During a couple of years, that is, once a week, I had a father. The ground was brown, muddy back then, grassy, humid, not desert-dry like in New Mexico. There are beautiful horses to watch in the corral, including Indian horses, leopard-spotted, Western saddled, mane and tail falling down their legs all the way to the horseshoe. After so long I prefer to try my hand on one such small Indian horse, easier to ride.

On one side, the high mountains of Colorado, whose peaks are no longer crystalline-white in the middle of summer because of global warming; and on the other side, the valley toward Santa Fe, hundreds of miles of slope leveling down to the boiling plains of Albuquerque.

The ranch is perched on a high plateau, few miles from the serpentine and spectacular canyon of the Rio Grande. Up here, it's hot under the sun, but there is a generous breeze. The sun-energized and protected bedrooms are furnished in the French style, adorned by low armchairs and overwrought desks in a flamboyant style reminiscent of some French king Louis. By contrast, the dining room exhibits the severe, functional modern style of Mondrian and Le

Corbusier; and again, there is a jump in style because the living-room is made of logs: floor, walls and roof perfect replica of a hunting den in the Far West at the time of the pioneers. Same style in the dining-room occupied by a long table whose blond plateau shines while its edges are rugged.

And, of course, everywhere one finds the latest screens, the ones that accept your touch and transmit your orders almost at the speed of light. I should not forget the translucent vases, some the size of a man, amphorae, made in the style of Bohemian glass vases circa 1900. They are filled with desert plants, roots and flowers that go according to the color of the room. In other words, Suzan's educated touch is everywhere.

Log 22

Suzan, John and Kathy are all about Europe now, the way European eat, dress, make love. John's manners are more refined, his garment clean, his jaw smooth like a log that has been recently honed. And what is particularly enjoyable about him, he hasn't turned self-righteous about alcohol, doesn't make it a rule *not* to drink, he drinks moderately. It is quite astounding; I am baffled by the miracle that radiates from his couple with Suzan.

Instinctively, I look for the imperfection, the defect and vulnerability in this entente, this communion of bodies and minds—but I can't.

Sister Kathy is no longer looking for a boyfriend, a rumor has it that she has her moments with a young Mexican. Power, fame and money are liberating. You become yourself when you have money. I didn't look into Kathy's affairs; but if that's true, good for her.

Everyone works nonstop at the ranch. Even break and recreation time are devoted to exchanging ideas that turn around the work at different levels of the site. Nathaniel is busy thinking when he sips his single malt and looks far in the distance; even when he rides his horse. At dusk, which comes after dinnertime now, late in the evening, he usually posts a nourished speculation that makes you realize he's been at his system all along. His famous *Treaty of Self-Annihilation* developed at dusk under the darkening skies of the high desert.

"There was a time when sacrifice worked because it was supported by a mythology the group believed in. A god was propitiated by the sight of blood, desirable flesh cooked to perfection—the God was especially satisfied by your giving away, your not having, your sacrificing *to* Him the most precious. The ancestral hero was killed and eaten in the guise of his animal totem by the native group and it mollified the spirit of discord. Once bleeding to death, victims were sanctified, they resuscitated in the entourage of the gods, high up there, in their clouds. In the Athens of 500 BC—in the same great city that invented rational discussion—they used to feed at the tax payer's expense a bunch derelicts, bums and foreigners called *pharmacoi*. Whenever the city went through difficult times, factions, partisanship, civil war... hey, the Senate could vote and decide to sacrifice one or several victims. The mob would beat them, parade them by the streets of Athens naked, "object of mockery and aggression" I have read somewhere. They'd skin them or burn them or dismember them, depending on the severity of the circumstances and the need for Athens to purge itself and feel good again. But a detail to remember and that Robert Grobard considers key for the human sacrifice to have worked—to have pacified the group—is that it involved victims nobody would claim, low-lives, strangers no one would die for. That's how the pharmacy of sacrifice worked: it absorbed the crescendo of violence, the deadly cycles of vendetta, for a time the ritual producing the impression that a chaotic force, a god was appeased."

"Now, I come back to this... and I know that for those who follow me, I am repeating myself, but some questions are worth repeating, mulling over and over again, and from one generation to the next... yes, what happens to the collective impulse to sacrifice when the ritual is lost and human beings are stripped of belief in myth and religion—but, notice, not of ideology? The fundamentalism you see flourishing nowadays among Christians, Islamists or Jews is not about religion. An Israeli Jew who kills his president does not do it because of his religion; nor did the 11 terrorists who killed thousands of people on Sept 11, 2001: it's not Allah who asked them to do it, but the ideology that says Islam must reconquer a Calafat in never had and wipe the Americans from the face of the earth... and I do not want to forget the Christian who burns the abortion clinic and kills the doctor with his bare hands; Christ never asked him to do it."

I put my viewing on pause and remembered how disparaging Nathaniel had been of the figure of Christ. He had changed.

"There is a multiplication of the impulse and no cure to calm the collective scratch, no designed culprit, no traditional punching ball, no more reason to bash this victim more than that one. So, the point becomes to experiment with more severe degrees of destitution in the victims; as the group becomes statistically significant and the social, moral, legal constraints grow, the need for correspondent sacrificial safety-valves also grow. The industrial age coincides with industrial wars, genocides, ninety percent of the planet colonized and many missed social revolutions (look at nineteenth century France). In modern times, to count as victims, you have to come by the millions; no mere token sacrifice will appease this beast."

"The Holocaust shows how alive is the sacrificial impulse in an age of waning belief in the old religions. No longer does the self-sacrifice of Christ work wonders; Lazarus stays dead among the dead. Old people believed; the young requested more vivid, I should say, more sanguine solutions. Though it was no longer a question of seeing the blood, this time. A more drastic pharmacy was required, a cure of metaphysical proportion. What could purify the engorged, putrid social pores and tissues of the Germany of the 30's and for 10 000 years, asked young Hitler in his *Mein Kampf*? We know who is the degenerate race. By the childish logic which makes all the magic of sacrifice, eliminating the degenerate race should generate a clean body, clean pores, clean genes to all the other children of Europe. It is the same old cure, but on a mega scale, and tinged with racism and pseudo-science. The Holocaust was *the* continental European project that engulfed every nation except England. The Final Solution was to unify Europe on the back of the Jews, fastest track; and it would have been done quite effectively had the Germans won the war."

Not for effect, but still producing his effect, Nathaniel had to pause and take his breath. This time he drank from a bottle of water.

"After the Holocaust, which it could be tempting to emulate and even overdo now that plan A, the grand plan of globalization falters, peters out and clearly fails most people on this planet—after Auschwitz, what happens in the realm of victimization? Allow me to be cynical: do we witness any progress?"

"We see more sophistication in the methods used to destitute victims, silence them, draw the line between them and us, use us to denounce them… and Terrorism. As a modern geopolitical tool, terrorism is new. Blow yourself up while sitting in a bus full of children belonging to your own race and "religion" (he wiggles the guillemets with both hands); sacrifice your life and that of these children to a vindictive god who, you say, asked you to trash false believers. In return, you become hero and saint to the true believers and will soon sit among a crowd of virgins. Twisted logic, contorted, yet still sacrificial logic. No longer are we using homeopathic solutions to tamp down violence; we are using violence to stoke more violence and spread its incandescence to the four corners of the flying carpet…"

I could not help during his speech remembering how my colleagues treated the psychiatrist and anthropologist Rober Grobard, as finished, and his theories, as tired. In Europe and in the US, waves of promising young academics had used his insights on victimization to write about everything under the sky: literature and customs and marriage documents; intimate events, historical events, revolutions and counter-revolutions. And then, suddenly, scapegoating theories seemed *passées*. After years of enthusiasm dissertation committees had soured on the notion of scapegoating altogether.

Nathaniel showed that what had expired was only the use of Grobard's scapegoating process for one's own career and promotion. The concept had to be expanded to account for new and more urgent concerns. Brilliant ideas don't just die; they are ready-made for the next generation of thinkers, ready to be transformed.

At dinnertime, there was a jovial conversation running around the massive quadrangular table, and then:

"By the way," said Nathaniel abruptly, "just a parenthesis, does anyone realize that the leftist accusation is right, the most powerful and dangerous group of cyberterrorists is to be found in the US Army, which can invest in cyberwar hundred times more than all the other terrorist organizations combined. It could blot the European networks into one mega weapon aimed against near eastern concerns. The American army has infiltrated viruses that could liquefy the industrial bones of Russia and China combined; and I am told by specialists that it could make a digital purée of Brazil's nervous system."

At the head of the table, usually John and Kathy flanked Nathaniel on either side, then came on one side of the table Suzan, her guest of the day and her personal coders. Jacques and I sat on the opposite side. The atmosphere was relaxed and the conversation pleasant. We could ask questions across the enormous table, but dinnertime was the occasion for Suzan and the Lagranges to speak their mind.

The Lagranges made long faces if you were clumsy enough to mention any of the disastrous US policies enacted locally, nationally or internationally. For them, America was about done for after eight years lost in the wilderness under the last Republican administration. She was a squeezed lemon, short of breath and spent like a whale washed on shore. Whatever the Democrats applied of common sense policy to stamp down the hemorrhage and bandage the wounds was coming too late. How much they preferred the nineties! Everyone around the table said something to this effect.

Suzan was slightly tipsy. "Wall Street has never done better, though, that's the fun part—so why worry and in the name of what morality? The immoral gods presiding over the realms of the economy are not interested in making sense and even less in appealing to our *conscience*. What conscience? Who has a *conscience* (she says it in a well-pronounced French), please, tell me? Chaos, mayhem, disruptions, diseases and catastrophic wars bring more insurance money, sell more weapons, bring higher price of oil, better for the market. The market is full-proof, let me tell you, there is enough trillions floating about the stratosphere to patch up holes big as the Grand Canyon."

We laughed. She has a gift for electric images.

"Pass me the wine, Nathaniel... and a cigarette." She drinks wine and sometimes, but rarely, smokes.

Nathaniel lights her cigarette. "Muhm!" he hums, "so far so good, but worse and worse tornadoes devastating the South, and winter storms unheard of on the East Coast, and the continental crack in California threatening to reopen, dryness in the heartland to create a desert like the Sahara—I don't want to sound like the angel of *Apocalypse*, but..."

"But, even if you do sound like him, John interjects, we won't take you seriously." John pats Nathaniel on the back, "we know you're a good man!" John giggles.

Kathy : "Nathaniel doesn't need to be the angel of Apocalypse to bring bad news, the good truth is bad enough. We should operate from the Galapagos."

"From Belize," says Suzan.

"Why, because less taxes?" asks John to tease her on her Jewish side.

"No, not to make more money, although what's wrong with that?" She receives amused approval from under the breath of all the participants. "No, because I remember Belize as the escape route for a thug in a bad American movie whose title I can't remember..."

"You're thinking about Nathaniel Douglas in *A Perfect Murder*?" says John. But then, he probably remembers the plot in that movie, a remake of Hitchcock's *Dial M for Murder* where the wife has a lover who is paid by the husband to kill her... and to not introduce a jarring note in the conversation, John pauses and looks through the bay windows and into the distance. Over the high desert and toward the mountains, few shredded clouds stretch high in the sky and put a touch of blackness on the dazzling sunset. The sun, which was ruby-red an hour ago, is a pale copper plate surrounded by an aura of pink. A minute later, it is an ash-gray disc sinking into the velvety blue.

Another night Nathaniel tells us a little more about his system. Jacques and I are in a better disposition than we were long ago, curious, anxious to know more of him, about him; and he feels it, of course. First, the three of us sit on the purple sofa big as a Buick that has accompanied *HighGuns* since L.A.. It is touching to see that Suzan feels nostalgia, wants like anyone some continuity in her life, keeps around her the objects that carry a soul.

I don't remember exactly how Jacques invited Nathaniel to give us, his oldest friends, his most advanced version of Desistence to date. Nathaniel demurred; but then, for the first time, invited us for a drink in his quarters, where we settled deep inside three mammoth armchairs. After the polite and necessary show of modesty, Nathaniel went to his desk, brought back his notes and spoke to us exactly as he does in front of his screen:

"My first step is a question: what happens when the sacrifice of a few for the sake of many does not work anymore?"

"Which you equate to the period starting after Auschwitz?" Jacques questioned sarcastically.

"Exact... Next question?"

Nathaniel cleared his throat, gulped down from a mug of single-malt and attacked: "Today the sacrifice of chosen victims does not work. What works is some kind of self-slaughter, of jumping in a bus full of grand-parents and little children, and exploding the belt."

"This is one kind of self-sacrifice, indeed, bringing everybody with you!" said Jacques with a hurtful face. Jacques had just written something on the buses exploding in Israel during the last Intifada. "Anyway, what do you mean by *it works*?"

"Good question, Jacques" says Nathaniel with a flourish of the hand. "It does not work like the sacrifice, by regrouping the entire group around one goat whose flesh was sliced, seasoned and perfumed. The Nazi still tried to make the Jews the universal goat in an industrial age and it almost worked, remember."

It was kind of funny to ask two Jews to remember the Holocaust.

"The booby-trapped terror agent of today is not a goat; he merely makes matters worse, he fights against solutions. That's simply what I mean by *it works*! Your regular terrorist makes matters worse and that's the goal of his self-destructive enterprise—destabilize, delegitimize, devalue the sanctity of life for the sake of an ideology believed as fanatically as religions were long ago."

"And so?" Jacques and I both asked in unison, looking at each other, dumbfounded by this flat result. It was like an elephant had given birth to a mouse. I could see on the side that Jacques was repressing hilarity, and it was contagious.

Nathaniel witnessed our readiness to mock him, he hesitated if it was worth his effort, decided it was, and said: "There is another way to self-sacrifice, the opposite way. It's called without playing on words sacrifice of self, get ready to give up on everything that you count dear, reassuring, all that you fear to lose for fear of losing your sense of self. And what if it was the very closed-in form of the Self that was hell? What if one had to burst out of this shell?

We knew who'd inspired these metaphors. We'd seen the hand-written calligraphy of the poet in the illustrated book Nathaniel had shared with us in New York; we remembered the colorful motif barring the top of one page, the pattern of siren-like women transforming into each other, their tails and limbs becoming one. And if we had been members of some sect and Nathaniel our guru, we would have just then sung in unison what was written underneath:

To Bathe in the waters of Life; to wash off the Not Human

I come in Self-annihilation and the grandeur of Inspiration

But we didn't say anything and merely hummed the words inside.

Jumping as was his wont to a very different reference, Nathaniel continued: "Give a limb if they pull on it, said Seneca the stoic. Abandon your leg If it grants you some leeway, breathing space. This house, this body is not yours; it belongs to the cosmos; what's yours is to make a choice. If they are about to turn you into a slave, take your life and disperse into the cosmos. Remain free of subjection and you will not die, not absolutely—you'll reappear, as in Ovid's *Metamorphoses*, scattered perhaps but transformed. You will be part of bigger and other than you. It's your self-definition that must go: *shackles of the mind...* your envelope, your carapace and covering. Your attitudes and mental ossification; your hang-ups, we'd say today. If you accept to lose your sense of self, your imaginary definition, then you can lose your-self into bigger than you. Drugs like ecstasy or psilocybin give us a glimpse of how consciousness may stretch beyond self-awareness. But drugs isolate and scatter individuals whereas Desistence turns isolated individual inside out and brings them together. You, your limited consciousness may die in the process, but you'll have reached collective consciousness, which is something classical philosophers never talked about; Descartes never explored with his *I think therefore I am*. Bigger than your paltry me, Monsieur Descartes, is a robust and sensible group of men and women and children. They were there before you were born and they will be there when you pass away. You see in which way the sacrifice of ego could be beneficiary?"

"And this bigger-than-you is not just another god?" I asked.

"No," he snapped. "Not at all, I've just explained to you."

I kept my mouth shut; it would have been stupid in me to remind him that it's me who had introduced him to Seneca the Stoic. When I met him, Nathaniel was full of big philosophical systems like Plato's and Aristotle's. A professor at the Sorbonne had mentioned unassuming Stoicism as a survival kit by stormy weather. I'd found in Marcus Aurelius and Epictetus precepts and a medicine for when things collapse around your ears. The first Stoics hoped to survive morally unscathed the destruction of Athenian democracy and, later, the collapse of Alexander the Great's empire. Over almost a thousand years, roughly from 500BC to 500AD, the stoics repeated one mantra: stick to your choice; you always have a choice, no matter how bleak the situation. You are free as long as you make a choice. Simple, concrete and practical philosophy.

"The group, what group? Who defines the group?" asked Jacques with a pointed smile. "What kind of Apocalypse do you have in mind? Are you asking us to kill ourselves? Do you want us to jump from bridges *altogether*? Blake was a mild British eccentric promenading naked with his wife amidst the flowers of a cottage right in London. He was a lone wolf who didn't have *the group of hearty men and women* at heart, he had God!"

Nathaniel let that pass as though he had considered this objection and said:

"Suppose the best and the brightest were to call it quits *en masse*… freeze; retreat inside… demure, refuse to give assistance… at chosen moments, say, regarding specific activities on the Webwork. Like the women in *Lysystrata*, who decide to not have sex when their men come back from the war: women's ultimate weapon, not to abandon their bodies into men's hands, sex strike. It does not kill anybody or temper with anything. No adolescent is pulling her belt among her people, no atrocity—you only threaten to call it quits, you desist. You prefer not to do what you're supposed to do."

He takes a swing of single malt.

"Now, we could do this all at once, let us suppose all at once for argument's sake, imagine that an entire generation meant to speak like Bartleby, the office clerk who answers 'I would prefer not to" whenever his boss asks him to do the same extra work all the other clerks on Wall Street are supposed to do. Melville writes that Bartleby didn't raise his voice to say 'I would prefer not to.' He stood there, in front of the head clerk, his tone 'mild, yet firm'—but I don't have to repeat to you guys, do I, our corridor discussions on *Bartleby the Scrivener*?"

I had read the story and found it fascinating, but not what Nathaniel had said about it. As for Jacques, difficult to tell; Jacques could lie better than me.

We were sinking in the ultra-soft leather of his armchairs and sipping single malt. For the first time, Nathaniel had received us in his chambers made of exotic teak wood and floor to ceiling wrap around facing the ominous mass of the Rockies with, at their top, the high jagged line of our red-blue horizon. The view was breath-taking—what a difference with living at mother's in the room of his childhood. It felt the more cozy inside that darkness was gaining outside.

Nathaniel invited us in; but there was a lot more to Desistence than he would let know during this first meeting. He'd send feelers, gauge where we stood; and, no doubt, have the proceeds recorded, in case he needed inspiration for his next blurb. Nathaniel was different because he no longer was alone with you anywhere; he came accompanied; what he would tell his following in the next hour was present in the room, you could palpably feel the progress of his thought reaching the Webwork.

Looking at me and Jacques alternatively, he continued. "Find the right tone, say it meekly, you know, with regret, 'sorry, it's not that I won't do it if you force me to, it's that I would prefer not to'... A désistant might say: You will end up doing what you wanted by me, through me, but without the satisfaction of my consent. I won't be the consenting victim, I'll merely watch you victimize me. Isn't that the most disarming kind of resistance? Picture a woman who coldly smiles in the face of the man who rapes her?"

At the risk of sounding like an academic, I said: "A kind of passive resistance like at the beginning of the XXth century, then?" I wanted to bring the political, historical aspect and calm the discussion, but my remark felt dismissive. For a second, which he couldn't avoid, Nathaniel looked down at me like he were up the ladder at the Annex and I was on the floor. Then, he mused and admired the shelves of books that lined the high shelves of his exquisite library carved out of a dark red mahogany wood, striking piece of furniture making you feel they had to cross the Andes and jungle to bring it to him. Now that he had the means to buy the books he wanted, and the edition he preferred, the space to stack them, including servants to keep them organized and clean, Nathaniel no longer read them; but he basked in them. One even wondered if these books had not been bought with the furniture, a meter of Nietzsche and two of Kant and Hegel. Nathaniel cared to give his rare visitor the impression that he was a regular businessman engaged in avant-garde pursuits. No longer did Nathaniel run for the books you asked nor did he read paragraphs to you out loud, but he lived in their shadow and recalled them passionately. Others might correct his thought, errors, misattributions. He could afford to cite by memory, accepting the inevitable distortions his mind would bring. Distortions are part of the transformation process.

I insisted: "Gandhi on the lotus and the British army at a loss? Is that what you envision would have pacifying effects on this digital world?"

"*Bartleby the Scrivener*, it's great on paper," Jacques dropped. "He doesn't have a desk; they don't know what to do with him, where to put him. So puzzled is his boss by his 'I would prefer not to'—the head clerk, the man who happens to narrate to us the story of Bartleby, well, he would obviously also prefer not to—and yet, he ends up doing the extra job."

It was funny somewhat. Remembering what my wife had told me about office work, I added: "All this works well when it's Melville who writes. In a real office downtown Manhattan, Bartleby is shown the door by midday or else he doesn't get the job in the first place."

Nathaniel received our objections like they were soft balls and deflected them without using a word. He no longer was in a hurry to make his point; his old forcefulness was gone. Jacques and I became aware of this when he took advantage of the lull to fetch himself a drink and, glass in hand, asked to be excused for answering few more of his e-mails before going to sleep.

We paused, sat further back into the leathery armchairs before springing on our feet and politely saying goodbye.

My wife had nothing against Nathaniel and his family. She was impressed by the place and relished its comfort, the presence of helpers to arrange lodgings and foods, prepare sauna and swimming pool, cleaning boys for the tennis courts and horse attendants. The sight of horses enchanted Isabel. Seeing her happy running in the vast open, and our not having to watch over her every second made us feel bad for our little girl, always confined to the cement of gritty New York. There were also several dogs and cats roaming the ranch, and a miniature monkey. Besides visits at the Central Park Zoo and reproductions in her books, she had had little contact with animals.

The ostentatious facilities made Gabriela roll her eyes and wince a little. Only at dinnertime did it become evident that intense involvement in their exclusive concerns made it difficult for Gabriela and Suzan to communicate. No animosity, more like respect for each other's domain. And it was likewise difficult for me to follow Nathaniel in the ramification of a metaphysical argument while answering Isabel's many questions about the place.

Fortunately, my work schedule was elastic and Gabriela eager to see the Indian ruins; me the eighteenth century Spanish churches scattered over the mesas like dominos; and Isabel the natural grandeur of the Rio Grande and its canyon. I drove us around in a cobalt blue Honda convertible.

I was relieved to put my mind into the more sensible considerations of love and family. Without jumping to conclusions, but thinking no less, Gabriela was sensitive enough to appreciate my position and not make a problem of the fact that Suzan and the Lagranges were perhaps doing a little too well for their own good. Looking at the way they worked, Gabriela said, they deserved it. Although, on the other hand, they were only a bunch of hippies. She laughed. My wife was working 9 to 5 (more like 6 or 7pm) as an education director for a big worker union. She did well, better than me at the university. However, nothing on the scale of this limitless wealth whose blurry provenance put her on edge. I confess it made me nervous too. There's got to be a backlash to outstanding success, and the greater the success. My wife didn't suspect traditional crime, petty theft, *bandoleros de alto vuelo,* as she said jokingly. The Lagranges didn't rob horse-drawn coaches on the high plain. The Lagranges were too intelligent for that, especially Suzan, who had taste and decency and an excellent pedigree all around. But Gabriela suspected that the Lagranges cut deep corners. And it was great for a while, *pero la ley es la ley*, the sky falls down on you at some point. They obviously cut corners, I agreed with Gabriela. No point in denying it to her. She would then really suspect me of lying. Whether the Lagranges cheated more than other businesses, she couldn't tell and it's not my vague explanations that helped. I agreed with her about keeping my eyes open, and no less my ears.

In a situation that modest origins made me suspect was too good to be true, I appreciated the weight of commonsense Gabriela brought. We agreed that I was not married to *HighGuns.* For now, I was doing nothing wrong working for them. After all, I was no more than a well-paid employee susceptible to pay more taxes, unless he found shelters.

We were approaching the deep ravine of the Rio Grande and gradually plunging into the belly of the golden sierra. As the road winds down the flanks of the canyon, the earth revealed stratified, slated. Isabel remembered our last trip to France and said we were like in a millefeuille, inside a creamy layered cake. I guess it made her daydream because she dosed off in her seat. Even though we had the air-conditioning at full blast, the burning hot air beyond our windows knocked you down. I went into a speech where I told Gabriela about the two basic categories of human beings extent on this earth: "those who have and those who don't." She was about to laugh at me, so I went on: "Nothing new perhaps, but much worse. It's less than ever a question of diploma, expertise, intelligence or education, only a matter of what you're worth at birth. It's gotten so hard to acquire a square inch where to rest your feet if you're not born into it. I want to leave something to Isabel; I don't want her to have to fight for a corner of ground like we've had to. And I am not saying 'a patch of grass' because we still don't own a patch of grass."

Gabriela liked it when I talked like that. I insinuated that, if there was a risk, it was my life that I gambled, not theirs. It was my choice, for our sake, the sake of the Zeltzki. And, yes, if something too troubling was going on, I could kiss politely goodbye to my friends.

Log 23

More, much more in euro (while the dollar continues to fall). And yet Suzan didn't feel the need to transplant *HighGuns* to Europe. The US still had an edge. It has changed along with the accelerating demise of the US economy. Then, hardly a few years back, America remained an easier option for the team to operate from. Europe still had less computers connected to the Webwork; you had therefore less chance of finding ways-in and selling imperfections. But on the other hand, it was easy to penetrate their networks from the US. The Europeans were behind in cyber-spying, counterterrorism and computer security; savvy, cutting-edge US hackers had a free ride. Suzan went straight for the jugular, the chassis, the nuts and bolts of a digital substructure that was to control, like it had done in the US, about every aspect of European societies. This daily treasure trove scooped at a long distance procured the team a regular high. Suzan explained at dinnertime that it was like splashing carefree in deep sea waters.

I progressively realized that Turkish, Greek, Italian, French, English, German, Norwegian, Chinese, American and even Russian geeks and hackers respected the Lagranges; they exchanged information, covered for one another, would not have informed against the Lagranges if you threaten to strangle them at the screen. Access to the Lagrange BBS was limited and required from the webworker an initiation, the proof of some exploit. It was not only difficult to consult their BBS; you had to show "merit" before depositing your loot. That's where Kathy's legal mind comes in. She'd convinced John and Nathaniel that they had to create an elite among the core followers of the idea Nathaniel called Desistence. An elite needs itself an elite, which stands beyond the hierarchy and decides on it; she proposed to give that role to the Lagrange family, exclusively (which included, of course, Suzan). In the course of my translations I discovered how much of an honor it was to be associated with the Lagranges, and Suzan in particular, when messing with the networks. And the beauty of it was that the leading team and their guests spent a neo-bourgeois life among friends and attendants in a tranquil retreat above Taos.

She was a master mind. I admired Suzan, and minor disappointments didn't change that; I mean, there were glitches. Suzan owed since their days in California I don't know which favor to the system administrator of an important porn site. She told me that she had needed a sudden influx of cash and had gone to extremes to get it. She gave back the sum, otherwise she wouldn't be doing so well, but she didn't pay back and with interest fast enough. Whatever the case, while in L.A. Suzan had let *HighGuns* be dragged into a dispute between porn kings from the valley that tarnished her Mulholland reputation.

It so happened that one of the bosses she had to ingratiate was Joe Minski, a Jew born in France. Joe came from the *Sentier*, the Garment District of Paris. He was born rue Saint Denis, the long and narrow, meandering old street not far from where I was born myself. We are talking about the busy center of *prêt-à-porter* boutiques and peep-shows during the day, and open prostitution at night, except Sundays. When I was a kid, before the computer age, populations of men came to the see the girls like you go with your grandpa to an amusement park. On rue Saint Denis now, no longer do whores beat the pavement nor do they line up the entryways of buildings, hustling passers-by with their whips. They stay undressed in their rooms and you meet them through the screen on your cell phone. It's more "private," cleaner and safer that way, arguably.

On behalf of *HighGuns*, I agreed to meet the French Jew owner of an important porn site. Physiologically speaking, Joe Minski could have been my uncle, a cousin. About five years my senior, he had the dark complexion, hairy constitution that I have; about-to get-fat, he was still handsome, less of a stud and more of a lion. The big difference, however, he had struck gold earlier than I, and something even told me he was born in money. Whether you considered me a professor or a thief, I felt next to him that I would always remain a secondary character, a petty entrepreneur, one timid animal eating at the hand of my master. He patronized me gently. Though, except for his dazzling success and the fascination he saw in my eyes, I couldn't pinpoint his condescension. He was extremely courteous; pushed aside the cables and the magazines, and received me without ostentation in the very house full of thick carpet and mirrors, long ruby red sofas and king size beds, movable walls, powerful lights and consoles where his porn stuff was made. It reminded me that in my family you had to push aside fabrics and boxes of buttons to make room for plates, salad and the chicken. His manners were telling me "just business, my dear." I imagined that more than willing asses, explosive bosoms and dripping slits had been exposed an hour earlier on the sofa where we were to talk.

First, we had Pastis with a variety of figs and nuts, endives subtly caramelized by his Martiniquais chef and paté, then *ragoût de mouton* followed by a copious *plateau de fromages*. He cared to show me his education by inviting me into his basement designed like a medieval cave to protect *Margaux* and *Pouilly Fuissé* from the California heat.

Outside, on the terrace, it was the same dry and breezy heat as in Nice, where my grand-mother had had an apartment with a large terrace and the same Mediterranean vegetation. I briefly mentioned that paradisiacal childhood of mine (without explaining how short-lived), and it turned out that we could have bumped into each other at the beginning of our French lives; we could have met on the Riviera in 1960 when he was a boy of ten and me five.

We exchanged a lot of impressions. The condescension I felt earlier disappeared and we had a good time reminiscing, smoking cigars and drinking cognac. We could have been in

France. Joe and I could have been family. As a matter of fact, our fathers seem to have been cut in the same cloth; same kind of fatherless men drifting through our lives. Both our fathers were sons of deportees who'd vanished in the Holocaust; both were sons of scrupulous and hard-working Jewish men given by the French to the Germans; both our fathers had turned out to be players, womanizers, men cynical about belief and skeptical of rule, law, nation, family included. Joe's father was a skilled and talented designer of men's clothes doing unscrupulous transactions on the fringe—my father did the same while he worked at the sawing machine producing women's outfits. Uncannily similar; except that his father had done it on a much bigger scale, employing factories, then settling the family in America to avoid disaster and never going bankrupt.

He was forty-nine and I was forty-four, and we were in his splendid house overlooking Santa Monica. You understand that I make up his name. Using the Yiddish word for scandal, he said that the whole *gratschke* with Suzan had been forgotten, erased out of his hard drive five minutes after I introduced myself.

"Amazing how in the fickle age of computers," he reflected, "it's become difficult to erase, to really erase something so that no one reads it over your shoulder, whether you're alive or in your grave."

"We cannot erase that there was erasure, I am told, it's built-in; it's like a safety net. Once part of the Webwork nothing escapes the Webwork." There had been intense discussions on the site about this.

He said in a voice full of overtone and looking nostalgically in the distance: "I wonder what is worse in the end, to remember or to forget? What pleasure, what chance it was, what freedom, to be able to forget, and to have to make an effort to remember! But, Etienne, I am struck by your: 'we cannot erase the erasure'? Sounds like something someone said at the Sorbonne last century."

This porn king had *also* gone to the Sorbonne in his prime time. He'd also read Heidegger and plumbed, in the middle of *Sein und Zeit*, the Log on anxiety—fundamental-feeling-about-being, as the philosopher puts it. All this before turning to more mundane considerations and remembering the kind of philanderer his father had been. Then Joe Minski took things by the horns. The best way to proceed.

"The image that comes to mind," I finally said, "is that of the SS organization, which not only eliminated Jews for the reasons made plain in the propaganda, but kept their actual elimination a secret, making sure the dust didn't settle in the gas chamber, so to speak. The squads of Jews assigned to the gas chambers were the first to be sent to the gas chambers. The executioner disappeared with the victim, erasing the evidence of genocide to the point that we cannot prove it happened other than by hearsay and mountains of shoes, circumstantial evidence. Hundred carcasses and corpses, not millions. The perfect crime is the one that never occurred."

He looked at me half-mockingly. "Sounds like what your colleague Nathaniel Lagrange tells his audience every morning."

Even the porn industry heard Nathaniel. I admitted to be, not only of service to Suzan and *HighGuns*, but an old friend of Nathaniel's. I didn't say that this kind of reflection came from me, who had taught Nathaniel Lagrange, my most gifted student. It would have sounded deliriously pretentious. In any case, the man assured me with a resounding tap on the shoulder that we should expect no more tug-of-war between him and *HighGuns*. The tomahawk was buried.

The more he assured me of this, actually, the less it reassured me. My having to travel to L.A. as a special emissary only confirmed his power over Suzan. We continued eating delicious sorbets, truffles and chocolates, and had a good time joking about how we could have had a youth together as cousins or even brothers. We could have met in France long ago and, who knows, we probably did but unawares. He found that amazing, like we were family. Meanwhile he was as perfectly aware as I was that we could not have met in France and be friends, even less family. If we had been playing soccer on the same beach at the same hour and in the same team we would not have met because of the difference of age, and because his father, as I have said, operated on a grander scale. Mine was not able to maintain the family on the Riviera for long. He sold grandma's apartment, the one with the terrace, when she passed away. We had never belonged to the same crowd, Joe Minski and I—until now.

Log 24

Should I continue to be surprised that, so far, the police have not pursued me, not even asked me to explain the bank account *HighGuns* opened under my name? I should be called back to New York and, if not arrested, at least interrogated. Instead of which I am let completely free to operate in Paris and sell my services to the best offer, including to the local police. Let us leave aside the many chores I did for the organization and my interventions on the site. I was not responsible for the content of my written translations or the phone interpretations I gave during conference calls Suzan weaved between Taos, New York and wherever the francophone client was. But it was clear to me and to Jacques that, with our help or without, Suzan was blackmailing blue-chip corporations in the crudest manner, letting them know that she'd *code exploit*, sell to others the vulnerability encountered in their backyard; and if they resisted, would marshal "zombie armies" and launch choking spam attacks.

Still; however hairy and scabrous the terms of the deal, I did not think it was illegal to translate it for *HighGuns.* Nothing criminal either in traveling to defend Suzan against the porn industry, itself perfectly legal. Neither Jacques nor Nathaniel seemed worried; why should I? Nobody worried because the idea now was that we couldn't lose: the more she garnered praises from her peers and her rivals—the more she worried system administrators and security officers around the country—the easier it would be for Suzan to turn over the operation and sell "us" to the best offer. One day, sooner than later, the site would be bought by the cleanest, greenest, coolest corporation. There would only remain the constant buzz of bees around the BBS of the Lagranges and the variations on Desistence coming out of Nathaniel's *corridors*. That's right, our website and all of us might soon be sold to the best offer: in keeping with the spirit of the first dotcom startups, Suzan made sure that from the receptionist, the gardener and the horseman, to John, Nathaniel, herself, Kathy, me or Jacques, everyone working for *HighGuns* in some capacity shared in the benefits, not equally perhaps, but generously. One heard no complaint about salary inside the compound. One shared *HighGuns'* destiny like the founding crew did at Yahoo and would soon do at Snapshat.

There was only one black spot in the picture, and it originated in Nathaniel's unexpected success, the assumption, the elevation of his person in the virtual. As we talked to him and heard him and saw him blabber on the Webwork, we wondered (I am strictly talking now about Jacques and I) what his dark teachings spawned in the heads of his phalanges of teens, the timid and tormented geeks he had under his sway in his corridors. Did they understand that his poetic references to Self-annihilation were to be taken with a grain of salt— as poetic metaphors?

Did I *really* want to share his fame? I wondered. Did I care to be *on top*? The next in line to be sacrificed to the whims of the crowd. Let *him* take the heat and let us see what comes.

What did Suzan think of the virulence in her associate's pamphleteering style? The self-sacrificing talk, was it good for business? It certainly was, so far.

Let me tell you, it was great to make money. No matter how she esteemed my repartee and respected me for having gone through the Ph. D. in America and the tenure and all that, nothing helped Gabriela feel that she had married the right guy like the fact that I *also* made from time to time unexpected money. I was not just one more innocuous intellectual and obscure academic. To make more money than the average is enough for you never to be reminded by anyone of your deficiencies or criticized for your flaws. Oddity, nastiness, gratuitous wrongdoings are more easily condoned in the rich man who, anyway, does not care; he has all the security he needs to close the door on you.

It was great to have two lives. Not that I continued to hid from my taxes all the money I made at *HighGuns*; an accountant had advised me against taking that route. I declared some and remained on a low bracket by sheltering more in IRA's and investing much more in a condo apartment. I made no mention at work of my lucrative adventures in a Far Western ranch. My university files don't contain one single mention of the name *HighGuns*. Why should I tell them? Acting deans and union members could only get confused by what I was doing for Suzan. Colleagues would be envious and find ways to make me regret my success. Most academics in public university feel like utter failures. You cannot teach remedial skills all your life; and I am not excluding graduate schools from this category. Each semester it breaks your heart to see the rare gem of a student graduate rapidly and the multitudes linger after they've outspent federal, State and city financial help. My colleagues imposed a moral grid onto others, more fortunate. In general, if intellectuals criticize the money-making machine and lament the devastation wrought on humanity by an unfair economic system gone wild, it's mostly because they have been excluded from the deal. Who among them does not dream of social ascension propelled by their demonstrations on what is wrong, what it is correct to think and what it is important to know? Maybe I was not meant to be an intellectual any more than Nathaniel was to write books. You imagine you're *this* and you work all your life for it, but you're good at something else. I had failed as an academic. I had also failed as a writer, had no story to tell, even though the number of my attempts at sci-fi novels and whatnot was impressive. I was not meant to create fiction, no. I was meant to be some kind of small businessman taking care of the material future of his family before it was too late.

Here is a feeling many Americans shared after 9/11, and it only got worse 2000 decennia progressed: finished the bonanza, adieu careless freedom and even relative comfort; long gone is the opulence of the Reagan years, including Bush father's indolence. Way behind us are the optimism of the 90's and the Clinton boom. Now, to access middle-class and stay in it, one has to cut corners. People who make big money cut bigger corners, and they have the means to cover their tracks.

My father had been a failure as a businessman in France. Perhaps I was meant to redress that on a larger scale. One finds personal success justified and I was comforted in this train of thought when speaking to Jacques, who was also flying high and thinking uncharacteristically optimistic thoughts. When returning to New York and our regular jobs, we would keep in touch and meet downtown in the jazz clubs and restaurants he patronized. Jacques no longer occupied with his big boys a minuscule studio on Leroy Street. He lived in a three-bedroom apartment overlooking Washington Square Park.

Jacques believed that making money out of hacking was fair game when it targeted men who made billions. Jacques also believed that Suzan could get caught if and when the police set their mind on her. No matter how difficult to get the system administrators she defrauded to press charges against her, "when the police are after you," Jacques said while rasping the table, "they pester you until they get their way. The police could blackmail the system administrators worse than her."

I believed what he said in this respect; being born American, he had more experience. "But then," he added, "there is the wild card of what Nathaniel might do with his zombies... his phalanges. What would a sort of hunger strike by some of the leading computer experts do to frighten the people who are in charge? I'm starting to wonder whether the police would not have to negotiate with the Lagranges, no matter what they have on them."

I agreed. Thanks to Nathaniel's *Fragments* even more than to Suzan's reputation as a hacker, *HighGuns'* notoriety on the Webwork was getting too big to fail, it had an aura of immunity.

It's then, however, that came the first warning that Suzan was pushing it too far. Fortunately for her, it was not her fault. It started with the best of intention, that of getting involved in the immigrant issue, so volatile and tearing people apart in the country. She made a good deal by buying for dirt cheap a several thousand acres *terreno* on the Mexican side of the border. She foresaw that tension would inevitably arise around the new thousand-mile long wall the last Republican congress had erected; and that, being there (albeit through proxy), we would have a foot right in the navel of chaos. To own a piece of the mess is a good start when you are in business nowadays. She could become mediator, at least make sure that the migrants were properly arrested by documenting signs of coercion, overuse of force. This last touch would varnish *HighGuns* image, always at risk of being tarnished by the last rumor.

For *HighGuns,* it turned out, owning the land and filming hundreds of illicit penetrations in US territory procured many benefits. It brought a cornucopia of advantages: playing the furious debate over immigration, the team sold images and video clips that comforted any side; that could be edited to fit any style, genre, form: from comic evasion to spooky retreat, tragic deportation and deadly gun fights; images that could be made to satisfy hardened protectionists as well as procure graphic ammunition against the Republicans and warm tears to liberals. Problem though, no one among us felt like going to the *terreno* and see with his own eyes what *HighGuns* had bought. A landlord must at least take a peek at his property.

Suzan had premonitions. "And what if it's covered with rats, rodents, all kinds of coyotes, hyenas... and wild dogs?" She grimaced in revulsion.

"How about snakes?" John answered calmly.

"I can live with snakes," she replied. "What I can't live with? I don't know. Smugglers and corrupt officials... snitches and betrayers making dirty money on our back..."

"There are probably a few of those; it's a big land you've bought, darling."

We laughed.

According to our information, there were smugglers and passers crossing our immense *terreno* while corrupt American officials took a siesta. And she could live with that, and when necessary assist the security apparatus in Texas or Mexico from afar. In fact, the border patrol, the helicopters, the armada of 4 by 4's, the teams of zealous agents making sure 24 hours a day that both sides of the wall were under control and relatively peaceful, all that was paid by public money. *HighGuns* had bought a *terreno* in a hot zone of human traffic, and in the bargain, received safety and security for free. Basic business conditions were provided by the US government.

On our laptops we could focus on and witness current evasions (or failed evasion) about to happen. John had had locals conceal miniature equipment: projectors in the bush, minuscule cameras on the wall. If his computer detected an escalation and concluded that occurrences out there could turn into drama—whether in the comic or tragic category didn't matter—from where he stood, John might procure a low, shallow or deep lighting to the scene, choose to focus on one immigrant, his family; or on the contrary, take ensemble shots, sky, wall and earth; and have the pack of migrants appear as a whole. Then, Kathy and her team would add colors, flashes and smog. They might decide to capture more of the sound, the human expressions and feelings during the climbing proper.

Our association with what was going on in that sorrowful part of the world was shameful; and Suzan, the Lagranges and their friends didn't exchange opinions about its profitability. But after a couple of years it almost felt natural and good for us to own the *terreno*. That way we kept our finger on the pulse of that psychotic patient named America; and we exposed daily, in real time, on our site the misery that the stupid and barbaric wall produced. Suzan would not have hoped for it, but if ever *HighGuns* had to retreat, "disappear" and immigrate out of America, the safest place would be that desolate, hot, dirty and dusty *terreno* stretching far into the Mexican side.

But then, some awful thing happened, a police helicopter crashed on the shack where fifty migrants were hiding in the hope of jumping the wall early the next day during the hour of lax patrolling between shifts. Two American pilots died, engulfed by the smoke coming out of the sordid shack. At the end, twenty-five bodies lay dead, the rest was burnt to various degrees or partially crushed, and all that was documented second by second. Since it was on the Mexican side, we witnessed how slow an administration can be when it doesn't intend to act. Already furious at American operations routinely taking place inside Mexican territories, the Mexican authorities claimed that the helicopter had played a dirty trick by brushing past the shack repeatedly, even pushing down on the flimsy roof, so as to freak the migrants out of the place and trap them. It was reckless behavior on the part of officials. The American side denied any wrongdoing and blamed the Mexican side for allowing dangerous points of penetration to proliferate. It's on tape: the helicopter was the target of repeated shots from machine guns and automatic rifles shooting from within the shack.

The *terreno* that night was turned into a raging battle field, and the results were awful to watch. This threatened to suppurate like an open wound on the flank of *HighGuns*, the owner of the place, shack included. What role had the company *HighGuns* played? The Lagranges were responsible for the torrid shack? Bloggers were already chipping away at the foundation of our reputation like termites.

We heard that lawyers and politicians from *San Antonio* were taking a humanitarian convoy to visit the desolate *terreno*, which was really out there, only accessible by long-winded dirt roads. Suzan decided to get the most expensive jet service. "Just to defend our name," she said. "If there is still something to defend."

John was against her going, they were too busy to waste precious time. "But someone has to go," she insisted. She assured him she'd hire the best security escort there was, and she'd bring one member of the team, someone who'd speak Spanish. Nobody offered to volunteer among the inner circle. Everyone was much too busy and didn't speak Spanish. She sent me an e-mail praising my Spanish (I do sometimes speak Spanish with my wife and Christmas we go to Peru, her native country, but I am nowhere close to fluent); Suzan was arguing that we were in mid-June, vacation time among academics. She used a little pressure and a little flattery: "We all know it's a hellhole; but we'll be safe, don't worry. I need someone smart at my side, just to hear my own thinking. We'll move under heavy security at all times; now, can you take it?" Her voice was soft but firm, she needed a friend at this delicate juncture. I couldn't deny her a serious service, and my family trip to France was only at the end of the month. I was thrilled to help her out of a difficult situation.

The only aspect that bothered me was that I had to use a white lie when selling the trip to my wife and my five-year old little girl. I said *matter-of-fact* that my employer in person was assessing the state of affairs in the *terreno* and had asked me to serve as translator; it would take a short week of hard work and I would be well paid. Of course, Isabel was not told about the disaster at the *terreno*. Gabriela understood that the business I worked for was in trouble. It was not so much Spanish that was required as cunning and a ruthless ability to get the upper hand during negotiations. She had noticed this in me and complained about it. My assurances regarding the security and the comfort assuaged her; and she was flattered that Suzan had chosen her husband.

But Gabriela had seen on clips that black wall barring the horizon; she'd noticed how dirty and eerily silent the dusty and shrubby *terreno*, strewn with remnants of luggage, garment, food, toys—as though a crowd had just left in a hurry, run for their lives. When she surfed into close-ups, she had probably felt disgusted by the huge and inform mass of brown and black muck. A spider web of chords and abandoned equipment covered it. And closer, you wondered what covered it, besides saliva, sweat and tears.

Gabriela was aware of the unfortunate "accident" which was for a day or two on all the news-page portals; but she was not aware of *HighGuns* selling 10 images of arrests and aborted evasions for 1 successful penetration; 100 clips where desperate people were in tears for 10 where they smiled and laughed, and cried of joy at meeting their brethren in a welcoming America. How would it all sound to my wife, if she had known, she who, like me, naturally espoused 100% the cause of the migrants? Perverse on our part to profit from such things, yes it was, no doubt. And I say "us" here because I flew to Mexico in first class and in the charming company of Suzan, visiting before departure and after arrival luxurious boutiques, spas and travelers' clubs without a scruple in my head and in perfect glee. There was a sore spot in the picture, though cries of guilt and the soliloquies of remorse didn't change the enticing quality of the situation.

We came out of the 4 by 4 and into the Martian heat and slowly walked into the compound, where we found our cool, wired and fully equipped lodgings in one entirely wood-paneled truck-container. Locked in there like in a safe, we immediately fell asleep each in his makeshift bedroom. We were merely separated by a flimsy latch; but I don't recall awkwardness between us. The next day we worked hard making it clear to the local governments, the international mafia and the owners of the *terrenos* next to ours, that we had nothing to do with the catastrophe, nothing at all. It was not an easy sell.

We offered our help to the victims of the incident, making sure they received adequate care. We provided them with food and medicine while they remained in their emergency tents, which we'd paid for. We assisted the Red Cross, channeled Amnesty International's questions to the administrations of both the US and Mexico. The operation cost *HighGuns* hundreds of thousands of dollars. Suzan created *LosDelTerrenoPerdido.com*, a site where *almas perdidas* from the border states could get information and support. Entire populations lived now in the shadow of the wall: those who couldn't climb; those who could climb but not climb off and were unable to make it free on the other side, yet couldn't go back to where they had come from since they had left nothing.

"I know you're troubled, Etienne, by all this," she said as we walked knee-deep in the swept-up dust. Half a minute out of the helicopter and you felt dirty, sweaty. The wind was too thick, unnaturally warm, the sun raw and ferocious. I had seen majestic deserts in California; this Mexican desert felt intentionally nasty, like a cruel and anonymous being flinging flat on your face greasy fast-food wrappings, slapping half empty cans of beer against your tibias, which in turn poured rancid and warm liquid down your socks.

"I am not going to bullshit you and justify myself for having dragged us into this."

I liked her use of 'us,' my being part of her inner circle.

"I am not responsible for the fact that business and morality are tangential functions that never quite intersect or meet, and if they do, only in theory, *ad infinitum*, in the best of worlds. This is not the best of worlds!"

I could only agree, and admire how she took me on my turf and easily obtained adhesion. Suzan the seductress. She knew she was still a beautiful woman at fifty-five and sexually active. Though we each were devoted to another person, until the end of the trip I thought—and I sensed that she entertained the idea as well—we might have sex after the champagne of success one night, the last night, on the way back. I never thought that we would henceforth start a secret affair and share an intimacy. We would do it for relaxation, for sport, to relieve ourselves from the sweat and the tears.

We never did, for once it was clear that we were out of that shit-hole of the *terreno* we were both too traumatized for sex. We cared for contact, plain human contact. She had me massage her neck and her back and her buttocks after we smoked Mexican pot. Her skin was pliable and finely wrinkled, yet tau; not an ounce of fat between skin and bone, delineated muscles. Soon, though, she'd have protruding bones, and the skin of her jaw might sag a little, enhancing her skinniness. *Carpe diem*, said the repressed libertine in me, you've been married for too long; but respect and admiration forbade me to desire her in the flesh. Massaging her fine body didn't result in a hard-on, not one that I couldn't conceal; and, of course, she noticed my disinclination. Better that way.

I don't know what we accomplished in remote Texas and beyond the frontier, Suzan and I. We merely added to the scandal: our efficiency, arrogance and luxury in the surrounding squalor were criticized by the Mexicans. American authorities not only looked down on us but added a mixture of envy, mockery and downright suspicion. They believed we were in cahoots with the passers and planned the sequences of our videos together; and they didn't appreciate that our products proved un-taxable in the US and exempt of charge on the Mexican side.

Did the incident alienate part of *HighGuns* clientèle on the Webwork? Maybe; dirty hands are good for business as long as you're not too obviously implicated. And at the same time, the faithful, our team and Nathaniel's following witnessed how Suzan channeled all the positive energies she could resuscitate from the worst of disaster. They saw her contrition; they watched her visits to the children who had lost one or two parents in the shack—clean, well-behaved Latino kids looking happy at the time of recording, well attended in plush clinics on this side of the border. No one really cared about the crushed migrant population, they had what they deserved since they tried to sneak in the US illegally. For a brief period, the whole thing was a way for pundits, lawyers and a mottle array of officials to advance their conflicting agendas. And I forget our enemies and competitors, the many critics of Nathaniel's *Fragments*, who were on a field trip, collecting the visual proves of *HighGuns* degradation. The only net result was that Suzan remained thankful to me; she could count on me, we had been very close in hard times.

She sold the *terreno* losing money and paid several individuals to disentangle our name.

Log 25

Suzan abandoned the project of generating photos from the source, which doesn't mean that she gave less thought to intriguing and pricy videos or less work to Jacques. More commissioned than me, he was the first to return to the compound after Suzan's decision to move the operation to Connecticut; and there, to settle the team not in a breathtaking situation, but in a nondescript tower in a boring and businesslike section of crummy downtown Hartford. In his usual way, Jacques said: "I guess it's like everything else that's too cool, must be taken apart and brought back to reality, which is commonplace. A way for Suzan to tell us, 'what did you think? We're no exception; we're just business people.'"

"She wants to fade into the crowd," I said. "*HighGuns* is too much in the public eye. There is more than one reason why Suzan does something."

"I know, you're in love with her, she can't go wrong!" he laughed. I blushed while answering: "Business is getting tough and the team has to buckle up. The Webwork is no longer a joyride; like everything else, tightening up."

"Yeah!" Jacques confessed, repressing a smile and turning pale. It's then he broke the news he had probably no intention of imparting to me just yet. "My last ride was not so smooth. I had better stay home, in fact." He revealed to me that for the first time it was his turn not to know what to think of a sorry deal now engulfing *HighGuns*. There were always sorry deals, the inevitable shadow of business: insolvent clients, evanescent solicitors not paying for the product so painstakingly wrested by the team and timely delivered; other hackers extorting concessions and fees out of Suzan upon discovering where she had been before sweet-talking an administrator. She was not the only shark, and not always the fastest on the Webwork. There were elite Russians and Bulgarian hackers she had to lift her hat and bend the knee to. Shit happens, as they say. But this time, Jacques was in a state of shock: Suzan had had to pay through the nose a black hat hacker who had first bought access codes from her, pretending to represent I don't know which legitimate business, and then used these codes to satisfy what had been, unbeknownst to her, vengeful intentions. No one in Suzan's team had paid much attention to the fact that the codes secured access to the computers in charge of dams and electrical plants, but also of prisons. She didn't care much about the content of her *exploit*; and she had interest, when the information appeared sensitive, in selling it fast and cleaning her hands of it. The hacker, a Russian just freed from prison, wreaked havoc in a prison upstate New York: not only were the guards and their officers locked in their offices for 12 hours, their TV and computer screens frozen; not only were the prison doors hermetically closed to outsiders, and the inmates free to roam inside the facilities and the open yards the way they pleased, drinking, smoking pot, snorting, shooting up, showing off, dancing, swearing, denuding and caressing in front of the cameras suspended to airplanes and helicopters and in the corners of their cells; bad enough were the photos going around the country, which I had glimpsed at from the corner of my eye that day, while reading at breakfast an article on the third page of the *New York Times*—still in the dark, thinking, the world is getting worse, business as usual… Jacques summed up his account: "The Russian is now going undetected both in real life and on the Webwork, and he threatens to send the police and the media a message associating the Lagranges to the mayhem."

This news freaked me out. Though less bloody (no one was hurt, actually) the prison rampage was worse than the accident at the *terreno*. I could lose my career over monetary association with this scandal. For a moment, Jacques was of a mind to quit *HighGuns*. "Forget the money, this is bad. Prisons, you don't mess with that."

Notwithstanding the fear that permeated me, I was in favor of giving Suzan the benefit of the doubt one more time. After all, she had done nothing bad herself—except stealing codes to prisons' doors and selling them to the wrong guy.

Jacques was rapidly swayed by my arguments. The truth is, we both loved mayhem. Nobody had died in the prison incident; the videos were truculent, outrageous, ferociously funny. They allowed a rare look at a negative universe in normal times safely concealed. She had trusted the wrong guy, that's bound to happen on the shadowy side of the anonymous Webwork. In all likelihood, she would pay off the bastard and move on like she had done countless times before.

Neither Jacques nor I needed much of an incentive to return to *HighGuns*, which now dwelled so close to New York. It's not only for the money, let's be clear, we were eager to witness what was going on, how they managed. Were they afraid? We felt solidarity in this taxing moment. If it were not for his family, Jacques would have stayed in downtown Hartford all week. We waited for Friday evening and took the commuter north.

Nondescript tower, gray office floor compartmented in dozens of empty cubicles where, a few years back an army of busy secretaries must have chatted and done their nails in front of the lulling screens; that was when Hartford was booming. The cubicles were eerily silent, though well-furnished and fully equipped for business. Desolation and dust accumulated under the low-ceilinged room; and yet, in one corner of the wrap-around window, the team had managed to push away the deadening brown-felted partitions and install a high-tech conference room anchored by a massive acajou table like for a board of directors.

The team is sullen, sunken into the purple sofa big as a Buick. Jacques and I pick our seats among an array of poufs, adjustable chairs, swivel chairs, reclining chairs, director-chairs set in front of the thick pane of glass which, I notice, has been cleaned just there. There are only other grey towers of glass and metal to look at; but the part "we" occupy is top-notch and gives the feeling of being suspended in the air.

John, Suzan, Kathy and Nathaniel are moping around and nursing their laptops. No hello. Coffee, hot chocolate and croissants circulate on a rolling tray, pushed by a muchacha. It's better not to say much; we play it cool and don't share our fears. There is nothing to gain in blaming anyone. We share the risk.

We have a fine dinner in the best restaurant of Hartford. Nathaniel is kind of hysterical, confiscating the audio foreground like he used to, in the old days. But this time speaking about details of his inexistent personal life that can't interest anyone. It's a smokescreen, I realize. He plays the idiot like Hamlet played the madman, while he is not sure yet how to act against his enemies. Later, in confidence to Jacques and me, he tells us how mad he is at Suzan; frustrated to the point that he is thinking of splitting with John and Kathy. He doesn't need Suzan to develop his practical philosophy on the Webwork. "On the contrary, it's people like her," he says between his teeth, "who are dragging the whole hacking enterprise into the mud and, of course, you know why, because they are greedy and careless. And you also know who gets their face, their names smudged in the process, only the family Lagrange, not her." A little later, he dismissively gestures towards the cubicles and adds "If it's to end like this, better go our separate ways, don't you think? I opt for New York, a small studio overlooking a leafy park will do for me."

He smiles maliciously at us, knowing full well that to Jacques and I, this mention of a return brings uncanny memories.

Nathaniel expands, he has lost nothing of his verve; he wants to cut lose, go from here and save what can be saved, "The principle of open source; that is, the widening the circle of people having access to information and collective organization: the know-how to appropriate the electronic devices that circle you and make them serve your ends, not that of administrations and corporations; the freedom of communicating what the hell flashes in your head—and people listening and answering what the hell pops up in theirs; and this, wherever they stand and whatever they stand for. It's as simple as that."

His speech was ready, main points scribbled on a piece of paper; recorded, it could later be posted *tel quel* or augmented. He rarely edited anything out, revised and corrected what came out of his mouth, preferring to keep the raw, inspired but also incomplete and desultory aspects of his thoughts, a choice which delighted his following.

"Oh! And I forgot to mention" he added abruptly and his voice going into a crescendo: "hacking is not about making money and not caring for the content of what you hack; quite the opposite, it's about knowledge, it's about acquiring the forbidden knowledge of the infrastructure that circles us so as to remain vigilant, conscious of what is happening. Even the rich who think they own the copyrights, patents and secrets of technology, own nothing in the end; it's technology that owns them. Technology and science that pile on themselves and ask for their money; but not their curiosity or even their interest. Our interest in hacking is noble and metaphysically engaged, and above all, stems from curiosity. I would say it's no less than a question of saving our souls, and in the process, Desistence, which cannot be about highwaymen of the digital age taking people hostages and asking for ransom. The désistant tries to make sure the digital tapestry on which his feet rest remains in the hands of every man. We want to know what is happening to us. So, you see, there is a fundamental difference here…"

His hesitation makes us feel uncomfortable; Jacques and I, we know against whom the tirade is directed. Even in the intimacy of his chambers, Nathaniel cannot name Suzan. His speech gives a sharp turn to his ideas; but it is clear that he is not ready to split in person.

Kathy and John are not ready either. Maybe they run the boutique, and the BBS, and the hierarchy of désistants who buzz silently around it night and day; but Suzan is the mind behind *HighGuns*. She *owns* the business, she has put it together and not only financially. Suzan is the elite, she is our samurai. To nobody else than Nathaniel, certainly not to Jacques and I, does it occur they could take over and kick Suzan out without paying a dear price.

The atmosphere in Connecticut is charged with almost catastrophic animosity; besides the Russian hacker, something has happened. Later, I notice that Suzan is well aware of Nathaniel's intentions. "Whoever is unhappy with the way things work at *HighGuns* may leave," she says loudly after a few drinks at the dinner table. From Suzan's standpoint, nobody is irreplaceable.

It cannot be the risk posed by one hacker that altered Nathaniel's discreet adoration of Suzan. Does he realize for the first time that he has been following her like a pet? Is he suddenly tired of playing the madcap at a kingless court? Or is he taking the measure that he is well on his way to becoming a famous man; his virtual following is growing on pace with the disorders and confusions of this world; and he is sharpening his message; Nathaniel should no longer depend on anyone. His thought should sustain itself, so to speak. Without brother and sister Lagrange, though, he wouldn't know where to start—how to create his dissident website, how to run their famed BBS strictly for the purpose of Desistence, even less make pocket money out of subscriptions. He'd be a bum, back at mother's, perhaps. In a way, my friend Nathaniel had not changed the old dependence; he still needed someone to hand him the framework.

In spite of the tension and the immediate cause for alarm, when we are the three Lagrange, Suzan, Jacques and I together in one room, it feels like we have never been so together. We want to close ranks and ready our resistance against the growing number of our enemies, the call of destiny. We drink and joke; and back at their fancy hotel, we smoke and dance to Latin and black music. Suzan has a device able to override bugs, in case. We can talk, so John and Nathaniel and Kathy talk about the humiliating end of the Iraq War, and the many aborted plans that reached all the way up the US government to bomb the nuclear facilities in Iran. The Lagranges had insider knowledge, classified information about what went on in the Pentagon. Luckily, the atomic power of Iran was more real than the inexistent Weapons of Mass Destruction that had justified invading Iraq, so the US government hesitated blowing up a good part of the planet by bombing their bombs. The whole Middle East mess is disastrous for America and its aura of strength; its grip on business around the world has cracked like a dry coconut on religious and archaic fault lines. Religion, Nathaniel has told his following, is about sacrifice. Who will sacrifice whom, this time?

There is a whiff of sadness in the air that is hard to shake: *HighGuns* no longer dwells in its own, unique cocoon. You wake up in the king size ultra-extra bouncy bed, and the hotel room tells you: you have no more past here than you have a tomorrow, you're a transient soul. So, get ready to pack and go.

Was *HighGuns* about to dissolve in the thick atmosphere? In her conversation, Suzan suggested that the group could realign, rearrange, vaporize, change name if need be, hibernate for a while, let things cool off. All this because of one nasty Russian hacker?

But then, Suzan regained some of her luster, she was back on top and managed the black hat hacker very well. I don't understand exactly how she got the better of the Russian. She'd intercepted something about Theodore the Obscure, nom de guerre of her nemesis. She often joked about the fact that Russians had their revenge against the West on the Webwork, which they controlled as a matter of course. From medical and police records, she learned that there was a convict, a Russian man of 53, who'd just been let go of an upstate prison where he'd spent the last ten years learning how to navigate the Webwork, downloading and hacking incognito. Quite a sophisticated fellow; yet not astute enough for Suzan and the team, who finally located him, traced him down to a hotel, a shabby dive on the last decrepit block of the Lower East Side in New York. She even learned his room number. She offered Theodore to have one of her coders reveal his identity if he didn't stop in his tracks; and she added that she would call *The Daily News* if he tried anything physical on anyone related to *HighGuns*. Pure bluff on her part, but it worked. Suzan had to hide her prison connection as much as Theodore. It's the way she pitched it that was inimitable.

Theodore the Obscure vanished like a frightened ghoul out of the cyber hell that had created him. And eventually the inmates of the prison upstate returned to their phlegmatic calm. They asked to be fed, organized and taken care of just like before.

Log 26

As the *Fragments on Self-Slaughter* became more popular, Nathaniel kept adding to them, reorienting and expanding the concept of Desistence in all directions. The tide of discontent was unprecedented, especially among the young, and he was better equipped than any other Webwork thinker to surf on it.

If I had to detail what fostered this discontent I would not know where to start. Everything around them brought home to the new generations the need of a radical response. Let me go over the obvious.

Winter 2010: New York is hit by unheard-of storms. Downtown Manhattan is named by Time magazine "the American Venice". From the tip of Wall Street to above 14th Street, sea water invades basements and first floors. Jacques and his family stay in their minute studio all day long. It lasts six months. "One feels like a refugee," Jacques texts me. I sympathize but am much less affected by the flood since I live on the Upper West Side. We learn that the geological crack has reopened for good in California. There are apocalyptic landslides in many parts of the planet; slums where millions squat like insects are inexorably sliding into the mud. And they still find a way of denying it on Fox News, but the heartland of North America is all but dust and dirt, a dry and desiccated sore. People migrate elsewhere like never before; they do business from abroad and leave the US, especially if they can afford. The very rich build transparent bubbles, green, warm and welcoming mansions on the other side of the Ural, in Patagonia or at the northern tip of Alaska. The political and financial worlds are finally aware of the global climate challenge about to overwhelm them as well, and this awareness impacts on environmental policies, at least in the so-called advanced the world (in the US, only when the Democrats have a say)—but it is too late to prevent Antarctica and Greenland from melting rapidly, thereby altering the temperature of the oceans.

For six months Manhattan shrank; the skyscrapers had their feet and ankles salty wet, hairy with seaweed and gnawed at by a population of crabs. The expressway circling the island was submerged; one acceded to the Freedom Tower by dinghy. Seen from the promenade in Brooklyn, towers stuck out of the bay of New York like myriad of desolate islands do out of the Yangtze River. Crowds waited on 23rd Street to take ferries to their work or to their college; and after that an ugly plastic wall was erected around the island, capable of resisting Tsunamis. The poor Statue had no more feet; I mean, they disappeared behind the plastic.

And nonetheless, business was booming. Debris were washing up on the very steps of the stock exchange building, where stocks fell to precipitous lows at first; but then, they climbed back and reached record highs again. A flotilla of yachts was at anchor around the tip of Manhattan. As a matter of coincidence, since then, rich people get richer twice faster; thanks to lax tax laws and deregulations, they need declare less and have easier ways to shelter money. I know something about it since I started to make real money. An unscrupulous oligarchy has taken over; there is little difference between China, Russia and the United States in terms of corruption and concentration of power by an international mafia that behaves no better than European kings and queens three hundred years ago.

The *Fragments* say something to this effect: "George Orwell, our guide into the future, predicted that the world would split in three competing, warring, yet grossly similar empires each run by a Big Brother looking at you from the screen installed in your very home; it is happening."

America does no longer pretend to be a paragon of legality, morality, religiosity; it's no longer a business model: aggressive commercialization feels dated, useless, forceful. So-called third-world countries in Africa, South America and Asia bypass Washington, Berlin, Moscow and Pekin's control, and deal directly among themselves, generating independent pockets of non-global commerce.

China is not doing better. It's growing and producing and overproducing; but obsolete reliance on coal and oil, on heavy and dirty industries paralyzes Russia, China and the United States. These mammoth organisms have missed the boat. Something statistics cannot explain, there is a shift in global priorities, a different rapport to the earth appears to boost "young" countries where, to put it simply, being human is still welcome and protected. Humanity, like a sleeping giant, raises her head, it opens an eye in the deep of oceans or at the top of mountains, far away from the metropolis. Nathaniel said in a more private *corridor* where I was invited even though I do not come from the ranks of a phalange: "This earth belongs to no one in particular; your great-great-grand-father was a pioneer who killed natives before establishing *his* America. I am still of a mind to say after Proudhon that private property is a theft. Let us take back not only the earth but everything *we* ever built on it, every tradition, every mode of production, from cutting the first stone and inventing the wheel to uploading the human brain on a computer; let us respect our trajectory as a specie now swarming on this planet, pushing elbow to elbow, and given to fractures and disunity at all levels. Let us re-acquire and then enshrine all our inventions from the start. Our BBS is already terabytes-full of algorithms of the most sensitive nature. Now, more specifically, I propose we make sure we have under our belt the secrets of the Pentagon and, in particular, we *know* how secure the nukes are in their silos... These days we cannot trust the military with *our* atomic bombs, even less the politicians, can we?"

But let me keep this last theme for later.

Nathaniel is right, there are places where traditional ways—barter, sense of community, customary arts and crafts are still weaving generations into the same routine—all that has survived and is kicking, and not only for the sake of tourists. The global shift I am talking about is transforming into desirable oasis regions that had altogether missed the industrial age: poor, ex-colonized Peru or Bolivia, Jamaica, Belize and Nicaragua, Nepal, even Pakistan—nations that boast of a youthful population, educated, eager to roam the cloud and work at enormous distances, usually for little pay. These are regions whose nature offers rich pockets of bio-diversity, impenetrable jungles and formidable mountains where the air is still pure.

Once the *terreno* and Theodore were behind us, nothing changed at *HighGuns*, except for the location and the sensation of being surrounded by hostile spirits. How eager one is to fall back asleep after waking-up calls. Of course, I continued to work for Suzan, but not as much as before, and not for the same providential money. The diverse police of the Webwork were on her heels; she had to build decoys and lure agents away from Kathy and John's every move. It took a lot of mental energy and was disastrous business-wise since it required the attention of the best in our group.

I remember feeling that the Lagranges didn't quite deserve the scrutiny and potential persecution they were submitted to. Whichever "handle" John, Kathy or Suzan chose that day, they said it was like the spies were in the room. Major companies hired hackers to provide security around their sites, chat rooms, virtual worlds. How to separate who had your back from who was after you? It felt abusive to single out *HighGuns* in an age of unprecedented violence—from the endemic junior high school rampage that left dozens of kids dead in their classrooms to outright terrorist acts committed against crowds and massive symbolic structures. Now that the Iraq war had ended and that the American armies were back, it was as though the worst of right-wing predictions about being attacked-at-home-by-Islamic-fundamentalists turned out to be only mildly prophetic. Reality was more shocking: the young who blew themselves up in our skies were white, college-educated, from Christian families, American born, British, Australian, French, Italian, Danish. Informed individuals were disgusted by the status quo; informed young people horrified by what was happening to the Earth. They felt guilty for the depredations perpetrated by previous generations, took the shame on themselves, accusing their own inaction; to express their repulsion and ultimate freedom, they took the road left wide open to anyone and concocted spectacular, unique endings. At least, these young people were killing only themselves.

A few among these martyrs may have been indoctrinated by the so-called "white arm" of Al-Qaeda, but most had no affiliation; they were godless, self-chosen sacrificial lambs jumping from bridges, towers or the top of mountains. And not only young men, women also dropped the backpack and pulled their auto-destruction kit under the vast vaults of La Gare du Nord, Grand Central; or they'd fall from a cargo plane in a pack, young military women, holding hands and not opening their parachutes. One would suddenly stand up in a packed amphitheater at Cambridge, Paris-IV, Columbia, NYU or Berkeley— and with one perfectly manicured finger one would gently push one key and liquefy like a robot in a Schwarzenegger movie.

Is it because Nathaniel kept discussing Eve's extreme defiance in John Milton that an astounding creativity was now devoted to the art of dying "the shortest way"? One was not the cause of the other, I think, one went parallel to the other. Nathaniel had the pulse of his patients under his fingers. He played them like an organ. And, it turned out, the more sophisticated were aware of Nathaniel's *Fragments*; and some took his conclusions a little too seriously, as young people do. Sometimes a printed copy of the *Fragments* was found in the remains of the backpack, the jacket, the pants or the skirt that had survived.

When evidence reached Connecticut, it generated a world of anxiety, contrition and guilt among us. Nathaniel intervened on the portal of *HighGuns* to clarify his position regarding suicide.

"I understand that this is a gesture with personal and very good reasons, but blowing yourselves up in our name, Desistence does not need it and does not want it, not in my interpretation. We don't blow anything, least ourselves, unless "they" come to get us and intend to destroy our humanity. Marcus-Aurelius, the Stoic emperor, could have advocated suicide to his readers; he didn't. 'Give them your arm, if they pull on it' does not mean 'stick your neck out and distinguish yourself from the crowd by blowing your brains out.' We are descendants of Bartleby the Scrivener, Gandhi, Camus' *stranger*—our resistance is, not passive, I don't like the word—it starts *inside*, it's in each of us like our personal secret, it's a virtual resistance that turns out to be very effective; and if we threaten, it's merely to retaliate while under attack. Notice, we only threaten…"

"This leads me to point out that we are not Luddites, you know, the English weavers who wanted to break every machine, starting with the industrial weaving machines that were taking away the bread from their mouths. They wanted to stay in their villages between sheep and cows. During the nineteenth century craftsmen had to transform and could no longer weave among sheep and cows. Henceforth clothes woven by hands were good for the few wealthy customers who could afford tradition.

For centuries, millennia, there has been too much technology and not enough nature, I agree with you. By now, the bit is everywhere—on you, in you; and you, whoever you are, you want to disintegrate and rejoin the elements the shortest way—air, water, earth, fire. Make your choice. I could not forbid you the power to die, were I the leader of the most efficient and exacting system. It's understandable, and laudable, morally irreproachable, for you to want to die because technology is robbing us of the last remnant of our humanity; but we're not going to blow the digital edifice. There is no way back to some savage state of humanity. Tekné (he used the Greek word) is mercurial and resourceful; she recovers from any attempt at destroying her and kicks back with a vengeance. And she never dies. To desist is to have a say in the direction of the long strides she takes, measure her intentions and weigh in the decisions, if we can—and to kill yourself so soon, and at such an early stage of our movement, I do not see how it helps."

"We take a pause and cry at *HighGuns* each time one lost her life in our name. I do not add this to grab you by the balls, and I am sorry if I sound melodramatic. Your decision is not part of the plan of attack I am talking about every time I open my mouth now. I beg the listener of the *Fragments* to spare life in her and around her for the sake of Desistence, whatever her personal motives may be. Reach out in the movement, the phalanges, the corridors; we need all the spirits of the air, fire, earth and water to breathe life into the idea."

Put in their context, the schemed hatched by individuals like Suzan seemed minimally responsible for any wrongdoing. As for Nathaniel's incendiary speeches, they appear to come from a distinctive voice now that they are regrouped, studied and the subject of monographs; but you can well imagine that Nathaniel was not the only Webwork preacher doing well. What was unique was the movement behind him, the tight organization of the phalanges, the wealth of information swelling the Lagrange BBS. His *Fragments* attracted many, yet still only a fringe of the population of geeks; and they were lost in the brouhaha coming from "the enormous, formless, indefinite echo chamber of the Webwork," to speak like Nathaniel.

But security work is policing, it amounts to some kind of scapegoating: unable to contain the evil forces unleashed by the cyber, agents had to do their job and single out someone. Nathaniel's impromptus were protected by the First Amendment, however provocative his arguments. But the connection between odd numbers of suicides coming from unexpected places and the oracular powers of Nathaniel Lagrange was starting to alert the authorities, the pundits and a few reporters. The Lagrange family was perfect; they were known, and in a sense, established. To go after them and catch them hand in the bag would not only chill the waters; it would be a victory for the security apparatus.

Suzan called herself at one point "Georgette," "Martine Ducasse," "La Comtesse de Lautréamont" "The Grand-Mother of Dr. Frankenstein," or "Emilie45678"—she would use several e-names at once, launch contradictory queries, meanwhile encircling the security man, having her cohort bombard his computer with spy programs and large enough pockets of data to put police hardware in denial of service. The agent couldn't retaliate; she'd numbed him, at least for the time being. I say "him" but it could very well have been a woman or a group of women. Astute, scrupulous, persistent young women procured top elite hackers now, whether at the service of corporations or the secret services.

There are reasons why women were attracted to Desistence much more than their mothers had been by hacking. The Mentor, Mitnick could not have been female adolescent. In its heroic age, hacking required testosterones, the arrogance and daring of males flaunting property laws and risking their reputation as human beings. Desistence occurs in a different context; the *Fragments* develop as a series of responses that don't involve robbery, extortion or any violence, but deepen a profound, an inner rejection already widespread in the population. Young women feel even more hurt than their counterparts by a world that makes of immorality, disrespect of nature and blatant inhumanity the normal; a world that don't seem to offer them a bright future. Their mothers were the first emancipated, independent and professional women; and, already for their daughters, professions close doors, opportunities evaporate. And this time it's not because of machismo: men are left unemployed as well, and we are not talking about low-skilled workers and drop-outs; Harvard, MIT-educated men. Engineers across the fields are going jobless. Entire sections of medicine become branches of robotics, a matter of programming the robots for the task at hand. Either you're a board of directors' member, a stock holder; or, most likely, among the shadowy cohorts who clean after the machines. Fewer professors are needed, each one a star who makes a fortune addressing millions on the Webwork.

I was lucky to be at the end of my career and that, until I asked for retirement, they couldn't do without me since I was tenured. But what would happen to Isabel if I could not help? I would make sure Gabriela and Isabel had what they needed.

Anyway, Nathaniel blurbs moved a moral chord in young women who had aspirations, high standards and felt disgusted. They liked his debonair style, his knowing the subjects he talked about without being pretentious and show off about it like an academic. They liked that the man lived by what he preached. Nathaniel was not a fraud; he came with surprisingly little of an ego, and if he basked in the virtual-presence of his following, it was not that adulation pumped up his weak self-esteem. Nathaniel gave you the impression of a wounded soul, an evolved specimen of a man who inhabited a gilded retreat but had no home, no wife and no children because he breathed entirely through his ideas.

Log 27

Suzan was not able for a time to give me more hairy projects; Jacques also stayed in New York. We suspected that she felt our commitment to her cause not written in stone. We two were not like the Lagranges or the young coders, for whom *HighGuns* was a matter of life or death. Money mattered to Jacques as it did to me. If she could no longer pay, it's not the *Fragments* that would sustain our expensive lifestyles. However, when it came to what we'd understood of the unorthodox methods used by the team either to make money or to get sensitive information, we'd be the last ones to go about telling. She could let us go, and have us back whenever she changed her mind. We wouldn't wander far, she knew that.

Reasons to go to Hartford dwindled, and we felt actually relieved to have to part like this, quietly, semi-officially, without being fired, without confrontation, before nasty words flew between us. It left open the return. I have no merit having phased out of Suzan's sphere of influence then; she had to trim.

We didn't need to show our face in Hartford to absorb the last trend at *HighGuns*.

There is an interesting sequence where Nathaniel wonder about *Nettwork*, the movie by Sidney Lumet, and he asks what it would look like in the computer age. The anchorman of a national TV network has a nervous breakdown while on the air. His show is cut and the delirious anchorman is fired. But, that same night, a new breed of executive (acted by Faye Dunaway) wakes up and realizes that the crazy man is perfect for TV. He should have his nervous breakdown on the air every day at 7:30 pm. He should shout "I'm fed up! I'm mad!" and fall, apoplectic, on the set all week long. "We want, they want, everybody wants someone who's that real," she argues in front of the old guard, the media executives who hesitate showing a raving maniac live on national TV and at dinnertime. Naturally, Faye Dunaway wins. The concept of reality TV is born, 1975. Nathaniel says: "What should be our rallying cry today that we face another machine, much more alluring? Should we switch off our computers and go for a walk? What if millions did it? Let us bring this down to thousands of experts and professionals around the world. What if they were to put their computer in a lull at the same time and not even go for a walk, stay there and look at what's happening on their screen? Nothing illegal. A moment of digital indifference in the middle of the afternoon; no crash and no blood. They could still be reached on their BlackBerries and sent emergency messages."

"At which point should *our* armies back off and not even stand up from their cushioned seat but, without leaving the screen, look into the distance, shout in unison like the madman and his public down the street: 'I'm fed up! I'm mad! Let me out of here!'? But, wait a minute, maybe they shouldn't even shout their outrage, *our* experts of today; they should say nothing and give no explanation to their sleeping at the wheel, which in reality is another level of vigilance. They should open their windows, breathe the stale air their street affords, and without a word, close the window and go back to their screen, there to amass a treasure-trove of information in case Desistence needs it. You see, Desistence is not about making money out of incompetent network administrators; it's about practical knowledge of the digital fabric ensnaring us without and within. We're not divulging secrets of state like Assange and Edward Snowden in the futile hope of gaining more transparency; we don't want to undermine mega corporations like Anonymous does. Why? Because we prefer capitalism to follow its deadly course. We don't believe in the good of revolution; we believe in the kind of togetherness that many can experience in the solitude of their chambers when they share a plan of attack. This is the moment when we are one beyond fragmentation; we share the same plan of attack. Desistence is not a passive resistance as some smart guys want it; on the contrary, it's active Desistence, absence at the job they pay you for, but active absence, tacit understanding and presence to one another through vast distances; attack, penetration, yes, but one that does not hurt anyone while it brings joy to some, one that leaves everything in place and turns what we witness on the Webwork to our end."

We had seen the movie at the ranch when we were all happily together and it had impressed me. Nathaniel resume his commentary from the start.

"In major cities people switch off their TV and shout in the night: 'I'm fed up, let me out of here!' They denounce everything and nothing in particular; for a moment, they shut down the bombardment from the tube and tap into an immense pool of anger and frustration, and we are only in the 1970's. They realize how little they normally speak to each other; how *mediatisés* they have become. 'There is a moment in each day that Satan cannot find.' No economy can tolerate moments like that, without mediation and organization, moments of pure human noise, refusal, revolt, raw abhorrence, and for no specific motive. Faye Dunaway is playing with fire by putting the madman on the air. He's calling off the universal bluff, telling the audience how his own madness is fattening the wallets of the board members; he is very lucid for a madman; and the media moguls are not duped, they are nervous in spite of ratings shooting through the roof; they convoke him; they like his foolhardiness, sure, but would prefer to not be the target. He could leave the board aside and let his delirium roam elsewhere."

"Let's rewind again. When people shout in unison with the anchorman and meet other shouts down the street, does it mean they are finally free? Are they? It's their subjugation to what is said on TV that makes them go to the window, obey the madman and shout; it's obeisance that brings the public to reach out. Tomorrow they'll grasp the control and wait in expectation of what the truthful fool has prophesied the day before. They are even madder than him perhaps. What do you think?"

Next time we meet, we look at each other, Jacques and I, and try to remember his sentences, the chill they inspire. There is a cutting, deadly serious tone to Nathaniel's recent monologues. He speaks like a military leader about a "plan of attack;" like a conspirator of "our armies;" though, it is true, he remains a Romantic about "the kind of togetherness that reaches many in the solitude of their chambers." He openly denounces Suzan's practices as fraudulent and often comes back to the threat as opposed to the act: "We are here to predict the worst; to up the ante of any possible catastrophe on earth, to threaten beyond whatever threat they have in store for us so as to make it look puny and ridiculous."

And down on our luck we were again, depressed at seeing ourselves back to ground level, the impression of looking at the train to the future passing by and Nathaniel waiving from the locomotive, smiling goodbye at us from ear to ear.

Jacques and I would meet downtown and beat the gray pavement kind of forlorn. If at times we felt like reproaching Nathaniel something and complained he had driven us nowhere, we had to recognize that it was not the same nowhere as before.

"We cannot reproach him this financial result," I told Jacques on the last return to New York. "It's not his fault if the sense of adventure loses steam after a while."

"No, it's not," said Jacques. "But I'm curious to see how long Nathaniel is going to go for this. Do you think, to the end?" Jacques was not exactly joking, when he added, "Do you think he's wedded, like in the tragic sense, to *HighGuns*?"

"The sacrificial sense, you mean?" I lowered the voice, whispering in spite of myself. "Sure he is, Nathaniel would love nothing as much as to end like a sacrificial lamb, offering himself on a silver platter, his neck to the knife. He's said it, hasn't he?"

"Suzan is going to bring us down because of the way she operates," Jacques prophesized; "and she is forced to operate that way if she wants to make money, which idealists like Nathaniel, you and me can't understand until it's too late." He placed his arms akimbo, ash fell from the dangling tip of his cigarette. He dragged on it strong, exhaling dense volutes of smoke with a nostalgic relish, fanning sadness from his dilated nostrils. Then he said, in a suave voice like Sinatra: "Nathaniel married to the mob! That's what it's come down to. Unless he pulls his stunt."

"What stunt?"

"I don't know what stunt and he doesn't know himself what his word can do on the Webwork."

"But it can do, we know that," I said.

"Maybe Suzan won't let him."

"She has not stopped him, so far."

One had to forget making piles of money, and forswear the sense of danger and thrill—back to ordinary middle class life in New York at a time when the price of things climbed to new heights and your dollar went down to new lows. No choice but to cut on extras, on distinction and deserved pleasures—don't pleasures always feel deserved? Meanwhile over in Connecticut, *HighGuns* was still off the hook: no arrest had been made. For what she declared, Suzan was up to date with the IRS, and that kept the FBI in step as well, taking its time. Come to think of it, no arrest will ever be made. It's amazing to think that the security men were never able, intent enough, ready to cuff the Lagranges. *Josephine* gave them a stupendous advantage, all the more effective that it could not be divulged. Police has let them fly the coop for so long.

It must be said also that Suzan found a way, not only to buy time, but to shake security off their back by moving fast, best way not to get apprehended. The Lagranges were not in Connecticut for long; when it got too hot, without warning, one day, they were gone.

We wrote adorned e-mails to Nathaniel and Suzan, John, Kathy, to no avail. Ultimate insult, the site sent back our e-mails as Mailer-Daemons. *HighGuns* was a shell, the dead skin shed by a snake. Which didn't mean *they* didn't read our messages. Jacques downtown and me uptown, we soon foundon our screens, in bold letters: "Do not worry dudes— kiddies stay behind, we adults move." This hurt, but it also comforted our hearts for it meant they were okay and they thought about us, whether it was Suzan or Nathaniel or the whole gang.

Later on, they reappeared, opened shop, were operating in the South, Georgia and Florida. I didn't care where, what they were doing when not on the Webwork; they were in business. There will be a way back in. They were taking it easy and flaunting their skills in Miami. Another grape of youth was clinging on to them, the cheap and constant handiwork they found among their primary clients. Slavery did not offer better conditions to the willing entrepreneur. Then, Suzan turned her attention toward South America and noticed that land, the price of houses and businesses were undervalued in places like Peru and Bolivia. She probably remembered our conversations about Peru. She had asked me about my impressions when traveling with Gabriela and I had told her that the country felt to me like the Far West of the 1840's, most up for grabs and lawless. She'd focused on Peru: much lower prices, expressed in *soles*, the *sol* being pegged on lower than half the dollar. In other words, you cut your overhead, and armed with a dollar that you still make in the US, you buy twice as much *there*, in Peru. The advantages of a country divided in three different echo-systems: one long strip of dry, moonlike coast along the Pacific Ocean; second, the colossal cordilleras whose peaks were once covered by snow; and on the other side, the hot and lush, forever humid jungle that merges into Brazil. Three ecosystems, Suzan liked that. The more she studied Peru, and including its rampant corruption and immense poverty, its 80% population under 20, the more she was inclined to move *HighGunsOnTheSierra.com* to Peru. It seemed to her a natural transplantation.

And she was right. They moved there and, buying the necessities, hiring the best available, did very well instantly. Middle-class Peruvian kids get a very decent education in prestigious Catholic schools. Suzan could navigate the local Webwork, set up shop for cheap, and in a flash wander back into her American haunts. Here, in Lima, they owed nobody a favor;

they could flourish just by teaching local companies how to secure systems against advanced attacks. Their reputation went the round of Lima in a few days.

I read the publicity that flashed on their new Website: "*HighGuns* en la Sierra, la mejor manera de asegurar sus viajes en el Webwork!"

They occupied a patrician property in San Isidro, the most luxurious neighborhood of Lima.

Lima is not New York. If you went out frequently you would bump into a Lagrange, that is, if they were in town and not up some mountain. For they might very well have a second home in greater Lima, a villa up the first slopes of the cordillera, up a few thousand feet from sunken and smudgy Lima. That's where the air is breathable; that's where you'd live, at least part time, if you had the choice, and that's where Suzan and her troupes went pretty fast.

People of means who could not stand the heat and the humidity of Lima went to fantastic clubs with swimming pools and tennis courts perched on the first big rocks steep mountains. On the photos, pulverized hills of beige rocks are baking in the sun. The team squints and tries a smile for the video clip. The sky is deep blue in Chaclacayo, a big village of some 15 000. Now, look at him, Nathaniel comes out of a sparkling 4 by 4 to buy cigarettes and a bottle of seltzer at a nondescript, decrepit bodega. As I said, except for San Isidro, everything in and around Lima looks decrepit, has not been painted or fixed in years. The club owners pocket the money and don't contribute to the village, which they squeeze since they are also mayors and their friends are the judges and the policiticans. Nathaniel does what he always does, he plunges his hand for the change at the bottom of his pocket. His jeans are reaped to the point of hanging by a thread. We see one knee, which is unexpectedly tanned, and his feet are visible through Indian sandals; he no longer bounces down the pavement grey of 6th Avenue in his stuffy white sneakers. Nathaniel is in his element, he whistles a tune you can't hear. He is the same thin and a bit nervous Nathaniel, no less and no more, when he lights up his cigarette. South America, it's the same planet, put on its head. Perfect environment for *HighGuns*.

Until one day, Suzan and the Lagranges discover that they are no longer welcome in Peru. For what I understand, it is done crudely. The club owner refuses to renew their membership; for all her money, Suzan has a hard time renting an apartment back in Lima, a house, a car—government pressure, she is told. Which government? The Peruvian authorities have nothing against rich Americans. The problem, of course, is that Lima depends on Washington.

The FBI is after the Lagranges and wants them back home where they can be monitored. Could not get extradition orders since there is no case against the Lagranges; but they could make their lives impossible almost everywhere in the world. The Lagranges are back in Miami and they are harassed from the moment they land. Stripped, fingered in the ass and in the vagina. Custom agents pretend they have received tips about drugs. Since none in the team is stupid enough to carry hashish, a blade of grass or a gram of coke, the custom officers have to let them go. They are all American citizens, after all; and there is no charge against them.

It's then, upon returning, that Suzan decides to implant *trojan horses* and other *rabbits* in programs controlling from water supply to medical management; from electricity to radio, telephone and cable hubs, and not in Miami, where they land, but in the New York Metropolitan area, in the mouth of the beast, whose digital organs they map for six months and a half until they can play them like a mechanical piano. Sensitive information is guarded and hard to access; but nothing is impossible in the realm of hacking, it's all digital and if you put in it persistence and métier, you get in eventually. As though *HighGuns* was its own nation, Suzan decides to create a deterrent, which she calls *Josephine*. It must be a threat powerful enough to intimidate the police. It is one more bargaining chip, only more sinister than usual: she doesn't really know how devastating, if authorized; she'll take an immeasurable risk by threatening to freeze the air-traffic controllers' screens seconds at a time. She would greatly prefer not to have to trigger the attack. But the threat might come handy.

It was manifest that Suzan would never shake the police off their back, unless she gave up hacking, and even then. Security agents and hackers have this in common: they don't give up.

Suzan didn't stay long in Miami. Now that her files are published by other hackers, anyone can read that she moved to the Upper East Side of Manhattan. In the mouth of the lion, she thought, she'd be as protected from detection of her Webwork intentions as in the eye of the storm. They took a large duplex on 61rst Street, between Lexington and 3rd Ave. No direct view, facades, other buildings hiding their sun; nothing ostentatious. Nothing too shabby either, decent; functional furnishing and carpeting in the conference room, the dining room. What made Nathaniel laugh was that the books had been glued to the shelves in the study room. Corporate life-style, plasma screens coming out of the sheet-rock. But after the Lagranges brought their gear, you also found in the duplex the fastest machines on the market.

What was unusual, they all used aliases, but made no secret about them, as though they were masks in a carnival. Nathaniel Lagrange posted under the name Hubert de Bauvais—research tells me it belonged to an obscure early 19th century French mathematician, small contribution, one of the pioneers of what would later establish Thermodynamics. Kathy was Countess Gustave (the provenance of this one is anybody's guess); John, Alfred de Musset; and Suzan, George Sand. Their screen-names were as extravagant: "Joshua-Premier," "Bob-Dylan-re-plugged," "Beelzebub-resuscitated" ... You may say, names like that will attract the attention of everybody, first off security agents, why do this?

Suzan knew she would attract attention anyway, so why not forestall the agent, why not move faster, a step ahead? Why not be in his face with a mask that proclaims *I am a mask*? And if he persists, jump in and confront the man. Why procrastinate and not meet destiny head on?

Log 28

I then found my way back into *HighGuns* by adding a footnote to Nathaniel's *Fragments*. I sent my comments to what Nathaniel had just packaged over the Webwork and since I was an old friend, from back during Nathaniel's forming years, from the old guard, they could not but add it to the flow.

"Before I left France, I remember going to a three-story house set between tall buildings on a boulevard just outside Paris. To own such a grand house indoors Paris would have meant André Stern was a very rich man. We would meet there on Saturday evening, once the Sabbath had ended. Guests would sit in the dining room on the ground floor around an elongated, classy oval table in mahogany acajou. Andre Stern and his wife had eleven children, all practicing their instrument after the forced respite of the Shabbat. From the upper floors came to us brooding over large books the sound of an orchestra that's warming up; the sweet cacophony during the minute before the concert starts. The quack of a clarinet clashed with the cry of a bow which had not yet found the pitch; perfect preamble to approach the Talmud.

"We were ten so that at some point we could pray and our prayer count as in a Synagogue. From the Sabbath, there remained on the table a big chunk of challah bread and some halvah. I had discovered that Andre Stern was an important French Orthodox Jew. He imported Israel's food for a good part of the religious community in Paris. His wife did not stay behind and ran a network of elementary schools. Even though he was a man of many obligations, André Stern spent his mornings in Le Marais discussing the Talmud between rabbis and fervent readers. But on Saturday night, to sober after the festivities and to entertain his mind with fresh questions, Stern invited men of diverse backgrounds, lawyers, professors, doctors, dilettantes like me—not Bible tourists, curious and serious people, unbelievers included. André would read out loud a short passage in the Hebrew of the Mishna (1st century); and then someone else read the Aramaic comments in the Gemara (2nd century). Then, one reader at a time, we naturally went from the medieval French of Rashi and Maimonides, to the present, and at some point I would finally be called upon to read modern French at the bottom of the page, in the footnote.

"To say that I did not always understand what was said at this table is an understatement. I couldn't fathom how much I didn't fathom. Have you ever had in front of you a hard copy of the Talmud in its original form? In the center of the large and brittle page, written in small, the Mishna, a few sentences attributed to two/three great rabbis who disagreed on the relevance or application in daily life of an injunction written five hundred years earlier in the Thora. Then, from circle to circle of comments, you see rabbis of different eras discussing the meaning to be given to the previous discussion. It never becomes clear enough that the next generation can stop discussing the previous discussions.

Thanks to the impromptu seminars that André Stern gave on Saturday evening, I realized that even for those versed in Aramaic, it was not all that clear what the believing Jew should do or not in certain situations, that's why he tended to overdo it and avoid these situations. I remember André Stern admitting sometimes that he was not sure himself, there were several interpretations possible and it was a matter of you making a quantum leap of faith. That's where belief fills the void, the lack of answers; when one can't understand, one starts praying. We loved it around the table, not understanding a 100%, and in my case, almost nothing at all. We came back to André Stern and his lovely home and asked for more.

I was amazed to see that at every step in the Mishnah there are links that open on windows where other discussions full of links take place that open... When Apple pioneered window-clicking, it borrowed from the Talmud, same abysmal structure."

"The paragraph chosen by Stern in the Mishnah one Saturday evening spoke of a difficulty in the life of the Jew concerning the recitation three times a day of Shema Israel: 'Listen Israel! Adonai is our God and He is one." These words are the center of the Jewish prayer. This portion of the prayer-book, the believer must believe in it with all the strength of his consciousness when he says it out loud among the congregation. He cannot afford to give lip service to this verse like it is permitted with other verses, otherwise one would spend the day praying. No man can put his heart in every moment of his life, it is not human. It is human to sometimes not pay attention; and Judaism is a human religion, aware of human limitations. Anyway, when reciting the Shema Israel a Jew has to give each syllable his attention."

"Then there is a problem if the Jew is at work," says a rabbi in the Mishnah. "Let's suppose he is perched in a tree, picking fruits. He will not pay attention to his picking while reciting the Shema; he will steal his boss, pay lip-service to his work; without mentioning that he might fall from the branch, if he pays too much attention to the word of God. But the opposite, supposing he gives lip service to the Shema, is even worse."

"'Let him come down from the tree and pray,' says another rabbi. What is a boss when it comes to God?'"

"But the first rabbi disagrees: a zealous Jew cannot inspire mistrust at work; not concerning the time spent praying which, if actually spent in fervent prayer, steals the boss who pays by the hour. After several objections by other rabbis, comes the decision that closes the debate and reconciles opposites: if a zealous Jew risks stealing his boss by a prolonged period of fervent prayer, he must compensate his employer, whether he is another Jew or a goy, by offering to work overtime freely. This was discussed two thousand years ago."

"You are wondering how this religious encounter once a week long ago relates to Desistence. Here it is. One can discontinue an obligation to marry another. Desistence consists, as Nathaniel puts it, in a disaffection on our part, a partial withdrawing of our adhesion to the systems and machines surrounding us, a suspicion, a distance and finally a desire to no longer be played by the rich men who rig the Webwork; the urge, for once, to play them at our roulette."

"Excuse me if I get carried away; if my perception of Desistence today is correct, then the movement must enter the workplace, and not only by quoting the disarming attitude of Bartleby the Scrivener. Desistence has to turn her malicious eyes toward good old businesses, shops, real offices down real avenues. What a company demands of its employees is that they not only punch in and be at work, but consciously at work, putting skin and brains into it. That's why they are paid, to be conscious and volunteer their best. As soon as the employee relaxes his mind, thinks of his last vacation, daydreams, drinks at work or breaks down, in terms of the contract of employment, he steals his boss. In other words, as soon as he does not care and undermines the effort expected of him, he desists. The désistant does his work just enough for his Desistence not to be noticed. He is a mole, a live-in spy. Following this line of thought, the attack could be directed not against the contract of employment written on legal paper but deeper, against the more personal, the implicit contract, the reliance that makes possible relationships between employers and employees."

"What this deeper breach of contract could bring is a trove of information on actual conditions of work, the treatment of employees… etc. Desistence could take over where unions and legal support no longer exist for the working men and women of today. Tomorrow there will be robots in the workplace doing all the repetitive and numbing tasks and more; but today there are human beings still doing that. The movement could help by collecting eye-witness information from their experience at work; it could hack higher echelons real motives and goals when promoting and firing, and finally it could threaten to reveal embarrassing stuff, get better deals for blue and white collars. The idea, which is central to the *Fragments*, that Desistence means being at the post, doing the job without being *there…* would then have serious consequences."

My blurb delighted the Lagranges, Suzan and, especially, Nathaniel. "You did your homework," he told me when I saw him. "as you've always done." There was no mockery, he was happy to have me back, and in times that were no longer so easy going and triumphant for the Lagranges.

After that my visits to the duplex on the Upper East Side were few but effective. I was back in business. That's when I contributed conceptually to *Josephine,* which helped return the confidence of both Suzan and Nathaniel. Given that the team was nostalgic of the good old years, teary about its past achievements and *HighGuns* entering, as ripe organizations do, a period of self-aggrandizement and embalmment, I received a warm welcome from Suzan and her coders, and including from Jacques. Yep, of course, Jacques had beaten me. Even if the circumstances were intense, we were all back together and that was fun.

Edging my bets, I took Suzan's side and Nathaniel's, both. John and Kathy had been expert at that, maneuvering their brother's *esprit* and Suzan's practical skills. They didn't see a contradiction and, indeed, it had been a match made in heaven. She was all about France and French history now. So, I advised Suzan on French restaurants, brands, perfume and high fashion, French literature and philosophy, customs, French habits, hang ups, shortcomings.

What was becoming evident to me is that I wanted to be there *until the end.* The operation was directed from the other side of town; it was pleasant to resume with having two lives. Soon I was anxiously conscious that, should *HighGuns* move—out of town, the country—

this time I would follow them. I would ask for retirement and leave the costume of professor behind. Was I also ready to leave my family for long stretches of time? Yes, if it meant making a small fortune.

For their sake, for *our* future in a world where the future was compromised, I'd cut corners, learn tricks and sleight of hands, live day and night next to Suzan and her coders, and make a bundle. Enough to finally settle us somewhere in the South of France, in a big house over a hill and by the sea. Little chance of realizing that—of realizing anything—if Gabriela stayed in her job and I only cashed in retirement.

I understood that my involvement could go severely wrong. I could one day bitterly regret the comfort of a lackluster career. It was reckless on my part; why take such risks at sixty years old?

Risk what, though? There would continue to be nothing criminal in my activities. Not talking about our deterrent to who wanted to hear was not a crime. Translating, interpreting forbidden transactions was reprehensible, but to which extent? Supposing *they* had something against *HighGuns* and dragged Suzan in court, then what? I was guilty by association. Even indicted and receiving *time*, my police records being clean, it would result in probation. No, the only difficulty would be the lingering pain of conscience associated with doing wrongful acts hurtful to other men: violent, abusive, exploitative action, causing pain; but there was nothing of the sort in what Suzan was doing, and me next to her. Nothing really wrong with my peripheral role in the making of *Josephine*. For instance, my inventing muggings and assaults, robberies that were not happening, and sending the gory details in high density pixel and video clips to NYPD detectives—was that criminal? This diversion occupied them for days when they had better things to do; there may have been victims of their disorientation. But police had more than started to get on my nerves; I was not against getting on their case and, with technical help from my friends, undermine the last shreds of their authority.

These were ideas that gave us a good laugh, more like pranks I passed on to Suzan, who directed the coders. However, I must admit, this was new in me, to confront the authorities. To be the cause of serious mischief. It's true, nowhere was my name showing; but as Jacques said, the police also live in the shadows. I was not afraid they'd be on my tail forever; it no longer mattered to me because I had also reached a point of no return in my refusal to adhere or submit or accept whimsical rules, brute enforcement and arbitrary justice. What I said earlier about making money should not mislead you; it was never just about money. Money would compensate for my shortcomings. This was my chance of making it once and for all in the eyes of my wife and child;

My own life no longer mattered, at least not enough to stop me from giving it all to Desistence; yes, risking it all, if it came to that.

I became a désistant.

Log 29

It turned out that making it a full-time job to embrace defiance was liberating; and belonging sincerely to much greater than myself was thrilling and took care of the remaining fears.

Suzan was getting older; she was pushing seventy. She was slightly bent, diminished in size; but she was still our brain, nothing escaped her gaze and she had acquired, with the patina of age, a new kind of beauty. This may sound trite, but intelligence in a person always brings out beauty.

There were still few crisis among us because Suzan was uncontrovertibly the leader, especially in difficult moments. Even Nathaniel, who could storm up a controversy against her methods and inform his phalanges to not trust *HighGuns*; particularly for him, Suzan was the captain. He would not know what to do, where, how to plant our tent, how to administer the site; and had no concrete alternative to propose when he did not like her decisions. He thought about launching a campaign against her to distance Desistence from black hat practices, and because he considered the deterrent "an aggressive weapon whose threat should never be used but for a pure purpose, in other words not as a racketeering tool for business;" but he dressed his rebellion in general terms and never named her directly. They sat each evening at the same dining table and discussed everything under the sun with a smile.

John and Kathy were in denial, couldn't believe the team was being treated as outlaws. Kathy saw them but she didn't register the cops lurking in alleyways; nor would John comprehend immediately why a car with invariably two men inside was in his rear-view mirror. It's to spare us this kind of encounter that Suzan had us, Jacques and I, leave the building by the service backdoor and rush into a taxi. To keep us out from under the radar, she said, "fresh and pure as cherubim," so she could use us later if the team got caught. We would remain behind as their antenna. And apparently, it worked, Jacques and I didn't feel like we were followed in the streets, the subway or in the taxi, say, if we happened to return home for a brief visit. However painful, it became normal for Jacques and I to hardly leave the duplex, and only at night between surveillance shifts.

Danger lurked at the border of our opulent life. This attached us all the more to the umbrella of safety and resourcefulness Suzan projected around her. She was as ruthless against our enemies as she was a good grand-mother for us, whether we were Lagrange family, friends, young coders or guests.

Nathaniel was waiting for his hour and did not contest Suzan face to face, at least not when I was around. He might point out the apparent inconsistencies of her actions in ironical terms; but, until that point, merely to accomplish his duty as parrot or court jester or fool. If you accept a distinction I read somewhere, there is a difference between the fool and the scoundrel. The fool is meek and self-righteous; he is a believer in a better world to come—he lives in the future and has problems actualizing his dreams. In politics, he's the die-hard left-wing apostle who's still expecting Trotsky's second coming to save us from capitalism. The scoundrel, on the other hand, is right wing to the bone, and he is not fooled by the event for he is the greedy force behind the event. The scoundrel acts. He makes and does. Nathaniel was a fool; Suzan was a scoundrel, even though she gave you the left wing blabla as well, playing both sides. She took advantage of situations, she never forgot her personal interest, which, didn't exclude her working for the greater good.

I started to wonder about her side of the equation. Was it only because of John that she kept working alongside Nathaniel? After all these years, John did much better, he drank much less. Their love was not on the rocks, it had kind of settled and become old affection. What did Suzan need the Lagranges for, and especially Nathaniel? He was right: her type of hacking, which amounted to an elegant form of extortion, had nothing to do with Desistence. They should part ways; they should have long ago. But they were attached at the heaps: he needed her for practical, imperative reasons; she needed him as cover, justification. She could hide beautifully within Desistence.

But what if, by now, there was more to Suzan's hosting the leadership of Nathaniel's movement (and spending big bucks doing that), than just manoeuver? More than one more camouflage? Desistence was in the air we breathed; there was a moment each day when we no longer allowed cynicism to pass our lips. Jacques had become a fervent a désistant. And we suspected that Suzan would also harbor a certain affection for the type of ultimate wager Desistence meant in Nathaniel's *Fragments*. We no longer felt like speaking in Nathaniel's back. We no longer made fun of him for his not having a woman when he only had to pick one. Our old friend had turned into a productive, effective, thoughtful, inspirational saint.

I remember this short exchange at dinnertime, in the main room of the duplex, around the conference table turned into dining table for the evening.

"They can go after us all they want," Jacques said while confronting marvelous foods and holding firm to his fork and knife.

"Fuck the police," she answered softly. "What we have should keep them in check, and it's better that way."

"Yes, added Nathaniel, "it's better for Desistence that they cannot snuff our explicit existence out like a candle."

Our being watched did not deter the team from launching a successful and legitimate Webwork photo-shop where for a price visitors could "create" the narrative of the lives they wanted to inhabit. At the end of their shopping spree, our clients came up each with "a singular" e-book of photos and clips, long shots with background and foreground sounds, music recorded from intimate and public moments of their own lives, now stored, categorized, sequences and plotted by our site. While on Facebook or Snapchat people posted snapshots of themselves, we took this mosaic and mixed it like a salad, adding for a price different seasonings. We invented Your Life Remade, which had a hard time taking hold at first. Who would want to remake their lives in the virtual? Ain't you happy the way you are? Why create a second existence you could feed and embellish for the rest of your life?

But when it took off, I recall that more than half our clients chose tragic-ended stories, while the rest preferred melodramatic or romantic dénouements. Open-ended, up-ended, unending—whatever kind of story they wanted was concocted and handed in virtual terms, but as vivid and felt as they come. There was, of course, an array of wrong and terrible second lives: scabrous, salacious, spicy, violent, criminal second lives… S & M, semi-retarded, brutally stupid or absurd existences. Plots that made absolutely no sense and could not possibly be lived through. Intrigues antithetical to human survival. For an added fee, your second life could have no connection at all with your own. Thanks to *HighGuns* (come to think of it, until the end sentimental Suzan kept the name and for the longest time police hesitated shutting it), you could buy dead persons' life-sequences, mega drives full of the entire treasure of data related to one person of your choice: photos collected from day one—before that, while still in the belly—and after that, lying in the coffin or coming out of the crematorium in a box small enough to hold less than a pound of ashes. The individual was sold to you, so to speak, the touch from his fingers recreated; education grade after grade and professional life inside out; marital or single status, inexistent or steamy private life; extra-marital life and abnormalities; accidents and hospitalizations, medical and psychiatric records, arrests, phone numbers, e-mail addresses of family members, files—and including secret files, for a fee—created by the subject and created about the subject by any kind of agency while h/she was alive.

Curiously, the law was not against us; it was okay to plunder dead people's lives since they themselves could not have been copyrighted. Once dead, their families and descendants no longer owned them. We were thinking about adding an extra fee and would start collecting from a wide array of living individuals we didn't like; but at the last minute a scruple got in the way, whether it was Suzan or Nathaniel who spoke against it.

Our clients adopted the character of Baron de Rothschild, Dupont de Nemours, Robert McNamara, John or Paul or Nicky Kennedy, Lennon or McCartney, Robert Mitchum, Ingrid Bergman, Brigitte Bardot, Burt Lancaster... *ad infinitum*. They were allowed into the most personal, trivial, humdrum; and where no record existed, our computer extrapolated. Naturally, clients were enticed into buying piece by piece the world corresponding to their identity in cyberspace, reproduced in superfine pixel on their screen; they were invited to wear connected gloves and 3D visuals.

Our database claimed to contain an infinite number of personal narratives which could be mixed and connected; and so, once he adopted a "handle," our client could choose to remain faithful to the actual life of the dead man or change it; be a John F. Kennedy who was not assassinated. A Rothschild who lost everything in the oil crisis of 1973; a Bill Clinton who kept secret his affair with Lewinski; and subsequently, a winning Al Gore, followed immediately by Hillary Clinton as the first ever female president, and not that reckless Bush junior who had two terms to plunder and ruin the country; followed by the corrupt semi-dictatorship of a buffoon...etc.

People flocked to *HighGuns* to buy virtual objects and properties; to be and feel and think and write in languages practiced three hundred years earlier. That they did not always understand and feared the parallel worlds they had bought into only added to the enjoyment.

On our portal, in fat letters: "No longer ashamed to be someone else, why be discreet about it? Express yourself, live vicariously!" It seems that Nathaniel had a say in this phrasing, like a joke to mock "the sheepish majority." Suzan snatched it, convinced it was indeed what the "sheepish majority," the multitude who don't take risk, don't make trouble, are not famous and/or rich nor intend to, craved for. She was right again: who wouldn't have fun being in the skin of someone else? Someone envied and that one could manipulate from within, someone admired that one might approach and shake hands with by shaking one hand with the other; someone hated and deeply scorned, on the contrary, one might devise to ruin inside out? How pleasant *not* to face your own danger, feed your own voracious mouth or commit your own crimes! Nothing happens to you, in the end.

Success, financial included, brought danger; to be in the public eye further exposed us. That you are ahead of the policeman when it comes to money and fame only adds to his obstinacy. The great advantage police have over the "criminals" they pursue is they have all the time in the world. There is presumption of innocence, sure; but since policemen snoop around, there must be something wrong with you. It's only a question of time before they nail you.

We drove upstate on weekends, and come winter, we bought state of the art skiing gear: parachute gear for mountain falling, equipment for glaciers that no longer existed. I've never heard of a group of people so able to live on at least two levels, one completely off the wall, risky, unlawful and brash; the other polite, refined, well-intentioned and politically correct to a fault. It takes talent to do that, a second personality seamlessly wrapping the first. Try yourself to be a two-face Janus, and see how long you can take the guilt and the cynicism.

The difference, and our saving grace: we no longer plotted for ourselves, I mean, each fragmented self for himself. There was a good part of us now that was given over to a bigger one.

The team needed to skip the scene. We skied at Hunter Mountain, which didn't offer the slopes that cater to the lonesome, privileged aficionado. "In Colorado, the glaciers must be wet as swamp," someone said to make us feel better. Hunter is more like family skiing; and so it pained Jacques and it hurt me to not have our families enjoy the artificial snows. I was then leaving Gabriela and Isabel for longer stretches of time. The team wanted me around; Suzan made it plain that you lived the life of the team or you didn't. She no longer needed consultants; she needed, she said laughing, "partners in crime."

Gabriela didn't question me this time more than she had before. I didn't give her a chance, in fact. It was in the middle of summer and I said to her that I would not go back to work come September; I had filed for retirement. I told her on a Sunday evening that I wouldn't be back in our apartment that night, nor the next. For how long, I couldn't tell exactly. It didn't come as a total surprise but it was a shock. She had hoped my participation in the *HighGuns* success would reach an apotheosis and die of natural death; and now, it was too late. Success seemed to have come and gone. Why was I more and more involved? I did not speak to her about my dedication to Desistence; it would only have alarmed her more. Again, I asked her to trust me on this one; she said she did, had no other choice.

I also talked to Isabel. It was hard to separate since we had always been together but for a few days here and there. I told her that my job required it. She could have asked, which job? But she knew it was not 'For how long?' she asked in her thin voice. When I told her "for a few months," it didn't quite register. She had not yet a fixed notion of the future; but she grasped it would take long.

From then on, whether we ski at Hunter Mountain, travel or go back to Manhattan, I inhabit the same tacky but spacious room on the same high floor as each member of our group, all registered as Webwork researchers from New York. Feeling lonely, I regularly end up at the bar downstairs, where Nathaniel further explains to me the virtues of the single-malt Whiskey.

Now that he was back in shape, John could ski, and so could Nathaniel. Kathy treaded more than she glided down the soft fields of snow; but she got through the job of going down the slope alright; skiing had been part of the Lagrange education since father was in station upstate New York. Personally, I could sky: before they divorced, my parents used to send me twice a year in the Alps, in *colonie de vacances*. It was good for my health, the doctor prescribed it. As for Suzan, she learned in no time to stand on skis more than on her arse, which had lost much of its redundancy since I'd seen her up close. She was very bony, but she was nervy also and strong. Her ability to physically learn at her age was astounding to me. She went down the whitish bed of snow slowly and rigidly perhaps, but without the resentment that may have come over Nathaniel when long ago, in his first life, he had not been the best at something. Now we skied head to head, we were not forcing it and Nathaniel didn't try to beat me to the line. Suzan elicited my sympathy and propitiated my help by admitting her shortcomings. She was on the slope to have fun and forget our concerns, our growing perplexity.

Was she afraid? Did she feel guilty? Not guilty; afraid, in spite of herself, probably. I was afraid. It would be difficult to explain that that was precisely the reason why I lived now on *HighGuns* grounds almost all the time, to embrace that edge from the second I woke up and put my naked two feet on the beige carpet. Although, in my case, there was actually little to fear, I kept telling myself.

Suzan was not intimidated by the short list of the FBI. She was good at this war of nerves. It's from ex-hubby Friedman she had learned shadow confrontation. Her husband had decided to kill himself rather than turn himself in. He'd avoided visibility to the end, deposited the mask only when dead. She was made of the same cloth, though she didn't mention his name before the family. She wrote at her computer in a secret file that I have hacked: "Tacky as it may seem, we are in it, John and I and the family until death do us apart." Another day: "Nothing cements a group like a threat." She was conscious of "persistent, potentially more serious fractures among us." Because, as I said, we'd all become désistants; but that did not mean we understood Desistence the same way.

Suzan read Dostoyevsky's *Crime and Punishment* after a day of exertions on the slope. She couldn't sleep more than three or four hours, so she read and wrote desultory notes. One thing was certain, no crime and punishment, Suzan wouldn't end like Raskolnikov, that is, overwhelmed by guilt to the point of going back to the scene of his crime, thereby giving himself to detective Petrovitch. Suzan had committed no crime, she said at dinnertime, visited no crime scene, axed no old lady's arteries and living bones. There was no reason for her to be overwhelmed by scruples: the filters she had jammed and the ciphers she had hacked did not exist, not like you and me, not like moral entities do. To eavesdrop on access codes was robbing no one you could kiss on the cheek. In a Nathaniel-like turn of phrase, she added that the infractions she practiced were "all metaphorical, just figures of speech." Hidden drawers of e-boutiques were private property only because you said so and made us believe so. What a Webwork creature is made out of belongs to anyone persistent and perspicacious enough to "own" it.

"It's a bit like the exoteric side *versus* the esoteric side of any religion," she said one time in the direction of Nathaniel. "When the intrepid searcher gets to the core, the fascinating center, the godhead of belief, what he finds is just hollowness."

Nathaniel said, "In the temple there was nothing to look at behind the curtain that curtailed your view of the sacrosanct."

"That's right," I added, sounding a bit too much like the professor, "the curtain is an old motif, a gimmick, a lure; you believe there is something behind. The curtain in the temple was perfect to create the illusion of a supreme presence where there was none."

I don't remember who added, "The castle of cards is the more labyrinthine that it needs to hide the hot air it stands on." Perhaps Jacques.

We knew Suzan's arguments; she didn't have to repeat that the security protocol had been botched here; elements of a firewall were missing there. That she sold cracks, gaps, defects and found bugs in expensive armors which she improved upon and corrected, made more difficult to penetrate next time. What could she be accused of? Suzan expanded *ad nauseum* on this theme and she was not wrong; but why did she have to convince herself that she was right?

John believed almost until the end that we would find buyers for the operation, sale it piecemeal; so, the hairier our situation the better. Once out of the woods, we might sell our memories and call them "the Family Lagrange Reality Show"—and make a racket!

"If the Lagranges don't fail this time," John writes in his blog, "then they will get richer and more famous." He was right: other teams had waded knee-deep in muddy waters and come out innocent like cherubim; why not the Lagranges?

Perhaps we were marked. We had the creepy sense that we were chosen, blessed like the tragic characters of old, *by being doomed*. Kathy writes: "Yesterday Nathaniel freaked me out when he pretended, and not as a joke but dead serious, that our story is no comedy – 'no tragicomedy, he said, not even melodrama or escapable, relenting drama, but pure and simple tragedy of the worst sublimest kind. It's Shakespearean—why? Because every major role on stage dies in the end, leaving only servants and confidents hired to wash the blood away and bring the coffins.'"

"It's not in the books you'll find true tragedy,' Nathaniel said to me in a bar where we sipped our single-malt, and where he harbored a more complex smile than before. 'It's in the life of a few folks destined to greatness. They don't have to be aristocrats, you know, kings and queens like in Shakespeare. They can come from more modest walks of life.'

"Yeah! Maybe you're right," said Kathy, who drank occasionally with us. "It's like Aeschylus and his furies? We'll all go up in flames !"

"We'll all writhe inside the poisoned robe of Hercules," I said—again regretting to sound like the professor. The reference was beautiful but obscure. They looked at me.

Kathy's joke about going up in flame was not funny. It's hard to poke fun at oneself when the risk is real. Okay we had *Josephine* and could by then threaten about any police outfit; but as I have said, police are not all stupid and they can be callous, if not brutal. They could set us up, for instance, by leaking what they knew of Suzan's soft gangsterism, her inflated income, her connections with the mafia. They could blow her cover, bring Desistence down. That's why Nathaniel's smile was bittersweet. His fame would only benefit from a tragic ending; after all, he'd inched toward being a martyr all his life. But what if circumstances forced on us a stupidly bad ending: a scandal, a mudsling disgracing the whole enterprise? How about a dent on the so far juvenile, innocent and ecstatic face of Desistence?

After many sedate years, I was rediscovering in my old age how I liked taking risks. Of course, taking risks without getting caught. I must have been eight or nine when I robbed francs in the cash register of the second-class hotel where my mother was raising me. Our poor clients generated a lot of small money; so, I would plunge my hands in the layers of francs and no one would find out because no one knew exactly how many francs there were; and also because I didn't go at it by the fistful and was discreet.

What if this time I was poking my hands too deep in the cashbox?

Log 30

One morning it became impossible to forget our being monitored. Unbeknownst to the team sleeping on the upper floor, the office, the conference/dining room on the lower floor had been visited during the night. I was out of town, on an errand in Pennsylvania. Always a step ahead, Suzan had sent me to prospect for a new base of operation. John and Kathy reconstituted the sequence from cameras on laptops. Where the team worked machines didn't sleep.

Two chubby gentlemen in blue jeans, hoods, official badges and thick jogging outfit had calmly rummaged the duplex, printed files, taken the time to copy entire hard drives. Scattered in the duplex, our makeshift habitat boasted of little privacy and reminded one of student life;

but it was decent, furniture design, kitchen out of a magazine, stereo and pick-up equipment and high-end laptops beyond the chubbies.

Another time, it was more serious. They started on the second floor while the entire team, including Jacques and I, were downstairs. Hateful and sneering men put their fat and greasy fingers on sweet angora sweaters; they trampled on Cardin jackets and wiped their shoes on my Peruvian carpet. Bastards sniffed Kathy's panties and salivated on her large bra with a malicious smile.

Finally, one chubby pointed his rubicund head at the top of the twisted stairs and said in the direction of Kathy: "Must be yours, eh?"

While the first started slowly down the stairs a second man, looking at Suzan, said, "More tetas than your bony ass, babe!" The first chubby detailed Suzan's flat chest and slim proportions like a pimp among his whores. It went worse than the worst B movie. John and Nathaniel had to be kept in check by Kathy and Suzan. They would have pounced on the two ridiculous men, who provoked them shamelessly, and whom they could easily have sent to the floor, had it not been for their hidden pistols. For a minute, Suzan succeeded in taking Nathaniel, John and Kathy to the conference room and closing the door on the chubbies, who banged on it but without much conviction, like they were following routine. She had the time to make it plain she didn't want to enter prison on charges of disrespect to petty officers. "That's what they're looking for, can't you see? A scuffle, a... At least, if we are cuffed, let it be as hackers, non?" She looked John and Nathaniel in the eye and they agreed. Without a word, she indicated her earphones and covered her ears to the rest of the team while opening the door. Jacques and I following, we all swallowed our saliva and put our earphones at maximum volume; then in unison turned our backs to the cops.

Though they didn't show a warrant and had no right to burst in like this, these street police liked to stretch the humiliation. Later, one or the other would come closer to Suzan, John or Nathaniel, Kathy especially, to nag them with a porn magazine, creams, pain killers, some equivocal gadget buried in the closet. Mine was not excluded. They duly noted the newspapers the team read, the letters we received; took photos with their IPhones—who knows if we could not be arraigned on political charges? The Lagranges are famous for giving a helping hand to the victims of this earth. Some terrorist connection was badly needed in the Lagrange file, empty as it was of evidence. Fact is, the team warehoused no drugs and had no guns; these police had nothing against us.

When she was sure the men would stay calm, Suzan turned around, took her earphones off, crossed her arms and looked brashly at the two footmen shouting questions in their cell phones. She was not worried about the image of her hard disk they were taking with them. What mattered breathed in some very well guarded corner of the Webwork. The Lagranges were no amateurs; a good analyst, someone trained like her, could exhume suspicious patterns from her Mac, but it would take time.

Humiliating and nerve racking as it was, this police visit calmed every one down, at least for now. Better to meet your enemy, especially if he's grotesque and laughable. Was that what we were up against? No one believed it. No one stated out loud his theory about why the chubbies had not been given a search warrant. Behind this dated apparatus, there were other police, light-footed, deft, coming from the best schools, subtle and more cold-blooded. Better paid and more powerful. Agents came in waves, like the biblical plagues. The second police let the first operate until it found them lacking and took over abruptly, discarding any chance for the first to ever getting promoted.

After that, it was not rare for Suzan to detect three Webwork security agents going after her from different agencies—that is, she knew of their whereabouts, their physical existence beyond their borrowing, like her, digital identities. They were good and they moved; and yet, they had all the time in the world. Although they had divergent agendas, they coordinated their effort and were building a case against her methodically, the way Scotland Yard worked before the computer age, by letting the target free and limiting policing to intense scrutiny for a long time. The less the "criminal" feels the Webwork is closing around his neck, the more he will reveal of himself. Record meticulously the drab, uneventful day to day of a "presumed criminal" and he's going to betray his "crime" one way or the other. The oldest school of police, the best, was coming at her.

The chubbies had only been a mistake, a desperate move from a pressured and reckless agency; whatever proof they'd obtained would not have been accepted in a court of law. It was strangely reassuring that there were functioning courts of justice in America, and a state of law, still.

I didn't have the skills before to crack into such high-profile accounts, and have discovered only recently, while in Paris, the important role Johnathan Levin has played in the precipitous events of the last two years, including this last escape from America well executed by the Lagranges.

Nostalgic of his womanizing past, on the Webwork he once called himself Richard Gere. Educated at Stanford (four years earlier than Suzan), first class corporate security executive in his twenties; independent businessman in his thirties; doesn't do much, lives off the family estate and his money in his forties; reassumes corporate prerogatives and pay in his fifties, only to suffer a case of premature exhaustion (what used to be called, a nervous breakdown). Upon coming out of the hospital at fifty-three, Jonathan Levine disappears into a high profile, top secret Webwork security police job. Strange. Why a man well-read, refined, musical, artistic, moneyed and surrounded by opportunities would want to become a policeman? Has a lot to prove in this respect at the time he starts reporting to the Secret Service on the Lagranges. He's accepted for a meager salary (considering what he had claimed in the private sector) an important, sensitive, but lose-lose and no-matter-what unrewarding position. He is one rare cop who doesn't need money, fame, medals and promotion. It comes from his well-to-do family, commitment to public service; the call, by now obsolete and nostalgic, to save morally this once-upon-a-time great country.

Brought on the case when the FBI had nothing tangible against the Lagranges, Jonathan Levine drew a portrait of the people behind *HighGuns* more severe, naturally, than the one we drew ourselves; and not always, it seems to me, accurate:

"A family of losers, and Nathaniel Lagrange the worst. But Kathy is no better, for she is a lawyer who has never defended a case; Suzan Friedman made her what she is, a known-quantity. Except for two acolytes—old friends of Nathaniel's: Etienne Zeltzki and Jacques Manassah, intelligent men who have succeeded in remaining secondary characters while making money in part because of their limited skills at computers—they all share this foggy belief in revolution on-the-fringe, 'out there' they claim, at the outposts of the Webwork, where it morph savage. Frontier mentality… kind of 60's memorabilia revisited in the cyber age. When it comes to justifying their attitude of defiance, which pretends to be extreme, they have developed this vague, undefined notion of 'Desistence' which, frankly, I can't make much sense of. There seem to be flashes of intuition that are brilliant in the *Fragments*; but then they remain fragments and coalesce and stick together. The concept goes every which way. What is clear, however, is that it has attracted a committed following on the Webwork, one which is well-organized, anonymous yet centralized and under the Lagrange command."

He had a keen view of Nathaniel: "A moral and sentimental cripple, great ideas, encyclopedic mind in a socially retarded body, until he hits the Webwork with the help of Suzan Freidman and instantly becomes a sensation. The kind of man who accuses the world of all the wrongs he is ready to inflict on it. And, of course, to this day no crime: interrogated, all would deny committing any cyber trespass whatsoever. They are not robbers and vulgar thieves; they have no blood on their hands. The wet work is done elsewhere by others; they come out clean. He does not look like Orson Wells in his heyday, but Nathaniel Lagrange makes me think of Orson Wells in *The Third Man*, when he justifies the viciousness of his penicillin smuggling ring by saying that Crime and Art go hand in hand: 'Look at Italy, he says, they had the atrocities committed by the Medici, who sponsored Michelangelo and Raphael. Now, look at Switzerland, peaceful, democratic and prosperous country, and what did they produce in 500 years? The cuckoo's clock.'"

"Nathaniel Lagrange spends his well-paid time scratching his balls and justifying his vulgar path of crime in the same vein," Jonathan adds. "In spite of their soft humanitarian touch, the Lagranges have blackmailed and threatened legitimate businesses into paying millions of dollars. They have been associated to troubling outbursts of violence in the prison episode and the *terreno* over the border. They have old connections with the mafia. They are one of the most dangerous, well-connected, well-financed, extremely skilled group of home-grown intellectual terrorists."

This is the draft of a report he'd polish and send later to his superior. What frustrated Jonathan for some time was what had baffled policemen before him: not only did the system administrators (those who had paid through the nose to acquire knowledge of their own network's shortcomings) prefer to conceal the transaction; but they usually established solid entente with the Lagranges, built on shared secrecy, and would shield *HighGuns* through misinformation, economic and political influence...etc.

Tycoons worked hand in hand with *HighGuns* and didn't hesitate to lure police away from them. No charge was brought against the members of the team; what the police had in file was misleading testimony. "Agents Hatchcroft and Erzlinger have duly established the image of Suzan's main disks," notes agent Levine, "but she must have done her core hacking on volatile memory, making sure it was gone at the end of the session, or else was copied on flash-drives that members of the team must have carried around. Neither Hatchcroft or Erzlinger has done the minimum of police work on the person of Suzan and her team!" It was embarrassing. Agents were intimidated by *HighGuns'* fame on the Webwork. It looked hopeless.

And nonetheless, Richard Gere got his break. One day he found Suzan Friedman hot handed, copying digital identities, access codes and security protocols for three days. She was on a binge. The detailed sequence of internal memory her computer sent to Jonathan's screen would have been perfect for any policeman. Jonathan could have cuffed her: it proved that Suzan penetrated charted territories and hacked against the law. For agent Levine, there never was a doubt that the Lagranges, and Suzan Friedman in particular, were guilty of breaking the law. Which law, he does not specify, didn't have to. He leaves that to the prosecutor and the judge, if there is ever a case brought to trial against the whole of them, which he doubts. Levine's instinct tells him to not ask for a warrant, to let Suzan go; this is small coin. He realizes that Suzan is sending him a smokescreen, for she is not a petty thief and is capable of much more dangerous hacking. She'd get two years with parole at best for identity theft, specifically since she has sold to the best offer what sensitive stuff she stole and not otherwise used it in any dangerous way; and has a virginal record. The image of her hard disk would only prove she did common theft for the first time, like she stole an orange at the corner grocery. She'd fall for nothing.

What has she done? For agent Levine, the Lagranges have penetrated and perhaps tempered with highly sensitive computer systems, top secret programs and crucial access codes to hubs controlling resources, the flow of information irrigating major institutions in the state of

New York and perhaps in the country. And besides that, there is no consensus among the intelligence community as to what the Lagrange BBS may contain of vital knowledge and access to the digital infrastructure.

"For all we know," he writes, "they may have access to the atomic code; normally, traditionally, constitutionally in the exclusive hands of the President and the Vice President; but, of late, we know that they have leaked and started to sell like other exclusive commodities." The F.B.I. tells him so and the C.I.A.. Nevertheless, Jonathan still thinks the power of the Lagranges and the existence of phalanges ready to do hara-kiri for the sake of an idea as elusive as Desistence are exaggerated.

But for Nathaniel—in the case of Nathaniel Lagrange, agent Levine sounds the alarm: "Let us keep watch over this one at all times. Nathaniel is a purist, a believer prone to enthusiasm and sudden breakdowns. The Lagranges, and Suzan in particular, their team of coders, their permanent guests don't have a consistent ideological agenda, they're about business. Nathaniel is about plunging head over heels in metaphysical extrapolations I am not sure he has the intellectual strength to keep under control. The fact that there has been a rash of suicide among young men and women claiming Desistence is not relevant to this dossier. Nathaniel has rejected suicide in his Fragments; he has posted against it and distanced his movement from it. Let's be honest here, a year ago Nathaniel did not intend to use *Josephine*. We have to thank rudimentary police work if the position of the group has hardened, if *HighGuns* poses a risk at this point in time."

Like with any terrorist threat, intelligence doesn't know how the attack will occur; but it knows that it will. Suzan has an advantage over Jonathan when she deducts who is after her from what she's detected of his spying. *Plus*, she has a weapon nobody can afford to let her use, and agent Levine less than anybody else. If she acts out under his watch, Jonathan falls, he's finished as a security police officer and perhaps as a man. After having conferred with his team of investigators and prosecutors, that is, after much wrangling, they have decided Levine can only pull one card out of his sleeve: offer Suzan Friedman some kind of immunity against future prosecution. They have come up with a strategy. What would be best from the police standpoint is if Levine could drive a wedge between Suzan and hard-headed Nathaniel; if he could have her agree to talk against him.

Levine should let her know she can iron the terms of her immunity with her lawyers; *they can't*. Not John, not Kathy, and especially not Nathaniel Lagrange. She should bite at the bait, if it's well presented. Jonathan rightfully assumes Suzan is more of a shark than the three Lagrange put together.

She's followed, listened to, seen, recorded, taped, and she cannot avoid witnessing it. To add to her predicament, the scrutiny can only get more precise. She sees it coming towards her like Antigone the walls of her prison. But she won't go down easy; and for now, she acts as though she won't go down at all. Full of energy, she crosses town, goes shopping on Madison Avenue; takes a taxi to SoHo to finish the spree; visits the art galleries of Chelsea. Or sometimes she takes the car from her parking lot around the corner and, alone, drives out of town, crosses the Tappan Zee Bridge, eats dinner beyond Nyack in some opulent inn overlooking the Hudson River. On her return, she gives the keys to the clerk at the parking lot on York Ave. There are very few cars allowed in that lot. Jonathan could not bring out a rotating light and park in the middle of the street. To keep track of her is no easy job.

Jonathan decides to approach Suzan at a café on the Upper West Side. You don't cross this line, it's not professional, but Jonathan couldn't resist seeing her in the flesh, serious and all, an old lady sitting alone at a small table under the charming sun of early June. Suzan, who knows she is on the FBI's short list, is relaxing after the completion of a wild shopping spree. She is surrounded by plastic bags full of shoe boxes. Right on Broadway, she's having lunch on the pleasant terrace of a French restaurant. When would he have her alone again, defenseless and in so good a disposition?

"You sit just like that, without asking me if it's okay; you're kind of brash, officer Levine."

"I am, I allow," he answers, "and so are you."

"How so?"

"You and your people have infiltrated my files and spied on the police!"

"And so what? Ain't you in the public service, aren't your files of the public domain?"

Jonathan blushes to the root of his hair. The funny thing was that he, the policeman, was disturbed by Suzan Friedman, the suspect. She came preceded by a legend among hackers and Jonathan had himself been a hacker, in his days at Stanford. He had been a handsome man, Jonathan. Now, at seventy, he was slightly overweight and overworked. Suzan didn't look so tired and she was only two years younger. She didn't seem worried, which amazed Jonathan. Perhaps she has a plan, he thought.

He had large brown eyes that were soft and shrewd. He took a perplexed, baffled, beaten, lost attitude, like he was humbly asking her to light the *tenebrae* ahead of him. He had no ready answer, no predatory intention. Acted as though he accepted to fall under her charm, which was still immense. Fortunately for him he was dressed loosely but elegantly that afternoon. Nothing felt better on him than a clear linen suit, worn-out but varnished moccasins of Italian origins, and a white shirt cut in a rich cotton from the Far West. Since Stanford he had gotten to jumping around his screen dressed like a young man.

"Go back to your grand-children and your wife, Mr. policeman," said Suzan without the least animosity, more like in sympathy for the man who had to stalk her. "This will take care of itself."

They looked at each other. "You're telling me Nathaniel is under control," he asked her. She didn't say anything, which meant, yes. Whether the agent taped her or not, she wanted to leave little trace of her collaboration.

Jonathan ordered a *Perrier menthe*, sign that he had taste. To order a sandwich he pronounced a few words in French that the French waiter seemed to understand. She was taken aback by his cordial manners, his elegant way to invite himself at her table and behave as though nothing the matter. Their entente was immediate. They talked about the city, bristling with activity, humanity and business intertwined. "Better than at any time," he said. "Doesn't matter if Wall Street stumbles or if the sea licks our heels... the city thrives, it's business as usual."

"Doesn't matter, you're perfectly right, agent Levine, because human life adapts. When it looks like it's going out of existence; it's back on the scene with a vengeance." They laughed at these platitudes.

At the word "business" Suzan had expected he'd press her to say something about her hacking and, in particular, *the deterrent*; but Levine didn't. He was tactful. They had named the fall guy. They spoke about music and Suzan showed profound interest in the topic. Of this encounter the unexpected result was that the policeman came out reassured and the suspect seduced.

Suzan was ready for a deal. One more meeting, and agent Levine had her. He had her by letting her go scot-free when she was the mastermind of the whole Lagrange thing; but he had her. She had to cough up her secrets, give away the recipes; start explaining the deterrent and instruct the security agents on how to dismantle it. Immunity is a big word. Immunity in court, perhaps; but not in the day to day, not under the thumb of the police.

Next time they met, Jonathan expected Suzan to bargain hard about this word "immunity" and take nothing for granted. Yet the fight occurred on a different front. Not clear how it got around that she had met Levine; I believe it's John who brought it out of her during a fight. She flinched, she weakened, perhaps stopped thinking only about herself and, for a second, cared to save him from the trap. Suzan wanted John on her side and felt guilty. Her drives along the Hudson River, all her promenades through the city had not prepared her to do it alone. Of course, she was aware that John couldn't keep a secret, not from his brother Nathaniel. But she still had to take him into the confidence. That was her mistake, especially since she had been meeting the agent unbeknownst to the Lagranges; Nathaniel raised hell and thought about ways to sideline her, to publically kick her out of Desistence.

However, Suzan did not share with John (or anyone else than me) the most shocking, that Nathaniel would be the fall guy; that Nathaniel alone would pay dearly (and perhaps also, to a degree, his brother and sister, but that was not clear); while the rest of us would more or less continue to live the life of the free.

Kathy, John, Nathaniel and the rest of us learned from Suzan at dinnertime that she was ready to talk to the police about *Josephine* and even about the organization of the phalanges. That produced a crisis. One brother spurred the other, Nathaniel enlisted John in the refusal to cooperate. Suzan enlisted Kathy in the desire to give in, and get away with what they could get away with, and have finished with it; at least, for now. The group cracked open like a dry coconut on gender terms. Jacques and I, we didn't count, we were secondary characters when it came to crisis inside the Lagrange clan.

Men say it's too early to surrender, not before having established a vantage point, leverage, bargaining chip. Kathy and Suzan are called soft skins, pussies.

"Sisters want to cooperate like that, bare-handed, naked," they jeer. "They're snitches, they want to *talk* their heart out...They want to spread their legs before the aged policeman..." These last words John regretted immediately, but they were said. There was a virulent, angry and resented split in the Lagranges between what you may call hard-liners and accommodators, and it cut right through the family. It tore at the couple...

Jacques and I, we sided with Nathaniel, we took a grand and pure stand like him, although we regretted it silently because she was the one who kept us on payroll. Suzan is the realist and she doesn't bullshit.

I remained her French confident and she could see how much I prized the position. I was not aware of her double play the way I am now; I made it plain to her that I could still prove a very useful friend. And she needs a friend. Suzan is placed suddenly, and for the first time, in a weak position. Kathy is not much of an ally. She has a name on the Webwork, but she is not much of a talker at the table, where her big brother plays her and John like yoyos.

Nathaniel doesn't frighten anyone as a hacker, but he has a big mouth and high principles, and a following; and Suzan has always known he is fragile, not whole, lacking, cracked. Nathaniel has less, much less to lose than her; or it's the reverse: Nathaniel loses everything in the conflagration of *HighGuns*. In order to rise from his ashes like the phoenix of old, he has first to disappear body and soul with *HighGuns*. He must sink with his ship—roped, harpooned to it like the mad captain Ahab in *Moby-Dick*. If he misses his chance, there won't be another. She has always suspected that Nathaniel is furious, enraged like Ajax when Euripides transforms him into a wild boar. There was in Nathaniel this defect of a loose cannon she was able to exploit and indulge in times of success; but no longer.

For Nathaniel, the mere idea of negotiation with the police means our demise, our destitution, our shameful rendition. Desistence undone, betrayed. He remains the old lefty, the Trotskyist that she regularly mocks. Prometheus forever chained to his transcendent Idea and falling down the abyss. For Suzan, talking to the authorities—and I remember that she mentioned agent Johnathan Levine as though it were an old, indifferent acquaintance from back in her years at Stanford—well, for her, it's business as usual. It may result in a blank check to operate otherwise. Immunity on paper, that should comfort everyone (she doesn't say, except one). As for being what the men call a snitch, she could live with that.

"We don't have to take on the ghetto mentality because they have branded us criminals; we're not *of the hood*. There's nothing substantial in our files; no reason to act the suspects and give them something to write about."

She had a brilliant argument: "What's wrong, anyway, with sharing our knowledge? We never said we would use the deterrent? We said we wouldn't. The know-how, the computing skills our *trojans* concentrate in their exceptional make up, all that painstaking logic we carefully put in making our *logic bombs*, gentlemen, *that* should also one day reach the public domain. What we preach about open source and free access applies also to what we do. Hacker's ethics should govern hackers' contacts with the police. After all, top police officers come from the same classrooms we graduated from. The fact they are police does not mean some are not gifted. Let's teach them!"

Another time, Suzan remarked nonchalantly: "Agent Johnathan Levine has been a hacker, not one of renown, I grant you. But the thing is, we know we can talk with an educated man like agent Levine."

This reminded everyone of the sad encounter with the chubbies.

"And so, does it make him an angel?" asked Nathaniel. "That only makes him more dangerous." There was this empty stare in Nathaniel's eyes, as though he talked to himself, listened to orders, voices he received.

"Nobody is an angel," answered Suzan smiling at the perspective of an extended metaphor. "There is an ongoing struggle in Hell between ghouls, the bad evil against the good evil, difficult to distinguish; but anyway, hazardous ghouls—open your book, or rather close it, Nathaniel, because we shouldn't underestimate our enemy in the case of agent Levine, we ought to negotiate with him, keep his elbows on the table."

She was convincing, in part because she used the line of reasoning her adversary (here Nathaniel) would. And nevertheless, Nathaniel succeeded to undermine Suzan by insinuating that her point of view didn't represent the majority of the group. She was too much business and on the side of government. The *raison d'être* that had fortified *HighGuns* in times of success and in times of distress was elsewhere: it came from the Mentor's *Manifesto*; from the commitment to impossible utopia, from doing business for the little guy, from taking vital knowledge away from the oligarchy and its myriad sycophants and employees. The deterrent could not be shredded or given away in any way. We needed it intact to counter the madness of this world and remain free.

Nathaniel was full of it and not easy to argue with. For the first time, I saw the old rigid and exaggerated Nathaniel creep back into the new soft and sure-footed Nathaniel.

"Maybe we are doomed, and so be it; I prefer to die than live forbidden to live," Nathaniel said. "And I'm not quoting from a tragedy." Here everybody tried a laugh. He repeated his arguments one by one, speaking so forcefully and fast that he lost his audience. Jacques and I, we looked discreetly at each other. We had a déjà-vu feeling, an uncanny remembrance.

Didn't matter: he had John's ear and Kathy's faith on his side; and beyond, when this conversation was rumored along his *corridors*, the enthusiasm of most participants. This time, he took Suzan's seat at the spiritual command of the enterprise. Perceived as prone to betrayal and corrupt, her technical prowess took a back seat.

Jacques and I would walk on our toes around him and observe how he'd go mute, stiffen; manifest the obdurate resolution of a boy. He grinded his teeth, refused to yield, reneged at negotiations, spat in our faces exactly like twenty some years earlier when you didn't give him enough of a chance to speak.

For John, it was bravado, a question of confronting Suzan for the first time in their long affair; and also, desire to give more time to his delicate brother, so as to prepare him for a brutal realization regarding his exceptional status. So far in denial, John did now accept it was the end of their free pass, or call it, free lunch; the end of the red carpet and the flatteries wherever they went. The police and the constant tensions between him and Suzan made it feel so. Now that he was all in a piece, not more drunk than any of us, just a regular man in his late fifties, gray haired and round bellied, Suzan had much less time to devote to John. They had long given up on passionate love and had navigated on affection, attachment, mutual respect. All that tedium which comes with plain habit in a couple had finally weighed on her; but even as she probably regretted it the moment she confided in John, when push came to shove, she could not shut him out of her deal entirely; she had to break a bit of the bread of truth to him.

Jacques lamented the situation; but he was like me, not that unhappy to witness the very end. Allegiances could shift in the course of one day and it was tiring and depressing. Silence gained between us at the dinner table, punctuated by conspiratorial whispers. Nathaniel mumbled and played again the idiot, but this time he acted closer to the retarded or the delirious than to the fool. It was not easy to fall from the sky of adulation; from a state of being carried by a human stream and no longer subjected to the laws of gravity that pin the common man to the ground. Suzan had to contend with despondency and insomnia. But at some point, she told herself "and so what, wake up, everything comes to an end.' All that mattered was to leave the stage gracefully.

She told me when we met in an obscure diner on First Avenue that she'd tolerate Nathaniel's rigidity only so far. John was not serious in his opposition, she could win him back; not Nathaniel—his was mad serious. Nathaniel had become some kind of fanatic. She was determined to shut him out on the one hand, and on the other grant John a few more weeks to daydream. Kathy also needed a few more weeks.

Suzan disclosed to me plan A: "Nathaniel falls without his demise implicating any member of the team, but only himself and his clumsiness. The police want Nathaniel; let's give them Nathaniel. No motive to wax sentimental. He does, after all, represent a danger greater than any *worm*. He may get rid of us faster than we think, Etienne." She was searching my soul with her bluest eyes, for she knew, of course, that Nathaniel *also* confided in me and Jacques. "His Idea will need illustrations written in blood, if you see what I mean; he'll crucify us to it, if he has to. Time to act, don't you think?"

She looked hard in me while telling me this *soto voce* and in a bland voice. I could have asked her what was plan B, but I simply strived to return her gaze. We looked at each other from head to toe and in silence. It was like we signed a contract, engaged our persons. Between us there would be this entente.

Log 31

Having located and maneuvered Suzan Friedman, agent Levine had to contain Nathaniel. Arduous task; Levine records in his log what he thinks of Nathaniel's derangement. His diagnostic mirrors Suzan's.

"Nathaniel is the most dangerous of the lot, the last to know what he's doing. Nathaniel doesn't follow a strategy like Suzan. To quote his patron-saint Hegel, he listens to *die Schöne Seele* in himself, *la belle âme*, the pure Romantic intention, which he perceives on impulse. He's against the group receiving their immunity through a bargaining process; so far, he doesn't know he's the only one excluded from the deal; though, between us, John and Kathy won't get much of a chance either. Nathaniel thinks it's sheepish, bad-ass and a major sin to sit at the same table with cops. It tarnishes the Idea and stains the man."

"So here is the risk: if I fathom the man correctly, he could, in response, ask his phalanges to walk up from their consoles and abandon their screens—let's call this Desistence 1; apparently, a benign response, although it would matter what kind of information does not get to circulate properly that way. Or, on the contrary, let's call this Desistence 2, Nathaniel could ask his phalanges that they bombard selected screens in crucial command control rooms with graffiti and nonsense. Let us suppose, not a far-fetch hypothesis, that pressure, sense of leadership, responsibility in front of his demanding Idea escalate, become too much to bear for his narrow shoulders; Nathaniel could, by Desistence 10 or 11, ask his following that they not only freeze their consoles and open their windows like in *Network*, which he rehashes so often, and jump out of these windows or, if they prefer, blow themselves up from the top of Liberty Tower."

Later: "After all, Nathaniel has prevented his désistants from committing suicide; yes, but it goes both ways. If he thinks he has that much power on them, he may want to authorize suicide at a moment he considers desperate for his movement—or his person, which is saying the same."

Of course, all this is pure speculation on the part of a policeman whose job is to predict and prevent the worst. I must say, though, that agent Levine was prescient. He continues: "Among his shadowy armies of youngsters many would inevitably take his call to arms to mean: Let's temper with basic services; let's paralyze the system for good. Nathaniel does not have to add details if and when he uses the word "attack" literally; what is clear to him is that the threat coming from Desistence must by then be so serious that the Lagranges would have to be let off the hook. We, the police, would have to let them go. That's how the famous Webwork thinker Nathaniel Lagrange thinks when it comes to the endgame of his survival. Suzan, on the other hands, understands that *Josephine* at play does not guaranty them losing the American police, certainly not once and for all; not on this planet. Nathaniel does not grasp that yet. He deludes himself. He does not want to register the scale of what is happening to him. When he does, on impulse he could press the keys since he has now access to the codes. He's wrestled them out of Suzan's treasure chest and this is the real reason why she sat in person at a terrace on Broadway waiting for me; and, before that, why she did all the shopping she could have done online, hoping our paths would cross. She is afraid of what Nathaniel can do, she needs help because, contrary to what she wants me to assume, she does not have him under control."

Later, Levine notes: "Emotionally, Nathaniel is still a teenager watching *Star Wars*. He's the last resistant fighter infiltrated in the black sphere of the Empire's command-center where me, agent Jonathan Levine, am a petty officer working under Dark Vader... and I had better not wander unarmed lest he blows me away with his exterminator. Rumor has it that, at sixty-one, Nathaniel is still strong, nervy, impulsive and fast on his feet."

Earlier on I said Nathaniel was mad again without providing much evidence. It's hard these days to draw a line between sanity and insanity; and I am not prone to pass judgment on who's crazier than whom around me. However, I must confirm that Nathaniel gave me the impression of slipping back into his old fury. He was not like Freud's case, the President Schreber, who's too mad to notice sometime that he is mad. But his awareness changed nothing to the fact that Nathaniel was falling apart inside.

Visiting his parents one weekend, he found a typed copy of his old paper on Hegel (typed by Nina twenty some years earlier). The pages were yellowed by time. He read it read and read it and became obsessed by it, convinced it was a breakthrough in Hegelian studies, a hidden jewel most representative of dialectical logic, if not Western thought. The fact nobody read his paper because it was still as illegible as ever after too many rewritings, that didn't change his considering it a major breakthrough. All his flashes on the Webwork were the mere result, he said to us, the pale, assuaged, cooled off, watered down consequence of this promising and juvenile article. That nobody had read it only proved that nobody had read him, heard him, paid real attention to his words. But there would come a time, for time catches up... the proof being this paper. In all fairness, if the written word still meant anything, on the strength of this unposted article alone, Nathaniel expected to be remembered like Walter Benjamin by his fifty pages on *Art in the Age of Technological Reproduction*.

While overblown, for Nathaniel *HighGuns'* material success had been welcome and justified. Suzan, John and Kathy, he himself had worked hard for their money. Material success has this advantage, it guaranties that you are not completely crazy or totally wrong: you make money, people appreciate your worth and are ready to grant you talent. You're a success, a genius, in the case of a Webwork thinker like Nathaniel.

Easy to be generous and pusillanimous and considerate when rich and adulated. It's when things started to go downhill that Nathaniel showed again his dark, relentless, heartless side, which had seemed gone while he led a reclusive and devoted lifestyle. What cracked him in the middle is a matter of conjecture. He felt that Desistence was being assaulted, and he above and before anyone was called upon to defend his offspring like a she-wolf her babies. In his delirium, he even saw himself the cause of the group's difficulties, in particular because of this goddamn paper of thirty pages nobody could read. It was dialectical, after all, that what had made his triumph precipitate his demise. It was already written in Hegel.

We laughed in his face: "Don't give your stuff so much importance," said John.

"Hegel has nothing to do with all this," Suzan sneered.

"Nothing has anything to do with anything," Nathaniel growled.

"We were doomed, something about the Lagranges," added Kathy.

"It's the return of the repressed," mocked Jacques.

"What went repressed in this case?" asked Nathaniel.

"Repressed my ass!" went Kathy.

"That they didn't love us, the bitches!" John hurled at Suzan. "That was the repressed," and with the glare of the drunk he used to be—or was he drinking again?—not without adding a nasty gesture at Suzan, John repeated, "all along, *they* didn't love us the bitches?" He was looking Suzan down grimacing and like she were a vulgar woman.

Nathaniel looked at John, Kathy and Suzan: "We should do away with her, then; was she not ready to do away with *me*! Denounce me and have me, eventually, locked up. What do you think they talked about with Levine?"

Nathaniel had recouped the nasty bottom of her secret, that he was, and him alone, the fall guy. One thing about Nathaniel, he is not an idiot.

Agent Levine wrote: "The Lagranges make no bone explaining to their public the outrageous persecution they are being subjected to for being the successful Webwork wheeler and dealer that they are. They have filmed agents watching them awkwardly from all kinds of place; the unsuccessful and grotesque intrusions at their domicile on the Upper East Side. They mix all and add caricature and mockery. Now, it appears that they have stacked guns, rifles, *mitraillettes*, the equipment of a *noir* TV series filmed today. The Lagranges are their own reality show, which they distill to the dark enjoyment of their public."

"One thing you learn in *Criminology* is to take the statement of a potential killer at face value, *tel quel* say the French. Don't discuss his madness with a madman. Listen to him, he's telling you something. Nathaniel now supervises their virtual shows, the weaponry to sustain a siege in their duplex and the codes that trigger *Josephine*. Must be something came back from his daddy's past, this low ranking military man the two brothers loathed while growing up. These white individuals from preppy Rhode Island (though the Lagranges lived modestly during their childhood), chief of them, Nathaniel the intellectual from Ivy league Brown University, though he never finished his degree; the thinker and acerbic moralist magazines and newspapers only a year ago found representative of our Webwork age—well, these guys have no qualms, no problem turning their attention to weapons. It looks like it comes naturally to them."

"It is quite possible for a human being to be driven by the fantasy of redeeming the grave wrong he imagines suffering at the hands of others, just when he is taking advantage of them and inflicting pain. It's called random retaliation impulse, and Nathaniel is, among the present agitators of ideas, precisely the one who has brought the notion of retaliation to the fore. The scapegoating, the victimization process central to his *Fragments* belongs to that collective impulse to make one body suffer for the shortcomings of everybody. But I worry that in a form or another Nathaniel may be the first victim of the impulse; victimization is working its way into him."

Not your usual flat-footed policeman, this agent Levine. Elsewhere, he notes: "Why would individuals want to impose their agenda on others to the point of crashing their lives and occupying it—yes, invading it, taking possession of it? No answer to this question in *Criminology* and that's what always bothered me with *Criminology*. Killers want to kill as many as they possibly can so as to be remembered by the living in the guise of missing children, missing brothers and sisters, missing spouses, aunts, uncles... They force their way into your family and disavow their own by their crime... Regularly parents do not recognize their sons and daughters in the terrorists they have become."

Another philosopher, though I am not sure how this last bit connects with Nathaniel. Agent Levine was never wrong; and yet, in reality, he was wrong. It's Suzan and not Nathaniel who first excited *Josephine* and unleashed her *worms*. I thought until recently it was Nathaniel. She said it was Nathaniel and like everybody else I went on believing her.

She waited for Jacques and I to leave the group before acting; I am not sure why. I need to shed the light of all the circumstances I can gather from memory and from the Webwork and correct the records where they can be. She set the ticking bomb and sent the alarm to the police at the same time. To prove that she was not a betrayer, not a sold out, not the "venial soul" John and Nathaniel accused her to be, she triggered what she could not a 100% control. It's Suzan, under the pressure to show the Lagranges and their following that she was not the chicken-who-flew-the-coop they denounced in the *corridors*, who pulled the trigger.

Nathaniel had erected around Suzan like a tribunal; he'd spurned the team to visit on her a good old and not so subtle witch-hunt. Result: instead of her doing business "out there" and us following her and *HighGuns* counting the coins, key members of the team spent their time spying on and smearing each other. Suzan's standing among désistants was in tatters. She was not only a snitch but a betrayer and a mole. Again, acting the docile flock, Jacques and I managed to appear siding with Nathaniel, while, discreetly, helping Suzan's life on premises, protecting her from John and Nathaniel's worst impulse by our mere presence.

Nathaniel had not changed, in fact; or he had changed again and wandered back to square one on a different plane. Same with John. Who said personal history is a spiral? Time and time again you revisit yourself from another standpoint.

Jacques winked in my direction when John and Nathaniel were ostensibly dismissive and he could not take it when John was offensive to Suzan. Jacques jumped and I had to restrain him. I could not take it either, but I would not have fought John and Nathaniel; they would have flattened us to the floor. It was time to leave again.

We didn't say much. We looked for a hotel we could afford on the Upper East Side and took two contiguous rooms. At least, we were glad to make it all in one piece and together. We agreed it was not desirable to settle back home among spouse and children *yet*. We kept in close contact with our respective families, and there certainly was a powerful tug to have the daddies back; but we felt we were too engaged in *HighGuns* business and it had gone sour. We were no Soprano, able to leave behind his crime as soon as he kisses hello to wife and kids. We felt that our worries would spoil and stain, if not our entourage, our comfort in it. We had better stay on the side and wait for things to cool down; but, of course, we didn't stay idle. We cleared the sunny side of one bedroom and plugged our machines. Days on end we watched, learned and tried to sniff the wind and mingle in the surf.

Log 32

Meanwhile, Nathaniel was not inactive in his *corridors*. His postings were getting sharper and more relevant as his life seemed to reach the edge of a cliff. That he was mad and becoming, as Suzan said, some kind of fanatic, did not impede in any way his thinking. For instance, Nathaniel added a canny note on the millennialism of the peasants in the year 1000; I copy here what he posted in the middle of the worst crisis.

"At the end of 999, at the end of December in the year 999 to be exact, peasants— actually, serves, according to historians—their wives and children, the old and the young abandoned their lodgings *en masse*. For once, they didn't fear the master's wrath: didn't care about army pursuit, punishment, and they were harsh back then. Throughout what is now Europe, in an amazing coincidence of determination when there was no Webwork and no mail even, serves left their villages, their clergy, their cattle... In the middle of the day they set out. They took with them only dogs and cats, family animals, and walked in a pack all the way to the end of cultivated land, which may not have been very far back then. There they kneeled and prayed, and we can assume drank and ate of the best since it was the end of time they celebrated."

"Millennialism is beautiful; but it is also true that it is a promise not kept. What happens the next day? I mean, the 1st of the year 1000. And the day after that, the 2nd and the 3rd of January, when serves realize there is no End of Time, it's not coming? The Apocalypse is tarrying? 1000 is a year like any other year; there is no direction in time. What makes it worse, they have finished their wine, sausage, camembert, and no longer feel the urge to pray. Give it a short week, what happens to the poor buggers? They return to their lord, his henchmen, get a whipping like they've not received before. Their villages have been plundered; the high clergy has eaten pigs and chickens. It's worse than before."

"Now, are we facing a new year 1000 when, in our *corridors*, we talk after Blake of a Desistence that would threaten Apocalypse *today*? No, we are not; there is no date to expect, no End of the World to come. Nothing to expect from time. The "now" does not belong to time like future and past. Now is now and breaks with time. Breaks time in half. Again, Desistence cannot mean waiting passively for the End of Time. We depend on no one, however great he is rumored to be. End of Time will never come *in time*. Each of us has in his own subjective-objective way to pro-act it, prepare it actively; we have to get to the point where we perceive infinity in each grain of sand. And I do not think perceiving is enough."

As I reconstitute what happened among the Lagranges while we (Jacques and I) were not around, I am confronted precisely with what Nathaniel said: each moment, each event, important event, no matter how much you access of varied information about it, is abyssal. There is a place where human agents are not explainable, reducible to cause and effect; one cannot a 100% account for one's decisions nor can one predict the consequences. Nathaniel didn't choose ponderously to start the program; once started on impulse, it ballooned in his face. My impression is that his body and his soul got to a moment and a place where he had to start the program. *Josephine* had become an extension of his hand, his will.

There were jarring asides in his blurbs. Getting a little too comfortable in his own style, Nathaniel's speeches would screech in your ears like wheels on rusty rails. There was this back and forth down the *corridors* about what it meant *not to* be Jewish; how to assert oneself and not feel bad about *not* being Jewish. The phrasing was unexpected and, at first, Nathaniel went into familiar forays and interesting remarks. And then:

"The thing with Jews is that some are very close to you, they are almost like you, they could be you. Only, they are better than you since they were there before and know better; and, in effect, you look more closely and discover they are just about to creep up on you and replace you."

The Jew as nuisance, parasite, virus getting into the blood... images as old as anti-Semitism. Of course, everyone understood that Suzan Friedman was the real target of the speech; and perhaps people like Etienne Ertzki and Jacques Menashe, Nathaniel's old turncoat friends, who had fled the coop when things got too difficult. That such an admirer of Jewish thought as Nathaniel Lagrange might drift on a slippery subject when edgy and freaked out, we

(Jacques and I) could accept. Prejudice cuts every which way: Jews are themselves anti-Semitic against one another. What was more painful was that it gave rise to interventions, blurbs, clips from his following I prefer not to quote here. I had thought désistants more intelligent than that.

Nathaniel, John and Kathy sensed that Suzan Friedman and Jonathan Levine were not like them, the Lagranges. Indeed, they were not like them. In many ways, Suzan felt closer to Levine than to people like John and his, excuse me, white trash siblings. Some will say that she had merely entertained the Lagranges to have company "out there" and not feel so alone in her private life. Now that she had finished squeezing the juice out of them, she could brand the Lagranges like cows on their way to the slaughterhouse. But I beg to disagree; we have seen that it's only reluctantly and after making painful mistakes that she thought about abandoning the team.

Family members formed the inner circle now, the gang in control. Suspicious of whatever Suzan said, did or didn't do at the computer, the Lagranges watched over her shoulder. They occupied different quarters, but promiscuity was unavoidable. She was old; he had gotten heavier, beefy. They had always been the strangest couple; only now, it went beyond the pale. Before leaving them, I saw John's fleshy hand pinch hard Suzan's little fat, rounded belly, push her around and, as she turned to face him, shout invectives at her. As a matter of fact, it is obvious that he re-started drinking then, so as to mistreat her with less scruples. What amazed me was that a woman like her would accept to be mistreated, even for an hour, even once.

Nathaniel didn't drink; he didn't mistreat Suzan; this was not his style. Having split the Lagranges from her, first he intended to drive a wedge between agent Levine and Suzan by threatening public expulsion from the team if she didn't denounce and explain in detail on *HighGuns'* portal the purpose of her meeting the policeman in a cozy restaurant uptown. He used his following as leverage against her. Nothing would have been more appealing to a good portion of our public than to see the Lagranges bring out their dirty linen. Some feel vindicated when the mighty suffer. To witness a group of people you have long admired and envied tear itself apart is bittersweet.

Nathaniel defied Suzan at dinnertime; he dared her to come clean in front of the ranks of Desistence. Nathaniel may have been mad, but he was sharp as a blade and lucid as hell in the hours preceding the disaster.

Suzan reneged, tried to gain time; she couldn't afford to confess publically her attempt at evading the ship and pushing the Lagranges over the precipice with the help of the police.

Second step, then: Nathaniel threatened to send a message to *Josephine* and have her attack in all directions if Suzan didn't come to the fore. That was not reasonable, obviously; that was obdurate. It would be like going after a fly with a hammer. Trigger *Josephine*, have her start the sequence was the last thing to do; but he was mad for not having the last word.

Besides being the hero of a transcendent idea, he was the old Nathaniel who had to win on the squash court (at the risk of losing his friends). Maximum destruction, the loser's urge to imprint his denture in the flesh of the winner. It's when Suzan realized that Nathaniel, John and Kathy were about to excite *Josephine* that she forestalled their move, triggered phase 1 of the deterrent, the attack on JFK, under the Lagrange name, using their signature, their style, and giving it a lag time. She did all this from the bathroom, using the screen that was there. She'd stored in a flash drive programs that described *Josephine,* gave her access codes and the protocol to rewrite her, the whole content of which she then posted right on the next police website. She figured it would take half hour for the right agents to wake up to the challenge and as much for the hierarchy to grapple with the appropriate decision. That left about an hour for them to neutralize *Josephine*; enough to dismantle phase 1 if they used every second (like a hacker would). She left the bathroom and the apartment under a pretext. The Lagranges still respected her enough not to lock her up; it had occurred to no one that Suzan might leave her post at the helm. Even demoted, captain is last to leave ship.

By giving the police two hours to stop the attack, she acted like a hacker, sending them the ball while putting the last touch to her indictment of the Lagranges. Nathaniel's unpredictability was no longer *her* headache; it was police responsibility. She had no idea yet of its proportions, but what was already evident to her is that her name should link to a disaster in which she took the last sensible stance.

Suzan left the duplex under the pretext of buying cigarettes, dressed as though she intended to just buy cigarettes. But she didn't come back and that night they learned of her denunciation on the police Website. After several minutes of shock, then utter fury, Nathaniel put on a face of resolution and maneuvered his brother and sister into playing with fire. Brother and sister were so anxious, so terrified by what was to happen as they made it happen—terror would feed on itself.

Nathaniel would not be robbed of the satisfaction to commit mass disruption. He had to purge the matter of the living around him and scoop out a pound of flesh to offer his concept, his abstraction. To pass through the needle-hole of reality Ideas have to force their way through. Nathaniel was mad furious, but not mad enough to not understand what his team of coders were telling him, that it would take just about the two hours predicted by Suzan for the police to locate and neutralize phase 1. And that after phase 1, there were other phases that would be automatically triggered if the overwriting failed. *Josephine* is an intelligent multiple-module bomb whose ravages progress by following several clocks at once. She is a fairly advanced AI once entirely deployed, who may help herself to a copious state of consciousness by feeding to the Webwork; and decide to shun scruples and remorse in the bargain. It is not easy to stop her once she is encouraged to follow her program and no longer function as a deterrent but a weapon.

For almost an hour *Josephine's* torpedoes had been on their way to clog switches, filters and routers all over the map, when Nathaniel, John and Kathy realized their error. Their bargaining chip was slipping away; they were shooting themselves in the foot. There was still time for the security agent to take advantage of the roadmap sent by Suzan. However, it was doubtful she had revealed the entire clockwork. Not only did she need time to explain, and for them to understand, but you don't just push a button, reality is multipart, infinite at each step, and to undo destruction more difficult than to cause it. And besides, reasoned Nathaniel, why should she do that, give it all to the police? Suzan may be corrupt; she is not stupid. She has not revealed the entire sequence. They might overwrite phase 1 and let phase 2 and 3 sleep for her—for us—to awaken later.

They tried to communicate with the police and negotiate their exit with Jonathan Levine; but they couldn't get through. Considering how much they were under the eyes of the police, it is astonishing. At about the time uniformed policemen were being ordered to arm to the teeth and go and arrest them, the Lagranges couldn't communicate with the police. Out of frustration, to let the steam out and show their muscle; and that they were not—as was obviously the case—outdone by Suzan, Nathaniel, John and Kathy Lagrange skimmed through *Josephine's* laundry list and triggered whatever minor dysfunction out there they pleased, giving it the lag time that popped in their head. Misinformation would scramble ambulance service on the Upper East Side for the next five hours starting in seventeen minutes; in about half hour there would be incoherent firefighter response in the West Village for three hours; prepare for a deafening noise in the channels of communication used by the NYPD, the coast guards and the Park and Recreation services; all three are about to receive, however, precise images and accurate information concerning real crimes about to be committed in all probability. Digital hubs disserving the Wall Street stock exchange might be sluggish next morning if...

"It's our last option as human beings," Nathaniel said without voice. John and Kathy were so anxious and wired up that they couldn't choose between the humiliation of surrendering to the pending arrest, or like Bonny and Clyde run grenade in hand toward the pack of their executioners. Why not use the deterrent for all its worth, turbo charging all the phases at once and send it to them like a warm grenade for them to dispose of? What could it do, really, if *the police* messed up? Nobody knew. What would happen at JFK if *Josephine* was not rewritten in time depended on the efficiency of the bots supposed to band together hundreds of computers and bombard the sky-controllers, their computers being already weakened by the inside job Suzan had done.

We had to derail the madness, somehow make it serve another purpose than destruction. This was not destruction destroying what destroys us. We couldn't simply watch blind fury take hold of our friends and of our entire life-project.

For a few minutes, Jacques and I succeeded to have a live conference with them. That they accepted to talk to us at all, us cowards, false friends, Jews and disguised agents who had teamed up with Suzan to save their ass, testifies to how desperate they were. Nathaniel was not so mad as to not see that he was mad.

"Fuck them!" was John saying. "Yeah, man! I've had enough of their shit! Let's show them what it costs to not listen to us Lagrange!"

"Do you want to be like the two illiterate criminals of *In Cold Blood*," I said with the intention to hurt, "and kill and rape everyone in the house, children, every member of the innocent family—for a fistful of dollars?"

This nasty reference to two infamous white trash killers seemed to hit home with Nathaniel. He stuttered: "Man, you really layer it on us! We are not the ones who started the whole shebang."

On screen, they were the same John and Nathaniel; and they were not. More disheveled, dressed haphazardly, eyes popping out of their socket for lack of sleep. We were all terribly pleased to be together at this hour. Kathy was biting her nails and smiling nervously, yet there was a glow of ferocity in her eyes she had not let out before. An enjoyment in evil. Like she was finally allowed to look in the face at the horror she had long wanted to inflict upon categories of people. John licked his lips and nibbled at them, and he also sneered. Though mad, or perhaps because he was so mad, I repeat, Nathaniel was in control, like he had not been before.

He was listening to our suggestion to look into another method like he was at one end of a long tunnel and we were at the other. Jacques asked him how he could forget the lessons of his own blurb? What about his speech on *Network?* How about Desistence? Was it just another vague idea made to serve no other purpose than illustrate the speaker in some vague debate of ideas?

Nathaniel was piqued, of course; he had never grown a thick skin. He kind of woke up and rubbed his eyes and looked at us looking at him; and softening his voice while speaking firmly, he denounced himself in the clearest terms for losing sight of Desistence, indeed, and being driven by competition with Suzan. "Self-aggrandizing pursuit" he said. "That's business for the Devil." He had started to make a terrible mistake but, with all his energy, all he wanted now was to reverse speed, not inflict but disavow violence, the very source of violence in him, the nasty impulse to retaliate, the root of which he would snatch away from his heart.

It all sounded a bit cheesy, staged, improvised. There was undeniably a groping, tentative, fuzzy quality to what he wrote then (correction: I say *wrote* since, even accompanied by visuals, it comes as written in his files; but he spoke to his machine). And it was all the more touching, since he was overwhelmed by regret, remorse, shame that may have been sincere. He had strayed from the pure perspective of his movement—which was to keep the deterrent a deterrent and safeguard our resistance—for a childish tic for tac with Suzan, which he could only lose.

Theoretically, among désistants the word has to be arrived after *corridor* discussions. But between theory and reality there is a difference. Nathaniel turned his back on *Josephine* and all that he could not handle and gave the code words for active Desistence. It is estimated that in the first minute no more than 10 000 people around the world intercepted his call. Most among us paid attention, however. Waiting for more incentive, some put their computer to sleep, except for the reception of further messages coming from *HighGuns*. The word spread fast. More walked out on their work at the moment, placed their cell phones on hold and suspended their conversation. There was something eerie and fascinating in the coming about of this inactivity across the Webwork a lot had been said about. But 10 000 or even 100 000 inactive players, even if in key positions to paralyze or lull or slow the flow, this is nothing, a drop in the ocean, not enough to make a ripple on the Webwork. Not enough to empty it, perhaps; enough to make holes where it matters. Or show that we could make holes; that was the message Nathaniel wanted Desistence to send through the Webwork. When he was convinced it had been sent, he asked his phalanges to return to business as usual and assess the consequences.

The phalanges remained devoted to Nathaniel; but for many superficial enthusiasts the name Lagrange was tainted, they were now terrorists and had, in retrospect, always been but a bunch of old lefty losers. Who would associate with people who hurled *worms* at airports?

Unless, who could tell, Desistence gathered enough momentum to change the face of the event, its dynamic. Events can be changed in retrospect. For now, the Lagrange BBS was amassing more digital treasures than ever.

It's when the Lagranges were ready to give themselves up and all their weaponry real and digital, that police came to cuff them. The taskforce that had gathered in the building stood dead still. From his computer at headquarters, Levine could hear the noise in the pipes and the crawl of insects on the walls, and to the last whisper between the brothers and sister Lagrange. That's what Levine wanted to hear just then, and Levine's orders were respected.

Levine had Nathaniel on his IPhone. There was no picture. At first, Nathaniel didn't say anything but, because of his nervous breathing, it was obvious to Levine that he was all ears.

"Isn't it enough?" asked agent Levine. "What more of a mess do you need to make?"

'That's just what I'm saying, agent Levine, isn't that enough?"

"Let's stop then!"

"Let's stop, yes, and embrace!"

"Not quite!"

"You're right, not yet; let's finish undoing the goddamn deterrent first. We are all in it now!"

He had this mocking tone, but Nathaniel was ready to undo *Josephine*...

Just then, enormous packets of information it couldn't manage overwhelmed flight control at JFK. The automated air-traffic controllers went blind. The plane to Caracas met the one from Sydney.

They had no time to prepare suitcases. They left the duplex and delivered themselves into the rough hands of the police as though they were going for brunch. The elite police were expecting orders. Levine didn't quite know what to do with the Lagranges, now that he had them. If they offered him a deal, he would accept. More important than anything else was to make sure the deterrent was neutralized a 100%. Only sincere cooperation of the Lagrange clan could assure him of that. He could trust Suzan, and yet, she had not told him much, not more than she had to. What about Nathaniel?

Nathaniel was brutal on the phone: "I have two things to tell you, agent Levine, the plane crash is your baby and me and my men we want to skip town. And nobody even dares putting a dirty hand on our blessed body (he spoke for the occasion as though he really were white trash). There is no lesser price to our cooperation."

Dressed as they were, they bounced down the stairs and into their car; only bringing zip drives and laptops, and their springy appearance: even Kathy and John were jumping in their sneakers according to the surveillance clips. Leaving New York and then riding on the highway, the I 95 shooting north, they drode straight up New York States to Canada—all the while supervised by a helicopter and nonstop on the phone with Jonathan Levine. They helped him dismantle *Josephine* further. There could not occur other digital disturbances affecting the sky. And then, layer after layer that took a couple of days to unfold over the phone—they didn't want to use their laptop, which would have made it easier for agent Levine to catch up and gobble them up—they meticulousness confirmed that ambulances in the city would reach destination; that Mount Sinai, Lenox, Roosevelt and NUY hospital centers would not experience intermittent blackouts; that NYPD detectives would not be dispatched to investigate violent crimes that had not occurred (what you may consider my most personal contribution to *Josephine*); and that the high speed network of information surrounding Wall Street would convey accurate data by opening time tomorrow.

From her hiding place, Suzan provided Levine with anti-bodies to several variants of the malware. The Lagranges started trading all they knew about the deterrent one click at a time and drop by drop. Undo evil is a slow process. *Josephine* had become adept at reforming after you cut limbs off of her. Erase her phase by phase and clock by clock required patience and persistence. Suzan sat at *Starbucks* on Madison Ave and 82nd St., sipping fancy coffee and watching the undoing of *Josephine* unfold on a borrowed laptop.

Log 33

Suddenly, Nathaniel's following was growing: more people considered the Lagranges (their brand and their persons) less as perpetrators of the crash at JFK than as victims of defamation. Dozens of websites were now following the Lagrange case, diffusing news and interpretations. Yes, Nathaniel had conceived in his twisted minds and implanted the cruel *worms*, but he had been ready to give up his error and diffuse the threat. Nathaniel Lagrange had been willing to spit out the poisoned bite and had not been allowed. He had cared to redress his wrong and come clean; and had been crushed by clumsy agents, silenced by an inhuman machine. Compounding the horror of the double plane crash, here was another case of blatant government incompetence and overreach.

The thing with this computer stuff is that it's supposed to free your time and make things easier. And it does: triggering implanted devices happens in a snap; but the programming, the putting together and the dismantling of ferocious programs takes time and hard work, even to an army of well-trained policemen informed by elite hackers.

Even a rare police genius like Levine can err. The slipping away of the Lagranges and driving to Canada is a blow, a dishonorable setback for him. Anyone else would have lost his job on this. But he is not taken off the case and sent to work on local thugs; no other agent is as versed in the Lagrange file as Levine. He is in fact given more back up and an international license to operate.

It didn't take a long time for brothers and sister Lagrange to put two and two together and to prefer France to Canada. France is slightly less under US influence than other parts of North or South America; and they were not ready for another plunge in the third world. I am sure Kathy loved the idea of being in Paris. I can imagine her saying something cliché like: "If I have to die soon, let it be in the City of Lights."

Once in Paris, the Lagranges—and a couple of coders and, I believe, a service person or two from the old days at the ranch—settled on the Right Bank, near Place de la République. After several weeks of conspicuous life awaiting their extradition and deportation back to the US, just when they were about to be extradited, they went under. How did they duck this one? My hunch is that they were known and prized enough by local hackers to find protection; and *HighGuns* (Suzan, actually) had long established connections with powerful leftist organizations, benevolent associations, Amnesty International...

I settled on the Left Bank, right on Place Saint-Sulpice. La Rive Gauche, more chic. I'd always wanted to live on that neo-classical square, in front of the baroque fountain squared off by four lions. I rented an apartment in the three- stars hotel that faces the imposant Jesuit church, l'Eglise Saint-Sulpice. After climbing up the stairs and refreshing my fingers at the fountain, I could admire the mural inside, a splendid diptych by Delacroix. It was cool like in a tomb inside the old thick stones; cool as it had been for hundreds of years. I ate my coffee and croissant or the sandwich *jambon beurre*, like the young tourists, sitting on the stairs. And then stepping inside the place of worship, silently, morning and evening, paid homage to *Jacob Fighting the Angel* and *The Desecration of the Temple*.

I was particularly interested by the first and came to the notion that Delacroix is asking his future public a question with this painting. While we turn the neck to look up the high wall, the painter whispers in our ear: Do you think he is doing well, Jacob, or he is losing ground under the assault of my flaming angel?" And you cannot answer. It's hard to tell because Jacob and the angel are entwined, fingers into fingers. They are of equal strength. Depending on the angle, the perspective you take on their strenuous bodies illuminating the small chapel, you may think it's the angel with his majestic wings, his strong legs—or on the contrary, it's Jacob in his furry shorts, who's winning the struggle. You may come to realize that there is no winner and only the struggle of passing the Jordan River. The palette is flamboyant, I suppose Delacroix used the oranges and the golden browns, the shimmer he'd found in Titian and Veronese. He borrowed all this; but Delacroix painted his own figures, his own version of the Biblical story. These thick-ankled legs, the robust wrists of the female-male angel belong only to him.

My coming back to France felt like reoccupying the very shoes of the intellectual dandy I had been before leaving France at twenty five. The difference was that now I came prepared. It was the necessity to purge myself that had driven me back here; to clean my life from your nefarious influence, Nathaniel. It's my turn to sound cheesy, didn't see any other way. I had to get implicated so that it would clean my name from the scourge of the Lagranges. And maybe beyond that, a greater good could occur and Desistence free herself from maniacs like you. My problem had not been with the movement and the idea, but with you.

Practical problem: from my first life I had no connection with the Parisian underground, no way to find the Lagranges before Levine and Suzan did. Part of the solution: I could bump into Suzan and Levine shopping around the corner of rue de Rennes. I looked for a hotel not far from them on rue de Vaugirard. We'd all instinctively settled in the vicinity of Boulevard Saint-Germain, choosing the most exquisite quarters our relatively abundant dollars could afford. I detect that Suzan stays in close collaboration with Levine. She has to be on his good side. After all, it's not Nathaniel who first triggered the *worms*; and Levine may want to remind her of that.

Since I worked for Suzan in LA, in my laptop there is a full address book of information about hackers and French system administrators of high and low standing; but who am I for them? I have no name; my presenting myself as a close associate of the famous Lagrange sounds arrogant. What do I pretend having to do with Nathaniel Lagrange and *HighGuns*? People don't refuse to talk to me but all the same, they don't talk to me. Parisians are not easy to talk to, anyway. And it's been like that between them and me always. Yet I am not retarded and have not lost my French. It's not that my American intonation gets in the way, simply that after many years of not speaking French daily, it is noticeable; I need more practice. They don't know where to place me, the Parisians I meet. I speak *almost* like them; and I may know from the inside their preoccupations and concerns, including their technical difficulties. And yet, my attitude is completely foreign.

But then, I meet American hackers operating in Paris and the communication is perfect.

I fish one of Nathaniel's e-mail addresses and we meet without any difficulty at the café on the plaza surrounding Eglise Saint-Sulpice. He literally materializes on the terrace and I am clueless as to where he came from. And when he leaves, he evaporates as well. It's all the more surprising that he hardly knows Paris, had never visited before.

Nathaniel is his thin self, wan, gaunt and sinewy, and getting gray and older, but maliciously happy.

"Boy oh! Boy!" he says to me upon shaking my hand, "I survived."

"You sure did."

"What do you want from me," he asks while sitting down.

"I want to help you fight Suzan and Levine, they're after you *here*, in case…"

"I know…"

He was the same Nathaniel who knew everything. But then he smiled and asked: "And where is Jacques? Where did you leave him? At the hotel?"

We laughed. Only the two of us facing each other, now, taking pleasure in the moment that passes by. Not in the past or the future, fully present.

For a while it was not difficult to play double game. I told Levine and Suzan about the little I got to know about the Parisian life of Nathaniel's; what I gleaned from his talk. He dwelled on generalizations. His whereabouts, address, recent habits and connections, he guarded well and hid from me. He knew how to keep a secret, Nathaniel. But we agreed on a game with the French police. I would make them believe he'd reveal more soon; and so, sometimes Nathaniel told me just a little more. That he resided in the northern suburbs. I was surprised to hear him refer to Saint-Ouen. Was it a decoy? My own grandparents on my mother side had resided in that forlorn suburb. In exchange for that kind of information, which gave the impression to the police that things were moving, for the time being I kept them at bay, not too close to Nathaniel, not into arresting him before they learned more about his protections. And then, I presented to Nathaniel as the fruit of *my* protection against Suzan and Levine the discretion of the French police, his not being harassed. This could last maybe a couple of weeks.

"They know where you are," I told Nathaniel next time we met. "Only they don't think storming the place will do them any good. I don't think this arrangement will last more than a few days."

"And what do you know exactly about Suzan and Levine?" asked Nathaniel. "What do they want?"

"They want to arrest you and put you on trial, of course!"

"On trial, you're kidding me?" he guffawed, contorted, jeered and then, turning dead serious: "They couldn't win in a public trial against us. They know that and you know that."

"I do. They don't. They are convinced they could nail you on the *worms* attack against Kennedy Airport."

"But it's Suzan, in cahoots with agent Levine—and this I can prove—who did it!"

"Perhaps," I answer. "But they think they have a case if they portray you as the attacker she forestalled by her preemptive attack. And there is the added fact in her favor that she gave the keys to the police after starting the engine; you didn't."

"Preemptive my ass, forestall yours. They want us dead. They'll find us to kill us under some pretext."

"I am not positive on that one," I said without blinking. "To this day, at the moment the accident it is not clear why the computers at JFK crashed since Suzan had *thoroughly*, she said, undone phase 1 with Levine. They think it's phase 2 that realized phase 1 backwards and that it's you and your coders who triggered phase 2 by trying to correct clumsily your first error... And that, Nathaniel, sorry to tell you, they can probably prove."

He lowered the chin in acknowledgement that he had, indeed, fucked up.

"They still think they can pin the whole thing on me, uh? They want me for the fall guy..."

"You know very well," I said, "that they need one."

It felt like saying a line out of a *noir* movie.

He looked at the white marble of the fountain, the lion faces on it, and then deep into my eyes. We were a few inches apart. "And you, Etienne, what's your take in all this? Why do you bother to sit here speaking to me? You wouldn't prefer to be at home with your wife and child? What am I for you at this point?"

"You're my friend, Nathaniel."

"Don't feel obliged to…"

"No, really," I said, "and to be completely honest with you, I want to continue making money like you, guys. I have never made as much money as I've made around *HighGuns*!"

"This is certainly true!"

We laughed and drank together fifteen-year old single-malt. Then we took a taxi and continued drinking Rive Droite, more populous and for the regular guy. After that, we shook hands, I turned around to not look at who was in the car as he'd asked me to—didn't even sneak an eye to the side so as to remember the car; I needed his trust—and he vanished.

Before leaving Paris thirty years earlier, I had hardly any friends. Could never find a decent job; lived like a small-time gigolo. Now, my address book being full of marvelous e-addresses, I am making money connecting would be French hackers to reputed Americans.

Nathaniel does not reveal anything about Kathy and John. How do they live, where in Saint-Ouen. It's a big town. Back in my childhood it was almost country. On Sunday, I remember, my sister and I would visit the crazy big house where uncles and aunts and their babies wandered from room to room; then had picnic on the overgrown lawn. They started a sentence in Yiddish and finished it in French. By late afternoon, my grand-mother would drink a little too much of the powerful red wine and would go off in imprecations, particularly against her husband, the grand-father who, she said, had failed them at every turn. Uncles would intervene and there was a fight, a crisis among aunts, uncles and cousins. Saint-Ouen is that disorganized, freakish place for me. I don't push Nathaniel to tell me more. It would not help, anyway. What helps is to remain on his good side.

Why had he accepted to meet me? Given his family's ignorance of all things French and his limited abilities in French, they could use someone like me. For a while I didn't see

Nathaniel, but I had a connection with the team in Saint-Ouen through the good old phone. For a transfer of money, I rounded the angles of the French planet for them. They were well settled, at least computer-wise, for they had excellent means of Webwork communication and protection. Not possible to tell from where they operated exactly; but they made money, through proxies. *HighGuns* accounts were not frozen and the site was still active, in fact, hyper-active, even after the "accident," even as its administrators were fugitives under international arrest warrants. One probable reason: money movements allowed police to keep track of what the team was doing. And Nathaniel could not be denied access to the Webwork, where he continued to express himself. It's called the First Amendment.

I then traced the Lagrange whereabouts in Saint-Ouen. It's Suzan who, unaware, directed me to them.

The Lagranges had no clue how close Suzan had been to finding them.

What was she doing in Europe? I wondered for a while. The Police had nothing against her: her side of the Lagrange file was classified, off the shelf; the computer numb against her. She would have been safe in New York, under NYPD protection. Furious as he was, Nathaniel might kill Suzan if he found her in Paris, and John would offer his assistance. And what if one of the young désistants who take Nathaniel's rhetoric against her literally, tracked her down like I have myself; then caught up with her physically? She has betrayed *HighGuns*, used and abused the name Desistence; there is no possible pardon for that. It's like there is a fatwa on her head; and that is why she prefers to know what the Lagranges are doing at all times. To make sure they could not hurt her anymore, she'd have followed her old companion John and his big brother to the African desert or the North Pole. She harbored no faith in the French police. Levine's ability to prevent catastrophes from happening were far from convincing.

When she was about to denounce them, it's me who did them in and I am proud of it. You may ask why I cared to be the one bringing them down, when they would have been denounced by Suzan and sent to their judgement all the same. I didn't want them to simply go to jail. I resented Nathaniel's vulgarity when he and John and Kathy had taken over *HighGuns*. It didn't have to go down that way. After what Suzan had done so elegantly with phase 1, to mess around with phase 2 and bombard right and left...

I understood the destructive bent, the abandon to violence; yet the more I related to it and could have imagined myself in Nathaniel's shoes, the more I thought the impulse had to be indexed, exposed, condemned and punished. Someone had to pay for the hospital rooms full of maimed and half-dead bodies. Not all involved should get scot-free. And, of course, I had my selfish motives; like Suzan, I wanted to make sure to not get swept up in the punishing sweep. Unlike Suzan, however, I also wanted Nathaniel to reimburse me for the fame he had acquired at my expense. And I sensed, to be fully honest here, that there may be a light at the end of the long tunnel; that is, there may be a way to wrest Desistence from his foolish hands.

Nathaniel had triggered *Josephine* for stupid personal reasons. Our movement deserved better.

Log 34

I was sitting alone in the elegant Art Nouveau place called Closerie des Lilas when Suzan walked right up to me. She noticed the single-malt Whiskey in my glass and sat next. Then, she ordered a Wild Goose vodka martini extra dry, some *oeuf d'esturgeon* and a couple of oysters, and said, "Well, Etienne, who would have thought you and I would be the first ones on this!"

"Or the last!" I answered.

She laughed. "Good old Etienne. You figure. Feels inevitable. You look good, I must say."

I had lost some weight in the turmoil of the last year, garments suited me better. She was quite elegant herself, still tall and thin on her high heels. A large white *mousseline* hat on her head, floating white linen pants and taffeta top, pearls at her neck and fine gold watch, diamond ring like she were a landlady from the 16th Arrondissement. I was quite taken by the metamorphosis.

I have always liked her; my reader knows that. But now she was my one competitor in a game where it was doubtful there was room for two. She could finish the process of her cleaning herself of the mess and of saving her ass and have Nathaniel fall or I would fight her to the finish and reap the fruit, and clean myself first, if I could achieve that without too much risk. You had to be the one denouncing the Lagranges and bringing them to justice to come clean when the hour of justice would come. Justice is not a charitable society that grants immunity like it were food and beverage.

A bit of information I have not revealed: I have not found Suzan's physical address in Paris by myself. It's Levine who, sending both of us on a similar mission, had set us one against the other like dogs. He didn't trust us finding things separately. He had to see what we'd do together under his discreet supervision.

Sipping at her vodka martini, Suzan lied without blinking about Nathaniel, telling me he was the one who had triggered the *worms* in a fit of acute madness. I made her believe I believed her and was ignorant of her part in the nitty-gritty sequence; that way I kept one step ahead. We'd regularly exchange polite and educated remarks about how beautiful Paris is and how it never changes on the surface; then we expand on how old hat, how frozen French people are in their senseless revolt against globalization; which, however, they equate to Anglo-Saxon dominance not without reasons. In the meantime, we observe how the digital format of their visual and acoustic environment becomes more American every day and how they go for it, buy it wholesale. Europeans never have enough Americana. You watch; they'll beat Americans at collecting and saving American art and crafts now that their museums are on a par, financially.

"America has always been good at selling its image," I said to her to say something.

"That's what we're doing here, ain't we?" she answered pointedly. "Selling her to the best offer? I hear you're doing well, Etienne."

"You hear well. I have good masters."

She had nothing against flattery. I admired her and let her know that each time I met her. If I was in the game at this late hour, I said, it was to have one more chance to learn among people like her… She placed her hand on my forearm, asking me not to exaggerate the flattery, she was not stupid. We detailed and observed each other like they do in Western spaghetti movies, waiting for who's gonna flinch, make first move on the gun, and lose because the other is faster.

She'd have denounced them, she was about to. I saw her in Saint-Ouen, lurking like me in the moon-like alleys behind their house. A frail old woman, not on high heels, wearing boots for the occasion. She had to be there physically and see with her own eyes what would unfold.

It boiled down to that shabby house, narrow like a trailer. A nondescript one floor house hidden behind a thorny front garden, and behind that there was a meager pebble where to park a car. No car on this one. A den for local gangsters in the lurch. It was not at all like my grand-parents' house, which must still exist somewhere, high, roomy and large, surrounded by a patio. The Lagrange shack, you'd walk next to it and not notice it.

Best way to find it was to comb the place from far away; comb it inch by inch with the help of a satellite, which is what Suzan did. For that kind of thing, I trusted her. Except for my striving to spy on her, I had no clue how to proceed. It all depended on the parameters she fed the computer. From my own I realized at the same time as Suzan did, that parts of Saint-Ouen were like Brooklyn forty/fifty years ago: overgrown abandoned lots; burnt out tenement houses and disaffected factories, empty warehouses, some re-affected to legal and illegal commerce. Nobody inspected the long, dark and semi-populated blocks, the shabby wooden houses suspended on cement hunks. Since the police stations had burnt a few years back, police never went to the best part of Saint Ouen, which the locals claimed as, not merely police-free, but French-free territory, *la Zone*. A succession of riots had left a sea of debris in the streets, which had never been cleaned; and the weird thing was to observe on my screen how every wall was covered by layers of American-looking graffiti; as the abandoned silhouettes of unkempt HLM's, which are large high buildings once upon a time painted in garish colors and now as dark as your brick towers in a Bronx project. The rare walker in that part of Saint Ouen is a French-born Arab or a hooded black who copies his gangsta' brothers from overseas; who wear the same baggy pants falling to his knees and showing his underwear, same outrageous sneakers, same heavy chains of gold around the neck. And you probably read on the Webwork that he smuggles military-grade weapons—not merely hunting guns like French people use—all exactly like his American counterpart.

Suzan fed the computer, which itself fed the satellite with the most concrete picture-rendition she could gather of their look, their clothes and belongings. The machine had John, Nathaniel and Kathy's proportions, curves, texture and appearance locked under any conceivable angle and distance.

In the portion of the back seat visible through the back window of a car parked on rue De la Feronnerie, her satellite located the beige collar of a Cardin suede jacket Suzan had bought him.

When she got into her car on rue de Rennes (three streets from my hotel), I was parked few cars away. I followed her and the way she drove, she had no clue. Right outside of Paris, façades were no longer so majestic and the streets so cute. Like most downtown Saint-Ouen, rue de la Feronnerie was apparently abandoned and where populated very poor. I felt pity for them. The Lagrange had to hide for good this time. I didn't see anyone coming out of the miniature trailer; but there were lights at the opaque windows and, by the way Suzan acted and looked when she had finished peeping through the thick bush, I could tell she was not disappointed. What had she seen through the dusty panes of glass? That they were packing up and about to escape one more time. She rushed to her car, visibly to denounce them.

I was a few yards away, playing the detective and lying flat on the back seat of my rented car, in the darkness. It was a cold autumn evening, and this time Suzan was not dressed in white silk but in blue jeans, marine coat, sweater and, as I said, boots. She ran back to her car. Only, this time, I was faster since I was already in my car.

In the first seconds, it is true, I could not read on her face obscured by the shade of the bush if they were inside, what they were about and what she intended to do. It's the decided way she broke into running that told me to rush things. Through the cell-phone connected to their webpage, I sent the police the street address the moment I guessed they were there. I composed Levine's cell number and whispered to him: "Get them before they leave." When she called seconds later, I have verified this since, Levine told Suzan: "I know, girl, you're late."

She must have been flabbergasted. Nobody ever beat her to the wire. I don't think she bears me an eternal grudge, however. The police were on the spot the moment Nathaniel opened his door to lead the way out. It's not like the police took half hour to show up. Levine was there, lurking down the street among us and letting Suzan and I go ahead; letting us take the risks but calling the shots. What if we killed each other? Wouldn't that be great for Levine? The same appalling idea that crossed my mind must have crossed Suzan's: what if the Lagrange resisted and were wiped out? Wouldn't that be much better than a trial that stirs things up and pokes into the past—*her* past? Besides, a savage ending is more cinematic; cable news are happy. But I didn't want the Lagrange group to be destroyed altogether, I wanted Nathaniel to pay for it all. In that moment of rapid action, I wondered how to crush him alone.

Other thought flashing in my mind: what if locals defended the Lagrange and came out of their dens and, indignant at our intrusion, broke into a riot until the media and the computer geeks stirred and came in throngs to visit the place? That's what's been keeping the police at bay. That's why Levine needs me and Suzan, to mellow things out with the Lagrange.

No one is coming to the defense of the Lagrange, obviously. They are all alone in their trailer, surrounded by a pack of wolves, and even the lambs, their local friends, seem to have turned a deaf ear that night. The underground has nothing to gain in defending the Lagrange to the bitter end. The elements are not there for a riot. I even smell in the air rejection of a foreign body, which they spit out of *La Zone.*

The elite French police climbed to their creaky door and cuffed the Lagrange as they gathered on the flimsy landing and before they sneaked out of the property. Facing the cops, they tried to return all at once in the trailer. Kathy and John did return and were about to seize the guns. Nathaniel was caught. Suzan saw all that unfold, and I was there behind her. In spite of the danger, I came out of my car in the cold night, as she did. And we looked at them from a hundred yards, Nathaniel lowering his head to pass it through the door of the trailer and speak to brother and sister. His hands are held back by a policeman. No raising of voice; no argument between them. What did he tell them? Police acted like pros this time. There was a gun in Nathaniel's back, and another at his temple. The Lagrange came to their senses in a snap: why die? Why play the heroes *to the end*?

There arrestation alone will be a sensation. And there is no reason to fear a trial.

Kathy balanced her weight around the small opening as she came out, empty-handed. John back on some kind of crutches smiled his ironic and defiant smile, which he'd lost for a time. Three in line coming out of the bush, shin down, rounding the back, hiding their face, shameful and defeated. Here come the mighty Lagrange, I thought. And I must say it was not all pity or even sympathy. Moving slowly with their guards and their hands cuffed in the back, they could not help looking surreptitiously around to verify how alone they were, deserted by the whole wide world; offered up to the god of retribution to atone for all the faults of mankind.

Nathaniel saw us, me and Suzan lurking separately in the dark street. Then I, for one, came out in the light and didn't hide. I stood in plain sight, walked up to him and camped myself, and looked at him denigratingly.

He had a jump. He growled and tugged on the chain; mere frustration and anger. Only, the policeman tugged back. In the hands of their respective agent, the family leaned towards him, instinctively trying to calm him down and protect him. You could hear the fists on the guns adjusting to him, the rifles nesting tight against the shoulders. Nathaniel would not contain his anger; he'd explode at any further aggravation coming from me, I sensed that. Therefore, I shouted to him:

"Now, Nathaniel, is this Desistence?"

Through the busy and cold silence my words traveled crisp clear; however, their substance sounded so out of place that nobody heard them at first. The arrest proceeded. Nathaniel was letting himself be brought to justice, he was giving himself in. His chin was down; but a supreme ironic smile was about to reassume its right on his face. Lawyers could drag his complicated case forever. All this, I felt in a flash, was going through Nathaniel like it was going through me. I repeated loud and clear:

"Is this Desistence, Nathaniel? Speak about plain subservience. You give in. You're a sheep, a slave. Also, you look like an ass hole! You're nothing, a piece of shit!"

Everyone was wondering what the hell. From the corner of my eye, I could see that Suzan was dazed, shocked and alarmed.

"And you, what the fuck are you?" Nathaniel shouted back. He couldn't camp himself like me, straight and proud. He was bent backward. The policeman not giving him an inch on the leash, Nathaniel tugged strongly on his cuffs, which created a commotion. Tugging back to stay in control, the policeman lost balance and brought down Nathaniel with him. They stumbled onto the uneven sidewalk, right in front of the police cars. Dust and brawl and the ticking of chains; rifles adjusting to their target. We were like in an American movie when dozens gyrating lights illuminate the murder scene. Next thing I knew Nathaniel was fighting to get control of the policeman's gun. He'd have quickly gotten the upper hand, for the policeman was overwhelmed by Nathaniel's strength and speed. Nathaniel was grappling the gun, he had it in his fist, he might have used it against the policeman—or against me, I had time to think—— had he not been riddled by bullets.

Nathaniel fell to his side. He didn't convulse nor tried to stand up swaying like some dead people do in movies. He collapsed on himself silently.

Log 35

Suzan has not quite decided if she should be furious at me and refuse me her friendship because I'm a barbarian and a brutal man, or consider that I have acquired the mettle to code exploit and belong to her exclusive club of hackers.

That night she looked at the team handcuffed and, over the shoulder, sent me envious glares; yet she managed to whisper in my ear something sarcastically funny once it was all over and Nathaniel was dead, and the Lagranges had tired of cursing my name, of shouting insanities at me from the police cars and scratching and kicking.

"Thank you," she said while brushing past me, "for nailing so efficiently the bastard. Alone all by myself I may not have been that successful."

The French government handed the rest of the Lagrange to the Americans, who brought them in front of what justice there still was overseas; and a storm of bloggers went crying over Nathaniel's corpse and defending the Lagranges, and calling them undeserving victims of a concerted disaster. One more signed by the police. Many people recalled the mishandling of the crash at JFK.

Desistence is doing very well, thank you. More adepts leave their station at premeditated times; more experts explain the concept. *HighGuns* is flying high, including making a lot of money, and this, even though the remaining Lagrange are in jail and for a long time. Who says you cannot pile money in jail?

And who says *HighGuns* belongs to the Lagrange forever? It was once created by Suzan, who is out of the picture. John and Kathy, even with all the time on their hands, don't have the minds it takes to make the *corridors* interesting day in and day out. And who is to say if another site, carrying less baggage, would not better represent Desistence at this point?

Suzan enjoyed Paris for a while, and then went south to Provence and the French Riviera. As for me, mission accomplished, I didn't feel guilty for my part in it; sad for my friend, but immensely relieved. I had certainly made enemies; but on the other hand, I had made friends. It's me, in truth, who had helped justice accomplish its old bloody process. Me who had precipitated a closure on the Lagrange affair.

I returned to New York under the protection of the police, there to dwell among my family for a few days, until I decided to go back to Europe, where I pronounce this last log. I played ball for a while, and convinced the Americans to hand me back to the French authorities, who couldn't refuse me. I still own a French passport.

Gabriela didn't ask questions. Nathaniel's death and my being for something in it, even if it is not clear what, has calmed the waters. She looks at me almost in awe. Perhaps it's unclear of what victory I come back victorious, but at least I do not return to my family a loser. I am not ruined.

Gabriela could not be happier about Europe, she loves France. I have not quite made the money I expected. I could not settle us on the French Riviera properly; but I harbor no regret. It must be too hot down there, too populated for one to appreciate the fine blond sand and the indigo blue wave circling renowned creaks. So, forget Antibes, Saint-Tropez and Juan-les-Pins, I had enough for a cottage-house in Normandy, and perhaps a horse or two. Who does not like to see natural storms these days, good old heavy gray cumulus? Sweet cooling rain? The English Channel brings a welcoming breeze, abundant rain and sometimes hail; but also sunshine. The drab Northern pebbled beaches, it turns out, are becoming very trendy. Étretat and Deauville are almost what they used to be in the time of Proust.

Isabel will grow up French for a few years; and then, when she needs New York later, she can live in the apartment uptown. Schooling and health are subsidized in France; and undergraduate education is good and free. I have required permanent protection from the US Federal Witness Protection Program, and it appears that my file is on the right track. Protection is no luxury, given Nathaniel's angry following. My name rings like a curse in vast quarters. They couldn't refuse me to go back to France, where it's easier for them to protect me. Only one condition, the police want me to stay on hand.

So far, no one has suffered from resurgence of the deterrent. Traces of *Josephine* that were deactivated and are still lingering have not come back to life. But we know that things don't die *out there*; they only fall in some kind of *black matter* from where *she* may sometime resurrect. As we speak an army of bees is already working at a new version of her *worms*.

Finally, Jacques and I have received convocation to explain our long-standing association with *HighGuns* and I've had to go back to New York and clarify my situation with the IRS. We corroborated, illustrated, clarified whatever the police wanted us to. Jacques had the same impression I had, routine work. We were in a throng of people; the Lagrange have been associated over the years with quite an interesting crowd in many cities, countries. Police were not after us two in particular and they had too much on their hands.

Nevertheless, yesterday, I learned that Jacques' name is in a pool, among second-tier circles of accessories and associates (to the Lagrange crimes). He has settled for probation. For three years, he's to receive counseling (a fifty-three-year old man, counseling!) and show up twice a month at his probation officer in New York.

I will undo the encryption that blocked access to the content of this file to the non-specialist. Levine won't be contented enough by the picture drawn here of the police under his leadership to brandish this against me. And even if Isabel reads this one day, then what? She'd be appalled by certain aspects; my greed perhaps, my enjoyment at doing the forbidden; a touch of cruelty here and there; but then, nothing will come to her as a complete surprise either. I didn't kill Nathaniel; I merely confronted him after he had messed up badly.

She'll see her father for who he is, someone who kept his independence and was not totally played, like she's been for a while, by the Lagrange. She could conclude that, after brushing past the law probably repeatedly, I did my best to save my soul, and hers by the same token.

The high poplars at the corner end of the property are like deep green flags whipped by the strong wind of late summer. Isabel stands in front of me; she is almost as tall as me now. She has grown when I was not around; and she has also grown as she suffered what went on. Then, we are sitting in lotus on the freshly cut lawn. I feel pain in the haunches, so I rapidly move to the bench.

I am passing through, in spite of my evident success, a moment of self-accusation and, naturally, she is aware of it. As though she has been mulling these ideas for a while, she says, "I know, Dad, you've made a tremendous amount of enemies, and some, well-heeled. Dad, one could reproach you the death of Nathaniel for personal reasons. It's not quite all right to have done what you did to your dear friend. Although, or, on the other hand, what did you do? You confronted him. So what? One could argue that he brought this all down on himself; and, don't take it personally, but in this case, you were merely an instrument."

"A willing instrument..."

"Doesn't matter."

She's going to be a lawyer.

The only trouble I can foresee bring more gray cumuli in my sky is Jacques. He will learn that I squealed. Who else could know that well the details of his dealings with *HighGuns*?

What can Jacques do to me? What will he want?

He will not bother Isabel and Gabriela. He can bother me, for me, who cares, I am like the bridge—scaffoldings that disappear once the building is built.

Desistence will survive Nathaniel and the Lagrange. Now that they are dead or in jail, the movement they helped organize no longer needs them. They are an impediment, a moral embarrassment. Their BBS is duplicable in all its fine structure and treasures; and besides, it is not theirs, it belongs to all of us, désistants.

Most of what Nathaniel said in his *Fragments* was well said and true and it's only a question of separating his troubled self from the precious ideas he developed over the years; then, of bringing them back where we found them, Nathaniel and I, when there was no *Josephine* and no phalanges yet. No noise, no distraction; only our dialogue and the clap-clap of small waves against the dock; the two of us standing at the handrail that protected us from falling into the bay of New York.

CPSIA information can be obtained
at www.ICGtesting.com
Printed in the USA
BVOW06s0600250517

485136BV00023B/121/P

9 781546 742623